PRAISE
and her S

"Deliciously edgy, sexy, and certainly not to be missed. A.C. Arthur knows how to deliver the heat."
—Lora Leigh, #1 *New York Times* bestselling author

"The shifter universe just got sexier with the kickoff to Arthur's sizzling new series, Shadow Shifters . . . intriguing."
—*RT Book Reviews*

"Arthur does a great job of building up the sexual tension . . . I'll be looking for the next one in the series."
—*Under the Covers*

"Romantic . . . exciting . . . fast-paced."
—*Genre Go Round Reviews*

"I am in love with A.C. Arthur's new series, Shadow Shifters. From start to finish, I was absolutely hooked . . . an incredible roller-coaster ride! With amazing suspense and sizzling sparks, Arthur creates a fantastic cast of characters that has secrets and lusts and so much more . . . Highly recommended to all paranormal romance lovers."
—*Romancing the Book*

"*Temptation Rising* has everything a good book should: action, adventure, suspense, mystery, and fiery-hot passion . . . The love scenes are intense and the detail, especially when they wind up in the jungle, is amazing . . . A.C. Arthur is a talented author and readers will eagerly look forward to the next one in the Shadow Shifters series."
—*Romance Junkies Review*

Also by A.C. Arthur

PRIMAL
HEAT

A.C. ARTHUR

St. Martin's Paperbacks

This is a work of fiction. All of the characters, organizations, and events portrayed in this novel are either products of the author's imagination or are used fictitiously.

PRIMAL HEAT

Copyright © 2015 by A.C. Arthur.

For information address St. Martin's Press, 175 Fifth Avenue, New York, NY 10010.

ISBN: 978-1-250-04293-4

Printed in the United States of America

St. Martin's Paperbacks edition / August 2015

St. Martin's Paperbacks are published by St. Martin's Press, 175 Fifth Avenue, New York, NY 10010.

10 9 8 7 6 5 4 3 2 1

Glossary of Terms

Shadow Shifter Tribes

Topètenia—the jaguars
Croesteriia—the cheetahs
Lormenia—the white Bengal tigers
Bosinia—the cougars
Serfins—the white lions

Acordado—the awakening, the Shadow Shifter's first shift
Alma—the name of the spa at Perryville Resorts Sedona. Means "soul" in Portuguese.
Amizade—annex to the Elders' Grounds used as a fellowship hall
Companheiro—mate
Companheiro calor—the scent shared between mates
Curandero—the medicinal and spiritual healer of the tribes
Elders—senior members of the tribe
Ètica—the Shadow Shifter Code of Ethics
Joining—the union of mated Shifters
La Selva—the name of the restaurant at Perryville Resorts. Means "the jungle" in Portuguese.

Pessoal—secondary building of the Elders' Grounds which houses the personal rooms of each Elder

Rogue—a Shadow Shifter who has turned from the tribes, refusing to follow the *Ètica,* in an effort to become their own distinct species

Santa Casa—main building of the Elders' Grounds that is the holy house of the Elders

The Assembly—three Elders from each tribe that make up the governing council of shifters in the Gungi

Prologue

"The time has come." Baxter Utiera spoke solemnly. His folded hands were weathered from the years, the manual labor, the strain of working within these tribes his entire life. This morning his chest was heavy, his temples throbbing slowly from all the deep contemplation he had done over the past few weeks.

Across the table Umberto Alamar, one of the tribe's Elders, stared at him knowingly. But he did not speak.

"Magdalena has foreseen it. The time is coming and I do not think there's anything we can do to stop it," Baxter continued. His eyes hurt, gritty from lack of sleep, his shoulders squared but aching from stress.

"We should not have come here. We should have stayed in the Gungi." Umberto spoke, his voice heavy and stilted with his Portuguese accent.

Baxter shook his head. "Hiding was never an option."

"They have *vantage*. They will *luta. Derramamento de sangue e morte virá. Derramamento de sangue e morte virá*," the Elder repeated until Baxter stood from the table, going to him and placing a hand on his shoulder.

"It may not be helped," Baxter told him, the words not

comforting but alarming to them both. "This is what they were created for, this battle that now comes. It is all that they have prepared for. They will prevail."

"They will die," Alamar stated solemnly. "We will all die if this is not handled correctly. Everything is on his shoulders now. How will he lead?"

Baxter frowned slightly, finally pulling his glasses from his face, using his thumb and finger to squeeze the bridge of his nose. This was not an easy assignment. He'd known when it was handed down to him that it would not be. There had been good times, moments when he thought maybe the presence of the shifters in the United States would be a good thing, that maybe they would be able to fit in as the Reynoldses had hoped and worked toward before their untimely deaths. Now it was their son, Roman, who led the Stateside Assembly. He'd put together a good group of shifters to carve out the blueprint of the democracy that would govern their species. Rome had also begun to forge alliances with human leaders, in hopes that when and if the time came, they would stand alongside the shifters and not against.

They would need that alliance sooner rather than later. They would need all the connections they could muster, including ones with their neighboring tribes. So far the *Topètenia* had been at the forefront of the Assembly. Now, however, they would need the strength of all the Shadow Shifters, they would need a united front to keep the bloodshed and death Umberto had predicted at bay.

In short, they would need a miracle.

Chapter 1

He bolted up in bed, sweat pouring from his face, his bare chest heaving with the rapid rhythm of his heart. The conversation replayed in his mind as if it were occurring right at this very moment.

Breathing heavily, Eli dragged a hand over his damp face and cursed. Elder Alamar and Baxter, the Overseer, had chosen to meet before dawn in a conference room adjacent to Eli's bedroom on the lower level of Havenway. The fact that Eli had been awake that night, as well as so many before and after, was not a pertinent issue. Still, he would admit that his senses had been in overdrive as a result of lack of sleep and lack of sex.

Upon pressing his ear closer to the wall, straining with all his power, he'd heard only whispers and murmuring, nothing coherent and nothing more about the bloodshed and death Magdalena had foreseen for the Stateside Shifters.

He'd cursed his shifter senses that had been off for weeks now. One minute they were magnified so that he could scent a person who was outside of Havenway, while he was inside the training facility with new recruits. And in the next, Eli was trembling with exhaustion and fatigue, plagued with a longing such as he'd never felt before. It was strong and most times at night, debilitating, as his limbs actually weakened, his erection so hard it was painful.

All signs that he expertly ignored.

Until the moment he'd needed to hear what was being said in the room next to him, because as long as he only had bits and pieces of the conversation, Eli would keep it to himself. There was no need to alert the Assembly Leader until he had all the facts lined up neatly. Roman was a stickler for accurate information being presented to him in a studious and efficient manner. As his guard for more than ten years now, Eli knew him almost better than the only other two closer to Rome—Kalina, the First Female, and Baxter, Rome's longtime butler. He knew that the Leader would want all the details of this conversation, especially with the situation the shifters now faced.

And he hadn't told him. Not yet anyway.

Since sleep was clearly a pointless endeavor, Eli pushed back the sheets as if they'd offended him in some way and climbed out of the king-sized bed. His room, the spacious corner dwelling in the lower east wing of Havenway, only had one window that didn't even span the length of his broad shoulders. All the windows in Havenway were small to prevent any break-ins. That was merely one of the security measures that X and Nick, the Eastern Zone Lead Enforcers, had designed to keep the shifters safe in their U.S. headquarters. The facility sat on six hundred acres of land just beyond Great Falls National Park in Arlington, Virginia. From the outside it looked like nothing more than an old dilapidated building, circled by an eight-foot-high electronic fence, marked PRIVATE PROPERTY. Inside, it was a technological fortress that housed over one hundred active shifter soldiers, including the First Family and their private security detail.

Eli didn't mind living here. On a personal level, he liked

the solitude he found in his room. A secret stairwell accessed through a door in Eli's bathroom led directly to an entrance into Rome's living space, facilitating his job as Lead Guard perfectly. To that end, he also wore a newly designed e-band that allowed Rome to communicate with him without using the global com links that would broadcast to all on-duty guards.

He made sure said band was in place on his right wrist after he slipped on sweatpants, a T-shirt, and his tennis shoes. In the next few moments he was outside of his room, walking along the steel-lined walls of the hallways that circled the facility's U shape until arriving at the training area. It was still too early for anyone to be here, but Eli punched in the code and pushed through the glass doors until he was inside the large room with all the latest weights and fitness equipment.

The treadmill was his goal because he wanted to run, and run fast. In truth, he wanted to shift into the cat and soar through the forest without stopping, but he knew that was dangerous. The United States government, through what they called the Genesis Project, now had a genuine shifter in their custody. With that shifter they'd produced a supersoldier prototype, aptly named ADAM, that Eli's twin brother, Ezra, had already destroyed. Considering those facts, they were all being extra cautious, even though Eli was aching to come across one of the supersoldiers so he could show him just what a born Shadow Shifter could do to a genetically engineered wannabe.

He was in a steady stride when he felt the first tingle at the base of his neck. It was just a ruffle of sensation that Eli let sit for a few moments. He continued to pump his arms, his breathing barely increasing as he entered into mile number one of his workout. His feet pounded the running belt, fists clenched, eyes focused straight ahead to the mirrored wall.

She was there. He couldn't see or scent her, but he could feel her presence and his teeth clenched with that knowledge alone. He'd been feeling this particular female for far too long, but not scenting her, which was the normal route of acknowledgment for a shifter. He'd ignored both those facts for he wasn't sure how long. Today, he wasn't in the mood to dismiss her.

He continued his run, working the full thirty minutes that he'd punched into the control panel. All while she watched.

When he stepped off the treadmill he stood in front of the mirror, stretching—which he should have done first, but having been so eager to burn the energy simmering inside, he'd bypassed that part of the workout ritual. Now he bent forward, came up, tilted backward. He lunged first to the left, then to the right, stretching his hamstring to its full capacity, loving the burn of the muscles inside. He stood up straight, put his hands on his hips, and did one squat before disappearing across the room.

The move had been quick, a practiced one he'd perfected for times just like these. Okay, she wasn't exactly the person he'd ever thought of using that little trick on, but since she was here and he was feeling particularly aroused by her scent this morning, he figured what the hell. When his feet stopped moving he was in front of her where she stood all the way at the other end of the training room, against the wall, hidden in the shadows.

She gasped when his hand went around her neck, the front of his body pressing tightly against the front of hers.

"Spying on me, guard?" he asked, his lips so close they rubbed along her earlobe as he leaned in to talk. "I'm not your assignment."

"No," she replied, her rich, throaty voice sending spikes of heat through his torso and downward until resting along the length of his dick. "You're supposed to be my trainer."

His thumb moved along her collarbone, smooth skin enticing him further, while his other hand found her waist, again skin touching skin. She wasn't naked, wouldn't dare leave her room and walk around a facility full of virile and virtually always aroused shifters without being fully dressed. He lowered his fingers quickly to confirm, feeling the band of her exercise pants and breathing a concealed sigh of relief.

"Then take notes because I'm about to teach you one of the first rules of spying on someone."

Eli didn't give her a moment to speak, but wrapped his arm around her waist and pulled her into a quick turn, then using his foot, clipped hers and fell to the mat on top of her without so much as a grunt. She let out a small gasp before she did what she probably thought was taking control of the situation and flipped them so that she was now on top.

"What rule is that, Mr. Preston?" she asked, looking down at him with a definite smirk of triumph on her face.

"Don't get caught," he said, seconds before grabbing the back of her neck and pulling her down to him. His lips took hers in a hungry connection that could have drawn blood if she hadn't reacted fast and opened her mouth to him. His tongue thrust forward taking hers for a wicked tangle while his other hand cupped her ass, pressing her hot little pussy right up against his rock-hard dick—just where she belonged.

Chapter 2

Nivea loved Eli's eyes. He didn't reveal them often, wearing those infuriating shades all the time. Most likely he knew how irresistibly hot they made him look.

Now, she thought with a quick catch of breath before sinking into an absolute abyss once more, there was another part of him to love—his mouth.

It was a clever mouth too, knowing and masterful, owning hers, directing, leading, guiding, actually fucking with complete potency. That was no exaggeration. From his kiss alone her already aroused center had reacted immediately. The tender folds were plump and now damp as her essence dripped from inside, just as his fingers had splayed over her ass and were now traveling downward. His tongue should be qualified as a weapon as he speared it in and out of her mouth, tangling with hers until she felt like he was doing the same thing between her legs. Or maybe that's just what she wanted him to do. It didn't matter. Nothing mattered at this moment except that Eli was kissing her, finally.

How long had she waited for this moment?

Six long, grueling years.

She'd watched him as a new recruit, mesmerized by the sound of his voice—deep, yet smooth like fine wine. The slow and methodical way he taught every aspect of being a shifter guard. While she hadn't been in any of his squads, ever, she'd always watched him and learned from the way he moved, the way he carried himself, how she should act as a shifter.

Whatever she'd done to warrant him being assigned to personally further her training these last few weeks, Nivea had no idea, but she would be forever grateful to whatever deity was responsible.

Her knees planted on the mat, she straddled Eli, her pussy rubbing over his engorged length, weeping with wanting. The blunt tip of his fingers rubbed against her scalp as he tore free the band she had holding her hair back. She barely registered him wrapping her hair around his hand, until he pulled, drawing her face away from his.

There were those eyes again, as green as the deepest depths of the sea, stormy and turbulent as they stared back at her.

"Your subject must never know you're watching them. If they do you're as good as dead," he told her seriously.

Well, she wasn't dead at the moment, but damn if she didn't feel close to having a heart attack. Her body was on fire, every part of her sensitive to his touch, her skin tingling at the sound of his voice. She was trying to catch her breath as he released his grip on her hair, his other hand pausing between her legs. Her thighs shook and she wanted to close them tight, to hold his hand right there until the aching subsided.

Instead, Nivea backed away. She came to a standing position, taking deep steadying breaths, concentrating on not showing him how much his kiss and his touch had rattled her. After years of being around Eli Preston, she knew him very well. He'd kissed her passionately, touched her like he wanted her, and then reprimanded her. This was not the way she wanted him.

"First, I didn't give my location away. You knew I would be here because we've been having these private training sessions every morning for the past few weeks, per your instruction," she told him, her pulse steadying with each word, eyes narrowing as he came to his feet just a few steps away from her.

His left eyebrow arched, something she'd seen only rarely since the sunglasses were normally his protocol. Her center clenched, minutely, at the action.

"Check your watch, sir. I'm right on time," she finished before he could speak.

He didn't look down at his e-band. No, his gaze stayed focused on her, which was uncommon, since during the weeks they'd been assigned to work together Eli had done everything in his power to only look at her when absolutely necessary. The same went for his touching her—the kissing part had been completely out of character. Nivea decided she would contemplate these inconsistencies later. She would keep everything professional, play on his level. That's the way she would handle Eli Preston, for now.

"Shall we begin?"

His response was to walk away, stopping in the center of the room where they usually began their sparring matches. As she walked to meet him she thought about the years she'd been obsessing over this particular shifter, all the hours she'd spent dreaming about the moment they would finally come together physically. It would be hot, no doubt, and intense, filled with all the emotion and energy they'd stored up over the years. And it would result in their mating, the beginning of all the most important goals in Nivea's life.

This assignment was a sign that her patience was about to pay off. The quick attack Eli launched when she was close enough to him was a sign that her calm dismissal of the kiss had ticked him off. Even as she worked through the maneuvers, countering his attacks, taking the falls to the mat while gritting her teeth, landing solid punches with a measure of pride, she knew he was off this morning. Something else was going on with Eli and it no doubt involved the Shadow Shifters.

Amina Cannon lounged on the small couch across from Nivea's bed absently flipping through a fashion magazine as Nivea changed into the newly designed guard uniform they all had to wear—navy blue mission pants and a lighter blue button-down shirt. Her boots lay across the room on the floor, where she'd left them last night. Immediately Eli's words echoed in her head.

"Guards should always be in uniform, Cannon," he'd said in that low, laced-with-death voice of his.

During this morning's workout she'd worn tennis shoes and exercise clothes. This had been in direct contrast to the will and the way of Eli Preston. Nivea had simply nodded in response, smiling as she walked out of the training facility because she knew he'd liked seeing her in her spandex capris and sports bra. His actions had spoken much louder than his words, in that regard. Still, she had no intention of disobeying him again, not so soon anyway. There was a meeting in the auditorium in twenty minutes. Not only did she plan to be there early, she planned to be wearing her crisp new uniform and to look damned hot doing so.

"Marriage is about love," Amina was saying when Nivea actually decided to tune in to her sister's conversation. "It's about respect and commonalities. It is not about a perfect union of the two biggest advertising agencies in the country."

Nivea shimmied into her pants, tucking her tank top in before buttoning them up and looking over at her sister.

"Shifters mate, Mina, they don't get married. The official ceremony is called 'joining' and it's far more intense than any human contract. That's what your argument to Mom and Dad should be," Nivea told her.

"Yes." Amina sighed. "Because that's exactly what the Cannons of New York want to hear. Talk about their origin in the dirty, sweaty Amazonian jungle instead of their rich and haughty new lifestyle that plants them firmly on the *Forbes'* most influential and wealthiest couples list year after year."

Nivea knew her words were absolutely correct. Richard and Michele Cannon wanted nothing to do with their *Topètenia* heritage. On paper they looked to be model citizens, successfully building and maintaining the Cannon Group and even starting a nonprofit agency that provided aid to underprivileged children. A good portion of those children were orphaned shifters. They looked like they were doing all the right things in this world. But Nivea knew better. She knew things her sisters did not and had made a deal with the devil himself to keep them from being exposed. Walking away and keeping her mouth shut about all that she'd endured had been the deal, and she'd taken it happily.

The older Cannons had come to the States as teenagers. After witnessing how humans of different races were treated, degraded, and dismissed, they knew without a doubt that a shifter would never be accepted as a part of this society. With that thought in mind Richard and Michele knew there would never be tolerance or acceptance in this country for their kind. The humans would brand them as outcasts and either kill or humiliate them until they wished they were dead. They swore then to build something bigger and better for their family, something normal, no matter what the cost.

Serene, the middle sister, had wholeheartedly subscribed to their parents' way of living, while Amina tried to straddle the fence as much as she could to keep the peace. Nivea, on the other hand, had always been extremely vocal about her disagreement with the way her parents chose to live. The day she'd gone to her parents with what would be her final and most disturbing complaint, the Cannons had decided to let their youngest daughter go. Forever.

"So what are you going to do? Not marry him? Walk away from the agreement, from your job at the agency, from your million-dollar penthouse, the BMW, the parties, the clothes? Are you really going to give all that up in your quest for true love?" Nivea wished daily that her sister would do exactly this.

Still, she knew without a doubt the answer to that question was no. With that in mind, she was having a hard time entertaining her sister's mostly contrived dilemma because Amina was the most materialistic person Nivea knew. Case in point: today her sister wore a pink silk jumper—her favorite color—silver stilettoes no doubt made by some extremely overpriced designer, diamonds in her ears and on her fingers, she had her hair perfectly coiffed, and a limousine was sitting outside the front entrance to Havenway, waiting patiently for Amina to finish with her visit and leave. Amina wasn't yelling about traveling to Havenway, which was essentially located in the center of a national park, but when she'd first come in she had scoffed at the size of Nivea's room, calling it "a glorified jail cell," even though she'd never seen a jail cell in her entire thirty-one years of life.

"I might," she exclaimed.

Nivea chuckled. "You won't."

"Look at you," Amina said as Nivea moved to where

her boots were, leaning over to shove her foot into one and then the other. "All dressed up in your war clothes, ready to go out and fight."

Amina waved her hand and the silver bangles at her wrist clinked.

"We fight the rogues, Mina," Nivea said with chagrin. It still bothered her that her own family didn't give a damn about the battle the shifters were in for their lives, for the lives of those coming after them. These were precarious times, Nivea knew that. Her family, however, refused to accept it. That fact made her sad, almost as much as the years-long crush she'd had on Lead Guard Eli Preston.

"Yeah, I know," her sister replied. "But I don't know why. They aren't bothering us. Besides, there's crime all over the world, killings and beatings, robberies, and all other sorts of evils lurking around out there. The Shadow Shifters can't expect to defeat them all. That's a futile mission if I've ever heard one."

Pulling her hair back into her favorite black band, Nivea shook her head at her sister. The band and the ponytail were the norm, the curliness of her hair and the soft flirty way it fell down her back was not.

"It's not that simple, not anymore. You should really tell Mom. She needs to come to the next Assembly meeting. There's a lot going on now that all of you should know about and get prepared for," she told her.

"That presentation came in the mail a few weeks ago. Dad didn't bother to look at it and forbade any of us from doing so either. But I did, at least some of it anyway. The new building is nice, much better than this dungeon-like place. Why don't you move there?" Amina suggested hopefully.

Snapping her utility belt around her waist, Nivea resisted rolling her eyes. Of course Richard wouldn't look at anything coming from Rome's law firm. He knew Rome was the Assembly Leader but since he hated all things to do with the shifters, he refused to respect that leadership or whatever came with it. He also knew that Nivea was working here with Rome, yet another reason Nivea was certain he wouldn't want to have anything to do with Havenway.

But Mina wasn't referring to that situation. How could she? No one but Richard, Michele, and Nivea knew the reason for her leaving New York and never looking back. No, her sister's remarks were much more basic. Yes, the state-of-the art facility that had just been completed in Prince George's County, Maryland that was the official Assembly Building with offices for visiting Elders and Faction Leaders and formal meeting space, was a gorgeous glass-and-brass structure. But it was so much more. Glancing down at her e-band, Nivea saw she didn't have the time to try and explain it completely to her sister, not that Amina really cared either way.

"Listen, I have to get to this meeting," Nivea told her as she picked up a bottle of perfume and spritzed.

Amina stood then, dropping her magazine to the floor as she came to stand behind Nivea. She looked at her sister through the mirror. "What?" Nivea asked.

Amina touched a hand to Nivea's ponytail, letting the long, fat curls fall from her elegant fingers. She smiled as she continued to survey her and Nivea shifted uncomfortably.

"What are you looking at?"

"You, little sister," was Amina's soft response. "Perfume, glossed lips, slightly shadowed eyes. You're a pretty little guard, huh?"

"Cut it out," Nivea said, swatting at Amina's hand and moving from the mirror.

"Got your eye on someone, sis? Another guard maybe?"

"No!" Nivea replied, loudly. Too loudly. "Dinner before

you go back to New York?" she asked, changing the subject as they both headed for the door.

Amina continued to smile. "Sure thing. But not here. You have to get dressed in real clothes and we'll go to a nice restaurant. I'll send the car back to get you around seven."

Nivea nodded. "Okay, I'll be ready."

She gave her sister a quick hug then ran down the opposite hallway, knowing she wouldn't be as early as she'd planned, but still hoping to get there before Eli. It was silly, she knew, and well on the side of playing feminine games, which she'd prided herself on never having to do. But as she'd attempted to tell her sister, things were different now. The position of the shifters was more than precarious, and as she would probably learn more about at this meeting, at a very critical state. If she didn't go for what she wanted now, would she get another chance? Would the shifters? She didn't have those answers and she wasn't about to take the risk.

"Captain Lawrence Crowe is the man behind the Genesis Project." Roman Reynolds, Stateside Assembly Leader, spoke to the three hundred and fifty guards that made up the primary defense unit of local Shadow Shifters.

Up and down the East Coast there were thousands more that were prepared to fight for the shifters' secret to be kept. But these were the men and women closest to the Assembly Leader, some that he'd trained himself—namely the Sanchez brothers—and others that had been trained by Xavier Santos Markland and Nicholas Delgado, Lead Enforcers, and Eli and Ezra Preston, Lead Guards in the Eastern Zone. Basically, these were the best of the best.

Nivea's heart hammered in her chest as she realized this. How long had she worked to get to this point? And how foolish did her parents think she was for doing so?

Who was she kidding? Richard and Michele Cannon were thinking about everything else in their socially elite and financially secure world, but not about their youngest child. No, that wasn't quite true, Richard would never forget her, just as she couldn't possibly forget him. Her chest ached at that thought, fists clenching in her lap.

In an effort to relax, to forget, Nivea moved uncomfortably in her seat, settling her gaze on the Assembly Leader and what he was now saying.

"We believe the goal of the Genesis Project is to successfully develop hybrid soldiers using shifter DNA to enhance their abilities. So far Crowe has only come close to achieving this goal. His latest attempt was disposed of in Arizona, where the project may or may not be continuing. Crowe has not been detained."

Rome looked up from the podium then, letting his gaze fall on as many of the guards as he possibly could. There'd always been a very personal feel to everything that happened here at Havenway. Even though the Stateside Assembly was now larger than most corporations, Rome had managed to keep this headquarters as relaxed and family-oriented as he possibly could. The Leader knew most, if not all, of the guards by name, as he often came down to the training center to watch them when time allowed. That had grown less frequent in the past couple of weeks, but everyone knew that was not to be helped.

The kidnapping of Shya Delgado, Nick and Ary's daughter, to try and obtain her DNA to aid in the Genesis Project, had put everyone on edge. Now, sitting here listening to even more information about this project that could force the exposure of the Shadow Shifters was more than a little alarming. And yet there was one person who didn't look distressed at all.

Rayna Corpeta sat in one of the seats along the side wall of the auditorium, closer to the stage than Nivea had been offered. The *Lormenia* shifter wore her uniform pants two sizes tighter than any other female guard, her shirt always unbuttoned to expose her cleavage, leaving nothing to the imagination about her voluptuous breasts. She looked exotic, talked with an accent, and fought almost as well as a portion of the new recruits.

And Nivea didn't trust her as far as she could toss the annoying bitch.

Rayna had one long leg crossed over the other, one hand with fingers running along the line of her throat while the other toyed with her long bronze-tinted hair. She looked around the room almost as if she were bored and Nivea barely resisted the urge to run up and kick the chair from beneath her. Just barely.

"Our number one goal from this point on is finding Crowe and whoever is helping him in this project. Although we are not sure of the others involved, we do know that somehow Crowe managed to obtain shifter DNA. If he has done it once, there is a likelihood that he will do it again, meaning other shifters are at risk. We are confident, however, that once we bring Crowe down this project and all he may be working with will crumble. To that end, I want him found and brought in," Rome said, looking among them once more, his voice ominous as the microphone immediately amplified and silenced it. "Dead or alive," were his final words, spoken with determination and clarity, albeit softer than his previous comments.

With perfectly synched movements, Nick and X fell into step right beside Rome as he walked down from the platform. Kalina, the First Female, stood from her seat in the first row to walk beside her mate as her personal guard, Jax, fell in with the others. As they neared the door Ezra and Eli joined in the ranks, slipping into the line behind Nick and X.

Nivea stood with all the other guards as they always did

the moment the Assembly Leader was on the floor. Their hands remained tucked behind their backs, chins up, eyes focused on the Leader as they silently declared their loyalty and service. Only this time her gaze shifted back a bit, until it rested on him.

His glasses were too dark to see his eyes, not even an outline of them, his chin held high, steps coordinated, strength oozing from every movement of his legs, his arms, his shoulders. She swallowed hard and had to be tapped on the shoulder when her row was ready to file out of the auditorium. She was just about to head to the gym to work off some of this energy she felt running wildly through her body when a touch to her elbow had her jumping.

Fists raised automatically to fight back, she turned, only to have those sunglasses glaring down at her, lips of medium thickness held in a stern line.

"Let's go," Eli told her. "We're running late."

Nivea didn't even bother to speak, wasn't 100 percent sure her voice would cooperate if she wanted to. There were times—like earlier this morning—when she'd been able to hold tight to her attraction to him. And then, there were times like now when just the sight of him made her feel like coming, right then, right there, just letting the abundance of his sexuality take over.

She hated that part. Damn, did she hate it.

Chapter 3

"So Captain Lawrence Crowe is now Public Enemy Number One for the Shadow Shifters," Nivea said, climbing into the passenger side of Eli's Assembly-issued Jeep Wrangler.

The vehicle was silver with windows tinted so dark nothing on the inside could be seen. Each vehicle was specially designed to assist guards in doing their jobs with skill and ease. They had been retrofitted with bulletproof steel. Weapons and ammunition were stored in side-door compartments that were specially lined to go undetected should the vehicles ever be searched. They even had a self-destruct mechanism that, once activated, would cause a chemical explosion that would destroy all evidence of the additions made to the vehicle as well as any other items that may have been inside.

They were pretty slick to look at too.

Nivea hadn't been issued one of her own yet. If Eli recommended her for this promotion, she would. If he didn't she would continue to drive the older-model Jeep with minimal security features that might at some point get her killed. Pulling out of the parking spot, Eli tried not to think along those lines. His job was to train her, to observe as she completed the assignment of investigating Agent Dorian Wilson. It was not to take care of her, protect her, or any of the other bullshit that had been roaming around in his mind where she was concerned lately.

"He's not working alone, we're positive of that fact. Still, the sooner we find Crowe, the sooner we can kill this supersoldier project before it goes any further," Eli told her as he turned right onto the trail that led out of the forest to the main highway.

She'd finished adjusting herself, pulling the lever at the bottom of the seat so that it was a little closer to the dashboard, snapping her seat belt into place, and pushing down the headrest. He had to admit it was too high up for anyone who wasn't at least six feet tall. Eli watched all her movements out of the corner of his eye, unable to keep his attention 100 percent focused on something as menial as driving the damn Jeep when she was around.

"I still can't believe he cloned a shifter. Who would ever think to do something like that, without considering the repercussions?"

The last had been spoken quietly but Eli ignored that. Denying the ability to pinpoint changes in her voice, her demeanor, her hairstyle, was all about self-preservation. It was about coming out of this assignment in one piece, without change. It was how he needed to proceed.

"Believe it," Eli said tightly, taking the Jeep into the busy midmorning traffic on Route 193. "It took Ezra, Bas, and Jacques, three pretty damned powerful shifters, to stop that bastard from killing every shifter in the police department out West."

In his front pocket his cell phone vibrated. Retrieving it, Eli read the message from one of his staff at the barbershop he owned and frowned. He'd been receiving similar ones for days now and chose to ignore them all. Gritting

his teeth, his fingers gripped the steering wheel as he re-
focused his thoughts on the scenario his twin brother
had described with the first hybrid.

Ezra had been there to save the woman who was now
glued to his hip, the human named Dawn who Ezra had
claimed as his mate. That was part of the reason why Ezra's new relationship status irritated the hell out of Eli. For
one, Eli didn't believe in the mating concept of the shifters. The notion that there was one perfect female for every
male was to Eli a lie, plain and simple. His past was living
proof of that fact.

The other reason he wasn't jumping with glee at Ezra
and Dawn's union was that his brother was the second
highest-ranking shifter to not only reveal himself to a human,
but to fall for one and bring her into the shifter fold. Sure,
there'd been two younger couples—two of the three Sanchez brothers that made up one of Rome's newest elite
groups of guards—that had mated with humans. The Assembly Leader thought the relationships might go sour and
cause big problems for the shifters, but Bas and Ezra were
the first two to openly defy the laws of the *Ètica*. Rome
hadn't tried to cover up either of those relationships, instead he'd made Bas's mate, Priya, the official spokesper-
son for the shifters and had welcomed Dawn, the one with
all the secrets, into the fold as well. Simply put, more situations that put the shifters at risk and pissed Eli the hell off.

"I heard about that," Nivea said with more enthusiasm
than he wanted to hear. "They said Ezra almost ripped his
head right off. I guess I can imagine how he felt knowing this 'thing' was going after his mate."

Eli spared her a glance before turning his attention back
to the road. "Don't sound so excited about someone getting
his head ripped off. You're a female, remember."

"What the hell is that supposed to mean?"

He sighed, wanting this conversation to be over, wanting this stupid assignment to be over, once and for all. "It means that you might want to start acting more like a female than a G.I. Jane. From the time you wake up in the morning until you close yourself off in your room after dinner, you're either in the field looking for a fight, or in the cafeteria picking a fight, or just always looking for some way to be physical. That's not what females do."

And saying what he'd just said to a female such as Nivea was the dumbest thing he could have ever done. She was a great guard and he respected that. On the other hand, she was a female, one who could be hurt or even killed being a guard. His thoughts were so conflicted when it came to Nivea Cannon and Eli didn't know why. Or rather, he didn't want to entertain the thought of why. All he knew for certain was that there was a war going on inside him where this particular shifter was concerned. A feeling he'd never felt with any other female in his life—the ones he'd allowed to get close or the ones he'd kept away. Nivea was unlike any of them, a fact that was more than a little disconcerting for Eli.

"First of all," she said, slapping a palm on the dashboard as she turned sideways in the seat. "I can do whatever the hell I want to do. And second, I'm as good a fighter, maybe even better, than half the guards back at Havenway. And if you don't like how I spend my days then stop paying so much attention to what I'm doing with them."

Eli wished like hell it could be that simple. If he could just tell himself to stop thinking about her, stop watching her whenever they were in the same room together, and even going so far as to follow her a time or two, he would have done it months ago. Unfortunately, like Nivea, he tended to do whatever it was he wanted.

"Calm down. Nobody's saying you're not a good guard. I'm just saying you could do other things with yourself instead of focusing so much on the job."

"Oh, really? What other things would you suggest I do, Mr. Preston?"

She could slide across the seat and straddle him, the memory of her soft globes in the palm of his hand was still fresh in his mind. He'd wanted to get his hands on her tight little ass for a long time and this morning, he'd finally had the chance. He almost cursed with the urgency to repeat the action. Or, for the sake of safety since he was driving, she could simply lean over, unzip his pants, and put her smart little mouth over his already engorged tip. She could suck until his release shot out of him in heavy tension-relieving jets. She could grip his length with her strong and capable hands and let him pump mercilessly into her mouth.

Beeping horns snapped him from his erogenous thoughts and Eli realized he'd swerved into the other lane while distracted by things like Nivea's mouth. He turned the wheel in the opposite direction, jerking her across the seat until one of her hands rested on his bicep.

"Need a driving lesson?" she asked sweetly. "Surely, a male shifter would know how to handle his vehicle. Or do you need a female to drive for you instead?"

"Funny," he replied tightly. "Just stay over there in your seat and be ready when we see Wilson. Rome thinks he might be connected to Crowe somehow, feeding him information he may have gathered from looking so closely into Rome and Nick."

"That would make sense," she added, immediately sobering to the business mode. "It's like he has no other cases to work on. All he does every day is sit outside of the law firm. Then when Rome or Nick leaves, he follows them. Never says anything to them, just watches wherever they go and whoever they meet with."

"And what's he doing with all that information?" Eli asked her.

She stared ahead, thinking, he surmised. Nivea Cannon was definitely a thinker. Sure, she was all about action, but there was never a situation she didn't contemplate, didn't analyze until the very last detail. She'd been tailing Agent Wilson for two months now so he was positive she knew everything there was to know about this guy, but so far none of that knowledge had made any difference in how they dealt with the man.

"He keeps a file, one of those Redweld folders. I don't think he trusts computers because I've never seen him with a laptop or a tablet or anything more technical than his cell phone. And even that's an earlier, out-of-date model. Pencils are all over his car along with balled-up pieces of paper. He's writing his notes longhand and the ones he keeps he puts into that Redweld."

"Notes about shifters?"

"Notes about everything he sees that he doesn't think is normal. I think he's beyond looking at Rome as if he's embezzling money or helping any drug cartel. I think he suspects something bigger."

Eli nodded. "Something like supersoldiers."

They'd been sitting in the truck for two hours outside of a cabin in northern Maryland where they'd followed Agent Wilson and two other agents who had exited the Bureau building with him late this afternoon. It was just after nine now, evening draped around the tree-lined ski resort with the whistle of a cool breeze outside.

Nivea answered another one of Mina's angry texts; standing her sister up for dinner was something she would never live down. That thought was soothed by their location and the fact that Nivea loved to ski. She adored the feel of the snow slipping with icy tingles through her fingers whenever she took off her gloves. There was a freedom she enjoyed while flying down the side of a mountain, cold air cutting against the skin of her face, the exhilaration that soared through each part of her body.

Those were good memories. They were the positive thoughts she'd sworn she would have had during her time with Eli. It was imperative that she did not allow Eli, or anyone else for that matter, to dictate how she would feel or think or work. She would not be controlled or handled, not ever again.

Eli had stopped the Jeep about thirty feet to the left of the cabin Agent Wilson had entered with his two guests. He'd parked alongside two other vehicles that they figured belonged to the occupants of the second cabin, a little farther down the hill.

"How long do you think they'll stay in there?" Nivea asked, already tired of sitting in the Jeep.

As much as she treasured her job as a guard, she absolutely despised any type of stakeout. Her legs ached from being bent in the sitting position for so long, her arms from being basically immobile. She'd never liked remaining still, preferring to move, to function, and to live. Still, she knew this was a part of the job.

"Depends on what they're doing," Eli replied finally, pulling his phone out of his jacket pocket.

"Three guys in a secluded cabin, hmm. I would say poker but it would be better with a fourth. Could be a guys' night out, but wouldn't they at least want a female for hire?"

Eli stopped pushing buttons on his phone to look over at her.

"Naughty thoughts always run rampant through your mind when you're on a stakeout?"

Only when I'm on a stakeout with you, she thought, but definitely did not speak.

Instead, she shrugged. "Just thinking out loud."

There was once again silence. It seemed they'd had a

lot of that for long stretches throughout today. That was weird since they could have easily talked about this morning's meeting and the priority search for Captain Crowe. They could have also talked about this morning's hot-as-hell kiss and the way his hands had explored her body with some type of ownership. She had a feeling that was the last thing Eli wanted to discuss.

Which was all the more reason she should bring it up.

"When you're finished letting Ezra and the others know our location for the third time since we've been here, maybe you can tell me why this morning. Why in all the time we've known each other did you decide this morning was the time to make your move?"

Eli's fingers stilled over the phone. He pressed the button to lock the screen and stuffed it back into his pocket before turning to her.

"It happened. It's over. There's nothing more to talk about," he stated, completely expecting her to accept and move on.

He had no idea who he was dealing with.

"It happened. It felt really good. And if we're not going to talk about it, are we at least going to take it a step further?"

He froze.

Nivea felt a small bit of triumph at being able to cause that reaction in him. Nothing ever took Eli off guard. He was always prepared for any- and everything, always had an answer, always knew what to do and when. Except for right at this very moment. He looked at her as if he didn't know whether to formulate another cool dismissive remark, or to give in to the arousal that crowded them both in the cab of the SUV.

"No," he said slowly, solemnly.

She frowned. "No, it didn't feel good? Because I can easily amend that to 'great.' It felt great."

The word came immediately and a bit more forcefully this time. "No, Cannon. We are not going there. Not ever again."

She could take his words as rejection and keep her hurt feelings and tingling nipples to herself. Or she could be the one to acknowledge that what happened this morning had been inevitable and that in the foreseeable future it would happen again. It was like taking that first tentative bite of chocolate, or sipping from that glass of champagne and feeling the bubbles fizz against your nostrils—one taste was never going to be enough.

With that thought, Nivea leapt from her seat. She moved over the console, planted her legs on either side of Eli, and lowered herself to a straddling position in about ten seconds flat. The shock combined with a slightly annoyed look on his face said he wasn't impressed. That was fine because she wasn't finished yet.

"This morning was about you, in your time, and on your terms." She cupped his face in her palms as she spoke. "That was cool, but I'm a take-charge type of female. When I hunt I don't settle for not catching my prey."

He opened his mouth to speak and she dove in, taking his tongue into her mouth and sucking deeply, until she felt his hands at her lower back, going even lower to cup her ass. She loved that feeling, loved how his fingers dug right into her skin, squeezing, owning. She lifted slightly, giving him the access to move his hands deeper, so that even as he gripped her cheeks, the tips of his fingers rubbed along her center, causing her pussy to pulsate with need.

"I said," he mumbled when she let her head fall back, absolutely loving the feel of his hands on her. "We are not doing this."

Nivea nodded, rotating her hips over the finger he'd now moved to rub right along her clit. "Yeah, you said that," she whispered, wanting desperately to step out of those damned mission pants so she could feel him, skin on blessed skin.

She leaned in once again, nipping his lip before reminding him, "But we are."

Her tongue found his again and Nivea felt like she was drowning. He tasted like peppermint, probably because he always kept some type of mint on him.

She moved her hands down to grip his shoulders, strong and rigid, which she'd already known from all the sparring they'd done in the last few weeks. Eli had a great body, all chiseled and muscled, glorious to look at and even more enticing to feel. Nivea pressed against him then, pushing her breasts into his chest, her pussy into his dick. He held her there, thrusting upward as the kiss deepened, their moans filling the interior of the truck.

Then the gunshots sounded and they both jumped.

Her face stayed poised just a couple of inches from his, her mouth still parted as she panted out her breath. His hands stayed on her ass but his gaze immediately went to the left, hers going in the opposite direction, their bodies taut. In the next second they were both out of the Jeep, weapons drawn as they made their way to the next sound of guns being discharged. Eli had yelled "shots fired" into his com link, the sound of his voice exploding in Nivea's ear. Breaking out into a run, they stopped at the back entrance of the second cabin, backs plastered against the wooded walls, arms up, guns in hand.

Every guard on duty would be patched in and would hear the call. They'd check with the controllers at Havenway for the location and head this way as soon as they confirmed. In the meantime, Eli nodded at Nivea. She took the sign and fell to her knees, coming up right beneath a back window. There was a light on so she could look inside. She held back a curse and held up two fingers indicating that there were two men, lying facedown on the floor, blood pooling from their heads.

They were just about to move again, possibly to gain entrance through the back door when there was noise and voices. In seconds, three others joined the party. Agent Wilson entered with his gun drawn, along with the two men that had accompanied him out here. They entered the room of the cabin where the dead bodies lay.

"Let's go."

Nivea heard the words but still did not move.

"Now, Cannon!" Eli said louder. "This isn't our party."

"They're dead," she told him as she got to her feet. "Those men are dead and we're just leaving them."

Eli stopped, turning so that he was now in her face. He grabbed the front of her shirt, pulling her up on tiptoe so that his nose was practically touching hers. "They're humans. Let them take care of their own. We have to move before more of them arrive and question why we, ones that Wilson will already know are connected to Rome and Nick, are here in the first place."

He was right. She knew it. But those men were dead. They'd been killed and Nivea wanted to know by whom. She wanted to know why. Mostly, after seeing the familiar tattoo on one of the dead men's wrists, she wanted to confirm that it had nothing to do with her father and the people he'd been working with for the last ten years.

Chapter 4

Eli was pulling out of the driveway before Nivea had a chance to put her seat belt on. Whoever had been doing the shooting inside that cabin had come running out just seconds after they'd moved from the window. Their guns were immediately raised and even more shots fired.

Did he want to pull his own weapon and shoot back? Hell yes! But Cannon was with him and if he pulled his weapon she was likely to do the same thing. Then they'd both be up against who knew how many flying bullets and if one hit her . . . he clenched his teeth at the thought.

"Why are we the ones running? We have guns too!" she exclaimed about ten seconds after he'd pressed his foot so hard on the gas pedal he thought he might actually break it.

"We're also all the way out here with no backup!" Eli yelled back at her, simultaneously looking into the rear-view mirror to see that not only had the guys shot at them, but they were now chasing them in their car.

"Fuck!" he yelled, making a quick turn off the main road. If he could keep them in the mountain terrain, cutting through the worn paths in and out of the trees, maybe he could lose them.

He cut the lights to the Jeep and spoke into the com link. "Being pursued, can't get back onto main road. I repeat, being pursued."

The first shots to hit the Jeep cracked the back windshield, which meant they had to be using a hell of a powerful gun or rifle. The windows to all the Assembly vehicles were lined with one-and-a-half-inch bulletproof acrylic. It didn't break completely but there was an indentation with spidery cracks instantly breaking away from it and the force rocked the vehicle as they sped over rocky terrain.

"To hell with this!" Nivea yelled.

"No!" Eli yelled right at her, but to no avail.

She'd already drawn her weapon and lowered her window. In the next second she was hanging out of it, aiming and pulling the trigger, bullets firing in rapid succession.

"Get your ass back in here, guard! Cease your fire! That's a direct order!" he yelled.

Nivea kept right on firing while Eli continued to swerve from hitting trees, fallen branches, and all other woodland paraphernalia that he wished like hell weren't in his way at this very moment. There was another direct hit to the back window and the Jeep faltered once more. Eli knew if they sustained another assault like that the window would completely shatter and they'd be vulnerable. Either something had to stop them from shooting or he had to find somewhere to hide. The odds of either one were slim.

Except Cannon continued shooting, and as much as he hated to admit it, whatever she aimed at, she hit. They were going downhill now at an extremely fast rate of speed. He pressed gently on the brake and yelled to her once more. "Either kill them or get your ass back in this truck, Cannon!"

She didn't acknowledge him in any way, just kept shooting until there was a loud noise and an explosion of light behind them. Eli swerved at the sight of the burning car twenty feet from them, his heart hammering in his chest. He turned the wheel so hard this time the entire vehicle jerked and jollied down the mountain. The vehicle was swerving now, going whichever way it wanted as Eli had lost full control. Because he had no headlights on, he saw nothing through the front windshield but darkness and heard nothing from behind but the remnants of the burning car falling to the ground, the flames cracking against the night air.

He reached across the seat, grabbing Cannon by her waist and pulling her back inside. Of course she couldn't come quietly, or limply, for that matter. She kicked and screamed and yelled and he ignored every second of it, opening the driver's side door and rolling out with her wrapped tightly in his arms, only seconds before the Jeep crashed into a tree, creating another loud noise and burst of fiery light on the mountaintop.

She was beneath him again.

For the second time in less than twenty-four hours, Nivea Cannon's strong, athletic body with all its barely there curves that enticed him more than he wanted to admit, was flush against his harder, tougher body, wreaking holy hell all over the place.

The tall licking flames coming from two downed vehicles had already invaded the mountaintop range. Eli moved, spreading his legs wider, grabbing the back of her neck and tucking it tightly into his chest. The heat surrounding them was palpable, sweat rolled down the back of his neck and spine prompting him to hold onto her even tighter. There was a crash and he figured tree limbs were burning and breaking, falling to the ground where, if unattended, this accident might actually turn into a catastrophe.

But he couldn't think about a forest fire right now, couldn't think along the lines of being trapped between the flames and the night elements—which were quickly turning chilly. His truck was gone and with it, backup clothes, weapons, and a first-aid kit he thought he might need soon.

Still, he didn't let Cannon go.

Until she squirmed.

She moved beneath him and goddammit, Eli felt like she was gyrating, like she was pushing her pussy up to meet his raging hard dick in an effort to join the two forevermore. His temples pounded at the thought. His temples and his dick throbbed while inside, his cat hissed.

They weren't safe. They were definitely not safe enough for him to be lying here thinking about fucking his trainee when he should have been thinking about how to get them out of here sooner rather than later.

". . . me."

The solitary word broke through his thoughts and he looked down to see the top of her head. Her hair was mussed, he thought with a frown. Then out of the corner of his eye he saw flames reaching higher into the evening sky and cursed.

". . . off!"

It was the next word he heard before he felt something rising between his legs. Something that wasn't what he wanted to rise down there at this particular time. He moved the lower half of his body to the side just in time to avoid the knee she had raised.

"What the hell?" he asked, looking down at her again.

This time she pushed at his chest until she was able to lift her head and glare back up at him.

"Get off me, you idiot! I can't breathe."

"You can't breathe because there's fire and smoke all over the place and if you hadn't noticed, I'm trying to protect your ass from that."

In reply she pushed at him again, this time with much more force. Cannon was not a weak woman. In fact, she was stronger than a lot of the guards Eli had trained. He'd always known that about her, just hadn't liked admitting it too much, and never to her. She was still no match for him, but he did move a bit to oblige her efforts. She let out a whoosh of breath and squirmed a little more, until he could swear he felt the tight buds of her nipples moving across his chest. But that was just TMI—too much imagination—on his part.

"They're dead," she said solemnly, her dark eyes looking up at him.

There was no emotion there and he hadn't expected to find anything. Cannon was, above all else, a professional at what she did. She took her job as a guard more seriously than he thought he did sometimes. With any other woman he would have expected tears or fear or whichever emotion she chose to cope with what had just gone down. But not Cannon.

Her eyes were focused, her hands steady as they pushed at him again, her voice clear and concise. She was right at this moment—aside from wanting him to get the hell off her—assessing the situation to see how they could get out of there before anyone showed up to ask questions.

"I gave them our location when we first heard the shots," he began. "They would have pulled up the Jeep's tracking immediately."

"The Jeep's gone," she said, coming up to a sitting position and looking around.

Eli looked around too. He glanced at the side reflection of her face—no cuts or bruises. Farther down his eyes raked over her body looking for blood or burns, anything to say that he'd been off in his protection and she'd gotten hurt anyway. A lump formed in his throat as he waited for the final results.

She was saying something but he didn't hear her, he was too busy grabbing her jaw and turning her so that he could see her whole face at once. Smooth caramel-toned skin, thick eyebrows arched perfectly, long lashes, high cheekbones, thin lips—the lower one plumper than the top, long neck . . . she was unharmed, he thought with a blink or two to get his mind back in the right place.

"I'm fine," she said with a little bite. "We can't sit here. The smoke's getting thick and the police and rescue units will be here soon. We weren't far enough away from the resort for no one to have seen or heard anything."

Eli nodded. "You're right. Can you walk?" he asked as he got to his feet.

She stood, reaching behind to pull her backup gun free from the band of her pants. "Can you?"

He removed his gun from his side, trying like hell not to notice how totally sexy she looked just now. "Highway's this way," he told her, turning his back on her and walking in the direction he wanted her to follow. "They'll come through the main roads to find us."

"Yeah, but they'll find the cops first. We should call them and give them an alternate route," she was saying from behind.

"You know an alternative route?" he asked.

"No," she replied after a few hesitant seconds.

"Then we'll head for the highway."

It seemed like they were walking forever and getting absolutely nowhere. The terrain consisted of branches and dirt-impacted leaves riddling the ground. It was rough going downhill, up a winding incline, and then back to level ground once more. Yet Nivea wasn't tired. Adrenaline buzzed through her body with a uniform rhythm.

Her muscles were bunched, her senses heightened, her steps sure and purposeful while moving through the night.

Above, the trees weren't as thick and tangled to create a canopy like in the Gungi, but they were full and mature, standing like guardians to the area, protecting what wildlife it could. Only they weren't humans and the hike to the highway was much longer than they'd anticipated.

Eli the Great would never admit that, nor would he stop to regroup or possibly ask her thoughts on which way they should go. He was following his instincts, she knew, but her instincts were telling her something else. They were warning her that this little escape was about to turn bad, quick.

"Stop!" she said finally, halting her own steps, knowing that if he chose to ignore her words, he'd hear that she wasn't crunching along the ground behind him.

It was well-known that Eli's and his brother's senses were much more acute than any of the other shifters. Nobody was really sure why, and the twins weren't the type to wear their secrets on their sleeves. Yet they were renowned for their added awareness and much more powerful shifters because of it. Nivea didn't think that made a difference in how she felt about Eli . . . until he kept walking.

"Eli?" She yelled to him once. "Eli!"

He finally turned, already about fifteen feet away from her.

"What is it?" he asked. "Why are you stopping?"

Even through the night she could see his features plainly, the sharp cut of his jaw and the light sprinkle of his goatee. His eyes were blocked as usual, but the wrinkle in his forehead told her he was worried. The muscle ticking in his jaw said he was angry on top of that worry. And the rigid stance he took when he was looking at her with nothing short of irritation said that now might not be the best time to question him.

Still, Nivea had never been known to take the easy way out.

"I think we might be lost," she told him.

"I don't get lost."

She nodded, knowing that was what he was going to say.

"I didn't say 'you' were lost, I said 'we.' "

He frowned.

"Look around you, there's no road in sight, nor is there any illumination from a streetlight."

"No streetlights on the highway," he corrected her grimly.

"Fine, but when's the last time you heard a vehicle driving by, saw some headlights?"

"In case you failed to notice, we're in the forest," he told her. "How would we hear cars or see headlights, if we're in the goddamned forest, Cannon? Think!" he yelled at her.

Nivea didn't speak, she was thinking, and not because he said so. She was very aware of everything around them, down to the creaking of the crickets pouncing about on the forest floor and in the trees. She could still scent the burning of the gas in the truck that had crashed, hear the crackle of fire that wasn't too far behind them. She could taste the rain as a shower was imminent and she hadn't heard any vehicles on the road or seen any headlights. If she was aware of all those things, why wasn't Eli?

She walked to him then, feeling the rage and something she couldn't quite name surrounding him like a barrier.

"Are you okay?" she asked.

He huffed. "I'd be better if we weren't standing here having a futile conversation. There's an extraction team on their way for us. We should keep moving."

"Maybe we should take a rest. The team will be able to locate us through our e-bands. We don't have to keep trekking around this forest, going in circles. I think we're deep enough in to have sufficient cover. Besides, nobody's following us."

"How the hell do you know that?" he asked, gritting his teeth.

"Because I don't smell them," she said slowly, eyeing him carefully. "Do you?"

Eli remained quiet, his lips tight, shoulders strained. "If you were tired of walking all you had to do was say so," he told her roughly, pushing past her and heading back to where they'd just passed a grouping of trees with protruding roots.

"Come," he demanded. "Sit here and rest."

Nivea didn't like his tone and might have considered arguing if he weren't her commanding officer. Her mind was also whirling around the possibility that Eli's senses weren't working as well as they should be, and what that might imply.

She walked over and lowered herself to the ground, folding her legs beneath her as she sat. Eli still stood, staring down at her like she was a disobedient child.

"Your turn," she told him, patting the spot next to her.

His movements were much more reluctant than hers but in seconds Eli's six-foot-three, two-hundred-and-twenty-five-pound body was folding down beside hers. He didn't cross his legs as she had done. Instead his long limbs were extended in front of him, his palms resting on his thighs.

"What do you think happened back there?" she asked, looking away from him and staring ahead into the night.

"Somebody was shot," he snapped.

"Don't be obtuse," was her quick comeback. "Dorian Wilson wasn't one of the dead bodies, but we saw him go into that cabin. So was he one of the shooters? And why? He's an FBI agent, not a murderer, at least not that I've seen in all the time I've been watching him. What if something changed? If somehow, now he is growing desperate."

"Assess the situation, Cannon," Eli said after a heavy

sigh. "Three men went into the cabin, we saw two lying on the floor covered in blood. Wilson wasn't one of them."

"Wilson also wasn't the one chasing us in that truck. So there had to be more than just those three men. Somebody had already been at the cabin waiting for Wilson and the others."

"And what did all these men have to do with us? How are they connected to Wilson's investigation of the shifters?" Eli asked.

He wasn't really expecting her to answer, Nivea knew. He was staring ahead also, contemplating. He didn't know what had happened in that cabin just as she didn't, but he was thinking about it, and he wasn't happy about his thoughts.

"Wilson's focus has always been on Rome and Nick. I didn't recognize those men that were with him. What if they were military men? What if they were connected to Crowe?"

"Only focus on the positives, Cannon. Crowe's our number one target, but Wilson's a threat as well. We need to keep them separate, consider they have two different agendas and work both issues separately, yet with equal vigor."

"Separate, but equal," she said softly, thinking over his words and trying like hell to ignore the heat sizzling between them as he sat closely beside her.

It was becoming enough of a distraction that Nivea had almost forgotten the tattoo she'd seen on one of the dead men's wrists before Eli had ordered her away from the window. She'd seen it before, the scaling length wrapping around the entire wrist, the head with its mouth open right at the vein of the man's arm. It was an anaconda and represented a reminder of certain death.

"If Wilson has help in his little crusade we're going to find out." Eli had continued talking.

Nivea took a deep breath, sitting up straighter and forcing herself to deal with the matter at hand, to keep the issues in her life separate but equal.

"Right," she said with a nod. "I've got a feeling he's still playing this close to the vest and today's little meeting may have shocked him as much as it did us."

"Why do you say that?"

"He doesn't strike me as an underhanded dealer. I mean, sure, he's hunting Rome and Nick, but honestly, he has good reason. He's a human and they're not. He knows something is going on and he's right. Hell, it's been in the news for months now. I saw some newspaper clippings on the desk in his home office. So I know he's following each one of those stories carefully, especially the one in Sedona where there were witnesses who actually gave statements of seeing large cats at the resort when it was burning down."

"Whose side are you on, Cannon?" Eli asked with a rise in his tone.

She looked at him, still feeling the desire drawing them together like being sucked unknowingly into some hypnotic trance. His entire demeanor was guarded, defensive, angry, but he was too stubborn to admit why. The scent she always associated with him was notches higher than the normal fresh, earthy scent of the Shadows. No, Eli, had a scent of his own. It was stronger, headier than anything Nivea had ever encountered, whether here in the States or in her visits to the Gungi. It was power and strength and primal masculinity all combined with a robust musky flavor that never failed to arouse her.

"How dare you ask me that!" was her quick and slightly overreactive response. "I'm on the right side," she continued. "I'm just stating the facts that I've gathered so far. Wilson is searching for the truth. He knows the answer is out there and that's why he won't stop."

"Until I stop him." Eli scowled back at her, a low grumble from his cat echoing through the clearing.

"We," she corrected. "We're in this together, remember?"

The way he cocked his head at her said he'd been trying to forget. But in the next instant his hand was at the back of her head, pulling her hard and fast to him, his lips taking possession instantly.

Chapter 5

Dammit! He was doing it again!

Why couldn't he keep his hands . . . and mouth . . . off of her?

Eli knew why and he wanted like hell to ignore it, just as he had been ignoring all the other signs. It wasn't easy, then again, nothing in his life had ever been easy. Not since he'd turned sixteen and experienced his first shift. From that moment on it had been downhill and only the cat within had ever been able to offer any solace.

But right now it wasn't solace that the cat was offering, it was a long, ragged purr as Eli's tongue stroked along-side Nivea's. She kissed him back with such vigor and intensity, just as she did everything else. Her arms wrapped tightly around him, offering him everything he'd been giving her. As if they were equal opponents in fighting as well as kissing. That thought made his dick hard, his kiss grow hungrier as he used his tongue to lick over her lips, sucking hard on the lower one as she breathed deeply.

Her cat was also at the surface, sending a clear message that it was ready and available and just as needy as his. At that point Eli wanted to pull back. He did not want their cats joining forces, their animalistic urges meeting and combining. He did not want to be connected to Nivea in any way.

Unlike what the other shifters wholeheartedly believed, there was no perfect mate for Eli. He'd realized that long ago. It seemed silly now to hang on to one of the human sayings for dear life, but he absolutely believed in the three strikes and you're out philosophy. Acacia had been his first, Leanne, his second, and now . . . no, Nivea was not next. He was not going to put himself in that position, or take her through what his track record had proven was an ordeal. He could not do that to her.

And yet, he could not pull away, could not release this hold that his attraction to her seemed to have on him. For months he'd been trying to avoid her, going to whichever part of Havenway was farthest from her. Then Rome pushed them together, giving the assignment for him to see her through her final training, to see if she was ready for a promotion. Eli understood that and he knew what his job was. But damn, why couldn't it have been another guard, any other guard? Why Nivea and why now?

"This isn't going to stop," she whispered through panting breaths as he bit along the line of her jaw. "We might as well accept it and get on with it."

Fuck!

Why was she talking?

Eli went back for her mouth, sucking her tongue deep into his mouth, feeling only a small measure of triumph at silencing her, even though her words continued to echo in his head. His hands were moving then, searching for something to silence the words, the logic of what she'd said. He ran his finger up and down her spine, then around to where his thumbs brushed along the slight curve of her breasts. She had her uniform jacket and shirt on, too many damn layers for him to feel the warmth he knew was awaiting him beneath. He was just about to pull away, just about to curse all that was real and complicated about this world they lived in, when his body went still.

His cat went on alert and he whispered over her lips, "Don't move."

She blinked as if confused, but remained still. Eli did not blink, he kept his cat's eyes open and focused on what, he didn't quite know. And then he did, he could see it as clear as day.

Agent Wilson alive and well, driving a dark sedan down the highway, surpassing the speed limit.

Eli did blink then, trying to figure out what he was seeing and why. He heard another sound and in the next instant, was up. Jumping away from her, Eli had his gun drawn and pointed into what was now darkness, not a car driving down the highway. His heart hammered in his chest as he struggled to grasp what the hell was going on. He was lost in the goddamned forest and wanting Nivea like he'd never wanted another female before. And he was seeing crap he knew wasn't there. He wanted to yell with the rage of helplessness, a feeling he despised more than fear, but admitted to feeling more of in the last few weeks.

It was as he was taking a deep breath, trying to convince himself that he was overreacting that Eli looked into the darkness once more, his finger tapping the trigger of his gun lightly, readily. That's when the tall, broad form appeared.

"Mom isn't going to appreciate it if you shoot me," Ezra, Eli's older twin, said glibly, taking the couple extra steps until they were face-to-face.

Eli lowered his arm with a scowl on his face. He'd heard the noise, the barest swipe of an arm against a tree trunk and he'd scented an intruder, the soft scent of warm chocolate. But he hadn't known it was his brother, hadn't picked up their blood connection, nor that of the other guards that came from the trees at that moment.

"She might be happy to finally get rid of you," Eli quipped, clicking the safety back on his gun and slipping it down the back band of his pants. He'd already turned away from Ezra, not wanting his brother to see his querying look.

"I doubt that since I'm her favorite," Ezra continued, moving past Eli to offer his hand to Nivea, who had shockingly remained seated on the tree stump.

Of course she refused the help, coming to her feet on her own and using her hands to dust the leaves and debris from her clothes. Eli watched her hands moving over taut thighs, the curve of her ass, then down her legs again. Cursing, he looked away from her as well.

"You ride with me and tell me everything that happened," Nick Delgado, one of the Eastern Zone Lead Enforcers, said once he'd made his way over to where Eli was standing. "Let Nivea go in the other car with Zach and Tobias."

"Where're X and Caprise? Why aren't their guards with them?" Eli questioned immediately. Ever since the first threats against Rome and Nick surfaced, each high-ranking Shadow had been assigned a personal guard. Zach was X's and Tobias was X's mate, Caprise's, guard. If those two were here, then who was guarding the other Lead Enforcer and his mate?

"They're at Havenway for the night so they're covered," Nick answered testily. "Now, follow me to the truck."

Nick Delgado was not one to be questioned. He was the most volatile of the Eastern Zone Shadows, with a reputation for a temper that preceded him in and out of the courtroom. Considering it had only been about two weeks since his daughter, Shya, had been kidnapped and returned, the fact that he was in human form and not a cat looking for everyone at Comastaz Labs to kill, was a high point. Eli was irritated and carrying a certain attitude himself, but he wasn't foolish enough to tempt the raging bull, so he followed Nick. But not before looking over to where Nivea was being led away by Zach.

"She's cool," Ezra said, clapping a hand on Eli's shoulder. "They'll get her side of the story and we're all gonna meet up with Rome when we get back to Havenway."

Falling in line beside his brother's sure gait, Eli continued to frown, his gaze averted. "What's with the divide-and-conquer routine?" he asked, being careful to keep his voice low since Nick was just a couple of feet ahead. Knowing the Lead Enforcer, he could probably still hear every word they were saying, but Eli wasn't going to be overly concerned about that. He had a right to know what was going on, and what the higher-ups were thinking about tonight's development.

"X got a tip from one of his FBI buddies that someone within the department has gone rogue and launched their own investigation into the law firm," Ezra told him as they made their way through the trees.

Eli noted they were going in the opposite direction from where he and Nivea had been traveling. No doubt, she'd noticed the same thing and was eager to rub it in his face that he'd been going the wrong way. Bad sense of direction, faulty senses, heightened sex drive. Damn, he thought with a sigh. Just, fucking, damn!

"Another investigation into Rome and Nick? Why? Didn't they already bark up that tree and get shot down?"

More than a year ago the First Female, Kalina, had been sent to investigate the firm that Rome and Nick ran together. She'd been unsuccessful in proving they were embezzling money, but positive in bringing out her true shifter form and joining with the current Assembly Leader.

"One of them never let go," Ezra said solemnly.

Eli sighed. "Wilson. We followed him from his office out here tonight. That's how this all got started."

They'd just stepped through the trees onto the bank of grass that led up a small incline to where six black Jeeps and one Suburban—all filled with shifters—were parked along the shoulder of the highway.

"That's why it's imperative we figure out who was in that cabin with him. Rome wants to know who else Wilson has convinced to help him with this witch hunt."

"He thinks it's someone from Comastaz, doesn't he?" Eli asked when they'd reached the SUV.

"Get in and we'll talk about it," Nick directed as he opened the passenger-side door.

Eli gave Ezra a questioning look but his brother only shrugged as he moved around to open the driver's-side door. Eli climbed into the back, avoiding the urge to look back once more to make sure Cannon was safely tucked in one of those Jeeps behind him. She wasn't his personal concern. There were other guards here now who'd be there if something should go down. They would protect her. Hell, she would probably end up protecting them, he thought, letting his hands fall to his knees as Ezra pulled out into traffic.

He had just about convinced himself not to think about her anymore when once again she was thrust into the forefront of his mind.

"Tell me everything you know about Nivea Cannon and her investigation of Agent Dorian Wilson," Nick said the moment the SUV was on the road.

Eli's forehead touched the tiles of his shower as he rested his head, wondering not for the first time in the last few months what the hell was going on in the shifter world.

The conversation with Nick had been tense to say the very least. Most of that was attributed to the instantly defensive stance Eli had taken against Nick's questioning of Nivea and her motives where Agent Wilson was concerned. No, correct that, the Lead Enforcer was hinting around at the fact that Nivea might not be as loyal to the shifters as she pretended to be.

"She's one of the best damn guards we have at Havenway, sir," Eli had responded tightly. "There's no other guard as dedicated to fighting for us as Nivea is. I'd venture to say sometimes I think she's too dedicated to her job and perhaps needs more of a personal life."

Why he'd said the last, Eli had no idea. The words had immediately been regretted as Nick—astute and practiced litigator that he was—pounced instantly.

"My point exactly," he replied. "All she does is work. Lately that's consisted of following Agent Wilson. But today, her sister came to visit her. All the way from New York. Did you know about that?"

He hadn't known.

"Should I have?" he replied instantly, drawing a look from Ezra through the rearview mirror and a glare from Nick as he turned in his seat.

"You were assigned to her for a reason, Eli. And that was to find out everything she knows," Nick told him. He'd been looking at Eli as if he should have already known what his job was, and that his question, along with his ignorance, was not going over well.

"I thought my assignment was to give her additional training and to see if she was ready for a promotion," he deadpanned.

"We can't promote her if she's working against us, now, can we?"

"What the hell do you mean working against us? Nivea's been dedicated to the shifters since the first day she came here. If you doubt that why not call Bas and ask him. He's known her since she was a kid."

"And that makes him biased," Nick snapped. "Besides, this intel we just received is about Nivea and the real reason she left New York. Considering how long I've known you I'll let you slide this one time if you don't know what that reason is. But I'm telling you right now that we need to know everything about her and her family and we need to know it soon. So do your job and get the information."

"So you think I know why she left and I'm not telling you?" he asked Ezra specifically. "You really think I would do that to you or the tribe? If I knew something about her that affected us all, I would have told you already."

Ezra turned in the seat, looking his twin directly in the eye as he spoke quietly this time. "You haven't been yourself lately and you know it. Maybe she's the one who will make this all go away for you. I don't know, so forgive me for having to ask where your head is right now."

Eli hadn't replied to that. He hadn't known what to say. Instead, he sat in the back of that truck for the next two hours, steaming over the fact that Nick actually believed there was something disingenuous about Nivea and that his brother obviously didn't trust him.

He yanked the cloth and the sponge roughly from the rack beneath the showerhead and began to wash, all the while grumbling about the newly focused assignment he'd been given. It promised to bring him even closer to Nivea Cannon, when in all actuality he'd been trying like hell to stay away from her.

There was no other choice for him where she was concerned. If she were dangerous to anyone at Havenway, it was Eli. Ezra's comment in the truck proved he still believed all that BS the shaman Dagar had told them after blowing that foul-assed black smoke into their lungs. Eli, on the other hand, believed none of it. He'd agreed to the shaman's treatment to ebb their sexual desire when they were in the Sierra Leone because the addiction to Acacia had gotten out of hand. It was interfering with their goal to become guards and their family's reputation. Not to mention, they'd learned that to Acacia it had all been just a sick joke anyway.

The damned smoke hadn't even worked. Eli had lain in his bed that night still wanting to touch Acacia, to taste her, to fuck her one more time. And when her minions had summoned him and Ezra, Eli had gone willingly. Just as he'd killed her readily when it was clear that she planned to kill him and Ezra.

The black smoke did not possess him as Ezra believed it did him. It did not control Eli's already acute senses—the senses that were jacked the hell up at this very moment. And the supposed remnants of that smoke in his system damn sure weren't going to subside and do his bidding the moment he came across his so-called mate. That was all myth and fairy tales that Ezra chose to believe because it worked well for his situation. Eli, fortunately, had learned long ago that if there was going to be a change in his circumstances, he would be the one to make it. He was the one in control of his destiny, not some spirit-filled holy man or his drug-induced treatments.

Even with all that he'd learned over the past years, everything that he'd come to terms with, Eli could not deny the obvious. There was something going on with him. Just as Ezra said in the truck, he hadn't been himself lately. He knew that and hated the fact almost as much as he hated his brother being the first to vocalize it.

Slamming his palm against the faucet, Eli turned off the water and stalked naked out of the shower and straight into his bedroom, yanking the towel off the edge of the bed. He was bent over, drying his calves when he paused, his head turning toward the door, his focus trained on who was approaching. He couldn't scent anyone, and wasn't expecting any company. Yet, he knew she was there.

The sound of her footsteps was muffled, but if he closed

his eyes Eli knew he'd see her as clearly as if she were standing right in front of him. He knew because he'd done so before. Her boots came up to the quarter point of her leg, black leather tied precisely. The bottoms of her uniform pants would be tucked neatly inside the top half of the boots. Her pants fit her tightly, had just enough space for her to run, kick, and jump comfortably and still managed to outline her delectable little ass in the sweetest way. Her dark blue T-shirt was more form-fitting, cupping hand-sized breasts and holding them high. She wouldn't be wearing her top shirt with the buttons and right breast pocket while inside Havenway and certainly not at this time of night. Her hair would be pulled back into that ponytail that drove him insane with the need to tear it free and watch the thick strands fall wildly around her face.

Coming to a standing position, Eli inhaled deeply, slowly, his eyes fastened on the door. On the exhale, about twenty seconds after he'd first sensed her presence, there was a sturdy knock.

He dropped the towel and walked slowly to the door, turning the knob and pulling it open just as she was about to knock again. She looked into his eyes, then down to his chest, then to his groin where his dick was growing steadily aroused in response.

"You gonna stand and stare or did you want to come in?" he asked after another few seconds of watching her appreciate him.

If he were a different type of man that appreciation would have gone a long way. It would have puffed his ego, maybe made him smile, and most certainly would have aroused him even more. As it was, Eli, the deeply scared shifter, was only wary of her look, of the desire she so quickly tossed his way. He had good reason to be cautious, to want to keep her as far away as he possibly could. But still he stepped to the side, inhaling deeply as she walked by.

Her scent was there now, when he should have picked it up before. Shifters relied 100 percent on their scenting abilities, of enemies, feelings, situations . . . mates, or in Eli's case, simply females. Gritting his teeth once more at the anomaly he was presently experiencing, Eli closed the door, locked it, and turned to once again find her staring at him.

"I want to know what they said to you in the truck tonight," she said, holding her hands down at her sides, looking into his eyes this time, as if she wasn't as sexually aware of him as he knew she was.

Eli walked to her. It wasn't by choice, he swore it wasn't. The cat within was instantly drawn to her feline, reaching out for the similar being, wanting desperately to forge a connection. The man knew better, he knew what would result from this and yet, he couldn't stay away. He'd never been able to listen to the warning and stay away.

"I don't think that's what you really want, Cannon," he told her seriously, standing so close to her now the buckle of her belt brushed against his thick length. The touch was cool and sent spikes of desire flaring quickly throughout Eli's body.

Every muscle tensed, every nerve stood on end, his breath growing more labored as he tried once again to make the effort. Pull away, back up, grab that damned towel, and get rid of her!

"I'm not here to play your games, Eli. Not tonight," she replied, breaking his concentration with the deep husky sound of her voice.

He reached around her then, grabbing the band from her hair before she could think to stop him and yanking it free.

"This is far from a game," he told her, watching with amazement as all that thick and wild hair fell loose, landing on her shoulders, framing her face. "Everything that happens from this point on will be serious and have consequences."

She kept her gaze level with his. Never backing down. It just wasn't in her nature to walk away from a fight or a challenge. How many times had he watched her in the sparring ring with shifters twice her size and weight? When she should have cowered or could have hidden beneath the "female" shield, she never did. She stood her ground and she fought, most times winning over the cocky male who thought far too little of her. Those thoughts made what Eli said next seem futile.

"If you plan to run away, now would be the time."

She squared her shoulders. "I was never the one running, Eli. That was always you."

Like dropping a match into a gallon of kerosene, her words sparked an inferno inside and Eli was immediately wrapping his arms around her waist, drawing her to him. "Not anymore," he murmured before crushing his lips down over hers. "Not anymore," he repeated as he pulled slightly away, only to plunge back inside again, his tongue taking hers in an intimate duel.

She tasted like fresh rain, like water to a parched thirst that threatened his speech. Her tongue was warm and tangled expertly with his. Her hands grasped his biceps, the palm of her right hand flat against the head of his cat tattoo. Heat pooled in his arm, grew into a ball of molten lava that seeped quickly throughout his bloodstream. The feeling was intense, immediate, and climactic. Inside Eli shook. Outside, he reacted.

He kissed down the line of her neck, loving the way she let her head fall back, giving him what he wanted without any argument. This wasn't the usual way she reacted to him. And this wasn't the usual way he treated her.

His hands gripped her breasts, loving the feel of the soft mounds against his palms. He squeezed and she hissed. He growled and she arched her back, giving him even more. Eli didn't want her giving him anything. He didn't want anybody giving him anything, not anymore. Not since Acacia had given him and Ezra all that they'd desired.

That thought spurred darkness to swirl around inside. To combat the ugly feeling Eli grabbed her by the wrist. She was standing with her legs slightly spread, her eyes half closed, mouth open as she sucked in a ragged breath each time he touched her. He glanced at her fingers—the same ones he'd watched handle a gun, dismembering it and then shooting its target precisely. When he hesitated, she continued, wrapping her hand around his thick and throbbing cock. Her fingers didn't meet around the flesh but she didn't seem concerned. Grabbing him at the base she jerked him once, then twice, then with a rhythm that had him pumping into her motions.

"That's what you wanted, wasn't it?" he said through clenched teeth. "You've wanted this for weeks, months even. Now's your chance to take it," he told her.

When she only kept her gaze fixed on his, her hand still working his length until drops of essence filled his tip, Eli yelled, "Take it!"

She lowered herself to her knees, still looking up at him, daring him to be the first to look away. Her fingers worked like magic had been infused in each tip, pulling from him every reason he'd had for staying away from her. She was dangerous. Being with her was going to lead to more trouble than it was worth. Eli knew this without a doubt, and yet he could . . . would not look away.

"Watch me," she told him, licking her tongue over her lips until they were shiny and damp. "Watch me, Eli."

She didn't have to tell him. Damn, an earthquake or a full-on attack from those hybrids couldn't stop him from watching her pretty fucking lips opening wide enough to fit the head of his throbbing cock inside. It was hot, god-dammit, so freakin' hot inside her mouth, and tight, the pressure was enough to make his balls swell. Pleasure zipped through his bloodstream like heroin through an addict's veins and he loved it. Everything in his past be damned, he loved it. He was heady with the sensation, his cat purring incessantly inside, that dark that dared to rear its ugly head with memories pushed far away until there was nothing but the light in her eyes. Eli couldn't look away from her any more than he could pull his dick from her mouth. He was stuck in this place, in this moment, regardless of how wrong he knew it was.

She used both hands now, pressing against the base of his cock, while her mouth worked the tip. She licked up and down the back and topside, letting her tongue play in the slit until she was slurping the remnants of his pre-cum. Her lips were drenched now, her fingers damp, her breathing erratic as she continued to work over him. And her eyes stayed on his.

That may have been the sexiest part of this interlude. The way her almond-shaped eyes remained open and stared at him, as if he were the only person in this room, this world that she wanted to see. His hips jutted forward and she relaxed her throat muscles to take him deeper, humming over the tip of his dick, bringing forth the release he figured she'd been waiting for.

Stop!

The word echoed in his mind but he didn't speak it or move out of her way.

"You can't have me," he said impulsively. He had no idea why he'd made the declaration. Why at this moment he felt he had to say those very words to her. But it didn't matter.

Nivea took them as a dare, as another one of his rebuffs that she planned to prove wrong. She locked her fingers around him, tilted her head, and flattened her tongue against the bottom of his cock. Then she sucked and sucked some more, her eyes glazed with pleasure. Eli felt it in his spine, his body vibrating with the intensity of the release ripping free. The next time she didn't suck, she swallowed and Eli growled.

Chapter 6

Nivea was sure she'd lost every last piece of her mind. From the moment she'd been struck speechless by Eli's gorgeously naked body standing in the doorway until the second she'd gone to her knees and taken him into her mouth, she'd been operating solely on autopilot.

"You can't have me."

There, he'd said it once more.

She shouldn't have had to hear it again. Except his words never seemed to match his actions. He hadn't walked away, hadn't thrown her out. No, he'd stood right there, giving her . . . him. And she'd taken.

Just as she was now as he yanked her shirt over her head and ripped her bra from her chest. His lips were fastened to her in seconds, his hands squeezing her swollen mounds, while his teeth and tongue toyed with her nipple until her thighs trembled.

Nivea reached for her belt buckle, trying like hell to help this moment along. She'd waited so long, needed so desperately. His words drowned in the buzz of pleasure, the adrenaline rush of anticipation.

Eli swiped her hand away instantly. "I got this," he

growled, his incisors longer and sharper than they had been just moments before. Shadows looked like humans, from their head to their feet when they weren't in full shift. They walked and talked like any other man or woman on the streets, hence the reason they'd been able to live amongst the humans without detection for so long.

But there'd always been something different about Eli. From the first day Nivea had laid eyes on him she'd noticed it. His jaw was stronger, more pronounced than his twin's, his muscles more defined right down to the strength in his hands and the corded veins that never quite went away. While Stateside Shadows trained to keep their animalistic nature safely secure, Eli was the only one who wasn't totally able to achieve that. Hence, the sunglasses to keep anyone from seeing the bright gold of his cat's eyes. He exuded strength and power and the keen hunter's instincts of the jaguar that he was inside. There was no amount of training or warning that could change that.

Nivea shivered at the thought.

His hands were rough as they hurriedly moved to the laces of her boots, pulling them off while she supported herself by holding onto his shoulder. When she would have allowed her fingers to wallow in the strength, the taut skin over trained muscle, Eli had a mission. He yanked her pants and underwear down, pulling them from her ankles before lifting her into his arms.

"You wanted it, now you're going to get it," he whispered in her ear just before biting down on the lobe.

The sting of pain was instant, rippling down her body in quick jolts. She couldn't help but cry out, no matter how submissive she thought it made her sound. When he dropped her to the bed Nivea didn't have a moment to catch her breath before he was over her. The hunter moving on its prey.

Later, she would swear his body glistened, skin the

color of chocolate, smooth and decadent, perfectly sculpted and cut in all the right places. With his knee he pushed her thighs apart and she gulped at the stretch and bend of the muscles in his thighs and calves. Holding his weight on the palms of his hands his biceps bulged, pectorals lifting and falling with the steady rhythm of his breath. When he lifted his head, his gaze searching for hers, Nivea gasped.

"Don't move," he told her.

She licked her lips. "Don't make me wait."

For an instant Nivea thought he might back away. It was there and it shocked her to her core to see it, Eli Preston blinked. As she figured she'd caught him just out of the shower, he wasn't wearing his shades, his turbulent green eyes had been keen, assessing but human. Until the second he'd touched her. The gold cat's eyes had appeared, calling to her cat, letting it know the game was on. But in the moment she'd snapped back at his comment, his eyes had shifted again. A second, maybe two, his shoulders shook, gold, then green, then gold again.

He growled in the next instant, baring those sharp-ass teeth, basically telling her to hold on, the ride was about to begin. Nivea gripped the comforter in her hands tightly and tilted her hips, more than ready to receive him. She held his gaze. "Now."

His thick, hot length was inside her so fast Nivea would swear she saw stars. The instant stretch of her skin, the fullness pressing quickly into her, sliding along the essence-coated walls, had her body shaking and her lips spreading in a grin. This was how she'd expected it to be, just what she'd known he would be like. It was perfect.

Until he wrapped an arm around her waist and lifted her up off the bed and onto his lap, quickly changing their positions. Her first instinct was to gasp as the length of his long, thick cock pressed farther inside her. Next was to hold onto his shoulders to keep from tipping over. Then, he bit her. Those sharp incisors touching the tender skin of her upper breast, just above her nipple. It was a strong enough sting, to ensure he'd broken skin, and lightning bolts of pleasure entered her bloodstream.

"Ride," he ordered when he lifted his head, touching those teeth to her ear. "Ride me like you want everything I've got."

It was an order and a dare, given in a way that only Eli could. There was no room for argument and if she cowered, there would be no living it down, no taking it back. Not that she wanted to. Nivea let her hands rub up and down Eli's arms, right over the slight ripple in his skin where his tat was emblazoned. The connection had her own tat, on the back of her left calf, twitching. Cat connecting with cat. Coming up on the heels of her feet, she leveraged herself and began to move. Rising high, pulling off his cock until only the tip remained ensconced in her heated core, then dropping down, sucking him in completely once more. Eli didn't make a sound, but his muscles bunched beneath her hands and she continued. Up and down, up and down, until her essence dripped down onto him, her breasts beginning to sweat, her breathing coming in quick pants.

Tossing her head back, Nivea rode the delicious wave that would soon carry her to complete bliss. Every nerve ending buzzed with the pleasure, the intense desire reaching its full culmination. This felt so right. He fit so securely inside her. He knew what she needed, just as she knew what he craved. He'd wanted hot and fast, she'd given him the exact scenario she'd dreamed of. When he closed his eyes and looked away she frowned, grinding her hips down on him.

"Look at me, Eli," she told him.

"Just ride," was his tight response.

Nivea shook her head. "No. You look at me. See that

I've got you. Whether in the field or in this bed, I've got you, Eli. I want you and I've got you."

"No!" he yelled instantly, lifting her off him before she had a chance to react, to defend.

Nivea instantly felt the loss, her heartbeat almost stopping at the disappearance of what she'd wanted for so long. She felt momentarily confused, blinking her eyes to try and refocus. But Eli didn't give her the chance. He was off the bed, standing at the side, reaching for her once more. He pulled her by the ankle until she was sliding off the bed as well, his big hands moving roughly down her neck to her breasts where he cupped her tightly, then down her torso to her hips where he reached around and squeezed her ass. He slipped down the crease until she was bucking, opening for him. His fingers pressed hard, deep into her pussy, then coming out, spreading her essence back toward her ass. Over and over he did that until Nivea's knees began to shake, her head lolling forward, forehead touching his shoulder.

As quickly as he'd moved before, he turned her so that his dick was pressed along the now-dampened crease. He put a hand to the small of her back and pressed her down toward the mattress.

"You never listen," he told her. "No matter what I tell you, you are determined to do the opposite."

"You wanted me too," she countered.

"You're fucking disobedient!" he yelled, spreading her cheeks, letting the tip of his dick rub from her anus to her core, still spreading her juices until the slick sound echoed in the room.

"You should be punished," he continued. "Punished."

The smack of his palm against her ass was quick, painful, and had Nivea coming with a rush that stole her breath.

"Eli," she breathed finally.

He smacked the other cheek and her arms shook, threatening to buckle and send her face smashing into the bed.

"Just . . . just," he started to say, then stopped, deciding to press his cock into her instead of completing the sentence.

He pounded hard, spearing in and out of her while holding tight to her hips with the same confidence and determination he trained his guards. The sound of his groin smacking into her ass was rhythmic, addictive as Nivea grabbed the comforter between her fingers again. With each thrust she moaned, with each retraction her cat growled. She'd tried to circle her hips, to meet his pumps, but he held her tighter, keeping her still while he worked.

"You don't have me," she vaguely heard him say through the haze of pleasure, the rise of her next release.

"You. Will. Never. Have. Me." Each word was punctuated with a thrust, retract, then a thrust again.

For what may have been the first time in her life Nivea couldn't respond. She couldn't give a quick quip, couldn't defend herself or tear him down with a smart retort. All she could do was grit her teeth to keep from screaming as her release rippled through her entire body.

He stilled behind her and she heard his cat purring, a soft curse falling from his lips as his dick pulsated inside her, his release escaping even though, she thought with faint alarm, he didn't want it to.

The shower wasn't meant for two. Each bathroom was utilitarian in design. So it was no wonder Eli felt claustrophobic as they both attempted to wash away the sweat resulting from their tryst. He'd done so with clear and present intent, while Nivea looked to be languishing in the moment.

She lifted one long arm, soaping the pit then up and down its length. Repeated those steps with the other arm.

All the while her eyes remained closed, her breasts rising and falling with the act. When she soaped the high mounds it was with great slowness, her hands resting over her puckered nipples, slipping slowly down her torso, where a trail of soapy bubbles followed. The moment the trail ended at the V of her legs was when Eli finally looked away.

His fists balled at his sides as he thought of how he'd fallen to the weakness. He'd fought for what seemed like so long against touching her, taking her. And now, here they were. Not even a foot away she was naked, her body available and waiting for him. All he had to do was reach out and take, again.

But he didn't. Instead he moved quickly to exit the stall, slamming the door behind him as he stepped into the coolness of the bathroom. The towel he'd used earlier was still in the bedroom, so he continued his hasty steps there, yanking the towel from the floor where he'd left it. Drying quickly he pulled on a pair of sweatpants and was just sticking his arms through a sleeveless undershirt when she emerged from the bathroom.

"So how are we going to deal with this?" she asked. "Uncomfortable silence? Awkward avoidance?"

She dried off her body as she talked, showing not an inch of modesty as she let the towel fall to the floor and reached for her clothes. Gritting his teeth, Eli refused to look at the lines and curves of her body as she moved, performing the simplest, yet most seductive task he'd ever seen.

"I have some questions to ask you and then we'll see," he stated, taking a seat on the edge of the bed, with the now-rumpled comforter.

Their scent filled the room—the musk of sex, combined with the earthy shifter aroma. It was intoxicating, wafting through the air like some sort of hypnotic agent, convincing him that the more important thing to do at this moment was to stop her from getting dressed and to sink inside her hot, wet pussy once more.

"Questions about what?" was her response. He would have been a fool to believe she'd keep quiet and let him do the talking.

"Your parents and some donations they've made recently," he told her, being careful to watch everything about her for a reaction.

It would be within the first few seconds of hearing his statement and digesting what he'd said. She would either look or smell guilty, or not. Seeing as his senses were operating at their own whim, Eli wasn't sure what he would rely on.

"I have no idea what my parents do," she replied slowly. Her hands had stilled only minutely as she stopped tucking her shirt into her pants and looked up at him. She hadn't broken the eye contact and she didn't look like she was guilty. As for the scent, Eli almost growled. All he could smell was their combined aroma, in all of its seductive and damning glory.

He frowned. "You're their child, how can you not know what they do?"

She looked affronted. "Where are your parents right now? What are they having for dinner? What was the last business transaction they completed?" she fired back.

"I'm asking you a specific question," he stated as calmly as he could because the attraction to her was slowly winning the battle over the serious nature of the conversation. On the one hand he was irritated as hell by the fact that Nick was questioning Nivea's allegiance to the tribe. On the other, his dick was already hard, his body craving hers as if he hadn't just been inside her a half hour ago.

"Why are your parents making contributions to the Comastaz Labs?"

There was an instant reaction to that question. Her eyes

widened and she swallowed, clearly thinking about how she would respond before doing so. Eli stood, crossing the room until he was in front of her. He felt safe in doing so now only because she was fully dressed, except for her boots.

"Answer the question," he prompted.

She lifted her hands, smoothing down her hair then letting her arms fall to her sides once again. "First," she said after a deep breath and even deeper exhale. "As far as the romance and holding a girl through the afterglow of lovemaking, you suck."

Eli didn't even flinch at her words, not at all offended by her declaration. If there was one thing he didn't want to be good at, especially as far as Nivea was concerned, it was romance.

"Second, in addition to their marketing firm, my parents own a couple of nonprofit foundations. I don't know where any of their money goes or why."

"How is that possible?" he queried, sounding as confused as he felt. He didn't live with his parents but he knew that his father had just retired from the government aide position he'd held for more than thirty years and that his mother, still as pretty as ever, supervised a showing of artwork that had been in her family for centuries.

She blinked then stepped around him, bending down to pick up her boots before taking the spot he'd just vacated on the bed. "Look, I'm not close with my family. So I don't know what they're doing."

"But you don't sound at all surprised that they would give money to Comastaz."

"It's a government laboratory. I'm sure if there's any type of monetary or social reward for their donation, that would be the reason they made it. My parents are really big on keeping up appearances."

"Even at the cost of betraying the shifters?"

She looked up at him then, her lips drawn tightly. "I answered your question to the best of my ability. Are we done now?" She'd finished tying both boots and was standing again. "I'd like to get back to my room."

"Before anybody sees that you were here, right?"

He had no idea why he'd asked her that question, or why he needed to be close to her again, but he moved forward. Lifting a finger he touched her chin, tilting her head up so he could see her eyes. What he saw in their depths left him breathless. Snatches of light and dark, pleasure and pain, suffering and turmoil. He wanted to yell in disgust, to force the images out of his head, but when she spoke, they all disappeared.

"You shouldn't keep your eyes covered all the time, they're beautiful," she told him.

Eli looked away instantly, turning from her and going to the door. "Nick and Rome know about the money your parents are sending to Comastaz. With all that's gone down they're concerned. I told them you were trustworthy, that I would take care of the situation. Don't make a liar out of me," he warned, his teeth clenching.

She moved behind him, her steps soft but sure.

"I'm not my parents. I stand for what I believe and I believe in the shifters. Whether or not that makes me a liar is not my concern."

She reached around him to turn the doorknob and walk out of his room, leaving him there to stare after her. To wonder and to regret. Eli closed the door with a growl that no doubt echoed throughout the entire dwelling.

Chapter 7

"We're not ready to proceed with production. ADAM was unsuccessful but we've had some new developments. I need at least six months to produce another prototype," Captain Lawrence Crowe said as he stood across from a huge mahogany desk.

To the left of the desk was the American flag, to the right the bright red flag of the U.S. Marine Corps. Lining the wall behind him were more citations and commendations than any one man should possess. All giving the impression of achievement and power, no doubt, only Lawrence knew better.

General Oscar Pierson, the tall, slim man with a sallow complexion and raspy voice, sat back in the executive office chair. He lifted a leg, resting an ankle on his knee, his fingers steepled in front of him.

Pierson was retired, had been for two years since the scandal erupted depicting him as the head honcho in the inhumane treatment of POWs in Iraq. Now, he worked closely with his partner-in-crime, Major Randall Guthrie, who had somehow escaped the scandal and still remained on active duty or at least active payroll.

They were all still being paid by the U.S. government, whether directly or through a government pension, even as they planned to betray that very entity.

"That's not an option," Pierson informed him. "The meeting's scheduled for four weeks from now, at which time we are expected to present an expertly designed killing machine. Buyers from all over the world will be here looking to write a check for the best weapon on the market. There's no margin for error and the stakes are succeed or be destroyed. Is that clear enough for you?"

Pierson had the political connections and the reputation to get him on foreign soil with the most powerful men in countries all over the world. Crowe was the mastermind, the seed that had put this little plan into motion. Guthrie was the muscle, or, more accurately, a fucking nuclear missile with its time clock ticking every second. The fact that he had been excluded from this meeting was cause for concern, but Crowe wasn't afraid. He held all the cards here, not to mention the ace in the hole that neither Pierson nor Guthrie knew about.

"That's too soon," he countered. "Rushing this will be disastrous for us all."

Pierson turned sharply, his cold gaze resting on Crowe. "You mean like the disaster you caused in Arizona? The press are still circling around the fire at Perryville Resorts and the break-in at your lab, like a bunch of vultures. Hell, your houses were even broken into and destroyed. Your name is wrapped in so much shit right now you should be wearing fishermen's waders instead of combat boots!"

Crowe didn't even flinch. "Exactly my point. ADAM wasn't ready. If we go in front of the buyers without being one hundred percent there's no telling what will happen."

Lowering his leg, Pierson turned to lean his elbows on his desk, now giving Crowe what he knew was his dangerous commander look. "I'm going to tell you exactly what's going to happen. You're going to get your ass to work producing a number of viable prototypes. Not just one, but another one to pick up the slack if you fuck up again. And another one as backup to that one. This deal is going through in four weeks. That means you're going to produce what you promised or I'm going to cut off your balls and feed them to you for breakfast. Are we clear, captain?"

Crowe gritted his teeth. He wanted to snap back, to tell the spindly old man that he wasn't scaring anybody in this room. Crowe could kill him right now, with his bare hands, just as he'd almost done to Pierson's whining and pampered son Sidney back in Arizona. But there was a bit of truth to the man's words. This deal was important to all of them and it was a one-shot occurrence. Arranging for the top foreign leaders to be in one place at one time, promising them a product that would make the three of them billionaires, was a pretty big deal. It was the fucking biggest deal of Crowe's life. He had to make it happen, there was no question about that.

He also had to stay alive.

"If this goes bad," he started to say to Pierson.

"It had better not go bad," Pierson interrupted.

Crowe nodded, knowing that if the prototypes didn't perform there would be hell to pay. Hearing the ghostly laugh of Boden Estevez in the back of his mind only reinforced that fact. Because when—not if, he thought—this all went bad, the world as they all knew it would never be the same.

He let his head fall back and laughed. Deep, rich, loud, reverberating throughout the expanse of his suite at the Four Seasons. The chip he'd had installed in Crowe's cell phone was proving to be one of the smartest things the beautiful Bianca had ever suggested.

Speaking of the goddess, she touched a hand to his shoulder, letting her long red-painted nails draw an imaginary path down his torso as she leaned in to whisper in his ear.

"He's going to create more of them, faster than ever," she said.

Boden chuckled again. "He sure is."

She slipped around him then, lifting a leg so she could straddle him on the bed. "The Shadows are going to fall hard."

"They are," he replied, cupping the plump globes of her ass.

"And you'll take your rightful place as ruler," she whispered in his ear, thrusting her pussy against his growing erection.

"Right again," he said, letting his hand slip under her dress and between her crease.

Everything Boden did was for the sake of revenge. First and foremost, against the Elders and the Shadow Shifters of the Gungi who had so easily and humiliatingly tossed him from the jungle and their tribe. The moment he'd arrived in Sierra Leone he'd begun to plan how he would take them down and eventually control the very tribes that despised him.

The next had come a while later, the twins that had so systematically taken away the one thing in the world Boden had ever cherished—his mate—by first using her body and then viciously killing her. Yes, that revenge would also be sweet.

"We'll rule together," she was saying, her tongue tracing provocative strokes over his ear and down his neck.

A growl rumbled in his chest, the jaguar quickly coming to life as three of his fingers pressed deep into Bianca's hot, waiting center. She hissed and began pumping against his strong strokes immediately. Always ready for him, Bianca rarely bothered with underwear or pretenses. Since the first time he'd seen her lurking around his hut in the Sierra Leone rain forest, she'd been submissive to his every whim. His control of her had come easily and proven almost invaluable. She'd done excellent work infiltrating Sabar's operation and securing the funds that would facilitate his highly secretive move from Sierra Leone to the States. However, he didn't love her, was not capable of such a basic and useless emotion. And she wasn't his mate— that ship had long since sailed the night Acacia was brutally murdered. No, everything Boden did in his life now was for a purpose, a bullet point being checked off on his long and sadistic to-do list.

When Bianca placed both hands on his shoulders, clenching as she continued to bounce up and down with the motion of his fingers, Boden's sharp teeth bit into his lower lip, the acidic taste of his own blood making his dick bulge to painful proportions. With his other hand he squeezed the right side of her ass, his finger slipping assuredly down her seam and over her anus. She was so wet his digits slipped back and forth over her plump folds and back to that tight bud where he pressed firmly, until she was breached.

She shivered in response, loving whenever he was there with her, whenever he gave her pleasure. He looked into her eyes, the ice-blue orbs shadowed by long black lashes. Her mouth, plump pink-tinted lips, gaped as she struggled to hold on, feeling the pleasure build and circle inside her but not daring to let it rip free. She knew better.

The knowledge of the complete control he had over her made Boden smile, his dick dripping moisture that would stain his pants. With more deep strokes he worked her pussy and her anus, loving the tightness, the gripping, the wetness dripping down his wrists.

"You'll continue to do what I say, my little tiger," he told her, leaning forward to lick down the line of her throat. "Whatever I say, whenever I say."

Her body jerked now, her long dark hair swaying with the erratic rhythm she'd begun in an attempt to keep up with his thrusts. "Yes!" she yelled. "Yes, sir, I will!"

He bit her then, his sharp teeth sinking into the tender and tasty skin of her neck until it was her blood that now flavored his tongue.

Come for me, now," he instructed her. "Come for me, now *Lormenian* cat. Now!"

Bianca convulsed over him, her nails-turned-claws sinking deep into his shoulders, cutting right through the material of his dress shirt. Her body bucked, her pussy walls tightening as she dripped incessantly, growling deep inside her chest as her release ripped free.

One week later.

Eli's head throbbed with every strand of the classical music that had been playing throughout the evening. For what felt like the billionth time tonight, he fiddled with the bow tie at his neck, rolling his head on his shoulders and tried to relax in the confining suit he'd been forced to wear.

"They're grown-man clothes," Ezra had told him when he'd shown up at Eli's door.

"I'm not the grown-up you are, Ezra," Eli had responded blandly, still not convinced he should wear the charcoal-gray suit and lighter toned shirt.

"It's a formal gig and we're all on duty since Rome, Nick, and X are going with their mates." Ezra had crossed the room then, reaching into the clothes bag and tossing the black-and-white paisley-print bow tie at Eli.

"Now hurry up, we're pulling out in twenty minutes."

His older brother had left him alone then, to Eli's relief.

Ezra was one of those men that could wear just about anything and women went out of their minds for him. Ezra was obsessed with designer clothes and accessories. Whatever the latest fashion was, he had it. And he worked it effortlessly, just as it seemed Ezra did many other things.

Ezra had come back from the Sierra Leone and trained like a shifter on a mission. He rose higher in the ranks with Eli right by his side, all the while meeting and sleeping with whatever woman he chose. He slept with them, he walked away, the next day he started again. Eli had only wished he could rebound as quickly.

Unfortunately, Eli had been drawn into Acacia's web. A part of him had known she wasn't for him, that what they shared would never be anything more than just sex, and another part had hoped. That hope had been dashed quickly with the revelation of Acacia's true goals. She'd been using Eli and Ezra to get back at her father for sending her true mate away. Once they'd found out, they'd gone to the shaman for his miracle potion to kill the desire they both still had so deeply for this shifter. For Ezra that had worked. For Eli, not so much. He'd still wanted Acacia, up until the moment he knew she intended to kill them. Then his instincts had kicked in, simultaneously with Ezra's, and they'd killed Acacia and her minions.

Eli came back to the States determined never to make that mistake again. Only to make another one far worse with Leanne.

That thought had Eli stumbling, his palms flattening on his dresser to keep his body upright. He blinked and all he could see was Leanne's lifeless body lying on her bed, the envelope with his name scrawled across the front taped to the mirror on her dresser.

Eli dropped his head, felt his heartbeat thumping throughout every pore of his body. Shaking his head, he tried to clear his thoughts, to get that picture out of his mind. He'd had memories before and he'd dealt with them, but this was different. He felt strange, as if he were a spectator looking in on the scene. Exactly how he'd felt a week ago in the woods after they'd left that cabin. He'd seen Agent Wilson in that car driving away like it was a scene on television, playing out in front of him.

He took a deep breath and then another, until his legs had stopped shaking, his head ceased throbbing. And then, still without an answer and not caring to delve deeper, he got back to the matter at hand.

Eli's gun bulged beneath the back of his jacket and he cursed, hating the dress clothes even more. After three tries he'd finally gotten the bow tie done in a vaguely acceptable fashion. With a heavy expel of breath he looked into the mirror, hating what he saw once again. Reaching down to his dresser he picked up his shades, slipping them on slowly then looking in the mirror once more.

That was better, he thought with instant relief. His shoulders had relaxed a little, the wrinkles that appeared in his forehead when he frowned had cleared, and hey, the suit didn't look half bad on him. His consensus about what had just happened, the memories and all that crap from the rain forest, was that they were all irrelevant.

Now all Eli wanted to do was find this Lawrence Crowe and hurt that SOB so bad he'd never be able to conceive another idea in his life, least of all an idea to create shifter supersoldiers.

Just when he thought the stigma of the fitted suit and too-tight bow tie would surely be the death of him, Eli walked into the ballroom of the Four Seasons where each table was filled with crystal and candles and classical music playing softly in the background. He felt like turning right around and running the hell out of there. But that wasn't going to happen.

"Let's check the room. Nick has another team checking the perimeter and vehicles parked within a three-block radius," Ezra told Eli as they both stood in the doorway of the hall. "Once we confirm it's clear we'll go out and bring Rome and Nick and their mates inside."

"Their mates, right," Eli muttered. He'd just turned to the left, opting to take that side of the room first when Ezra's words stopped him.

"You don't think about mating anymore?"

Eli looked over his shoulder. His brother may have been walking around the room, checking under each table and chair, but he was definitely waiting for an answer.

"No. I don't."

"But you did before," he continued.

Eli ran his hands along the fabric-covered wall near a doorway marked EXIT. He pushed the door open and looked up and down the mustard-painted hallway. He'd thought he'd put the memories of the rain forest and all that had happened there on the back burner for the night. He hadn't anticipated Ezra bringing Leanne—another one of Eli's failures—into the picture.

"That was a mistake," Eli replied, more to himself than to Ezra, who was across the room anyway.

"We all make mistakes, you know. Then we get over them and we try again," his twin responded.

Eli tried not to act surprised that Ezra heard him. Of course he would hear him no matter where he was in the room. They were twins with extrasensory abilities. It just so happened that Ezra's were working perfectly and Eli's, well, hadn't he earlier declared that issue irrelevant?

"There's no 'try again' in my world. Two strikes and

I'm out," he told his brother honestly and before Ezra could speak again, added, "Now, let's just get the job done without the small talk, okay?"

Ezra touched Eli's shoulder and Eli had to fight like hell to keep from jumping out of his skin and embarrassing the crap out of himself. He hadn't heard Ezra's approach, nor had he picked up his now-familiar *companheiro calor*.

"This isn't a small issue, man. And ignoring it is not going to work forever. Hell, it's probably not working now."

Eli shook his head. "You don't know what I'm going through."

"I don't?" Ezra asked, raising a brow. "You're my brother. My twin. I know just as much about you as you do yourself."

"If you knew so much about me, you'd understand that I'm still baffled about you having a mate," Eli spat back without thinking of why he shouldn't. Or possibly why now was not the best time to have this confrontation.

Ezra only blinked once, before a muscle in his jaw twitched. "That's right. Dawn is my mate. I love her more than I've ever loved anything in this world and I would do anything to make her happy and to keep her safe. That's what mating is about. That's what shifters are supposed to find."

"That's a bunch of bullshit designed to make us just a little more unstable than we already are. I'm never taking part in that process, never putting myself in that position again."

"That asshole bought his own death ticket, Eli. You were defending yourself and . . ." He paused. "You were defending a human."

"Right! A human whose life I ruined!" he roared back. "By all accounts I should be in prison now, repenting for my crime. Instead I'm here and I'm walking around trying to do this job and you keep getting in my face about shit I don't want to revisit."

Ezra sighed and took a step back. "You're right, Eli. You're trying to do your job and you don't need me in your face."

There was a second or so of remorse for having yelled at Ezra, but it had to be said. Not only did he not want to be dragged down memory lane in the rain forest, Eli definitely did not want to remember the night he'd murdered a human and got off without any jail time thanks to Nick's expert legal skills. He just didn't want to deal with any of this shit, not tonight.

"Let's just get this done," he told his brother.

"Right," a female voice added to the conversation. "X sent me inside to check on your progress. Neither of you were answering your radio calls."

Eli immediately reached up to his ear to touch the small com link there. Then he pulled back his jacket sleeve to make sure he'd put his e-band on when he'd been donning this monkey suit. What he really was doing was trying like hell to keep his eyes off Nivea Cannon.

She looked like sex walking. In the few seconds he'd glanced at her, every item of her clothing, or lack thereof, had been emblazoned in his memory. The shoes were sky-high, a natural color with a gold spiked heel. The dress was short—fucking crazy blindingly short—barely coming to her midthigh, a copper color that made him think instantly of new pennies. Her long hair was pulled over one shoulder, exposing the line of her neck and giving her a sultry, come-get-me look that had him wanting to race across the room to do just that.

Instead, he turned and resumed what he'd been doing. Fifteen minutes later he yelled, "All clear!" and then went back out of the room and to the parking lot where the SUVs were parked. He did not look at her again, could not.

* * *

Eli Preston was an ass.

An arrogant, pigheaded ass that needed some sense knocked into his head. An hour after arriving at Rome's pro bono defense fund's charity event of the year, she stood against the wall near the front entrance, watching the hundreds of people mill about, but only able to think about one.

He'd slept with her, then quickly crawled back into that shell he loved to hibernate in. In all the years she'd fantasized about how their first time would be, she'd never thought the word *regret* would surface. After the most exhilarating sex she'd ever had in her life, Nivea was afraid she might have to think twice about wanting anything more to do with that bastard shifter.

But then she picked up his scent and it was like déjà vu. She could feel his thick length pressing into her, the sting of his fingers as they dug deep into the skin of her hips while he worked inside of her. Each thrust had left her breathless, each retreat sending shooting pangs of loss throughout her entire body. And just like that she wanted him again, needed to feel all of him, if only one more time.

She hated that fact and at the same time refused to cower from it.

Following the scent, she moved through the crowd. There were a few politicians in the room, some high-up law officials and of course, lawyers, all schmoozing around, eating great banquet food and hopefully writing huge checks to the pro bono fund. Briefly, she thought of her parents and of what they were doing. She hated having to keep their secret, especially when she knew without a doubt they were wrong. But telling would be worse, it would hurt the two people she cared most about in this world, her sisters.

With practiced restraint she pushed those thoughts aside. What the Cannons did was their business. That was the deal Nivea had made in return for the agreement to let her freely walk away from the freak show they called a family. No matter what Nick and Rome suspected she was loyal to them. She only wished she could show them by giving them information on her parents. But that would never happen.

She was across the room now, looking around, searching for the owner of the scent that had drawn her here. He was nowhere to be found. He'd looked so damned good in that suit, she'd wanted to run to him and wrap her legs around his waist when she first saw him standing in the ballroom. But he and Ezra were arguing so the air was filled with tension and the undeniable scent of two male shifters, their cats dangerously close to the surface. By their hushed, but volatile tones, she suspected they'd been talking about what had happened to them in the Sierra Leone rain forest. For years she'd wondered what had made Eli the closed-off shifter he had become. She'd heard rumors about his time in the rain forest with the *Lormenian* and *Serfin* shifters and thought maybe he'd been thinking of defecting to one of those tribes, even though he was a jaguar. But no, Eli and Ezra were inseparable. He would never leave his brother, or Rome and Nick for that matter. He would, however, give her enough of a cold shoulder that she couldn't wait to get out of his bedroom, when she should have been still lying in his arms, basking in the afterglow of sex.

Heart-stopping, invigorating sex—

Nivea's thoughts were terminated abruptly, her arm grasped hard, and her body pulled back through a door, all before she could think a coherent thought.

"Fucking insane!" Eli roared into her ear after he'd slammed her back against the wall. "You're driving me insane!"

Nivea finally caught her breath, about two seconds before Eli's hand was up her dress, thrusting past the barrier of her thong to slip between her folds.

"Eli," she breathed his name.

His head was down, his forehead resting on the bare skin of her shoulder as his fingers—oh god, his magnificently talented fingers—stroked her clit, then sank back into her center, and then went back to her clit again. She opened her legs wider, had no other choice really because it felt so damned good.

"Why won't you stop it? Why won't you just leave this alone?" he asked. His voice sounded as tortured and ragged as she suspected he felt inside.

She wrapped her arms around him, rubbing her palms over the back of his head.

"I can't, Eli," she admitted hoarsely. "I don't know why, but I can't."

"No," he told her, licking along the cleavage bared by the bodice of her dress. "I can't. This can't be," he whispered. "It can't be. I want it to stop. But if you leave—"

His words halted abruptly as he sucked on the plump bulge of her breast. He sucked so hard Nivea was sure there would be a mark. Then she felt his teeth, the sharp pinprick breaking her skin. She moaned deep and long and came all over his hand.

When he jerked back she wanted to reach out and punch him because she saw the look on his face. It was similar to the blasé look he'd had in his room. But then he opened his mouth and Nivea knew it was different.

"They're here," he said, his voice thick, eyes roaming the area. "They're here, right goddamned now!"

Tall, muscled, and seething mad, the Sanchez brothers were already at the entrance to the ballroom. Rather, they blocked the entrance, backs facing the guests. The one in the middle, Caleb, the youngest, was built like a battering ram. This last year of training constantly at Havenway had beefed the younger shifter up, adding to his sharp Brazilian features and giving him a definite lethal look. To his left was Aidan, the oldest, his strong jaw locked, nostrils flaring as he held on to the shift that was battling for control. To the left stood Brayden, the strategist of the trio, the narrowing of his eyes a telltale sign that he was thinking of an attack plan.

"They're in this room," Eli said, coming up behind them.

Aidan nodded. "X and Ezra are in the back of the room. Whatever is in here will stay in here. Contained."

"We're going out to deal with whatever's waiting," Brayden told Eli.

"I'm going with you," Eli announced sternly. His cat was scratching at the surface, the sure and certain scent arousing the hunter inside.

"There are too many humans here tonight. Too much collateral damage," Caleb added.

"That's why we're going out, to minimize the damage," Eli said, stepping around Aidan so that he was now in front, leading the guards as they went out to battle. "No shifting," he said. Then he added with a wary look over his shoulder, "Unless absolutely necessary."

The threesome nodded and they walked out of the ballroom, trusting their counterparts to deal with whatever was inside, while they handled whatever lurked out in the dark.

They were on the street in less than a minute, Eli's shoulders bunching at the tension resting heavily over them. He inhaled deeply, knew that behind him the others were doing the same.

"It's not quite a shifter," he mumbled.

"No," Aidan added. "It's not."

"Stinks just the same," Caleb told them. "And the fucker's coming right at us!"

The youngest guard was right, about twenty feet away and big as a bulldozer, what looked like a man stomped down Pennsylvania Avenue.

"Sonofabitch!" Brayden yelled. "They made another one."

Eli rolled his head on his shoulders until his neck cracked. He felt the sting of his claws ripping through the skin of his fingers, the domino cracking of bones beneath that tight-ass suit he'd worn and growled in rage because he'd already ordered no shifting.

Instead he took off at a run, not bothering to listen for the steps behind him, knowing that the Sanchez brothers had been expertly trained to divide and conquer. They would move quickly, like blurs through the night and effectively disengage this scary-looking bastard before it had a chance to do whatever it planned to do.

As for Eli, all he saw were its eyes, an eerie green, bright and glowing. Its focus was intent, its goal death and destruction. Eli knew this because there was a strand running deep inside his body that was similar. The recognition was quick and cut through him like a heated blade, just as he rammed into the seven-foot monstrosity. It barely budged as Eli's right shoulder yelled in agony from the contact.

The hybrid lifted an arm, swiping at Eli with his long and sharpened claws. They didn't look normal, like that of a cat, but instead piercing and glinting, like steel. He'd escaped the cut of them by about three inches as he leaned as far back on his feet as he could without touching the ground. His right arm came around like a slash of lightning, his fist connecting with the hybrid's chin, causing its head to jerk back at the assault. He followed with a left to the midsection and then another right to its face again. There was no sound of agony or even of contact. The thing simply reacted, throwing its own punches that slammed into Eli's body like concrete blocks.

Inside his cat roared, teeth pressing sharply against his lips. His ears rang from the contact of each blow delivered by the hybrid, until what filled Eli's mind was the sound of the rain forest, the scent infiltrating his nostrils now damp and tropical, his eyes seeing like the nocturnal cat through the human sunglasses he wore. There was a weakness in the hybrid, Eli sensed it and before the beast could strike him again he looked it up and down, assessing every spot he could for where it was until he found it. Right beneath its ear, where a thick green ooze had begun to drip. There was some sort of crack there, slicing down the hybrid's neck and Eli simply reacted, not knowing for sure it would work.

With a vicious roar he came off his feet, claws bared, right arm reaching out and sinking into the hybrid's cracked skin. More of the ooze spurted into the air, the hybrid releasing a sound that echoed through the night. At that very moment its legs were taken out, Brayden and Aidan used the strength they'd honed in their lower extremities to kick away the hybrid's balance by attacking it at the knees. Caleb came next with a blow to its head and the monster crumpled to the ground. The ooze seemed to suck all of the insides out of the hybrid as right before their eyes it became a shell of a distorted body. Its face was a twisted mask of sharp teeth, whiskered muzzle, flared nostrils, and eerie eyes. The carcass still moved up and down as if breathing its last breath.

Eli caught himself mimicking the motion, air moving in and out through his lungs so that his chest moved in sync with the hybrid. Then the sirens sounded, screams erupted, and Eli turned back to see humans bursting through the doors.

"Shit!" he yelled and ran toward the hotel.

"Clean that up!" he shouted back to the Sanchez brothers, not wanting anyone to see what was left on the street. He wondered if there'd been any witnesses of the fight with the hybrid in the first place. He hadn't thought for one second about spectators, only concentrating on dispatching the monstrosity before it could hurt any humans or shifters. Now, he raced toward the building praying that everyone was safe, and for the first time in he had no idea how many minutes, remembered he'd left Nivea inside.

Chapter 8

Chaos had broken out so quickly and definitively that Nivea had only a second to catch her breath from being extremely aroused to ready for battle. Every guard in the ballroom was on alert the moment she stepped from the stairwell alone.

Obviously she was the only one getting the memo a day late. At any rate, she was ready for whatever was going down in the next moments. Inhaling deeply, she searched for whatever had warned Eli. Her body trembled as the scent filtered through her. It was strikingly familiar, so much so she'd placed a hand to her heart to still its rapid beating. Swallowing deeply, she looked around again to make sure she'd seen the other guards on alert as well.

X and Ezra were on their feet at the back of the room near the table where Rome, Kalina, Caprise, Nick, and Ary were still seated. Jax, Leo, Zach, and Tobias flanked that table. There was an identical EXIT door across the room and Nivea noticed the guard standing there was poised for battle as well. Then her neck snapped to the left, her nose twitching as that familiar scent grew stronger. For one heart-stopping second she thought she'd see him standing there, dressed in that perfect suit, fitting him as if it had been made just for his expertly cut body. She found herself searching for those damned sunglasses, the tight line of his lips as he glared at her impatiently, the warmth that emanated from any place his hands touched her. Eli. The name was a whisper in her head.

But he wasn't the one she saw. He wasn't the owner of the scent. It was the enemy.

"Three o'clock. Black pants, white dinner jacket, long curling auburn hair, and green eyes. Glowing, green eyes," she spoke into her com link, already moving toward the target.

Out of the corner of her eye she saw the other guards moving in the same direction, following her lead.

"Do not engage," she heard loudly through her earpiece. "Do not engage, Cannon!"

The directive was from Ezra. She clenched her teeth, totally prepared to ignore the Lead Guard. This wasn't an invited guest, she knew that instinctively. She also knew without any doubt in her mind that whoever this was, he was somehow connected to Eli, or had been in contact with him in some way. Why else would they share the same scent?

She didn't stop moving, had no intention of not saying something to this person, trying to find out what his connection to Eli was. But as she grew closer, and as he turned to her, locking her gaze with his own, she started to reconsider her plan. Taking deep breaths and slowing her steps minutely she figured she'd approach him as if he were just a man and she was just a woman. She would talk to him, get information from him, then turn him over to the other guards—the ones that were moving through the guests as quickly and discreetly as they possibly could.

But the moment she reached him, her plan changed, for the worse.

The man opened his mouth, baring sharp teeth and a long thick tongue that rolled out as if on command. The growl was loud and rattled the chandeliers above. At first the guests froze, then they screamed, and panic ensued.

He reached for her, grabbing her arm with claws that immediately locked into her skin. Nivea didn't think about how powerful this sonofabitch was, or how she planned to take him down. All she could do was react. With her left hand, her claws bared, she sliced at the man's neck, twisting her body so that he would release her arm. He didn't, so ultimately it felt like he was actually ripping her shoulder from its joint. With a slight bend she was able to propel herself into the air, turning quickly so that her free arm could wrap around his neck. Locking on, she pulled and pulled, all while searing pain radiated from her other shoulder. When he still didn't let go she bent forward, teeth bared now, and bit the side of his face. The next roar was of rage, not pain, she was almost certain. The beast reared back and Nivea was once again air bound, falling back to what she was sure would momentarily be the floor.

If so, it was the best-smelling and warmest floor she'd ever encountered as strong arms wrapped immediately around her, holding until her feet were able to touch the floor.

"Stay back!" Eli yelled in her face before pushing her behind him and running straight at the beast.

Fuck that! she thought, rolling her head on her shoulders and mentally getting herself back in order. When she turned again Eli and Ezra were tag-teaming the beast, the two stronger guards attacking with timed precision. Eli knelt to the ground, sweeping the beast's legs from beneath it while seconds later, Ezra straddled its neck as it hit the floor, punches raining over its face.

"Below the ear!" she heard Eli yell. "Get it below the ear!"

Nivea was already moving, not sure if Ezra had heard Eli or not. She came around the left side of the beast, the other guards shuttling away the guests that were too shocked to run out of the ballroom. As the beast continued to roar, slamming its huge fists into the floor causing the entire room to shake, Ezra continued punching it in the face, his thighs covering the beast's neck. But she glimpsed something, a crack just beneath its ear.

"Get the hell back!" she heard Eli yelling. Knowing he was talking to her and clearly prepared to ignore it, Nivea's clawed hand was in the air swinging downward, just missing Ezra's cheek by an inch or so, before landing right along the line of the crack in the beast's neck.

Its mouth opened, tongue lolling to the side as it made a half-roar sound and green ooze shot up into the air. Ezra and Eli both yelled as the ooze splattered on them. Nivea backed up but still managed to get splashed.

"What the fuck is that?" Nick asked, pushing past the two guards that had helped to form a circle around where the beast, Nivea, Ezra, and Eli now stood.

"I'm guessing what serves as the blood of a hybrid," Ezra said, coming to his feet and removing the tuxedo jacket he'd been wearing.

Eli had already pulled his jacket off, the seams of both arms ripped after all his movements. He had it balled up and was currently using it to wipe his face, just before he looked over to her with what she'd already deemed his death glare. He was angry with her because she hadn't listened to what he'd told her to do. She knew that just as she knew she'd hear an earful at some point tonight. Funny how he was never suffering from lack of words when it came to chewing her out about something. But after they'd made love—radio silence. Typical arrogant shifter behavior? No, typical Eli Preston behavior.

"Two more down in the bathroom," Brayden announced, entering the room with his brothers flanking him.

Rome cursed. The First Female was right beside him, placing a hand on his shoulder, her light complexion in stark contrast to the black of his tuxedo jacket. She wore a shimmering silver gown that earlier this evening had caught every twinkle in her hazel-colored eyes. Now, those eyes looked worried.

Ary Delgado also stood beside her mate, her gaze transfixed on the hybrid while Nick scowled.

Caprise Delgado—a woman and shifter that Nivea admired for her strength, beauty, and tenacity—had already walked up to the hybrid, kicking the now disintegrating carcass, frowning when that part of its leg melted into ashes.

"They aren't worth the tainted DNA they're using to make them," she stated.

"How many were outside?" Rome asked sternly.

"One," Eli replied. "One big-ass motherfucker with only one objective—to kill."

"What makes you say that?" X asked him.

"Its eyes," Eli told him, tossing the jacket onto the closest table. "There's no comprehension there, no movement or focus. They're blank, like a robot. A programmed robot that was coming for us but able to take out anything in its path."

"They've been tagged," Aidan said to Rome. "Each one of them had this little pin just beneath the right ear."

"So, the crack beneath the left ear—the one that makes them look a little like Frankenstein—is their Achilles' heel and the pin at the right ear is their GPS?" Nick asked, his eyebrows drawn so close it looked as if he had one wicked unibrow.

Aidan nodded. "Right. We're going to take these and work our magic. Meet you back at Havenway," he said concisely, but still waited for Rome to respond.

Rome looked to the younger shifter that he'd brought into the fold. "Good. I want a full report within the hour."

Aidan's reply was a tight nod to Rome, and another one to his brothers as he turned and headed for the doors. Caleb and Brayden followed him out.

"Get Priya on the phone. I want a conference with her and all of the other FLs the moment we arrive at Havenway. Jax, take someone to get the vehicles and bring them around to the service entrance. We'll be there in ten minutes."

Jax mimicked Aidan's previous nod, turn, and walk-out motion as Eli immediately moved to Rome's side. With Kalina's guard gone, he would assume protection detail for both the Assembly Leader and First Female. Without being asked, Nivea went to stand at Kalina's side, noting the First Female's nod of acceptance as she moved past her.

"X, I want you to stay behind to make sure all of this is cleaned up. Nobody gets in this ballroom until it's done. And check those bathrooms before you leave," Rome directed. "Caprise will ride with Nick."

Nivea almost thought Caprise would say something in response, but in the months since she'd come to Havenway and mated with X, the female shifter had begun to take the hierarchy seriously. Nivea had worked hard to train herself for the same allegiance, but taking Eli's orders was becoming harder and harder the more personal their relationship became.

"Their DNA is still unstable. They'll turn to ash to be swept up," Ezra told Rome.

The Assembly Leader looked down at the floor where the beast that was terrorizing them just minutes before was now nothing more than a steaming pile of gray ash. "Make sure we take care of it. I don't want any human sweeping it up and trying to figure out what it was. It's apparent that Crowe somehow got his hands on a shifter through our carelessness. I'm not used to making the same mistake twice."

With that, X moved to whisper something to one of the other guards. They in turn left the room, no doubt to find a broom and trash bag to sweep up the ash, Nivea thought.

"The trucks are here," Eli said to Rome.

"Fifteen minutes after we're at Havenway I want all of you in the debriefing room," Rome told Nick and X.

Eli and Ezra would attend as the Lead Guards. Nivea would not be in attendance, which meant she'd have to wait to find out what their next step would be. As she walked behind Rome and Kalina—Eli moving quickly in front of them—she thought there would be definitive next steps in finding out where Crowe was so they could stop him. Apparently what happened in Arizona had not slowed the man down one bit.

"What the hell did you think you were doing? I told you to stay back!" Eli yelled the moment he'd found Nivea and pulled her out into the hallway at Havenway.

The conference call was over, and to say the shifters that had been in the room were running high on tension was a vast understatement. He was angry and irritated beyond belief that because of her he'd been distracted in the meeting. When he should have been listening intently to every word that was being said, every facet of the new game plan being laid out, he was instead thinking of what that beast could have done to her.

As it stood now, the image of her being twisted around the beast's back, her arm about to totally dislocate from her body, had him simmering with rage. He'd wanted to rip that bastard apart with his bare hands and only because he might have injured her in the process did he hold tight to the heated rage that bubbled inside of him. He couldn't take it if something happened to Nivea. That, for Eli, would be the last straw, the third strike where females in his life were concerned and he had no idea what he'd do after that.

"I was doing my job," was her calm reply.

She'd been sitting in the cafeteria, her hands holding a cup of coffee, her gaze forward. He'd wondered what she was thinking so intently about but had been more attuned to the scent he'd picked up the moment he entered the room. It was the first time he'd scented her in he didn't know how long, the first time his body reacted before he'd actually seen her. Did that mean his senses were back on point? Was whatever had been going on with him over now? He couldn't tell, but was certainly hoping for that.

"I told you to stay back. I am your superior!" he yelled at her.

"You're an asshole," she snapped back. "I did what I was trained to do and I helped take that bastard down. So why don't you just say what's really on your mind, Eli? Tell me why you're really so angry with me, so intent on pushing me away."

He loved to watch her lips move, to see the sparks of emotion in her eyes when she was angry or aroused. He did not like what she was insinuating.

"It was dangerous out there tonight. You don't know anything about those hybrids. Nobody does," he countered.

"You knew where to strike to take it down. How is that?" she asked, her back still pressed against the wall. "This was your first time seeing one, right? How did you know what to do?"

Eli took a step back. He wanted to look away, to regroup, but he couldn't. Her hair was curly at the ends, hanging loose down her back. She'd changed from that sexy-as-hell dress to sweats and a loose-fitting T-shirt and yet he still wanted to wrap her legs around his waist and pound into her warm, wet pussy until his mind cleared, until his body and his cat felt finally free.

At his sides his fists clenched, jaw ticking with the pressure of gritting his teeth. "Instinct," he told her. "I've been training longer than you. It was just instinct." Only Eli wasn't so certain that was it entirely. He'd seen the spot beneath the beast's left ear and then he'd seen the beast falling, crumpling to the ground and he knew. In the next moment he acted. It was as simple and perplexing as that.

Nivea shook her head, the left corner of her mouth lifting slightly. "Another thing you suck at is lying, Eli. You knew something about that hybrid. And now, I do too."

"What?" He stepped closer to her again because staying away was just futile. "What do you know?"

She looked around then, her head moving from side to side, her gaze searching for someone. Finally she came up on tiptoe, pressing her lips to his ear and whispered, "It shared your scent. I thought it was you but it wasn't. Why is that, Eli?"

He jerked away as if her words had somehow scorched him.

"Why did that killer smell like you and how did you know how to kill it?" she asked again.

Eli kept moving back, trying desperately to get away this time. Not from her, he thought, as his legs continued to move. From everything.

"You know, don't you? You can tell me, Eli. You can trust me."

"No!" he yelled. He couldn't trust her. She was just like the other females that had come and gone from his life. They were soft and smelled like heaven. Highly sexual and desirable and he wanted them. No, correct that, he needed them. For the moments it took for him to get off and to move on, he thought finally. Because now, after all he'd been through, Eli would never allow anything more.

With his mind in check once more, Eli took a steadying step toward her. Then another and another, until her breasts rubbed against his lower chest. He waited until she looked up at him, as he knew she would. There was never any backing down from her, never any turning away because things got tough. For a second he wondered if that would be true in any case.

Then he blinked and realized he didn't give a damn. None of that mattered.

"What I want to trust you to do is be a better guard," he said sternly. "To take the orders given to you and to protect the ones you're assigned to. Do you think you can do that, Cannon?"

She swallowed, her lips thinning only slightly before she replied, "I can do that, Preston."

Chapter 9

"He asked about you," Amina said simply, her voice sounding strained as she spoke over the phone.

The fingers that had been drumming over her steering wheel while Nivea sat outside the barbershop on the corner stilled.

"Why?" she asked after a few seconds of silence.

"I wondered that myself," her sister told her. "It's been years since he's even acknowledged you existed. Then out of the blue he asks, 'Have you heard from Nivea?'"

"And what did you say?"

"What was I supposed to say? He *is* my father. And yours too. Whatever falling out you had with them all those years ago was probably silly and should not have kept you all from speaking or seeing each other for all this time."

This wasn't the first time Amina had shared her views on what she thought was Nivea's chosen exile from the Cannon family. It was normally Nivea's practice to simply ignore her sister, changing the topic and moving on. Today, Eli's questions from a week ago resonated in her mind. Why was Richard Cannon giving money to the Comastaz Labs?

"It just is, Amina. We've been over this before."

"Right. And before I always let it go because you seemed happy and so did they. But he wanted to know when the last time I saw and talked to you was. He wanted to know where you were, what you were doing and I thought, maybe?"

A car sped past and Nivea looked up and out the side window. She tried to keep her breathing steady and remain alert. The press had been all over what happened at the charity ball. Even with Priya's statements on behalf of Reynolds & Delgado, LLC, that there was a disagreement arising from hotel guests that were not on the invite list and things quickly escalated, the whispers of "cat people" were circulating once more.

"Maybe what?" she asked her sister, trying to keep her personal life from overlapping with her work, and not 100 percent certain that was going to remain a possibility for much longer.

"Maybe you would like to come home," she said slowly. "Just for dinner, I mean," she quickly added.

"No!" Nivea replied just as fast. Going back to New York—not home because that place would never be Nivea's home again—was not an option.

"But—" Amina started.

Nivea was shaking her head even though she knew her sister couldn't see her. "But nothing. I'm never going back there. Ever," she added adamantly. "Look, Amina, I have to go. I'll call you later."

Nivea immediately took the phone from her ear and ended the call, her fingers shaking as she held it in her hand. Lowering her head until her brow rested on the steering wheel, Nivea closed her eyes and continued to focus on her breathing.

In slowly, out even slower. In and out until her heart rate steadied and her temples ceased throbbing. That's what the shrink had taught her. Whenever the memories came on hard and swift, to breathe her way through them and to remember, no matter what, that it wasn't her fault. It was Richard's.

Still, the weakness each memory provoked was all hers and Nivea hated it, each and every time.

"Dammit!" she whispered vehemently. "Just goddammit!"

Shaking her head slowly as if the motion could actually clear all the dark and degrading memories that lived inside her, she rose up until her spine was straight. Her cat, also rising to its full length, filled her human body until she felt every ounce of its courage and strength pouring through her veins like some sort of intravenous injection.

With pursed lips she thought about Eli's questions once more. Was Richard Cannon somehow involved with the creation of the hybrids? And if so, how was she going to handle that? She was sure that Rome and the others thought she might not remain loyal to them, even though—to their credit—none of them treated her any differently than they had before.

Leaving the ballroom a few nights ago she'd been able to assist in guarding Rome and Kalina as they'd left. She'd ridden in the truck with them and had seen Kalina back to her private rooms.

"Thank you very much for taking the initiative," Kalina had said to Nivea before ducking into her room.

Nivea had felt prouder than she had in a very long time because this was what she wanted to do with her life. To protect those that she was loyal to, to uphold the laws of their kind, and to work with the other guards doing the same. She was not a traitor, or a murderer—or anything else that made up the complex composition of Richard Cannon. No matter that his blood ran hot through her veins. She was nothing like him. But she did know him better than probably anyone else on this earth. He'd made it that way the moment he'd pulled his nine-year-old daughter into his adult world with that first inappropriate touch to her bare shoulder and visiting her nightly for the next seven years.

Hence the reason she could never go back.

Unless she really had no other choice.

Nivea prayed she would have another choice, her gaze moving to the door of the barbershop as she stopped fighting the indecision over whether or not to go inside. Eli owned the barbershop and three others just like it throughout the city. He employed men that he'd met over the years, ones that had fallen in some way and needed a helping hand. She'd admired that about Eli, the compassion he had for people. The fact that it seemed to be all people besides her only stung a little. Well, a lot, but she wasn't about to start with that complaint at the moment.

Instead, she slipped her cell phone into her jacket pocket alongside the keys she'd previously taken out of the ignition. She climbed out of her car and seconds later was opening the door to the barbershop, all while trying not to think about Eli's reaction to her being there.

They weren't out on assignment today because Dorian Wilson had seemingly disappeared. After the incident at the cabin they hadn't seen him at his house and X's friend at the Bureau had confirmed he hadn't shown up for work. He wasn't dead, Eli had seemed certain of that fact when she'd suggested that maybe he'd been shot at the cabin but managed to drive away, thus dying someplace else. But he didn't seem to be in D.C. either. And after the incident at the charity ball, Rome wanted all shifters focused on training to deal with the hybrids, since it seemed apparent that Crowe wasn't stopping his development of the species.

Eli had left Havenway hours ago and she'd been—like a stalker—following him around the city. Why? She'd asked herself that question several times today and had only been able to come up with one answer—he was her mate.

Nivea was as sure of this as she was of her name. Especially after their little tryst, no matter how long ago that seemed to be. The shrink said she'd one day be able to love and trust and care for someone the way she was supposed to have been loved and cared for, and she believed it wholeheartedly. Just as she was certain that Eli was the one, if he could ever get past that chip the size of a boulder on his shoulder.

The moment she walked into the shop a couple of things greeted her. The quiet: a barbershop, similar to a beauty salon, was rarely ever quiet. The people: all eight of them were standing at the back of the shop, huddled together, staring toward something behind her. And as she finally turned her head to the left, she saw the knife that was being held to Eli's neck.

"Fuck!" Eli murmured the moment he saw Cannon walk through the door.

Up until this moment he'd had the situation under control. Or at least he was getting there.

Pedro Rimas—the man currently holding the sharp blade to his neck—had been stopping by the barbershop, leaving messages for Eli for the past two weeks. Malik Drake, Priya's brother who had been kidnapped two months ago and was still attending outpatient rehab for his decades-long drug addiction, had taken each message and made sure Eli knew about them instantly.

Eli's first inclination was to ignore the messages. To forget that time in his life, the weeks when he wasn't sure if he'd be sentenced to human jail for the rest of his life. Or if his cat would overrule the justice system entirely and carry them back to the forest. Nine years ago he'd killed

Rimas's brother, Lonzo, in a pool hall because the bastard had hit Leanne Campbell, Eli's ex-girlfriend, knocking her unconscious. Rimas had been in jail at the time. Today, now that he was clearly finished serving his time, Rimas had come after Eli for revenge. Eli understood that motivation all too well.

"We don't do your kind of hair," Eli managed to say to Cannon, glaring at her from the bent back, headlock position Rimas had him in.

"Shut the hell up!" Rimas yelled, his arm tightening around Eli's neck, the hand with the knife shaking so that the tip of the blade nipped Eli's skin.

Blinking, Eli opened his eyes again to see Cannon's lips moving but no sound coming out. Dammit, she was speaking into her com link, alerting the others that he was in trouble. They'd be here in no time, especially Ezra. He had to diffuse this situation and quickly. It wasn't as if Rimas was stronger than him, or his cat, for that matter. But Eli had been trying his best to handle this situation differently, to not react the way he had the night he'd killed Rimas's brother. It had been taking a hell of a lot of his strength but he'd thought he was making progress since the nutcase hadn't sliced Eli's neck open as of yet. Then, she showed up.

"I want you all to get out of here," she said, moving back and opening the door.

She was talking to the barbers and clients that a few minutes before Eli had ordered into the back of the shop.

"Come on, get out now!" she continued, moving her arms to direct them.

She stood with her back to him and Rimas while she waved the people out. Malik had looked at Eli, then to Cannon in question.

"Get moving. I've got this," she told him.

From behind her, Eli nodded, telling Malik it was okay

to listen to this unarmed female. Well, Malik would think she was just an unarmed female. Only Eli knew better.

"This doesn't concern you, bitch!" Rimas yelled at Cannon when everyone else had cleared out of the room.

She turned slowly, refusing to look at Eli.

"He's right," Eli said. "This doesn't concern you."

A brow arched, the right side of her mouth lifting in a partial smile as she took a step forward. Nobody looked as sexy as she did in that guard's uniform. Even with her hair pulled back tight in her signature ponytail, she was every bit as alluring as any model on the front page of a fashion magazine. Only better because there was an edge to her along with a bit of poise that he only now admitted had been the first thing to attract him to her.

Now that personality trait might be what got her killed. No, he corrected himself instantly, he'd never let that happen. Not again.

"Looks like we're having some type of disagreement here," she said calmly. "And hey, if he overcharged you, I can believe it. He's a shady character if I've ever met one."

Eli frowned as she talked to Rimas, ignoring him and probably thinking she was helping. Inside his cat growled, ready to strike, needing desperately to shift. His spine tingled, moving beneath his shirt, all too ready to bend and conform to the cat's will. But he couldn't. Exposure to this human at this time would be too detrimental for the shifters. Besides that, once the cat was released, Eli would lose all control, just as he had before.

"I'm not going to tell you again," he said tightly. "Get. The. Hell. Out of here!"

She didn't even look at him as she took that next step, didn't seem to care what she was walking into.

"We can resolve this without violence," she told Rimas.

"He's dying here today. I'm gonna gut him the same

way he did my brother and if you don't get lost I'm gonna do the same to you!" Rimas yelled at her and something inside Eli vibrated, his body shaking with its intensity.

"Are you going to let him get away with that?" she asked Eli, finally looking at him.

Her intention to diffuse this situation was clear in the set of her shoulders and the glare of her eyes. Eli watched with growing trepidation. He stood up straight then, pulling Rimas's arms with him.

"Keep still, you prick!" Rimas yelled. He was shaking and yet trying to keep his hold on Eli.

It was useless. Eli flexed his back muscles, jerking free of Rimas's hold, simultaneously elbowing the guy in the gut. All actions he could have taken before. He hadn't because to do so would have further enraged Rimas and possibly pushed Eli to shift into his cat to take care of the bastard once and for all. That was not a scenario he wished to play out, not here and not now that the shifters had so many other issues going on.

Just as he was patting himself on the back for keeping the worst from happening in front of his staff and customers, Rimas came up quickly, lunging forward, knife held high. Eli leaned to the side to avoid the stick of the knife and punched him again in the jaw. His claws had extended, leaving a long scratch across the man's face that leaked with blood immediately.

He frowned, trying like hell to bite back all that boiled inside, the anger mixed with the power. Eli took a step back, praying the cat and all the darkness from that stupid shaman treatment kept it together. They had to work together, the three entities to keep the peace, the balance . . .

There was a movement behind him and the next thing he saw was Cannon lifting a leg to kick at Rimas. The man grabbed her leg quickly, bending it and stepping into her, thrusting the knife deep into her shoulder before Eli could even blink.

But blink he finally did and when his eyes opened again, they were the cat's. On a deep inhale he picked up the scent of her blood, rich and acidic, and fury darkened his gaze, pumping into every muscle of his body. Eli lunged, cat's teeth and full claws bared, only his prey in his sights.

He swiped at Rimas from behind, pulling him by the shirt off of Cannon and tossing him into the wall with such force the drywall caved with the outline of his body. Rimas slid to the floor and Eli was on him, swinging and striking, seeing nothing but bloodred.

Eli's vision blurred for a moment as his fists continued to batter the man on the floor. When it cleared there was blood everywhere. It filled the room, ran down the walls onto the dirt floor. Acacia's body was limp and still they'd attacked. The sting of betrayal had only been the tip of the iceberg. The shaman's potion laced with damiana had reportedly enhanced the warrior instinct the twin shifters had been born with, turning it into something darker, deeper, more tainted than either of them had foreseen. They'd killed her men too, just before taking Acacia down, so that their bodies were drenched in blood, their chests heaving with the exertion, cats roaring at the conquest.

"Stop, Eli! Stop!"

It was Ezra yelling into his ear, holding onto his arms, and pulling him across the room. The room that was no longer in the Sierra Leone. Eli's back slammed against the wall, his heart pounding against his rib cage as his vision finally cleared, the curtain of red slipping away so that his brother's sea-green eyes stared back at him, a grim look on his face.

His cat roared, so loud the sound vibrated throughout Eli's entire body and he closed his eyes tight to endure the tremors. Then the scent wafted into his nostrils and his eyes shot open. There was blood, again, this time dripping onto the floor from her arm as she stood. She was looking at him and Eli bolted up onto his feet. In seconds he was on her, his hands shaking as he took her arm, felt the warmth of the pouring blood, and saw the angry gash at her shoulder.

"She's going to be okay," he heard a voice from behind. "Aidan's on his way with a truck now. He was the closest to us when I headed this way. He'll take her back to Havenway and Ary will fix her up."

He knew the voice. His brother, his twin. Alongside the voice was another sound. A heartbeat, Ezra's maybe? Eli felt totally open, vulnerable to every emotion, every nuance of being a shifter and then some. But it wasn't Ezra's heartbeat he heard echoing in his ears. It was Nivea's, he knew because he was touching her and the sound matched the pulsing at her wrist.

"He hurt you," Eli said, his forehead furrowing as he couldn't tear his gaze away from her wound.

"I'm okay," she said with a nervous chuckle. "Just a little cut."

She was trying to reassure him. It wasn't working. He turned from her then, his teeth bared, the cat's roar sounding loudly throughout the room.

"Just hold on," Ezra said. "Hold the hell on! She's going to be okay. And he's alive."

The latter wasn't what Eli wanted to hear. He lunged forward, ready to complete the task he'd begun, but Ezra was there, blocking his body with his own, pushing Eli back. This time Eli didn't fall away so easily. He pushed against his brother's barrier, trying to get to the bastard that had hurt Nivea. She was bleeding, a lot, and the sight had Eli's stomach churning, his temples throbbing with the need to retaliate, to kill.

"Take care of her, Eli! Go back to Havenway and take care of her!" Ezra continued to yell into his brother's face.

Eli roared again, his claws clicking against each other as his fingers clenched and retracted. His chest felt full, like the breath coming through was a terrific struggle. He wanted to yell "no," to tell Ezra to get the hell out of his way or end up on the floor as well. But he couldn't. He roared again, this time in disappointment and confusion. He wanted the death, felt the power of it rippling through his veins. Inside him lived a killer—all he had to do was unleash it completely. It would be so simple to let go and move forward, to take the life that had harmed hers. To end it as it had begun, with violence.

Then his entire body warmed and he stilled, the war raging within him ceasing immediately. She had a hand on his shoulder. It was her good arm, the other one slack at her side, drenched in blood.

"Let's go home," she said quietly. "The truck's out back. We can leave right now."

He didn't want to leave, and yet, there was a part of him that did. It wasn't running, no, he convinced himself that wasn't the case. But he could walk away with her, with Nivea, and not have to see her die because of events he'd set in motion. Not this time. She would still be alive. Unlike Acacia, and eventually Leanne.

Eli took a step.

"I've got you," he said, bending slightly and picking her up in his arms. "We'll go back and get you some help."

She looked like she was about to say something, but in the end, simply nodded. He walked to the back of the barbershop and out the door to the waiting SUV. Aidan had already gotten out and was holding the back door open. Eli only nodded to the other shifter before climbing onto the backseat with Nivea still held tightly against his chest. With each inhale he smelled her blood. That scent permeated every crevice of his body, until his heart pounded, his cat hissed, and the thought of ever losing her settled like a dark cloud in his mind.

"Your bath is ready," Eli said an hour after they'd been at Havenway.

Ezra had been correct, and Ary had neatly sewn the gash in Nivea's shoulder closed. In a day or so it would heal completely, the stitches dissolving on their own and Nivea's shoulder returning to normal. That was the way Shadows healed, fast and neat, unless the injury was fatal; then they died just as any ordinary human. Other than that, cancer was the only human ailment that could also kill a shifter. It was complex, the ins and outs of their genetic makeup, which made him realize how foolish it was to ever try and duplicate it. Unfortunately, Captain Crowe was obviously not privy to that same knowledge. Either that or he simply did not care, which Eli was personally putting his money on.

Nivea was sitting on the side of Eli's bed where he'd left her. She'd wanted to go to her own area, had said she was perfectly capable of taking care of herself. Still, he'd brought her here. Her room at Havenway was on the other side of the complex, near the western exit and supply room. He wouldn't hear her if she cried out in pain from all the way over there. With his shifter senses, he probably should have, but he wouldn't. Or at least he wasn't certain he would, and so that had not been an option.

When she didn't move immediately he went to the bed, reaching for her hand to lead her.

"It wasn't your fault, you know," she said when she looked up at him.

Blood still stained her clothes. Half the white tank top she'd worn beneath the guard T-shirt was red. The skin along her chest and one arm was stained with the color.

Even the side of her face and jaw had blood on them. It made him frown, even though the cat had long since calmed to an almost normal state.

"It shouldn't have happened," he told her frankly. "Now, let's get your bath."

She took his hand then, her fingers feeling thinner than he ever remembered before. Rising from the bed she moved only a fraction slower than normal and she walked with the same sure steps. Still, Eli held onto her, forcing himself to move with her and ushering her through the bathroom door before him.

His hands were steady as he bent down to untie her laces. She leaned into him while he pulled off each boot, putting them to the side. Her ankle socks rolled off easily and he held the heel of her foot in his hand for just a second longer than he should have. With resignation he undid the buckle of her pants, unzipped, and began pushing them down her legs.

"Really, Eli, I can do this myself," she told him, her tone steady.

It wasn't that she was modest, he already knew that wasn't true. The physical contact between them wasn't an issue either, because they'd been there and done that and if he wasn't completely off the mark, she would be willing to do it all over again. As much as the case should be different, he had to admit to himself that he was in the same boat. He wanted her again, and again.

"Be quiet and let me get this done," he implored. If she could just do that he'd have her in and out of the tub and tucked securely into his bed in no time. Then he could find Ezra and learn what happened to Rimas.

He hadn't killed him, Eli was certain. But he'd been on his way to that end, he knew without a doubt. Drawing his lips tightly, he pushed down Nivea's pants and panties at the same time, averting his gaze so that the clean-shaven triangle between her legs didn't tempt him any more than the memory of how slick and plump the skin was there. When he touched the rim of the T-shirt he felt his brow knot, his shoulders tensing as the damp cloth rubbed along his skin. Hurriedly he yanked the material apart, not wanting to ask her to lift her arm. The sports bra she was wearing came off the same way, ripped and unable to be worn again.

Nivea didn't seem to mind as she turned and was ready to climb into the tub. Of course Eli reached out to pick her up, moving close before kneeling to set her into the tub. There were no bubbles, only hot water to soothe the aching muscles he was sure she probably had.

When she sat back, sighing as the steam immediately went to work on her body, Eli was about to stand up and walk away. He would go to the sink to retrieve the cloth and soap to wash her. Then he would carry her out and cover her delectable body up before he did something he knew was selfish considering the circumstances.

"Why did he want to kill you?"

The question stilled him instantly.

"He said you'd killed his brother. Who was he?"

Eli did not want to answer either of those questions. He did not want to talk about this situation, especially not with her. But how could he deny her? She'd taken a knife in the shoulder because of what he'd done all those years ago. How could he not tell her everything that had led up to the moment she'd been assaulted?

To keep his thoughts focused Eli moved across the room to obtain the cloth and soap. Going to his knees beside the tub he dipped them both into the water until the cloth was soaped then proceeded to rub gently at the blood on her cheek.

"His name is Pedro Rimas," he said, speaking quietly. "His brother was Lonzo and he'd been involved with a woman named Leanne."

Eli hadn't said her name for so long it felt awkward slipping past his lips. He moved the cloth down her neck, rubbing softly until the streaks were gone.

"One night I witnessed Lonzo assaulting Leanne. He knocked her out cold like she was some guy on the street. I just reacted," he said, not shrugging the way he felt like doing. Instead he kept his gaze on the cloth and all the places that blood needed to be cleaned from.

The words were coming and he was minutely grateful, because denying her this explanation was just simply not an option. But his mind was quickly losing focus. The darkness of his past combined with the sensual feeling of the present. He'd never bathed a woman before, never wanted to do something so intimate, and yet, right now, all he wanted was to wash her completely clean of all the anger and rage he'd sent her way this afternoon.

Clearing his throat of the lump that had slowly begun to form there, he continued.

"Leanne and I dated for almost a year. Then it was over and eventually she began seeing Lonzo. When I saw them that night it was the first time in months. And when he hit her I just reacted."

Dipping the cloth into the water then lifting it up to her shoulder, he let the water drip down her chest and arms. If she was uncomfortable, it only showed in the quick jolt of her chest. She never spoke a word. Eli continued to rinse the upper portion of her body, then soaped the cloth again and washed the lower parts, being as gentle as he had been before. He did not continue with his explanation even though there was more in his mind about what happened, more thoughts, concerns, regrets. He'd reenacted that scene so many times.

From the moment he'd first struck Lonzo, until the last punch to the back of the man's head as he was crawling on the floor. It was straight to his skull, his sharp teeth bared but not penetrating—because while he was the cat in every other aspect, his human body was still intact. The man had died and Eli had been arrested that night. Two weeks later, while he was out on bail, he'd gone to see Leanne, apologies on his lips. But it was too late. That's what her letter said, the one that lay next to her lifeless body strewn naked across her bed. She'd overdosed on pain pills. And the guilt had hung around Eli's neck like metal chains.

"You killed him to protect her."

Her voice was soft, her fingers wet as they touched his cheek. He'd been staring down into the water for who knew how long. But when he heard her speak he'd looked up slowly to see her gaze intent on him.

"And she killed herself to get away from me," he admitted for the first time in all these years. "I couldn't give her what she wanted or needed so she turned to him. Then I killed him and she had nothing. So she died."

"And your penance is to continue to have nothing because that's what you think you deserve," she said while shaking her head. "Oh, Eli."

"It is done," he said, moving so abruptly water splashed over the side of the tub. He stood then, walking to the small closet and pulling out a towel. "Let's get you into bed. You should rest."

"I don't need to rest," she said disdainfully, coming to a stand in the tub so that water dripped in quick succession over her lush nakedness.

He breathed in deep, his chest constricting, temples throbbing incessantly as he wrestled with imminent desire and constant inner betrayal. He shouldn't want Nivea. He'd decided long ago that there would never be another female in his life that could ultimately end up hurt or worse. Yet, he did want her, and in the last few hours felt as if he wouldn't take another breath if something happened to her.

"And I don't need you handling me with kid gloves," she exclaimed, extending an arm to grab the towel he'd been holding with a death grip from his hands.

Wrapping the towel around her, shielding all that he wanted from his view, Nivea stepped out of the tub.

"This is ridiculous and then again, it's not. I completely understand your guilt, but I'm here to tell you it's unnecessary. You can't live your life blaming yourself for other people's faults or actions."

"You don't know what you're talking about, so it's probably best to stop talking altogether," he told her.

"Is that your way of telling me to shut up?"

His reply was to walk out of the bathroom, leaving her and whatever else she thought she wanted to say to him, alone. In his room Eli ran his hands down his face. He tried to steady his breathing, to get a grip on all that was going on around him and to stop thinking about fucking her again and again!

"Okay, let's just talk about this. Something really bad happened to you and you reacted. But it doesn't make you an awful person, Eli. You're stronger than this. I know you are."

"You don't know anything about me!" he yelled.

Then he clapped his lips shut and turned away from her. He tried counting from one hundred, taking in slow and deep breaths, each method of relaxation that was supposed to work. He did not want to talk about his past, and most of all not with her. Eli was certain she wouldn't understand. Hell, there was still so much he didn't understand himself.

"You will not go into the field until I say so. You are officially on medical leave," he said, walking to the door with every intention of locking her inside if that's what it took to keep her safe.

"What?" she yelled back. "Are you out of your damned

mind? I'm not a child that you can just dictate to, Eli. I'm an adult and I'm—"

Whatever she was going to say was lost in the next three seconds as Eli spun around, crossed the room, and grabbed her into his arms, smashing his lips down over hers in a hungry kiss that stole his breath, his mind, and almost every single dark part of him at once.

Chapter 10

Kissing Eli was like being engulfed by a raging storm. He took everything from her, air, thought, inhibitions, it all melted away with each stroke of his tongue. She fell into him at that moment, being dragged under and struggling to breathe. His strong hands cupped her face and she grabbed his wrists to keep herself standing upright. His teeth scraped along her lips, her chin, then his tongue was plunging deep again. Their breathing was erratic, hearts beating wildly as hunger threatened to consume them both.

Then she was lifted off her feet and dropped onto the bed, the towel she'd been holding around her body falling to the side, coolness from the air-conditioned room slapping against her exposed skin. He grabbed her ankles then, pulling them apart and pushing them back until her legs bent, feet planted on the bed. She hissed his name, but he ignored her, leaned down until his lips were touching her plump folds, his tongue delving deep into her center, swirling around until her hips jolted up off the bed. When she shivered all over, his tongue moved upward, circling around her clit until she was biting her bottom lip, the cat inside purring with complete glory.

Nivea couldn't close her eyes. She couldn't fall into the pleasure, the warrior in her held her from succumbing so easily. "I won't do as you command," she said through clenched teeth.

He barely paused, but his attention slipped from front to back, his tongue swirling over her anus, dampening her there. Her teeth chattered, fingers gripping the sheets of the bed. All the while she shook her head, refusing to let his words stand. She would not allow him to control her. Regardless of whether or not Eli Preston was her mate, he would not dictate what she could or could not do in her life. She'd vowed after leaving New York to never live that way again.

"I won't," she whispered.

He pulled his mouth away from her and Nivea felt like the wind had been knocked out of her. She missed his mouth on her immediately, but would not make a sound.

"You want to act tough?" he asked, not looking up at her, his gaze still locked on her soaking wet pussy, on the remnants of his clever ministrations.

"You want to tempt me and yet defy me," he continued, rubbing a finger up and down her slit until her entire body trembled. He circled her clit, rubbing in teasing circles until her pussy pulsated, her essence dripping onto the bed.

"I won't see you hurt," he told her, his voice tight, restrained. He dipped a finger inside of her, pressing deep then pulling back. In went two fingers this time, stretching inside her, pressing with delicious pleasure against her walls.

"You can't . . . control . . . me," she gasped, her chest heaving, eyes still focused on the top of his head.

He looked up then, their gazes locking, holding, simmering. His fingers slipped from her center, down, back, until one wet digit was pressing into her anus, stretching the sensitive skin there, breaching a barrier Nivea had never known the feeling of before. She drew in a breath, loving the feel of how tight her body sucked on his finger.

"You sure about that, my little hellcat?" he asked, one of his thick brows rising.

Nivea struggled to keep herself still, her eyes open and her gaze focused on him. This was a battle for control, for everything she'd ever worked for and she felt like she was losing. Her body wanted this pleasure. The cat inside wanted everything Eli, its mate, was offering her at this moment. But was that enough? The human in her knew it wasn't, she knew the game Eli was playing. He would use her pleasure to control her, just as Richard had once used her innocence to keep her quiet.

"No!" she yelled at him. Then with all the strength she could muster she closed her legs, rolling to the side until his finger was dislodged, her shoulder throbbing with the pressure of being pushed into the mattress.

He'd been about to say something, to rebut the single word she'd been able to speak, when there was a knock at the door. A soft, tentative knock, as if someone knew he'd need a moment to respond. Nivea inhaled deeply, their *companheiro calor* so strong and assaulting to her senses that she almost wanted to cry out. Instead Nivea rolled completely off the bed, grabbing the towel, and headed back into the bathroom, leaving Eli and the anger surrounding him like a cloak behind.

"The press is all over what happened today," Rome said solemnly. "Ezra dropped Rimas off at the hospital. His wounds were deep scratches in a clawlike pattern. He's mumbling about hearing growling, seeing weird animal eyes and long sharp teeth. As of about ten minutes ago the police had finally been allowed back into the room to question him more. Reporters are all over the hospital and your barbershop. They're looking for a connection to the reports of loud, animal-like growling the night of the charity ball. The rumor of the cat people grows stronger every day."

Only a leader such as Rome could make a statement that long seem like one single death sentence. There were equal measures of compassion mixed with the bitter sting of guilt being thrust at him for what he'd done. He'd run out into the open to confront the hybrid the night of the charity ball. He and the Sanchez brothers engaged without thought to who might have been on the streets to see them. And today, he'd seen that knife sink into Nivea's skin, smelled the strong scent of her blood, could almost taste it in the back of his throat as he watched it drip down her arm, and he'd reacted. It was that simple. And Eli could truthfully say that if put in the same circumstances, he would do it again.

"I didn't shift and I didn't kill him," was what he finally said to the shifter he'd grown to care for and respect a great deal.

"No. You didn't, not this time," Rome agreed.

Eli's jaw clenched.

"I'm not here to blame you, Eli. Things are happening around us that none of us are able to control right now. But you are trained for this," Rome continued. "You are a leader and you know the consequences."

He stood up straight, squaring his shoulders and holding the Assembly Leader's gaze. "You are correct."

"There's a press conference scheduled for tomorrow morning. You're going to make a statement about the violence in your barbershop."

"Why? Rimas is going to tell the cops tonight that I beat the crap out of him. They're going to arrest me. Giving a press conference is admitting my guilt before the entire city."

Nick stepped forward then, his face grim, cat's eyes

bared. "You were defending your shop against an intruder. Rimas had a knife, he held it to your neck for at least five minutes before Nivea came in. Then he stabbed her. You have witnesses so the self-defense is clear," he told Eli.

"Just like it was clear when I killed Lonzo," he replied.

"Don't do that, man," X said, moving around Rome to stand near Eli. "Don't make this more personal than it is. That man came after you with the intent to kill you. The reason doesn't matter. You did what you had to do to stay alive. Nobody is going to penalize you for that."

"Unless I'm one of the cat people," Eli added, then shook his head. "Look, I hear what you're saying. I'll do the press conference and whatever else I can to make this go away so we can focus on the important matters. You don't have to worry about me."

All three men looked at him skeptically and Eli felt like growling with rage. He hated their concerned and wary glances, the looks that said they thought he was completely losing it. And the feeling inside that they might actually be right. Clenching his fists at his sides, he turned away, moving to the nightstand, and looking down at the empty table. No clock, no pictures, nothing but the lamp that had been here when he moved in. His clothes hung in the closet and rested in the drawers but that was the extent of his belongings in this space. There was nothing else and had never been. Eli felt like this on the inside as well. He was a jaguar and a human, and at one point in his life he'd required something extra—the shaman's healing potion. That was all that he was, nothing else.

"I'll do the press conference and whatever is necessary to minimize the attention to the shifters," he stated again. "I should have reacted differently."

"No, he shouldn't have," Nivea said, coming out of the bathroom wearing one of his button-down shirts.

When he turned to see her he realized all she had were

her pants and they were lying on the floor on the other side of the bed. The shirt she'd worn in here, he'd tossed into the trash can. For a mere flicker of an instant he was struck by how naturally beautiful she looked with her hair hanging down to her shoulders, her feet bare, and his shirt nearly reaching her knees. Something, other than his cat and the dark he was so used to being inside him, shifted with the sight of her. Irritation won over the unknown and Eli frowned.

"He was trying to diffuse the situation. He let that lunatic hold a knife to his throat for who knows how long before I came, in an attempt to protect our secret. The man meant to kill him, I saw it plain as day in his eyes. He would have tried to kill us both," she told Rome and the others adamantly.

The room grew silent after her outburst and Eli, not really knowing why, had moved closer to her while she spoke. Now he stood right beside her, his body slightly in front of hers.

"You're right." X spoke up first. "He wanted to kill Eli and he would have tried his damnedest to kill you both. I know you reacted the only way you could," X said, looking at Eli. "But now the situation is more precarious than it was before. We're dealing with exposure from so many outlets at this point."

"Including from you," Nick said, his gaze aimed directly at Nivea.

"I'm no threat to the Shadows," she told him vehemently. Her body had lurched forward slightly and Eli had extended his arm to block her from moving any farther, and also ready to prevent anyone from striking out at her.

"I've trained for years to defend us and our secret. I don't care what you think you know, I'm no traitor," she finished confidently.

Eli believed her. In that moment he knew what she'd said was the absolute truth. While he had no idea what was going on with her parents and their apparent connection to Comastaz, he knew without any doubt that Nivea was not involved.

"She's telling the truth," he told them. "She doesn't know what her parents are up to."

Nick frowned. Rome folded his arms over his chest, his hand lifting to rub along his bearded chin.

"Whether that's true or not, you should know we're keeping a close eye on them," he told Nivea.

"That's not my concern," she replied coolly.

"Your issue to deal with," he told her. "Right now, one of my issues is that you were injured today, pretty badly from what Ary told me. So you're on security monitor duty for the next week, until that shoulder is completely healed. Eli will do the press conference and continue to try to find out what the hell went down at that cabin and where Agent Wilson ran off to. The Sanchez brothers are also on hand to help with tracking Crowe."

Eli heard her intake of breath over Rome's orders and knew she was about to go off.

"We've already had that discussion," he interjected. "She knows she will not be going out into the field until I say she's cleared."

"What the hell? Are you all crazy? I'm fine!" Nivea yelled. "You know how quickly we heal. I'll be ready to go out tomorrow. Why are you doing this to me?"

"Enough!" Rome yelled, raising his voice for the first time since coming into this room. "One week in the security monitoring room. And you, press conference at ten tomorrow morning. Tonight, both of you need to get some rest."

The Assembly Leader turned and walked out of the room before another word could be spoken. Nick followed right behind him without looking back, while X gave Eli what was as compassionate a look as the big man could offer.

"You're an idiot!" She rounded on him the moment they were alone. "Why didn't you tell them that I'm okay? That I can go out tomorrow?"

"Because you're not and you can't," he said somberly. "Look, I know that you're feeling okay. I don't like not being able to go back out tonight either. But I understand their reasoning. We're too pumped up right now, the cats are too close to the surface, ready to pounce. We need to lay low for a minute."

"Your minute consists of one day while mine is a week. How is that fair, Eli?"

"It's fair because you're the one who had a stab wound that went so deep that bastard nicked your bone!" he yelled at her. "You lost a crap-load of blood and . . . and . . ." He couldn't finish because the memory was too clear, the pain searing through his body at the sight flicking through his mind once more. It was too much to bear.

"Look, just hang around Havenway and do what he says for the week. I'll be following up on some things with the Sanchez brothers and I may need your eyes and ears here," he told her, suddenly exhausted from the events of the day, from this unnamed emotion rippling through his veins like an infusion.

"I'm a guard. I fight for these shifters every damned day," was her solemn retort.

Eli looked at her then, stared right into her light brown eyes and felt like her gaze was reaching deep inside of him, pulling something out he'd long since buried. "You're a damned good guard and you do fight for the shifters every day. I'll be first to vouch for you. But part of being a good fighter is knowing when to sit and wait."

When she didn't respond Eli took a deep breath, letting

it out in a whoosh and dragging his hands down his face. "I'm going to grab a shower," he said, turning away from her and heading to the bathroom door. He had no idea why he stopped and couldn't really bring himself to turn around, but before going inside he said, "I don't know if I can protect you if you go back to your room. If you need me in the middle of the night . . . I just don't know," he admitted, his voice so quiet he didn't even think she'd heard him.

"Ask me to stay, Eli," she replied.

He gritted his teeth then, his cat scratching at his insides as if eager for his human mouth to let the words slip free. He didn't know how to ask, what to say, how to do this male-and-female dance with her. All Eli knew for certain was that when he came out of the bathroom, he wanted to see her sitting on his bed. When he lay down to go to sleep, he wanted to feel her beside him. And when he awoke in the morning, he wanted to roll over and see her there.

"Stay," he finally replied, not waiting for an answer but going into the bathroom and closing the door quietly behind him.

Chapter 11

"This is where the signal stops," Brayden said, coming up to the bushes at the backside of the estate they were looking for in Prince George's County.

"Do you know who lives here?" Aidan asked, walking around his brother, flattening his hands on the brick structure and leaning forward to look into the window. "Lights are on in this hallway but I didn't see any cars in the driveway."

Caleb stood back from the others, tilting his head upward to look at the second floor of the structure. "No lights on upstairs. Probably some type of alarm system though. We'd have to disarm it before going in. Either that or get in and out in about ten minutes before the alarm company can dispatch the police."

Eli stood farthest from the brothers, looking around the entire space. To his right was a thick line of trees about forty feet away, lush grass all around. To the left was the same scenario. Directly in front of them were patio doors, the windows Aidan had looked through, heading to the left side of the house. Above was a deck that wrapped around the right side. Behind them, an in-ground pool, more grassy acreage, and a thicker line of trees, tall and full for privacy. The driveway was in the front, going to the dead end part of the block, where they had parked and walked down. This was a pretty secluded neighborhood, high-end, but not gated. Dumbasses.

"We'll take our chances," Eli told the group. "Let's go in."

He knew exactly whose house this was as he walked closer to the patio door where Caleb had already begun picking the lock. In seconds they were in and sure enough, the shrill buzzing of an alarm went off. The shifters moved with stealth, not speaking but using hand signals to split up and head in different directions.

Eli took the main level, heading up the basement stairs and moving through the expansive space on quiet feet and using his nocturnal vision. There was an office and he immediately slipped inside, heading straight to the desk and the computer. Running his hands along the sides he searched for flash drives. He wanted all of them. There weren't any, but when he opened the first drawer he smiled as a clear box with four flash drives inside came into view. He ditched the box and stuffed the drives into his pockets, not worried about leaving any fingerprints, since Shadows didn't have them.

When he was satisfied the desk was clear and knew that their time was winding down, Eli was just moving around to the front of the desk when something caught his eye. He grabbed the piece of paper quickly and ran out of the room. Aidan had been coming from the upstairs, giving Eli a thumbs-down signal as they passed in the foyer and then headed back down the basement stairs.

Brayden was coming from the garage and joined them on the descent. Caleb had stayed in the basement and shook his head when they ran into him. But Brayden held up a small plastic black bag and smiled. They rushed out of the house, moving quietly and quickly down the street to where they'd parked the truck. While the alarm still blared there had been no movement or lights going on at either of the neighboring houses. He considered they might still be asleep since it was only around four in the morning and the sun had yet to rise.

"Cut through that clearing down there," Caleb yelled from the backseat up to Aidan, who was driving.

"This street has no outlet. You have to turn around," Brayden interjected.

Aidan tossed his brother a sly smile. "I can make one."

"That's what I'm talkin' about!" Caleb yelled as Aidan took a hard right.

The truck rocked back and forth as its wheels rode up over the curb and onto the grassy property of the third clueless neighbor. They went straight through their backyard, coming out on another street and speeding away from the scene of the crime, while sirens blared in the distance.

Caleb and Aidan were high-fiving, Brayden was scowling, and Eli was trying not to smile at the younger shifters' antics. That hidden smile turned into a frown the moment his phone vibrated in his pocket.

"Yeah?" he answered.

"Press conference is cancelled," Ezra said gruffly.

There was a minor relief that was quickly followed by intense foreboding. "What happened?" Eli asked him.

"Rimas was killed sometime during the night. Papplin just arrived at the hospital for his shift and heard the news. Nurses went into the room to check his vitals at three a.m. and he was unresponsive."

Eli's teeth clenched as he listened, his cat awakening to press persistently against his spine. "What else?"

There was more, Eli was positive of that fact.

Ezra sighed heavily. "On a hunch, Papplin went to the room where Rimas was found. He picked up a rogue scent."

"Fuck!" Eli yelled, and the background chatter in the interior of the truck ceased.

"Don't go there, Eli," Ezra warned immediately. "Wherever you are right now, head back to Havenway. Don't go to the hospital or to your shop. Police are swarming both places. If you show up they're going to question you and Nick doesn't want you alone when they do."

"I'm not going into hiding," Eli countered.

"We're all going to be in hiding soon if we don't get a hold on this hybrid issue. Now that somebody's clearly out to expose us, we don't need to help them by flying off the handle and shifting right in front of them."

"Is that what you think I did? You think I flew off the handle and beat the crap out of Rimas?" Eli asked.

"I think the man was trying to kill you and when Nivea showed up his assault on her pushed a sensitive button. I'm not blaming you but I'm warning you not to put yourself in a situation you can no longer control again."

"Because I can't possibly control myself due to the poison that I voluntarily breathed into my body the way you can now?" The words were bitter and matched the complete distaste for everything he and Ezra had been forced to do back in the Sierra Leone rain forest.

Ezra was silent and Eli was annoyed as hell.

Ezra's revelation that his mate, the human named Dawn, had been his savior from Dagar's tainted smoke, was a sore subject between the two. Eli refused to believe that relinquishing control of his feelings to a female, again, was necessary to live a normal life. The last thing he needed, after Acacia and Leanne, was to let another female claim any part of him. Besides, Eli wasn't sure the symptoms he was experiencing had anything to do with the shaman's potion, after all, Ezra had never complained about seeing things that weren't presently right in front of him.

Yet even as he pressed the button to end the call with

his brother he knew that he'd already made a possibly deadly mistake. He'd slept with Nivea Cannon. Not only had they had sex, acting on the attraction that had been brewing between them for years, but he'd actually slept in a bed with her curled into his arms last night. He'd fallen asleep with her scent permeating his senses and awakened to the same. And dammit, it had felt fucking fantastic!

Thrusting his phone back into his pocket, he filled the Sanchez brothers in on what was going on. "I need you to be my eyes and ears down there," he told them. "Go to the hospital and see if you can get a lead on the rogue scent. Stop by the barbershop to see who might be there. If a rogue's responsible for Rimas's death, the question is why? If the answer is what I think it is, then we're all screwed!"

Agent Dorian Wilson sat on the back deck of his older sister Miranda's D.C. suburb house. On this early fall afternoon, he stared out at the two trees that were barely in their prime, yet already had golden leaves falling to the ground. The swing that his niece, Jasmine, loved to go higher and higher on, sat idle, as today was a school day. Miranda and her husband, Eric McCoy, the chief of the Metropolitan Police Department's Homicide Division, were at work. They'd graciously welcomed Dorian into their home when he'd shown up in the early morning hours two weeks ago.

He hadn't dared go back to his apartment. Wasn't sure who was watching him now, in addition to the tail he'd already known he had. Taking a pull off the Budweiser he held in his right hand, Dorian recalled how he'd come to be in this place at this time.

A little over two years ago he'd begun investigating a money-laundering scheme originating at the Reynolds & Delgado law firm and stretching down to South America. At the same time, Eric had the murder of Senator Baines and his daughter on his hands. The connection had not come immediately to Dorian, but eventually he'd put some of the pieces together. Kalina Harper, the ex-cop turned wife of Roman Reynolds, hadn't been able to come up with any hard evidence against the man or his law firm—no surprise there once she began sleeping with him. But talking with his brother-in-law one day at his office, Dorian had come across some strange pictures. He'd copied them and taken them back to his house where he'd begun his own investigation.

As if it had been yesterday, the images played back through his mind. It was of a man—the body, face, legs, arms of a man—with the claws of an animal. Dorian wasn't naïve, he knew all about Photoshopping pictures and airbrushing images. But something told him this image wasn't a fake. Or at the very least, if the claws were fake, they'd still been used in the commission of a crime.

Months later there'd been another murder, Diamond Turner, a stripper from Club Athena's. The business card of Xavier Santos Markland found in Diamond's purse had given Dorian another crack at Reynolds and his gang. Unfortunately, he'd hit another dead end. At that point he may have been willing to concede that he was chasing the ghost of a story, but then he'd seen it for himself. The eerie, glowing eyes of the female that had begun watching him on a daily basis. After much thought he'd finally figured out what the eyes reminded him of—a big cat. That revelation had pushed Dorian in a whole new direction with his investigation into Reynolds and as things began to unfold throughout the States, pieces of the puzzle that had been an enigma to him for the last two years had finally begun to fall into place.

In the last two months Dorian had been in touch with other agents across the state and just two weeks ago they'd finally agreed to meet at a clandestine location, to compare notes on the cat people and the connection to Roman

Reynolds. There'd been reports as far out as Sedona, Arizona, where just a month ago there was a break-in at a government lab and one of Roman's friends', Sebastian Perry's, resort had been burned to the ground. All amidst reports of animal roaring and vicious deaths.

The meeting location had been brilliant, a civilian-owned cabin in the western Maryland mountains. Nobody within the Bureau would find them there, and nobody else would be looking for them.

Dorian had been wrong. And he'd almost been killed.

One of the agents had stood up just a few minutes after their meeting had begun and started shooting. His name was Kegan Charles and he was stationed in Dallas. They'd just finished introductions and were each about to pull out their own files compiled on what had been going on in their jurisdiction when the shots rang out. Dorian had quickly rolled to the floor, clutching his Redweld to his chest. He'd crawled into one of the back bedrooms and escaped through a window. But not before seeing her again.

Nivea Cannon, graduate of George Washington University and otherwise unemployed. She was the one with the cat's eyes, the one that had been following him for months now, and she'd been at the cabin with one of Rome's bodyguards, Eli Preston, owner of two Southside barbershops in D.C. Taking a leave of absence from the Bureau and using these past days to dig deeper into the background of these new players had been how Dorian spent his time.

This case, these people, had been Dorian's focus for almost a year now. At first it had just been another case, but once Kalina had entered the picture it had taken on another layer. The moment he learned that Kalina was sleeping with Roman Reynolds and had subsequently married the guy, Dorian knew without a doubt he had to find out what was going on. He'd never told Kalina how he felt about her and doubted that it mattered now, but if there was something he could do to save her life and possibly the lives of others, it was his sworn duty to do it. No matter how long it took.

With that in mind, this afternoon he was mulling over the loose ends, trying to piece it all together in his head before he could formulate a plan to expose them. Because now it wasn't only a matter of his reputation but also of his sanity.

Speaking of which, Dorian had just taken another long swallow of beer when he saw her. He lowered his arm slowly, until the glass bottle clinked onto the metal top of the table sitting beside the deck chair. He blinked, not wearing his shades and wondering if the unseasonably high summerlike temperatures they'd been having the past couple of days were causing him to hallucinate.

No, she was real and she was gorgeous. So much so, his dick twitched as he watched the sway of her hips while she came closer. The high heels of her shoes clanked on the wooden steps leading up the deck, long tanned legs bringing her closer to him as if he'd beckoned her from some long-lost wet dream. She wore her skirt short enough to make his mouth water. Her top was tight, like a second skin hugging breasts he knew would spill out of his now sweaty palms. Her hair was pulled back from her face, long dark brown tresses that fell in a sexy tumble of curls down the center of her back. And when she was finally on the deck, standing right in front of him, she looked at him, bringing her hand up to slip the wide-framed shades she wore down her nose a couple of inches until he could see her eyes.

"Agent Wilson, I have something you desire. And you can help get me what I want. I'd say that makes us a perfect team," she said boldly. Sky-blue eyes too bright to be contacts and just eerie enough to be real, glistened against her sun-kissed skin.

Chapter 12

First Lady Kalina Harper wasn't one to give in to pressure or stress. She'd survived growing up in an orphanage, a sexual assault, an undercover operation that had changed her life, and the realization that she was a Shadow Shifter. To say she was resilient was an understatement. But watching her mate deal with the biggest battle to ever face the shifters was rubbing her the wrong way.

For months she'd stood by Rome's side as he'd taken on one bad announcement regarding the shifters after another. They'd both stood shaken to the core when they found out that Shya Delgado had been kidnapped and that the damiana inadvertently slipped into her bloodstream during her mother's pregnancy might possibly kill her. Nick was one of Rome's best friends so Shya was like their own child, and knowing she was in danger had led to countless sleepless nights for both of them.

Today, however, in the midst of everything that was going on around them, Kalina had desired at least an hour of normalcy. She wanted to have lunch with her mate, to sit at a restaurant with him and talk about their day like two normal humans.

That apparently was not to be.

"You're hardly eating," Rome said, snapping Kalina out of her reverie. "Lunch was your idea, remember?"

Giving up the pretense and letting her fork fall to the side of her plate, Kalina looked at her mate. "I scheduled lunch for one thirty," she informed him. "It's now almost three."

He sat back in his chair, already finished with the North Carolina mountain trout entrée he ordered each time they visited the District Commons restaurant. Kalina's first thought was how deliciously handsome this man was, all day, every day. From the root beer tone of his skin, to the broad build of his body that wore the custom-made suits like no other man she'd ever laid eyes on, to the way his eyes grew even darker when he stared at her hungrily, her heart did a flip-flop every time she looked at him. The cat inside purred with the knowledge that he belonged to her.

"I told you the meeting ran over, I had no other choice but to push our lunch back. Now, why don't you tell me what's really bothering you, because I know it's not about the lunch that you're not eating being a couple of hours late."

Kalina inhaled deeply, watching him with eyes that were familiar with every inch of his body. He looked at her similarly, as if there was nothing she could hide from him, ever. And yet, there was.

"There's something I need to tell you, Rome." She took another breath, hoping to steady herself, to gather that confidence she was known for and to get this over with.

"I know that there's been a lot going on with getting the Assembly Headquarters ready and all that's been happening with these hybrids and Shya. I swear it feels like I've been on a roller-coaster ride ever since the first moment I met you."

"Are you regretting that?" he asked seriously. "Do you wish we'd never met?"

"No," she replied hurriedly, shaking her head as if to solidify the answer. "Never that. I just mean that it seems like we haven't had a moment's peace. I keep trying to think of the last normal dinner we had when you returned from the office, but they're usually turned into meetings with Nick and X, or with the guards. And since Elder Alamar has taken up residence at Havenway and he and Baxter have been walking around whispering like conspiracy theorists, I haven't had a moment alone with you." Kalina sighed this time, feeling like this wasn't going the way she'd wanted.

"I just want to be with my mate, my husband, and have a regular day, just like any other couple."

Rome reached across the table then, signaling for her to give him her hand. She did, and he rubbed a finger over the diamond ring that he'd given her for their joining. "There's nothing in this world more important to me than you, Kalina. Absolutely nothing," he told her solemnly. "With that said, I do have a responsibility. And you've been more than accommodating in that regard. You've actually been a tremendous help in developing the Assembly and the plans for our future. But at the same time, I hear what you're saying. Tell me what I can do to make this better for you."

Kalina had just opened her mouth to speak when a wisp of cool air floated over their table. She looked up because a scent had traveled with the breeze, a soft, yet still undeniable smell that had both her and her cat going on instant alert.

Her dress was red, like a siren's song in silk. The halter-top dress hugged her breasts, wrapped around her waist, and lay on her toned legs until midthigh. Alabaster skin was highlighted by shiny black hair, crystalline ice-blue eyes, and a smile that went straight for the gut . . . or the dick, Kalina wasn't sure. Yet, she didn't spare her mate a glance, keeping her gaze on the female interrupting their lunch date.

"Assembly Leader," the female said with a slow nod to Rome. "First Female," came next when she finally spared Kalina a glance.

"Rogue," was Kalina's quick response.

Rome remained still, his palms flattening on the table. Eli and Jax, who had been sitting at a table across from them, nursing a glass of water, stood immediately, but were slowed by the almost imperceptible shake of Rome's head. The guards did not sit, but they did not approach either.

"They said you were smart," the rogue continued. "I didn't believe them." She shrugged. "Still don't."

Kalina didn't even blink. "Not smart would be walking into a room full of Shadows alone and believing that you'll walk out unscathed."

"What do you want, Bianca?" Rome asked, interrupting the stare-down between the females.

She'd heard that name before, Kalina thought with interest. Rome and the other FLs had mentioned it during one of their phone conferences. Afterward, there hadn't been a lot of talk about her, but Kalina was certain now that she'd heard Jace Maybon, the Pacific Zone FL, bring her up because she'd been on his radar as a potential client in his talent agency. Looking her up and down again, Kalina was certain what Bianca Adani's first and most prized talent would be.

The tramp leaned over then, flattening her palms on the table so that her cleavage was perfectly aligned with Rome's line of sight. He kept his gaze on her eyes and Kalina's chest swelled with pride.

"I have a message for you, Assembly Leader," she said, her voice going to a hushed tone.

Out of the corner of her eye, Kalina saw Jax and Eli step closer, until they were directly behind Bianca. Their gazes locked on her but not in the sexual way the rogue may have intended.

"A message from whom?" Rome asked.

He would remain calm and play this entire scenario out. Rome was a leader through and through, so his actions would be carefully considered and as discreet as possible since they were sitting in a public restaurant.

Bianca chuckled, a deep, rich sound that was followed by a toss of her head, the sheet of her dark hair flipping over one shoulder with the motion. "The leader you never anticipated would return," she replied cryptically.

Rome shrugged. "So what's the message from this leader-in-hiding?"

His tone was nonchalant but Kalina knew he was on high alert, the rogue's words piquing the interest of all four of the Shadows.

"Oh, he's definitely not hiding and neither are the rest of the tribes," Bianca told Rome. "Not anymore. We're all here, all around you. *Lormenia, Serfins, Croesteriia, Bosinia,* and even more *Topètenia* than you'd ever imagined. We're here and we're ready."

Kalina did not gasp, but she did sit up straighter in her chair, her cat ready to lunge at the Bengal tiger. Rome reached forward then, letting his palm rest on Bianca's, which he patted as if she were an insolent child. "If you're ready to follow, you will be safe. If not, you should warn them to stand down."

Bianca looked down at Rome's hand on her own, then over her shoulder to Kalina whom she smiled at knowingly. Or at least the rogue thought it was knowingly.

Kalina had no doubts where Rome the Leader or her mate were concerned. She showed that by smiling at the rogue in return.

When Bianca looked back at Rome it was with her seductive smile still in place. "We only follow one leader, and it is not you. Or your pregnant little cat over there."

Rome's gaze flew quickly to Kalina as Bianca stood up straight, looking over at Jax and Eli as she chuckled.

She took a step away from the table and then paused to add one more thing before leaving. "You've been warned."

Eli followed Bianca out of the restaurant while Jax stayed close enough to the table to hear Rome's surprised inquiry to his mate. "Pregnant?"

This had been one of the longest days in Nivea's life. It was nearing dinnertime and she was bored out of her mind. For nine hours straight she'd sat in the tech room watching security monitors, reviewing news feeds, and monitoring the Internet for any mention of cat people, the shifters, or the hybrids. It was a daunting task, one she'd shared with forty other guards that for whatever reason actually enjoyed being cooped up in a room with no windows and jugs of coffee.

Earlier this morning she'd awakened alone to a note from Eli. She'd thought she would roll over and cuddle her face against his chest as she'd done frequently throughout the night, but the paper had crinkled against her skin, instantly waking her up.

He was going out in the field and would be in touch by cell phone. Initially she'd been pissed by the note and the fact that she'd been ordered to stay inside, even when her shoulder was relatively painless at the moment. Then, Nivea had lain back on the bed, reveling in not only where she was but how far she'd come. She'd slept with Eli Preston last night. Not had sex with him as they'd done before and then been sent on her merry way, but she'd lain in his arms while he held her close and they'd both slept, peacefully.

Once upon a time, so many of Nivea's nights had been riddled with nightmares, with dark and disturbing memories that refused to let her go. She'd gone through years of therapy, possessing a determination her therapist had said she'd never seen in another female victim of sexual abuse before. But Nivea had wanted to be normal, she'd wanted desperately to move past the things that had happened that had not been her fault. She'd wanted to forget but to be smart enough to remember at the same time. Because remembering was what kept her sane and focused. It's what kept her from killing the man who had tried to destroy her life.

Just before, Nivea had received two text messages and one picture message from Eli. The two texts were of an address and a list of the contents of a bag he'd found. She'd run everything through the computers, coming up with a name, Robert Slakeman of Slakeman Enterprises. Slakeman was a defense contractor. His weapons armed the U.S. military and some high-level cartel members, as recently alleged by a few FBI agents on the West Coast. Nivea had no idea what any of this had to do with the hybrids or what the shifters were dealing with now, but she certainly planned to ask Eli when he returned to Havenway.

She'd just finished viewing the picture message when there was a knock on the door. Her bed was on the far side of the room, her dresser and a desk closest to the door. She moved past both and pulled the door open, not in a million years expecting who was on the other side.

"Long time no see," Richard Cannon said, making his way inside her room without an invitation.

Nivea's heart immediately pounded and while she would have preferred he'd stayed out in the hallway, she wasn't about to make a scene that would alert everyone that he was here. As she closed the door she wondered how he'd managed to get inside anyway, considering Rome and Nick were looking into his financial dealings. Maybe that wasn't public knowledge as of yet, which would be the only reason the guards at the gate would have allowed him passage. That and the fact that he was a shifter and her father.

She sighed with that thought.

"What do you want?" was her question the moment the door was closed and she was relatively sure nobody would overhear what was going on.

Some would say he looked good for a fifty-seven-year-old man, with his black suit, crisp white shirt, and slate-gray tie. His hair was midnight black and combed back from his face so that his thick eyebrows and expertly cut mustache were prominent. Money really did do wonders, she thought, because the asshole that lived in those clothes would never be more than a dirty, scumbag pervert in her eyes, no matter what he wore.

"Is that any way to greet your father, whom you haven't seen for years?" he asked, looking around her room as if there might be something there he had interest in.

Nivea knew that was not true. There was nothing at Havenway that interested her father. Nothing the Shadow Shifters were doing that he wanted to be a part of. After all, his number one goal for the last thirty years had been to kill off whatever shifter children he could in an effort to end the breed entirely because he believed the world would never accept them. He was the biggest, sorriest kind of hypocrite there was. While his nonprofit foundation boasted how many children they helped and saved from abusive homes and sickly situations, the man—Richard Cannon—had the blood of thousands of shifters on his hands. The wretched bastard.

"No, but that's how I greet the man who made me swear

not to ever tell what he was doing to me to anyone or he'd terrorize my sisters the same way he did me," she replied vehemently.

Richard didn't even have the gall to look affronted by her comment. Actually, his shoulders almost lifted in a shrug, but he took that moment to step closer to her instead.

"I specifically recall telling you to keep your mouth shut. So imagine my surprise when I find out you're now spreading your vicious lies to this so-called Assembly Leader you insist on following."

She took a step back, hating that she couldn't control the instinct to get as far away from him as she possibly could.

"You're the last shifter I would waste my time talking about." Nivea spat. "Now you can just take yourself back to New York."

Richard shook his head, clicking his tongue against his teeth, creating a sound that echoed through her small room, sending wary shivers up and down her spine. He used to make that sound whenever she cried. When she'd run into the corner of her room, turning her back away from him, and thinking that would be enough to send him away. It hadn't been, and the sound had represented his first show of disappointment in her. The leash around her neck had been the final clue. It had meant he could control her, that she was his to do with as he wanted. And he had.

"Someone's been asking questions. They've been digging into my financials, talking to my shareholders, putting doubts in their heads. Your mother's friends are acting as if they no longer want to talk to her. I think you know why."

Nivea shook her head. "I don't go back on my word. I don't lie or betray like you and she did."

"Just tell me what you told him and then we'll go to him together and explain that you lied. That you've always been a liar, always a troublemaker looking for attention. We'll tell him that and see just how long he wants to keep you here among this little army he believes he's building."

"I did not lie!" she yelled at him. "I didn't lie when I told her what you were doing to me and I didn't lie when I said if you put one hand on my sisters I would make you pay."

"Don't threaten me, you little bitch!" Richard yelled, stepping so close, so quickly that his chest pushed against hers.

The movement caught her off guard and she stumbled back a step. Trying to regain her composure, Nivea moved around Richard, going deeper into her room, her back to the wall but her front to the door, where she planned to kick his ass out in the next few seconds.

"Don't talk to me like that! You are no longer allowed to talk to me like you own me. I'm an adult and I'm free from you," she countered. "I don't have to tell anybody a damned thing about you if I don't want to. And guess what, I don't want to. I don't want to mention your disgusting name!"

The hand that came up to slap her was quick, but Nivea was quicker. She blocked the slap, grabbing hold of Richard's wrist and twisting it until he frowned back at her. He didn't yell out. No, Richard Cannon was too strong for that. She bristled at the fact that here was where her inner strength had originated. The very part of her that she'd relied on so heavily to get over all that he'd done to her, had come from him, the sick bastard.

"You think you're so tough, but you're not. Remember Amina and Serene are still with me. They're still mine."

"I kept my part of the deal," she told him, releasing his hand as if it had been on fire. "I did what I promised so you would keep your filthy hands off of them. They don't deserve what you did to me."

"I did nothing that you didn't want," he taunted, his eyes filled with the same glint they always had when he came into her room, just before he . . .

"You were always front and center, singing the loudest in the school plays. Shining brighter than any other star in the Christmas play. You outran your sisters, outdanced them, and outlearned them. No matter what they did, you did better. And when I finally opened my eyes to that, when I finally gave you the attention you fought for, you cried foul, running to your mother of all people!"

"I was your daughter!" Nivea yelled, her chest heavy and heaving with each breath she struggled for. "You were not supposed to do those things to me."

"You wanted it, Nivea," he told her, taking a step closer to her. "Just like you want it now. You're not getting the attention you want, maybe from one of these misguided shifters. That's why you brought up my name, and it's why you're telling these lies about me. You want them to think you're special, that you're worthy." Richard grinned. "They have no idea."

Every muscle in her body trembled. With the blink of an eye Nivea was sixteen and back in the Manhattan condo where she'd lived with her sisters. She'd just come home from school—from track practice—and was all sweaty and tired and had already peeled off her shirt, toed off her tennis shoes, and was headed to the shower, when he'd walked into her room. It was daylight outside. He never came to her during the day, was never home. Why was he now?

Why was he here at Havenway?

She felt dizzy, her throat clogging, hands sweating. In her mind, she knew the difference. She knew the here and now, that she was a guard for the Shadow Shifter Assembly

and that Havenway was more heavily protected than the
humans' White House. But another part of her, a part
she'd thought she'd closed the door on long ago, had just
been revealed. He was back and he was close and she
was . . .

Richard was on her in the seconds she hesitated. She
should have known better, should have never given him the
moment to act. Nivea fell back onto her bed, the force of
his quick launch knocking the air right out of her. With a
gasp she looked up at the ceiling, at the plain dark-gray
paint that covered all the walls in her room.

His body was pressing into hers, familiar and sickening all at the same time. He was hard and strong and she
wanted to scream. No, she wanted to fight. All those years
it had taken her to stand up to her father, to stop the cycle
of his vicious abuse. She shouldn't be in this spot now. He
shouldn't be here and she wasn't about to take this shit
from him again.

Nivea lifted a knee, aiming right at his groin, but he slid
off her just in time to avoid the contact, wrapping his hands
around her neck and squeezing as he rolled partially off
of her.

"You were always too stubborn, thinking too damned
much to do you any good. You should have just listened
like your mother and sisters did, then I wouldn't have had to
punish you," he told her, his hands tightening at her throat.

Nivea smacked at his wrists, kicking her legs up and
down, struggling to breathe.

"I told your mother we should have taken care of you,
but no. She wanted to make the deal. She said that even
though you were the youngest, that you were the smartest
of the three and you would do what was right. You would
protect them all and thus keep our secret." Sweat dripped
from his forehead down onto her cheek. "I knew she was

wrong. She wasn't smart, not at all. I should never have listened to her. Should have . . . done . . . this . . . before!"

He continued to choke her and Nivea felt like she was falling, her limbs dangling in the wind as she plunged to her death. Then her hands wrapped around his wrists and she squeezed with all her might. Her watery eyes focused on his bulging, erratic ones, and she centered her mind and body on all that she'd learned, on how to kill this bastard.

Something inside Eli's chest pounded, a hurried rhythm that moved from his shoulder blades all the way down to his ankles, propelling him forward from the moment he stepped out of his truck in the parking lot of Havenway. He moved quickly past Jax and Rome and Kalina, reaching the door to the side entrance before any of them. His fingers punched in the code so quickly they looked like a blur of movement.

Inside his cat hissed and swiped so that Eli's human body reacted by moving even faster. In the back of his throat was a sour taste, similar to the night in the Sierra Leone rain forest when he'd been on his knees in the shaman's hut, inhaling the thick smoke that he'd been promised would heal him. He swallowed deeply, hoping the memory of the taste would subside, but instead it increased and Eli's heart pounded, his legs breaking into a run.

Without knowing exactly where he was going he moved through the hallways of the H-shaped structure, passing other guards who looked on with concern, cutting around the corner that separated the dining hall and training facilities from the guard quarters. His cat was chuffing now, announcing its arrival, which it never did. Jaguars stalked their prey, watched and circled until it was time to pounce. This was different, he wasn't hunting, he was avenging.

Nivea's face appeared clearly in his mind, her eyes wide with fear, mouth opened to scream but no sound coming out. Eli ran faster until stopping in front of a door. Taking a step back he kicked the steel-lined door with all his might. It creaked, then buckled, and his shoulder slamming into it next did the rest.

When his eyes focused on the room, on who was in it and what was going on, he knew he had to continue to react now, and think about the consequences later. He pounced on the back of the man, his sharp teeth biting down into the back of his neck. He pulled back, yanking his prey off the bed, pulling him to the floor.

"Eli! No! No!" she yelled.

Her voice was familiar, rubbing along the spine of his cat until it trembled. But it wasn't enough. He shook his head, tossing the man caught in the grip of his strong jaws and sharp teeth from side to side.

"He's not worth it, Eli," Nivea continued. "He's just not worth it."

There was only darkness, only the heavy cloak of black and anger, pain, and despair. He wanted to stop that, wanted to put an end to the pain and the abuse that he now knew she had suffered. In his mind's eye he could see it clearly, could piece together Nivea's reluctance to go home to her family in New York, to even talk about them. This man was her father, the blood seeping into Eli's mouth was kin to his mate. With a stinging burn at the base of his spine, that word settled over him and Eli released his hold on the man, tossing his head back as he roared in the deepest despair he'd ever experienced in his life.

"It's okay," she was saying now. "Just let him go, Eli. It's better if he just goes."

Eli heard her words, had heard everything she'd said since barging into the room. Only now, her voice sounded different. Sad, no, desolate maybe. He didn't look at her because he knew there was no way he could do what she'd just suggested, no matter how much he wanted to give her whatever she needed to make her sound happy again. Even if she were cussing at him, pressing adamantly against his authority as she did so often, anything but what he was hearing in her voice right now.

Taking another heaving breath, he moved to stand in front of the door just in case the asshole who now had blood running down his back got the sick notion in his head to run.

Eli dug into his pocket, pressing numbers quickly into his phone.

"Yeah. I need you down in Nivea's room right now. Bring some cuffs and shackles, and another guard with you. We've got a prisoner."

Disconnecting the call, Eli ignored the burn at the base of his spine that said the cat still wanted to break free. It recognized the scent of another shifter—the one lying on his stomach across from him—and one who had been in contact with rogues. The rogue scent could have been left over from the crazy as hell run-in he'd just watched Rome and Kalina experience with Bianca. But Eli was betting it was the cat across the room struggling to breathe that had recently been with a rogue shifter. His body moving with uneven breaths, the coward refused to stand. He wouldn't get up to face Eli head-on like a man. No, he'd rather pick on a female. He'd thought he could pick on Nivea.

The older man had no idea how stupid a move that had been. There was nothing Eli wouldn't do for this female. Absolutely nothing, he thought as he turned his attention to her, wanting to ensure that she was all right. He hadn't anticipated anything less from Nivea, was actually counting on the superior strength this female shifter had that rivaled her other counterparts. But he'd been wrong, and the sight of her curled into a fetal position in a far corner of the room had rage boiling deep inside his gut once more.

Chapter 13

This was ridiculous.

This was not her.

She did not cry or give in or succumb.

She was stronger than this, had been for the last ten years. Nothing could get her back to that place in her life when everything had seemed so bleak and all that she'd believed in had crumbled so completely. Absolutely nothing.

Except him.

His hands had been on her again, rubbing along the bare skin of her arms, touching the curve of her hip. He'd pressed his body into hers and she'd felt everything about him, from the buckle of his pants to the sickening erection, even so deep as the vile blood running through his veins. She was nauseous, her stomach roiling at the mere memory and she curled up even tighter. Wondering if somehow she could be that fetus again, the unsuspecting and unknowing creature that had yet to breathe the same air as the asshole who had helped to create her.

A shower would rid her of the disgust, of the tainting marks that had to be left on her after he was finished. The signs that everyone would see how defiled she'd been. But it never worked. After hours beneath a stinging hot spray she'd still felt the touch of his fingers, his lips, and his tongue. She'd felt it and had been repulsed each and every time. It was a wonder she'd been able to be intimate with anyone else, with memories like that bouncing around in her head.

But that was because of her strength, because the jaguar living and breathing inside of her would not surrender.

Nivea reached for that strength, she called out to her cat, to save her, to bring her back. The fact that she hadn't moved, her body still huddled tight in this corner said the call had fallen on deaf ears.

Then there was another touch. It was warm and comforting, so she didn't bother to fight against it. She was being lifted, her entire body feeling light and trouble-free. They were moving, she and whoever carried her, to where she had no idea. She had no strength to question or even wonder. Her head lolled forward, the left side of her face resting against a muscled chest, eyes remaining closed, having seen far too much today.

She breathed in his scent, let it filter through her body like salve against an open wound. She hissed at first, then settled into the feeling of safety, and of home.

His voice still sounded in her head.

"You wanted it, Nivea," he father had told her. "Just like you want it now. You're not getting the attention you want . . ."

But this wasn't what she wanted. It wasn't how Nivea wanted to feel, how she wanted to live her life. Who in their right mind wanted their father touching them intimately with his hands and his mouth, doing things to them that at nine and ten years old nobody should be doing? That hadn't been her request, hadn't been her intention when she'd achieved good grades in school or performed well at a sport. She had never looked for that type of attention from him and she would not let him blame her!

"It's not my fault!" she screamed out, just seconds after hearing a door click softly closed behind her. "It's not!"

"No, it's not," Eli whispered quietly against the top of her head. "It's not your fault, baby."

Nivea kept her eyes closed. It was the only way to stop the tears. "It's his fault," she continued, her chest heaving with the effort of each word. "He's the one that's deficient, not me. He's sick and he's wrong and I'm, I'm just . . . his . . . victim." The last word came out in a whisper, yet it still burned her throat to say.

"You are not his," Eli replied vehemently. "Not one part of you belongs to him and I'll be damned if he touches you ever again."

His voice held only the slightest semblance of control, his arms tightening around her as he spoke them. Nivea couldn't help it, she tilted her head back and looked up at him then. That muscle in his jaw was twitching, his lips held tight. She couldn't see his eyes because of his shades and without thought, she reached up and pulled them off. He didn't resist, did not complain, simply looked down at her. And she was lost.

Eli had the stormiest green eyes she'd ever seen. In them was all the turmoil and intensity that came with this man and beast. There had never been a time that she'd seen them and not felt the power of all that was inside him.

"You're right," she admitted. "I do not belong to him."

They sat on Eli's bed now, while he cradled her in his lap. A couple of hours ago, or maybe even yesterday, she might have thought this the most insane position. She would never have relinquished enough of herself to sit in his arms this way, to have him hold her as if she were his child to protect. But right now, hell, it felt damned good to have been protected, at least one time, from her father.

She took a deep breath, wondering for an instant if what she was about to do was a mistake or not. Instinct told her it wasn't. For so long she'd known there was something different about Eli, something that existed only between the two of them. And while he'd yet to accept it, she had vowed not to run away from it, from him. So her words, which she was trying to consider carefully, were going to come, no matter the repercussions.

"It started when I was nine. I'd just finished my first piano recital and I was so excited that I'd received a standing ovation. Amina, that's my oldest sister, she didn't like the piano, but she loved the pretty pink dress she'd had to wear to the formal affair. Serene is my other sister, she's older too and she was just happy that it was me playing the piano and not her. Reading was her thing. She lost herself in all those books she had. But me, I liked to shine."

Nivea could admit that because it wasn't a bad thing. She'd done good work in her life and there was nothing wrong with being proud of it. No matter what he'd said.

Eli pushed a strand of hair from her face, tucking it softly behind her ear.

"I was in my bedroom, getting ready for bed, when I heard the door open. I thought it was Amina because she was always sent to check on me. There were so many things my oldest sister did that my mother probably should have been doing." Nivea sighed. "But it wasn't Mina. It was my father. He congratulated me for doing such a wonderful job and for being his star daughter. He was so proud of me, so happy for me."

She shivered with the memory.

"All the while he talked his hand rubbed over my bare shoulder. I'd already taken off my dress and now wore just my slip and my tights. I didn't like how his hand felt on my shoulder, but I didn't move because he hated having to tell me things twice. Always yelled that I was the most hardheaded of his daughters."

Eli had gone completely still. Nivea didn't look up at his face again, just kept staring off at nothing in particular. But she could feel how rigid he was even though his arms stayed wrapped around her. His anger was palpable and she hated that with each word she said, it continued to heighten. All she knew was that she had to get this out now, or she'd never be able to tell him. How would they build a future with something like this between them?

"He touched my shoulders then, and eventually removed the slip from my body. It seems he was right about one thing, I was his most stubborn and hard-to-control daughter. I questioned everything he was doing. I even told him I was pretty sure it was wrong. But he didn't stop, not until I was naked. He touched me everywhere that night just with his hands, and then told me to go to bed."

"Stop," Eli said then, touching a finger to her lips. "Just stop before I leave this room to find where he is and break his fucking neck."

Nivea shook her head. "You don't understand," she mumbled over his fingers, until she finally lifted her hand to move them. "I knew it was wrong but I let him do it because he said if I did he wouldn't touch Amina and Serene. For years I accepted that as the excuse to endure all that nastiness. Then when I was older, when I turned seventeen, I found the files. I saw the tattoo and I knew I had him. I could make him stop, I could keep him from touching my sisters, I could get out, and I did. I confronted him about the papers I'd found in his office and threatened to go straight to the Elders if he didn't let me go. I'd tried running away before but they always found me and when they did it . . . he . . . was worse." She paused, taking a deep breath and releasing it slowly. "I made him promise to let me go and not come after me and to not touch my sisters because I knew they would never leave. He wanted my word that I would never speak of those papers or tell my sisters what had happened. I knew it was making a deal with the devil, but I didn't think I had any other choice. I had to get out of there and I did. Eli, I got out and I healed and I'm not a victim anymore."

"I never thought you were a victim," he told her earnestly. "You're the strongest, most sensible shifter I know. Never in my wildest dreams would the word victim be associated with you."

And just like that, all the pain and misery Nivea had endured all those years of her childhood slipped away. She'd had other men in her life. It had been a part of her personal therapy, to become comfortable around men, to be able to talk to them and allow them to touch her, when she gave permission only. And she'd passed that test with flying colors, her hatred for her father seeming to give her even more strength to move forward. The knowledge that her sisters would forever be safe from his touch was even more of a reward. But Eli was different. Everything about him, right down to the way she'd finally ended up in his bed, was different and uncalculated and unplanned. She'd wanted him, yes, but she had no misconceptions about the fact that when they came together it would be because Eli made it happen. His concession had always been important to her, and now his honesty had released the grip around her heart.

Nivea let go of the breath that felt as if she'd been holding it forever. She stared down at her hands in her lap, then up at Eli.

"He thinks I told Rome and Nick about what he's doing. I promised I wouldn't. And he promised never to touch my sisters."

"They're adults now," Eli countered.

"But they're still under his thumb, still within his reach and I just don't trust him."

"What about your mother?"

She sucked in another breath. "She's so brainwashed by him. She'll never leave or betray him. Not even for her own child."

Eli did something else that shocked her, as if she hadn't experienced enough surprises for one day. He touched his fingers softly to the line of her jaw, tracing all the way around, then going slowly down her neck. It was a butterfly-soft touch that immediately silenced her words, but ramped up the beat of her heart.

"You're so much more than I ever expected," he told her. "Probably more than they anticipated as well."

Nivea didn't know what to say to that and she didn't know what to do. The cat inside, however, knew what it wanted. It seemed to communicate with Eli's cat because his eyes shot up to hers in that moment, changing from their human green to cat gold. Heat immediately circled around them, wrapping in the sweetest embrace she could have ever imagined.

In that moment Nivea decided not to wait. She leaned into him, lowering her lids just a bit as she stared down at his mouth. He lunged before she could complete her mission, his lips crashing against hers. Their tongues touched instantly, circling in an age-old dance that never ceased to get her blood pumping. He had a hand to her back and the one still at her neck, pulling her closer as he practically devoured her.

Nivea arched into his embrace, loving the feeling of his power raining over her. She felt like she was about to be taken, but liberated at the same time. The anticipation was too strong, her heart pounding mercilessly in her chest, her pussy throbbing with expectation. She wrapped her arms around his neck, immediately pulling him closer, opening her mouth wider to him. When his hand slid down lower to cup her breast, squeezing until she arched and gasped, Nivea's entire world shifted.

Feeling as if she were caught in a funnel, breathless and air bound, Nivea wondered what would happen when she landed. Would she confess her love to this shifter, putting herself and her heart on the line for him to do with as he pleased, or would she somehow keep the control she'd worked so hard to maintain?

Questions dissipated when he dragged his mouth from hers to clamp down on her nipple, his tongue soaking through the T-shirt and bra she wore. Her head fell back as she gave him all the access he wanted. Sharp teeth ripped at the shirt until it was in shreds, hanging off her arms. The bra snapped, the sound echoing throughout the room alongside that of Eli's muffled growl. It all seemed so fast and so fevered, but he wasn't rushing as his tongue lathed over her bared skin, flattening over her nipple, then licking up and down the curve of each breast.

She wanted to scream out his name, to declare that every part of her belonged to him, but Nivea held firm. She gasped and quivered in his arms but she did not speak, did not believe that she could just yet.

"I can't get enough," she heard him mumble. "I'm never going to get enough of you."

His tone sounded troubled as if his words were true, but he hated that it was so. Nivea didn't hate it. She loved hearing those words, loved knowing that he was drowning in all that was between them the same as she was.

"I'm not going anywhere," she admitted, her own sharpened teeth biting into her lip before she gasped again. "I'm right here with you, Eli."

He seemed to ignore her words, otherwise preoccupied with sucking as much of her breast into his mouth as he could. The feeling sent a rush of desire shooting straight to her pussy. Dampness filled her pants and she squirmed, letting the crotch of her underwear and the mission blues she still wore rub against her aching clit.

Still holding her tightly at the back, Eli used his other hand to rip the belt and buckle of her pants free. A part of her thought she'd be visiting the commissary for a replacement uniform in the morning, but she just didn't give a damn. Instead, she opened her legs in anticipation of his touch, which came almost instantaneously. He yanked at the thin wisp of cloth that served as underwear, tossing the material aside.

Then he was there, his fingers parting her swollen folds, slipping slowly into the wetness and sending shivers up and down her body. With one arm she held firmly to Eli's shoulders, hoping it helped her stay upright but almost certain it was more his strong hold that kept her from falling onto the floor. With her other hand she cupped her bare breast, loving the feel of the weight of it in her palm. There was something slickly erotic about her own hands on her body and the immediate pleasure spikes that came from the motion. While Eli continued his exploration of her tender folds, moving up to toy with her clit, then back, so far back he rimmed her with a quick, damp digit, she squeezed her breast harder, letting the turgid nipple roll between the tips of her fingers just as Eli had done before.

Her tongue licked along her bottom lip, and Eli slipped two thick fingers into her dripping center. Nivea tried to open her legs wider to take him in deeper, but her pants hindered that movement.

"I got you," she heard him say. "I know what you need, baby, I know."

If he did he wouldn't be taking so damned long to give it to her. But Nivea was soon silenced when Eli's fingers moved quicker, pressing deeper, drawing her essence out to drip over her folds, creating a slapping sound that echoed in her ears. She pumped into his hand fervently, grasping her breast with vigor as the climb to bliss had begun. She could see the end, could envision herself slipping right over that cliff of satiated relief. She wanted to run there, to not miss a step to getting there and grabbing every ounce of what promised to be a pleasurable release. Eli said he understood but she was almost sure he couldn't possibly know, when his fingers slipped quickly from her center, back to her anus where he pressed certainly until her sphincter was breached and she gasped with relief.

The moment was now.

Her vision was blurry, her breaths racing to break free. The cat inside had long since roared its way to submission and now there was only this. The feel of him filling her there, so tight and yet so deliciously sweet. She wanted more, needed . . . needed . . .

He pulled out, pressed back in, spreading his two fingers as wide as he could inside her passageway and Nivea couldn't stand it a moment longer. She screamed out his name, or was that a roar that sounded like his name? She had no idea, all she knew was that her body was being transformed, all that she'd known and ever experienced was in the past. This, right here, this deep-seated pleasure was the here and now and she was loving every minute of it!

The cat would not be ignored. The urge to take her, to own her, so far unheeded was now inevitable. Eli moved off the bed, carrying Nivea with him before letting her feet touch the floor. She looked spent, her cat's eyes slanted and slightly blurry. Her chest heaved and for a moment his mouth watered with the thought of tasting her delicious breasts once more. But he was determined not to be distracted, not this time. The shreds of her shirt slipped from her arms as she moved them, her bra doing the same. Her pants and panties were partly down and Eli made quick work of pulling them completely off, getting stuck on her boots but yanking them free as well.

When she looked up at him, her lips wet from her licking them, eyes hooded from the release that had just overtaken her, he thought about tossing her onto the bed and slipping inside her wet pussy as soon as possible. But the cat wouldn't let that be. It pawed at him, pressing insistently against every part of him, including his mind, that he'd been trying to keep the animal clear of.

It was too late.

That realization had him moving, yanking his shirt over his head, toeing off his own boots, hating when they were stuck because of the tight laces. Once they were off, his pants and boxers were finally freed and he was once again in front of her.

Nivea Cannon.

The guard that had taunted him with her compact body and resilience. She was smart and pretty and vicious on the battlefield—everything, he thought with a start. Nivea Cannon was everything to him.

With a growl that started deep in his gut, rumbling forward until it ripped right past his vocal cords, Eli grabbed her by the shoulders, turning her away from him.

"Eli?" She'd whispered his name but he didn't reply.

He couldn't.

Words would not do. They would not explain all that was soaring through his system at the moment. And most importantly, they wouldn't change a damned thing.

His dick was so hard it hurt. The incessant throbbing, the burning need had him sliding his hand down Nivea's spine, pushing her gently until her palms flattened on the bed.

He leaned forward, one hand gripping his thick length, and kissed her vertebrae, moving up one at a time, letting his tongue swirl in moist circles, coming back down again until he was dropping heated kisses over her upturned ass.

"On your knees," he whispered over her smooth flesh. "I want you on your knees."

Never in his life would Eli have described Nivea as obedient, but she moved without a word, planting both her knees on his bed, spreading her legs so wide the plumpness of her folds and every drop of moistness between her legs was visible. His mouth watered, his nostrils flaring as the cat enjoyed the scent of their mating.

Closing his eyes, Eli stepped forward. He held the tip of his dick to her, moved up and down, coating himself with her essence. She wiggled back against him and he purred. Her ass was perfect, the way she was arching her back and extending it out to him, offering him the world. The entire fucking world, he thought, right here before him.

He couldn't resist. How could he have ever considered resisting?

His fingers had spread her wide for him, the remnants of her release having dripped all over until it was as wet on the tight pucker of her anus as on her pussy. He wanted her here, wanted to claim, to conquer, and for once in his life, to just be.

Eli pressed forward, the tip of his dick moving past her rim. He clenched his teeth, closed his eyes, and let his head lull back. He gave her a moment to adjust to the feel of him back there, the promise of what was to come. Then he pressed forward, loving the tight sheathing around his length. He felt like she was squeezing the life out of him, taking him for every last drop of breath he had.

Wait, wasn't he supposed to be claiming her?

With a vicious shake of his head, Eli pulled out slightly, then thrust in with more pressure than before. She hissed, he saw her fingers clenching in the comforter, and then she backed up on him. He licked his lips, his hands going to her hips where he held firm. His hips began to move then, thrusting in, pulling out, matching her speed and velocity.

All the dark Eli had seen when he'd closed his eyes up until this point dissipated. Now, there was only light, and in that light was a cat. Nivea's cat. She was waiting for him as if she'd always expected he would come.

Come.

Come.

The word echoed in his mind even as he stroked her harder and harder. She was so freakin' wet, her excitement building all over again, her ass cheeks smacking back against his groin, his strokes went deep and long and made him feel like he was being milked of every hidden emotion he possessed. When his entire body had begun to shake, the cat's shift running along the base of his spine, Eli couldn't hold on any longer. His fingers dug into her skin the moment she whispered, "Come for me, *companheiro. Vena para mi, por favor. Por favor.*"

He hadn't needed her words, but damn, they sounded good. With her voice, as her ass pressed back against him, her walls so tight around him, the release was sucked straight from his cock, along with the breath from his lungs.

Later that night Eli lay with Nivea stretched out so that half her body was across his, the other on the bed. They'd been sweaty from their last round of lovemaking but now the air had chilled his skin. But he didn't dare move. His eyes closed even though the last thing he wanted to do was sleep. His body was acutely aware of hers and Eli wanted her again and again. He had no idea what the morning would bring for either of them so he'd wanted the night to last . . . forever.

But his eyes did finally close and the dream did eventually suck him in again.

He was back in the Sierra Leone rain forest, standing in front of Acacia's hut once again. Ezra hadn't wanted to come and on the outside, Eli had acted as if he agreed with his twin. But on the inside, this had been exactly where he wanted to be. Dagar's potion was supposed to curb this hunger, to make them need her less so that they could finish the training they'd come here for and not embarrass their grandfather any further. Acacia had betrayed them. She'd taken them in and fucked both of them senseless, making them believe that the pleasure was mutual, when in actuality all she had been doing was using the jaguar twins to get back at her father for taking the other jaguar she'd loved, her true mate, from her.

Ezra was livid. Eli was too, but for an entirely different reason. He still wanted her, a part of him believing he could still claim her. So he and Ezra had followed Acacia's minions when they'd come to collect them. They'd entered her hut knowing what they would find. Acacia was naked, her beautifully tanned skin glowing in the candles' illumination. She'd wanted them and hell, Eli had wanted her. He was sure she'd read his mind. Ezra had immediately lashed out and she'd had him bound to the wall. But Eli, he'd remained calm, ready. She'd had him lie on the marble slab that he was used to. She loved having him there and he enjoyed it immensely. So when she climbed on top of him, lowering herself down onto his dick, Eli had almost instantaneously come. Yet, there was something different. The way she looked down at him, the scent in the air, the sound of the crickets chirping loudly from outside the hut . . . something that even to this day he wasn't entirely sure of.

Acacia had just rotated her hips on his dick, sucking him deep into her pussy. Then she'd reached back and the next thing Eli saw was her arm arching over him, the glint of the knife she held in her hand clear as day.

Ezra roared, ripped free of his shackles, and grabbed Acacia by the back of her neck. At Eli's angry growl his twin dropped Acacia to the floor. But in seconds her minions were on them and the next thing Eli knew, he'd shifted and he was killing them. Murdering them all, including Acacia. Only minutes ago, he and Ezra had walked into the hut with three other shifters. Now, the two cats paced around the dead carcasses of three shifters, blood and flesh littering the ground, the acrid stench rising quickly in the air.

Ezra's cat had looked at Eli's. Silence, but communication, as it always had been between the twins. They each regretted, each hated, each felt the boiling dark anger taking its rightful place inside them.

It was the same, this haunting memory. Each time it came, it left Eli breathless and sad from the continued streak it had created in his life. And yet, she had entered and taken her place in his destiny without him noticing, without him being able to stop her.

Nivea's cat stood outside the hut when Eli's cat exited in the dream this time, as if she'd been waiting for him all along. Again. Only this time when Eli went to her, when he let down his guard and gave in to the mating he felt inexplicably drawn to, Nivea turned to run away and before she could get far, she was captured. Grabbed at the base of her skull by a bigger, deadlier jaguar that was hell-bent on revenge.

Chapter 14

Richard Cannon sat with his dress shirt rumpled, his face fixed in a scowl, across a short table from Rome. They were in a section at the far end of Havenway that had been blocked off from the rest of the facility.

They'd taken to calling it lockdown even though up until a day ago, they'd had no one to house in it. But with tensions rising for the shifters, Rome had decided that they definitely needed a location such as this. There were four rooms with steel-reinforced doors with automatic locks on either side of a narrow hallway that also had its own bolted and electronically secure access. X and Nick had been sure to design this part of the facility as if it were the humans' Fort Knox. There were even magnetized beams that, once activated, would prevent anyone from moving throughout this part of the facility without being detected.

Today they were interrogating one of their own. Richard was not a rogue but he wasn't aligned with the Shadows either. He'd never taken a stance on either side for as long as Rome had been working with the Stateside Assembly. In fact, Richard had been one of the few rich and influential shifters that had ignored all of Rome's invitations to join him at the Assembly. For the past couple of years Rome hadn't thought much of it, as he figured there would always be those shifters that had a greater desire to be considered more for their human attributes than those of their cats. He'd respected that choice. Until now.

"You're sending money to the Comastaz Labs. Why?" Rome asked without preamble.

Richard's response was rude but factual. "This is a free country. I can do whatever I want with my money."

Rome had only nodded. Nick, on the other hand, had moved quicker than either Rome or Richard had anticipated, grabbing the man by the back of his neck and slamming his face down on the steel table. Blood oozed instantly from Richard's nose and Rome casually reached into his inside jacket pocket, extending his arm slowly to offer the man a tissue.

Richard snatched the tissue as Rome said, "I'm not going to repeat the question, but I am still expecting an answer."

He used the tissue to blot the blood, an angry glare aimed at Nick as he pulled from the obviously bigger and stronger shifter's grasp. Nick allowed that little action, but he didn't move from standing right behind Cannon, just in case he had to do more convincing.

"Tax credits," he replied with a roll of his eyes. "I get a certain amount of tax credits for my donations to government agencies."

"Bullshit!" Nick replied immediately.

"You run a marketing agency but that's not where the checks originated from. Your nonprofit—the one that's already qualified for certain tax credits—is the one cutting the checks. There's no legal gain to that donation unless it's somehow connected to the work the nonprofit is doing. Is that the case?" Rome inquired.

"I guess you wouldn't know anything about business

since you're so hell-bent on acting like savages. The more I write off of the nonprofit, the bigger my tax breaks are," Richard replied with distaste.

Nick grabbed his neck once more.

"Hey!" he yelled, trying to slip from Nick's grasp. "You can't do this! We're not in the jungle, you filthy animals. In case you didn't notice, this is civilization. We walk upright and behave like we have some decency in America."

The man might have continued with his rant but Nick lifted him out of the chair and slammed him front first into the cement wall, angling his forearm on the man's neck to keep the side of his face pressed against the dark blue paint.

"You sure you want to keep calling us names, asshole?" Nick asked, his face close to Cannon's.

Rome remained seated.

"We cleared our schedules for the day just so we could spend this time with you, Mr. Cannon. Now, this can take another few minutes or it can take much, much longer. It's up to you."

It took Nick ramming his fist into the guy's back to get a gasping, "All right, all right, get this Neanderthal off me!"

"Neanderthals couldn't crack your skull with their teeth," Nick said before dropping Cannon's limp body onto the floor. "I can, you sorry sonofabitch."

In the time they'd had Richard Cannon in their custody they'd learned a few more disturbing things about him, one of which started with the pictures he'd had on his office computer of Nivea posed in a way a father should never see his child. They'd also found receipts from Comastaz and invoices that they hadn't quite figured out yet. All of that, coupled with Cannon's apparent distaste of the Shadows, had Nick a little on edge and a lot repulsed. Rome didn't blame him, and so he hadn't bothered to stop him or to help Cannon get up off the floor.

"I'm still waiting," he said after the man had attempted to get up only to land flat on his face again.

Finally, he simply rolled over onto his back, his hands flapping like a fish out of water over his chest as he continued to heave for his breath.

"It's research," Richard finally coughed out. "Research to help the humans catch up to where we are. I'm only helping them to even the playing field when this shit finally hits the fan!"

Nick had been about to kick him when Rome stood abruptly, blocking Richard from his friend's reach. Leaning down, he grabbed the front of Cannon's shirt, lifting his top half off the floor.

"How exactly were you helping them, you piece of shit? What else did you give them besides money?"

Rome hadn't thought about it until just a few seconds ago, the moment Richard said he'd been helping to level the playing field. He thought about those invoices they'd found in Cannon's office. The papers that documented hundreds of units shipped directly to the labs. Rome frowned. If Cannon was saying what Rome thought he was, so help the sick bastard. If Nick didn't rip his head off, Rome was very likely to.

"The unwanteds," Cannon said, looking Rome directly in the eye. "I gave him what your people in the rain forest didn't want. They cast them aside, said they were born of the wrong class of shifter and could not stand with them. So I brought them over here. I found somewhere for them to be useful since, because of their unfortunate lineage, they had no place on this earth."

"What the hell are you talking about?" Nick asked.

Rome let Richard's body drop to the floor, standing and backing away from him as he felt his cat rising up inside, ready to shift, ready to pounce. To restrain himself, he turned away from the man, rubbing a hand down his face as Nick repeated, "What the hell are the unwanteds?"

At his side, Rome's fists clenched as he dropped his head. "That's what they call the children in the Gungi whose parents have been found to be rogues, or descendants of rogues. Elder Alamar reported on this when the Stateside Assembly was just being formed. The tribes in the rain forest were now afraid that the rogue trait was hereditary. I didn't believe it until Lidia Morales arrived here with Brayden Sanchez. She's Sabar's niece and apparently was ostracized for that relation. That's why the Sanchezes finally took her abroad with them. She was a big part of the reason Sabar had targeted the Sanchez brothers when he first began building his army."

"Wait a minute," Nick said incredulously.

Before his friend could start speaking again, Rome turned to face him, nodding his head. "Yes, that's exactly what I mean. This piece of crap's been sending shifter children to Crowe at Comastaz and Crowe's been picking them apart to continue building those damned hybrids."

"Because he couldn't get his hands on my daughter," Nick finished for Rome. "He couldn't get her DNA so they settled for what they thought was distorted shifter DNA. And the only way they would have known that was from a sneaking traitor like this."

The kick that landed in Richard's gut could not have been prevented even if Rome wanted to. The man curled into a fetal position and Nick landed another kick to his spine.

"Don't kill him," Rome said in a level but commanding tone. "He should suffer the same way he made those kids suffer. Spend some time with him and then lock him up again."

He was leaving the room when he heard the man land

another kick. Nick was fuming; everything they'd learned from Cannon coupled with the still fresh memory of his daughter being kidnapped had the shifter at his breaking point. Now, with the knowledge that Richard Cannon had sent other shifter children to the fate that could have been Shya's—that was a rage that Rome could not begin to explain. As angry and as hurt as he was with the discovery, he knew it was worse for Nick. And so he'd left him with Cannon, but he'd given the order not to kill. This meant Nick would not kill the shifter, but he would beat him until the bastard wished he were dead.

"I was just on my way out," Nivea said when she'd opened the door to her room, only to find the First Female and X's mate, Caprise, standing in the doorway.

She'd awakened once again to Eli being gone. That man sure did like to perform a disappearing act, especially after sex. Emotionally drained from seeing her father and telling Eli all that had happened between them, and more than a little agitated with her so-called mate for leaving her once again, she wasn't really in the mood for chitchat. And she especially was not in the mood for two of the highest-ranking mated females in the Assembly and whatever they felt they needed to say to her.

"We won't take up much of your time," Kalina said. "We just thought it might be time for us to talk."

Realizing that she was standing in the doorway, actually blocking the First Female from entering her room, Nivea moved to the side, swaying her arm as invitation for them to come in. When the door was closed she took a deep breath and prayed she would handle this the way she should, that she wouldn't show the attitude that was brimming just beneath the surface, that her agitation would remain in check, that . . .

"Look, I can tell you're not in a very good mood."

Caprise spoke first. She was a tall and exotically gorgeous female with thick black hair hanging almost to her waist. She'd just begun guard training a few months ago, but Nivea had seen her in the training center and knew she was a natural at defensive tactics, just like her older brother, Nick. Caprise was also a trained dancer and had a grace about her that bordered on the overtly sexy, which kept her mate, X, on his toes. Of the two ladies standing across from her, Caprise was definitely the most candid. Nivea could so appreciate that.

"No. I'm not," she admitted and then took a deep breath, expelling it slowly. "But I do not want to take it out on either of you. So if we could possibly do this later . . ."

Kalina shook her head.

"No. Unfortunately, there are a couple of things I'd like to ask you about the incident at the cabin. Did you or did you not see Agent Dorian Wilson there that night?"

Okay, that was a little better, Nivea thought with an inward sigh. She could talk about Wilson and the cabin. That was her job. What she didn't want to talk to them about was her father or Eli or anything related to those two people.

"Eli and I followed Agent Wilson to the cabin," she started, willing her hands to remain still at her sides. "Fifteen minutes after he went inside, two other men showed up, and then two more."

"So there were five men in total in that cabin and two ended up dead?" Caprise asked.

"Right," Nivea conceded. "And I have no idea where the other three went, mostly because I hadn't been able to identify two of them. As for Wilson, X received reports from his contact at the Bureau that the man is MIA. I've been to his apartment twice every day. No car, mail falling out of its box. Nothing."

"And you think that's normal?" Kalina asked her.

Nivea shook her head. "No. Not normal. Then again there was nothing normal about Wilson's obsession with us."

"He thought he knew what we were doing," Kalina said, turning away from them and walking a few steps across the room. She turned back, a finger resting on her chin. "From the start he thought he knew who and what Roman was. Then he decided to come after X. I told him he was wrong and I warned him to back off."

"Hardheaded S.O.B., ain't he?" Caprise added with a smirk.

"But he's not stupid," Kalina replied. "And continuing to come after us was just stupid. Dorian should have known better, he should have backed off."

Nivea could see where the First Female was going with this conversation as she'd been down that road herself. She just hadn't had the time to follow up on that particular hunch. "Unless he found others who shared his assumptions. If those men in the cabin were ones that thought they knew everything about us as well, they would have had a common bond. A reason to meet in a secluded spot."

"And if there was somebody that didn't want them to really figure out what we are, then there would be anger, blood, death," Caprise added. "All three of which were found in that cabin."

Nivea let out a shaky breath.

"You think a shifter was in that cabin?"

"X said there was a rogue scent in the hospital room where that guy Eli beat the hell out of was killed," Caprise offered. She'd been moving around as they talked, looking at everything on Nivea's dresser, from her deodorant to the Betty Boop lunch box where she kept her fancy jewelry.

Now the guard had turned to face them, crossing her arms over her chest as she thought about what she'd just said.

"Rogues usually don't care who knows about us," Nivea commented, thinking about what was being said. She'd relaxed a little having the women in her personal space, thinking of them as her two sisters for a moment. She leaned against the wall by the bathroom.

"Their goal is to wreak as much havoc in the human world as possible," she continued.

"And killing a human that's just been beat down by a Shadow in a hospital room surrounded by other humans would be right at the top of the wreak havoc meter, don't you think?" Kalina asked.

"Sonofabitch!" Caprise yelled.

Nivea had to agree with her. "So whoever killed the wannabe investigators in the cabin is the same one who killed Rimas at the hospital. Because what better way to get humans riled up than to start killing them off without any regard? We all know rogues don't give a damn who they kill, just that it gets this war between humans and shifters going a little sooner."

Kalina was nodding. "Right. The question now is who is controlling these rogues, because there's no doubt that the real way to get humans up in arms would be for one of them to simply shift in a public place."

Caprise snapped her finger as if she'd just thought of something. "Just like when Sabar was alive and running the rogues. He wanted to kill humans, but he also needed them to keep buying his drugs, so he didn't have the rogues just running through the streets in cat form."

"So somebody new is pulling their strings. Just as Eli and the other guys believe someone is working along with Crowe. What are the odds that this 'someone' could be the same person controlling the rogues and Crowe's hybrid project?" Nivea asked.

Kalina cursed. "We need to figure out who this bastard is."

"And take his ass down, now!" Caprise completed. "Are you off your house arrest?" she asked, looking over to where Nivea stood.

She couldn't help it, Nivea gave the female a warning glare, which resulted in Caprise's impulsive laughter.

"I'd say her shoulder looks pretty healed to me," Kalina added. "Besides, it's gonna have to be the two of you on the outside. Ever since Rome found out I was pregnant, I've been living under a microscope. I'm actually surprised he hasn't sent Jax to come in here and haul me back into our room and into that bed that I'm thoroughly sick of lying in."

"What?" Nivea asked, coming closer. "Wait, you're pregnant?"

"I am," Kalina said with a proud grin, her palm going immediately to her stomach.

Caprise shook her head. "All this domestication around here is really cramping my style."

"Ah, congratulations," Nivea finally managed after she tore her gaze from Kalina's stomach and her mind from the loud scream of disappointment.

Ary and Nick were mated and they had a child.

Ezra and Dawn were mated and could barely keep their hands off each other. Bas and Priya were talking about a huge wedding. And Caprise, she was so in love with X she didn't know what to do with herself, despite her bravado.

"Thanks," Kalina replied. "But I'm not an invalid."

"Yeah, I'll send that memo to the Assembly Leader right away," Caprise chirped. "You might as well give it up, he's never going to let you out to look for Wilson, or a rogue killer for that matter."

"Me, on the other hand," Nivea added. "I've already been assigned to Wilson. So I can dig a little deeper. Find his next of kin and pay them a visit."

Caprise pointed in her direction. "Good thinking. I'll get into X's database and start searching the rogues."

"Search all tribes," Kalina added. "Bianca the Bitch said they were all in on this—cougars, cheetahs, tigers, and lions. We should consider any of them the enemy."

"Don't I know about enemies," Nivea said out loud and instinctively knew it had been a mistake.

Kalina took a couple of steps until she was standing right beside Nivea. "I don't know the specifics of what went on with you and your father, but I know it was bad enough to have Eli roaring in anger. I heard him all the way in my room. Rome said they have Richard Cannon locked up tight but I don't get the sense that you're afraid of him."

She'd thought this was the last subject she wanted to broach with these women, or with anyone for that matter. But Nivea's response came surprisingly easy.

"I've never been afraid of him. Disgusted by what he did to me, maybe. Terrified that he would turn his attentions to my sisters, yes, but never afraid of him. He's a spineless coward, always has been."

"And now he's either going to grow some balls and do what's right or rot in that holding tank for the rest of his life," Caprise added. "Don't think about him or what he did. Your life is your own now."

Nivea nodded. Caprise had endured her share of pain at the hands of a man she once loved so Nivea could relate to her sincere words. As for Kalina, she'd grown up an orphan and had met Rome for the first time after she was sexually assaulted. None of them had been blessed with an easy life, but here they all stood now, united and ready to do whatever was necessary to keep their secret and their species safe. Nivea took pride in that fact and nodded to them both.

"Let's get started," she told them.

* * *

Eli hadn't seen Nivea all day. After meeting with Rome in the morning and learning that the Assembly Leader planned to stay around Havenway for the remainder of the day, he'd decided to go and check on the barbershop. There was no doubt his staff had questions. Malik had already sent him numerous text messages. In addition, he had the sinking suspicion that the rogue that had taken care of Rimas would also take a personal interest in the barbershop with hopes of drawing Eli out.

Never being one to run from a threat, Eli had gone alone, stepping out of his SUV and moving slowly toward his shop. He scented the air as he moved, his cat's eyes protected from public view by his sunglasses, surveying his surroundings. All looked to be in order.

He entered the barbershop, standing in the doorway for a few more minutes, surveying, scenting. The rogue had definitely been here.

"Hey, man, glad you decided to stop by," Malik said, approaching him.

Eli extended his arm, shaking the man's hand and appreciating the eye contact. Sometimes people who had battled with addiction and such needed a helping hand and could feel a little embarrassed by that fact. Malik Drake did not.

Eli and Nivea had rescued Malik from rogues that were probably also drug dealers. The rogues had kidnapped him in an effort to get Priya, Malik's sister, to report on the existence of cat people. Of course, that never happened and now Priya worked for the Assembly. As a way of helping Priya to rest easily about her brother's well-being—and to ensure she was no longer vulnerable in this area of her life—Eli had offered Malik a job at the barbershop as long as he maintained his sobriety and attended the outpatient rehab facility. So far, all had been working out well.

"Got a little caught up yesterday," Eli replied.

Malik nodded. "I bet you did. All you missed was the press camped out here like they expected another fight to break out." Malik gave a wry chuckle as he walked toward the back of the shop.

Eli followed him, nodding to the barbers and customers as he moved through the room. As always, he admired how his staff kept a clean and pleasant atmosphere. The walls had been painted a warm green, the floors black marble that matched the chairs and stations. He'd considered adding a couple of stylists to at least one of the shops, but figured he liked the mostly male clientele much more. His thoughts momentarily ventured to Nivea and all the conflict he was having with regard to her being in his life—or, more like his bed—now.

"Got a package back here for you," Malik was saying when Eli snapped out of his Nivea-reverie. "Came early this morning. I was going to call you but then it got busy and I figured I'd get ahold of you later in the day."

"No problem," Eli said as they moved through the hallway.

The last door to the left was the business office. It had only been in the last couple of weeks that Eli had given Malik more responsibility around the shop. The added duties had seemed to work well to boost Malik's confidence and Eli was proud of the way the man had stepped up to the plate.

"Here you go," he said once they were in the office. He tapped his hands on the top of a white box sitting on the edge of a table across from the desk.

It was a medium-sized box and when Eli moved closer to examine it, the first thing he noted was the lack of a return address.

"How was this delivered?" he asked Malik.

"It was on the steps when I came in this morning. I got

here around six because we have a few customers that come in right at seven and I wanted to make sure the floor and booths were clean before everybody started to arrive."

Eli nodded. He slid a finger along the length of the box and down the sides, all the while his senses going into over-drive at how strong the rogue scent was at this moment.

"I'll take it with me," he said finally, lifting the box and moving over to the desk to act like he was looking at other mail that had accumulated.

"Heard that guy that was in here died at the hospital," Malik said and Eli's head shot up to look at him.

"Somebody else killed him there," he stated coolly.

Malik nodded. "Long as the deed got done," was his reply. "You pull a knife on a man, you better be prepared to kill or be killed. That's what my pops told me before he split."

The last was said with a careless chuckle that Eli sus-pected held more emotion than anything the man had ever said to him before. A few minutes later Eli and Malik had walked out to the front of the shop again and he'd bid him farewell, telling Malik how proud he was of his progress.

For the next few hours Eli had driven around town, that box sitting in the passenger seat of his SUV. Finally, he'd pulled to the side of I-66 in the building rush-hour traffic and opened the box.

His chest constricted, his fingers tightening on the box as he stared down at its contents.

"Fuck!" he yelled in the interior of the car.

Later that evening, Eli sat at the table behind the one that Rome, Kalina, Nick, Ary, X, and Caprise occupied. He and Ezra sometimes sat at the table with them, but tonight Ezra and Dawn had gone out to dinner and Eli had no de-sire to feel like the odd man out. He hadn't wanted to consider why he gave a damn about that either.

"Let's go for a walk," he heard a voice behind him say.

He knew that voice, just as he knew how being alone with her would turn out. Considering the way his afternoon had gone, that probably wasn't the best idea.

"No, thanks," was his chilly reply.

She didn't speak for a second or so but she didn't leave either.

"So, what, I'll see you if I come to your room tonight and then you'll leave before I wake up in the morning?" Nivea inquired, her tone as chilly as his had just been.

"Don't do this, Cannon. Not right now." If he'd been thinking straight Eli would have known immediately that wasn't the right thing to say to her.

She came around to the other side of him, standing so close Eli had no choice but to stare up at her. She wore pants that looked like the ones she did her training in and a white T-shirt that was long enough to cover the majority of her curves but just sheer enough to give a good indication that there was much more to see. His teeth clenched so hard they ached.

"Don't do what, exactly? Call you out on how ridiculous you're acting?"

"No," he replied slowly. "Don't make a scene. There's a good reason I do not want to go for a walk right now and if you'd just relax and move on I can continue trying to figure out how I plan on dealing with it."

"What happened?" she asked immediately. "Is it the rogues? Did you find him?"

Eli's eyes narrowed.

"Did I find who?"

Nivea didn't reply. In fact, her lips had clamped closed so tightly they thinned and Eli was instantly concerned.

"Who do you think I should be looking for, Nivea?"

She shook her head. "Nobody. I mean, I know that Rome questioned my father today and I thought maybe he'd given you a name of someone to look out for."

She wasn't being completely truthful with him, Eli could tell by the way her shoulders tensed, her scent wavering between that of a lie and that of anxiety.

"Do you know who your father was working with? Is there someone else we should have in custody?"

She'd been shaking her head before his question could be completed.

"No. I was just wondering."

It was more likely she was just lying, but Eli truly did not think he could deal with her tonight. He couldn't take her somewhere private where he could ask the questions he wanted and possibly get the answers, or get a lot of pleasure from being alone with her instead.

"Well, stop wondering. And in answer to your question, you do not have to come to my room tonight." Eli stood and walked away from her, feeling her angry glare against his back in sharp painful pricks. He'd hurt her and he hadn't meant to. Yet, he'd known he eventually would.

Damn his dysfunctional makeup and all the bullshit he'd allowed into his life that made him more fucked up. With purposeful strides he walked out of the dining hall, intent on locking himself in his room until he could figure out what the hell was going on and how to stop it before everyone he cared about ended up a victim.

Before he'd even realized it, Eli had slammed into Baxter. The older man moved throughout Havenway with such quiet accuracy it was never really a surprise to see where he'd turn up. Except Eli hadn't been expecting to see him, or rather, bump into him right at this moment. His intention had been to get far away from people for a while, but it seemed as if that was not going to happen.

Baxter's weathered hands reached up to Eli's shoulders, just as Eli mumbled, "Pardon me."

"No pardon necessary," Baxter said, his voice slow, steady, and wise.

Baxter had been with Rome's family since before he was born. Just a few months ago they'd all learned that the butler's service to the Shadow Shifters went well beyond cleaning up their houses and washing their dirty clothes. Baxter was an Overseer. His job, as a human, was to watch, to teach, to preserve the legacy of the Shadow Shifters. He was the only human Overseer and had worked very closely with Elder Alamar as the Stateside Assembly had been constructed.

For that reason, and because Eli had been brought up to do nothing less, he'd always afforded Baxter a great amount of respect.

"I was actually looking for you," Baxter continued.

Eli took a step back, not only feeling leery at Baxter's words, but also uncomfortable by the way the man was looking at him.

"Is this about Rome? Is something wrong?" Eli asked, his muscles already tensing.

"Relax, shifter. I know that we are all a bit on edge these days. But what I have to say I think will bring some relief to you."

To the contrary, his cryptic words had Eli's jaw clenching so hard he could have cracked a tooth. "What is it?" he asked without further preamble.

"I know what happened to you and your brother in Sierra Leone," Baxter began.

Eli sighed, truly sick of thinking and hearing about this subject. "Look, I don't have time for this," he said. "I'm busy right now. Please excuse me." Eli turned to walk away before Baxter could reply, only to be stopped by the man's hand on his arm.

"You need to listen to what I have to tell you, son."

Eli looked down at Baxter's hand, then back up at the older man. "I'm not your son."

Baxter released his hold on Eli, giving a slight nod of his head as he pushed his wire-framed glasses up higher on his nose.

"In some ways that is exactly what you are now," Baxter replied.

"What the hell are you talking about?"

"It starts in your temples," Baxter began. "The pain from seeing so much in so short an amount of time. It bothers you, I know because I've watched you in the meetings. You don't want to believe it, cannot think that you have changed. But at the same time you cannot deny what you are experiencing."

Eli shook his head. "I have no idea what you're talking about." But as if on command, his temples had begun to throb the moment Baxter spoke of them. At his sides his hands clenched as if that action could dispute the pain somehow.

"Your brother's reaction to the damiana-laced shaman's treatment has been different from yours. His mate's DNA contributed to his healing from the poison. Once he completely embraced her, he was able to fully take hold of the powerful shifter that he had become."

"I'm. Not. Ezra," Eli told him through gritted teeth.

He was angry with Baxter, but didn't actually know why. Sure, the man had halted his search for solitude but there was something else, something that had Eli's heart beating rapidly.

"Your reaction to the smoke has only started the inevitable."

Eli did not respond this time. He was almost afraid to. Not wanting to hear what the man was going to say next, while at the same time, on some distant level, already knowing exactly what his words would be.

"They've already begun, Eli," Baxter continued, clasping his hands in front of him.

The man spoke with an air of old wisdom so much that sometimes Eli thought he should be wearing a long belted robe, like most of the Elders did, instead of regular everyday clothes like the rest of them.

"With all due respect, Baxter," Eli began, then stopped as the man only nodded at him.

"You have seen the visions. They've come while you are awake as well as when you are asleep. They are of the past and of the future, sometimes of the right now. You wonder how or why, but think if you do not speak of it, they will cease to exist." The older man shook his head.

"You are wrong. The visions will get stronger, clearer. They will come more frequently and eventually at your command. Your senses will return to one hundred percent, possibly even stronger. That is how it is for Seers."

Eli listened to his every word, felt something warm spreading throughout his body, a familiar sense of knowing and still replied, "I am not a Seer. I am too young to be one and there is no lineage throughout my family."

"You are correct," Baxter told him. "You are very young to come into your power. It usually does not present itself until forty or forty-five years into a shifter's life. You can thank the damiana in that shaman's smoke for bringing it to the surface so soon. As for the family lineage, the bloodlines have been so diluted after the tribes began to migrate from the Gungi, there is no perfect familial trace on the Seer power now."

"No," Eli said, shaking his head and closing his eyes. Lifting his hands he cupped them to his ears. It was foolish he knew, but what else could he do? He couldn't take anymore. Not one more goddamned thing. From Acacia and all the drama and death that followed, to Leanne and her tragic end, and now Nivea and the problems the shifters as a whole were facing. Eli felt like he was on an emotional roller coaster and about to explode with anger at any moment.

Then Baxter touched Eli's right hand with his left, placing his full palm over the guard's with a touch that was both warm and light. The pain vibrating from Eli's temples down to his shoulders and resting in the pit of his stomach ceased, a shiver moving down his spine.

"You know this to be true. It is the answer that you have both sought and struggled with. Your time in Sierra Leone changed you. How you decide to embrace your destiny is the only thing in your control. You are a Seer; that will not go away. To fight against it or continue to deny it is futile. It is who you are."

"Stop it," Eli whispered, his legs going weak beneath him. "Just stop it."

Baxter removed his hand from Eli's. He took a step back and walked away. Eli watched him go, wishing he had never come and spoken to him. He saw the older man walking slowly down the hall until he turned the corner, leaving only the scent of knowledge and despair in his wake. Eli inhaled the scent deeply, the man's words replaying in his mind, just as he realized he'd watched Baxter's departure through closed eyes.

Chapter 15

More than a week had passed since Eli had been to the hospital room where Rimas died, and less time than that since he'd visited his barbershop and received the gift that was left for him. Today was finally the day.

He braced his hands on the bathroom sink, letting his head fall as he tried to center his thoughts. Nivea was sleeping in his bed, an even bigger part of her stretching alongside his cat, living and breathing inside of him. After a couple days of her going to her own room at night and keeping her distance throughout the day, he'd had enough. Last night he'd gone to her.

She'd been in the training center practicing with Caprise, or at least he'd thought the two females were practicing. Thinking back on it now they'd appeared to be doing more talking than actual training. But he hadn't paid much attention to that at the time. All he could think about was how badly he'd wanted her in his bed, his arms, beneath him, on top of him. Damn, he just needed her.

"Well, if it isn't the long-lost twin," Caprise greeted him as he'd approached.

She'd taken to calling both him and Ezra *twin,* only

distinguishing by which one she was looking at during that time. Eli mostly let it slide because he'd never had a younger sister before, and especially not one who liked to believe she could take him on the training field.

"Does your mate know you're in here at this time of night?" had been his sarcastic comeback.

Caprise hadn't batted an eye, but delivered her immediate retort. "That depends if yours knows how moody an asshole you can be. Oh, wait, let me ask Nivea since she's right here."

Eli's lips clenched as he moved between the two females, his back facing Caprise. He looked at Nivea just as she was adjusting the band holding her hair back from her face.

"We need to talk," he said. "Now."

She arched a brow and let her hands fall to the bare skin of her hips. Those damned training pants were riding so low he could see the tip of her hip bone, the sweet indentation of her navel, and the diamond dangling from the ring she had there.

"I'm training," she replied.

"Take a break," he answered, knowing that what he wanted to do to her would take much longer than a break.

"She can't, unless her trainer says so," Caprise chimed in from behind. "Or her mate. I don't know, which one are you, Eli?"

"Please," he'd said through clenched teeth, wanting to throttle Caprise and then pick Nivea up and toss her over his shoulder. He'd carry her into his room and have his way with her and this burning need that had been growing steadily in the pit of his stomach would go away once and for all.

She looked like she was going to deny him until he stepped closer. Eli could feel it, like a blanket covering him, the reach of her cat calling out to his. Nivea opened her mouth to speak, then snapped it shut because she knew, just as he did, that refusing would be futile.

Turning quickly, she walked away from him and after exhaling the breath he hadn't realized he'd been holding, Eli followed behind her.

"Be careful, twin," he heard Caprise calling from behind him. "That's not a cat you want to toy with."

Eli didn't even turn to acknowledge her warning, but wondered if the females in Havenway had some type of loyalty pact.

Once in the hallway, he realized that Nivea had continued walking. Eli picked up her scent, following it dutifully, his mind focused on only her, the cat and the human. There was something in that combination that had been calling to him for far too long. He'd tried to ignore it, felt he had no other choice but to do so. Here he was, the great alpha that he'd always assumed he was meant to be, following behind a sexy and headstrong female destined to reel him in and keep him tightly within her grasp.

He was shaking his head even as he approached the door to his room where Nivea now stood, arms folded over her chest, shoulder leaning on the doorjamb.

"This doesn't mean you've won, Eli," she said to him, her cat's eyes flashing fiercely.

"I should have never entered this competition," he told her as he reached around, touching his fingers to the new print-scan security device Nick had installed on all the higher level shifter's doors.

When he heard the click of the locks, he pushed against her until they both fell into the room. With his foot he pushed the door closed behind him and knew it would automatically lock again. His arm was immediately around her waist, pulling her close to him and lifting her feet off the floor. She didn't gasp or act shocked in any way at his quick motion, but instead wrapped her arms around his neck and parted her lips in anticipation of his. He did not keep her waiting but latched onto her bottom lip, sucking it into his mouth and moaning at how good she tasted. When his tongue slipped inside her mouth and was stroked by hers, everything everywhere stopped.

Walking across the floor until his bed was right behind her, Eli laid Nivea down, falling on top of her as they went. He grabbed her leg, lifting it up so high it finally rested on his shoulder. His hand was sliding down again, cupping her ass, fingers stroking between her legs, feeling the heat through the spandex she wore. Their kiss was hungry and fevered, her teeth scraping along the line of his jaw and down his neck. When her tongue delved into his ear, Eli roared. His sharp teeth latched onto the collar of her shirt, ripping the material straight down the center.

She did exhale quickly then, her back arching so that he could peel the rest of the shirt away. Grabbing the center of the sports bra she wore, that too came off with a ripping sound. Unbound breasts with darkened nipples, taut and begging to be kissed were appeased, his tongue lathing over each turgid bud. He cupped both breasts in his palms, squeezing and rotating from one to the other, licking, sucking, kneading.

Her palms smacked against the back of his head, her fingers slipping forward to pull the sunglasses from his eyes. She tossed them across the bed and in the distance Eli heard them hit the floor. She cradled his face then, forcing him to look up at her.

"We're in this together," she whispered. "Like it or not."

He didn't like it. Or rather he didn't like the word *together*.

As for the way her tongue slipped past her lips in offering and his mouth closed over it, sucking so deep he felt as if he were actually inhaling a part of her into himself, Eli was too far gone to complain. As their bodies tangled together in the here and now, his thoughts wandered to their cats running, stretching, scents mingling, hearts molding, and their eventual joining . . . dammit, another vision.

Eli tore himself away from that thought, released his mouth's hold on her, and ripped away her pants and the tiny wisp of lace that served as her underwear. She was naked and ready, the scent of her essence and the sight of it dampening her plump folds was all Eli needed to know, all his mind needed to fixate on at this moment.

With a trembling finger, he parted her tender folds, loving the suctioning sound of her opening to him. His mouth watered at the sight of her clit, so taut and eager to be pleased and her center dripping with sweet nectar. In one quick motion his mouth was on her, devouring all that she had to offer, all that she was. Her hips lifted from the bed, her hands now gripping the back of his head, holding him steady as she pumped into his mouth.

It came with a rush and Eli's shoulders shook with the intensity of it. Emotion, that's what it was, and the moment he realized it, he pulled back, ripping the snap from his pants and freeing his erection. She said something, whispered his name, told him what she wanted, something. Eli didn't know. He didn't want to know. And he didn't want to see, not her face, not her gorgeous breasts or the glistening goodness of all the desire she had for him. He did not want to *see* anything, anymore.

He just wanted to feel.

He thrust into her fast and furious, leveraging himself on his knees, fingers gripping her thighs as he held her legs up. She gasped and her hands moved to cup her breasts. Eli closed his eyes, pulled out, and thrust in once more. Out and then in, deeper and deeper until his cat stood on its haunches and roared so loud Eli's ears rang. The cat was fierce and hungry, the man horny and conflicted. Together they worked, moving in and out of her, loving the feel of her slickness against his rigid length, the clap of her soft thighs against his, the sound of her voice echoing his name.

No. He shook his head. Just feel the pleasure and let that be all.

But it was useless.

"Eli."

He could hear her loud and clear, each and every time.

"My *companheiro*," she whispered. "My *companheiro*."

Shaking his head did nothing. Her voice was too loud, too soft, her cat too persistent rubbing alongside his.

"All for you, my *companheiro*."

Eli gritted his teeth as she shivered beneath him, wanting, no desperately needing, to see now. He looked down at her, saw her eyes half closed, her back arched, nipples hard. She was in the midst of her release, her body trembling, lower lip clenched between her teeth, fists gripping the sheets. She looked so sweet, so deserving of something better, someone with more sanity, more normalcy. She deserved the best, and yet this was all he could give her, all he had.

With guilt pounding at his temples Eli wanted to pull out, to get off this bed and walk the hell away. But when he tried, something held him still. Her walls gripped his length, her thighs holding him tightly. She opened her eyes and looked right at him. Eli blinked, but she did not go away. The soft curve of her lips, the high tilt of her cheekbones, her smooth brown skin and her eyes, the golden hue of her cat, held him captive.

"Nivea," he whispered as that painful clutching in his chest centered. He didn't think he'd be able to take his next breath.

"Come for me, Eli," she said, lifting her hands to flatten her palms on his chest. "Let go and come for me, darling. For me, Eli, just for me."

He couldn't and yet, how could he not? Breath eased through his chest as the warmth from her touch spread throughout him. Inside his cat purred and Eli watched her undulating beneath him, whispering over and over again, "Come for me, darling. Come for me."

Until that was all he could do. His hands came to her wrists and he held tightly as his body stiffened over hers, his essence being pulled from him in thick jetting pulsations that felt more like he was emptying his soul.

Later, Eli would believe that he had done just that.

He'd left her in that room asleep, moving even more quietly than he ever had before, knowing that facing her at that moment was not going to be a good thing. As he left the compound he accepted that he was being a coward, as if the word were scrawled beneath the tattoo of his cat for all to see.

Now, hours later, he was pulling up in front of an old run-down apartment building in the south side of D.C. Cutting off the engine and letting his head fall back against the seat, he inhaled deeply, exhaled slowly.

The rogue was here.

She thought about him. Even now as she stepped out of her car and walked toward the building, Nivea could not get Eli out of her mind.

Something had changed between them this morning. She'd felt it in every stroke of his hips, every thrust of his hard length inside her. It was a feeling of completeness, a full and intense feeling that fit like the missing puzzle piece in Nivea's life. She'd fallen asleep with a smile on her face and a lightness in her heart as she realized that

Eli had just accepted the fact that they were mates. He probably hadn't liked it, but he hadn't been able to deny it as he'd locked gazes with her and gave her his release.

Nivea hadn't moved a muscle when he'd awakened this morning, his hand moving softly over her hair, his breathing slow and steady. For once, in all the time she'd known him, Eli had seemed content. His lips had touched her forehead in the sweetest of kisses and then the air shifted, a coolness settled over the room, and Eli had eased from the bed. She'd known he was showering and getting dressed to leave and that he would not say a word to her as long as she lay pretending to be asleep.

She did not open her eyes or speak, but watched him through partially opened lids as he slipped out the door. Rolling over onto her back just seconds afterward, she wondered what the hell she was doing. Why hadn't she said something? Called him on this foolish resistance he insisted on continuing?

With a sigh she realized she knew very well why. She wasn't going to tell Eli what to do with his heart or his destiny. Sure, a Shadow knew its mate and once it found its true partner, none other would suffice. But Nivea believed in free will. She believed in love and commitment and loyalty—in spite of the fact that she'd never truly experienced them. No matter what her father had done to her she'd always vowed not to let it dictate her life, her happiness. So while there were some victims of abuse who could not sustain healthy relationships, or refused to even try, she was different. She wanted the normal, the real and pure love of two people, and if she couldn't have that honestly and truly, then she would have nothing at all.

Eli's silence had seemed to make that choice for her.

Shake it off, Cannon. Now's not the time.

If she didn't tell herself to move on, she might not be able to. That alone told Nivea she was in pretty damned deep with Eli Preston. Taking a concentrated breath, she yanked open the door that almost fell off the hinges with her efforts. With a frown she thought of how she wasn't supposed to be on this little trip alone.

The plan had been for Caprise to join her, but she'd been drafted for babysitting duty. After the kidnapping, Nick and Ary rarely left Shya alone and when they absolutely had to, they only trusted people closest to them to care for her. Today was Caprise's turn since Ary had a very important appointment with Kalina for her first ultrasound. So the hit they'd received from the shifter database on a group of suspected rogues in the south side D.C. area was on Nivea to investigate. Caprise had asked if she wanted to wait, to go the next day, but Nivea knew what they were up against. If these rogues were going around killing then it stood to reason they were just as hell-bent on exposure as Crowe and his hybrids. She'd decided to come alone.

Taking the stairs two at a time, her adrenaline buzzing with the scent sifting surely through the air, she came through a door on the top floor. Her cat was wide awake, moving just beneath her skin so that she had to roll her shoulders to appease it.

"Just chill," she spoke aloud to the cat inside. Nivea loved the feeling of her heritage, knowing the power that rested just beneath the human skin, but she'd always been sure to keep it under control as well, to not let that hellion of a feline get the upper hand. If she hadn't, Richard Cannon would have been dead a long time ago.

She walked slowly and steadily, knowing exactly which apartment she was headed to without checking the address she'd programmed into her phone. The rogue scent was calling to her, and . . . there was something else, someone else . . .

Her heartbeat thumped, her cat hissing the closer she came to the door. She didn't dare speak, but kept her gaze locked on the door, and she heard it. The thinking was over, adrenaline pumped through her veins, the cat inside taking over as Nivea kicked in the door.

This wasn't what she'd been expecting to see. Then again, there'd been no way she could have known what was going on behind that door.

Eli stood in the middle of the messy apartment. More than six feet long, over two hundred and fifty pounds, his mouth opening wide as the second warning roar was released. In front of him, with their backs to her were two more cats—a cougar and a cheetah, poised and ready for battle.

"Shit!" she cursed just as the cheetah turned in her direction and charged.

They were fast as hell so Nivea barely had a second to drop to all fours and shift before the cheetah was on her back. She reared back quickly, not giving it a chance to sink its teeth into her, tossing the cat across the floor. Then she was charging and pouncing. The cheetah moved, jumping onto the back of the couch. Nivea was faster this time, leaping up and taking a bite out of the cheetah's flank. It hissed and fell back off the chair. Nivea continued battering the cat until it was in a corner, hissing and swatting until finally, tired of the nonsense, Nivea jumped on the cheetah's back, sinking her teeth into its skull and biting down until its bones cracked and the cat crumpled to the ground.

Turning quickly, blood dripping from her teeth, flanks heaving from her efforts, Nivea saw her mate battling the cougar. It was a strong and well-trained *Bosinian* fighting Eli with vigor and even though Nivea knew full well Eli would emerge the victor, it didn't stop her from leaping to his defense.

She jumped in front of the cougar, distracting it momentarily while Eli leapt from the marble countertop down onto its back. That didn't immediately stop the cougar from hurtling at Nivea. She charged back and while Eli bit into the back of its head, she attacked its underbelly, both jaguars biting to kill.

When the furniture had finished being broken and scattered about the room and the roaring and hissing came to a stop, two cats stood, breathing heavily, glaring at each other. He was a big and beautiful panther, where Nivea's jaguar was golden with rosettes so close they sometimes looked to be big black blurs.

"What the hell are you doing here?" Eli yelled about two seconds after he shifted.

His naked body was in the face of her cat's, staring down at it with rage unlike any she'd ever seen in him. No, that was not true, she'd seen it before, the day he was beating the crap out of Rimas.

The cat took a step back before Nivea shifted, shaking her head because the quick action always made her a little dizzy.

"I could ask you the same thing," she shot back.

"But you won't because I'm the commanding officer. And goddammit! What the hell, Cannon? Why are you here shifting and attacking fucking cats?"

"Attacking rogues, you mean? Last time I checked that was my job," she snapped back.

"Your job is to do what I say, when I say."

"That's bullshit, Eli! My job is the same as yours, to keep our secret safe."

"Well, you're doing a hell of a job, coming in here shifting like that," he roared back. "That cat could have killed you! It could have bitten down on your neck and . . ." His words trailed off as he closed his eyes, pinching the bridge of his nose as if he were in some type of pain.

"Oh, you mean after you'd already shifted? What the hell was that? I walk in on two cats about to tear another's throat out. What did you think I was going to do?"

There was nothing else she could have done. He was her mate and there was no way she could stand by and watch him be hurt, no way she wouldn't fight side by side with him. Pain radiated through her chest at the thought that Eli wouldn't understand that.

When he stalked past her instead of speaking another word she called after him, "Running away again, Eli? You're becoming a pro at that."

"Shut up!" he yelled over his shoulder as she tried valiantly not to look at the dimples in his muscled ass, or the power of his bare thighs.

She clamped her lips shut, not because he'd told her to, but rather because he wasn't likely to listen to a word she had to say. Instead she turned around, staring at the brutalized rogue carcasses, wondering what the hell their connection was to all that was going on around them. Seconds later her face was covered and she stumbled back as Eli roughly put a shirt that smelled like cheesesteak subs over her head.

"What the hell? Are you crazy?" she asked as he lifted her arms and stuffed them through the large openings of the shirt.

"No. But you are if you think I'm going to let anybody come in here and see your naked ass!" he yelled before moving past her. "I'm calling this in."

He reached down on the floor to where the shreds of his jeans were, picked up his cell phone, and put it to his ear. He'd obviously found some cargo shorts that fit without falling down his hips. His chest, however, was still bare, the jaguar tat on his arm taunting her.

"Use your com link, it'll be quicker," she told him.

"Don't want everyone on duty to know about this."

Nivea shrugged, not bothering to ask why, and pulled on the hem of her shirt to make sure all her assets were in fact covered. She walked around the room, thinking these rogues weren't cats, they were actually pigs. Dirty and disgusting pigs that didn't know the meaning of a trash can or Pine-Sol. Moving around she looked for anything that would connect these two rogues to what was going on— either at the cabin with Agent Wilson, or the hospital with Rimas. Something that would pull all of this nonsense together.

"We've got to get out of here," Eli said from behind her. "I'm sure somebody heard all the noise."

Nivea kept moving.

"The Sanchez brothers are on their way," he said.

She turned to him then. "Did they know you were coming here?"

Instead of supplying an answer, Eli asked a question. "What are you doing here, Nivea? Did you follow me?"

Nivea rolled her eyes and moved into the kitchen area, looking over the filthy countertops. "Get over yourself, Eli. I have a job to do too."

"And how did your job land you here?" he asked. "And don't give me another flippant remark. Answer me, Nivea. What the hell are you doing here?"

She sighed then, figuring it didn't make sense for both of them to try and keep a secret that was bound to come out anyway. "We're on the same team here. Caprise, Kalina, and I pieced together the fact that a rogue was in that cabin with Agent Wilson. Why? A rogue was also in the hospital room and killed Rimas. Why again? They're trying to get our attention," she said finally. "Or rather trying to keep our attention diverted so we won't focus on the true threat, Crowe and those hybrids. Or possibly someone who is controlling both Crowe and the rogues."

Eli was already shaking his head. "Rogues would not be working with hybrids."

"All I know is that we're here chasing after them instead of hunting Crowe as we should be. Don't you wonder why that is? Why were they with Agent Wilson and why kill Rimas?"

"This is not how rogues work," Eli said, but she could tell he was thinking over her words. He was looking around now, just as she was.

They both stopped when they heard a phone ringing.

"It's not mine," he told her, going completely still.

"Not mine either," she announced, moving out of the kitchen and following the sound.

She kicked it when she was about two steps away from Eli. He bent down and picked it up, gliding his finger across the screen to answer.

"Hello?" he spoke into it. "Hello?"

When there was no answer he pulled the phone away from his ear and looked down at it. With a frown he turned it so that Nivea could see the screen as well.

"Boden," she whispered.

Nick tossed the cell phone onto the conference table. It flipped over and landed flat just a couple inches shy of the speaker console in the center.

"If Boden Estevez is alive, you can bet he's not working alone." Sebastian Perry's voice sounded throughout the room.

"I knew that bastard wasn't dead," Jace Maybon, Pacific Zone Faction Leader, added, a string of curses following that declaration.

"How did you know?" Kalina asked.

The First Female had been seated next to her mate, a tall glass of milk centered on a blue square napkin in front of her. The milk was flavored, strawberry, because Kalina couldn't stand the taste of white milk. Jax stood two steps to her right, and Baxter two feet behind her, hands clasped in front of him.

To say that security around Rome and Kalina would be heightened was an understatement. Eli stood directly behind Rome, while Ezra was on the left side of the table, within arm's reach of Nick. Every high ranking leader of the Assembly would now have their first guard and a second one. Females would have four. Everyone would be armed and ready to kick ass at a moment's notice, no questions asked. This was the state of the Assembly.

"A few months back I reported that Bianca Adani was looking for representation through my agency," Jace began. "Now, I know I'm damned good at what I do. We represent the top A-list actors in the world so I can see why someone serious about breaking into the business would look our way. But resumes very rarely make it to my personal e-mail and they're almost never followed up by a video delivered right to my front door."

"You never told us about a video," Cole Linden, Central Zone Faction Leader interrupted. "It must have had tits and ass in it for you to keep quiet."

"Don't be crass, Linden," Jace shot back. "I didn't say anything because there was nothing to report. I just found it odd that all her information was coming straight to me. When my assistant checked with others throughout the agency, none of them reported receiving the same submission. We all know there's no such thing as coincidence."

"How does any of that relate to Boden?" Nivea asked, receiving surprised looks from everyone in the room.

Everyone except for Caprise, who was barely hiding her knowing smirk. Eli frowned, because he didn't like Nivea being the center of attention, for any reason.

Bas, Cole, and Jace were all on speakerphone so they couldn't see who had asked the question.

"She's right," Kalina interjected. "That doesn't sound like it relates to Boden at all."

A throat was cleared but Eli couldn't tell which one of the FLs on the other end of the speaker it was.

"My grandparents spent their later years traveling the globe, visiting all of the rain forests that had become home to Shadow tribes. During the time they were in the Sierra Leone rain forest they heard of a grand love affair, the re-joining of the tribes some had called it because it was a *Topètenia* and a *Lormenia*," Jace told them. "When my grandmother finally had a chance to see this couple she couldn't believe it. Boden was mated to Acacia, the daughter of the *Lormenian* leader, Teodoro."

There was an audible gasp from somewhere at the other end of the room and Eli saw Ezra's lips going thin, a muscle ticking in his jaw. He was glad to have the safety of his sunglasses. Nobody could see his surprise or possibly the anger that was growing within him, without access to his eyes. He stood with his legs slightly spread, hands fisted in front of him, a rush of emotion swirling around like a growing storm inside.

"Wait a minute." X spoke up this time. "You're saying that your grandmother had proof that Boden was alive years ago and never thought to tell anyone?"

"She told my mother, who assumed her mother was going senile or something, possibly suffering from some disease she'd picked up throughout her travels. She dismissed the rantings of an old woman who wanted things between the shifters to be like in the old days. My mother didn't speak of it because she feared the Elders may have hunted down her mother, issuing the same death sentence they had to Boden."

"That would not have happened," Elder Alamar spoke up.

He didn't usually attend these meetings but after Eli and

Nivea had brought the phone back to Rome, the Assembly Leader had called in everyone immediately.

"We did not take killing our own lightly," the normally quiet shifter said.

"But you would kill them!" Jace yelled. "If you saw fit you would kill them because you thought you knew best who should live and who should die."

"Calm down," Rome stated evenly, yet dominantly. "We cannot erase the past. The Elders of the Gungi ruled the way they deemed appropriate. We will do differently because we now know more."

"So if Boden wasn't killed when he was supposed to be, instead taking refuge in the Sierra Leone rain forest and falling in love with the tiger princess, why is he here now and how is that tramp Bianca connected?" Kalina asked.

"At the end of Bianca's video there was the *Topètenia* insignia intertwined with that of the *Lormenia* and the *Bosinia, Croesteriia,* and *Serfins*. I'd already known Bianca was a shifter but I was curious when I saw this so I did some background on her. That's when I found out she was Acacia's younger sister, born to a *Lormenia* female that was not Teodoro's mate and so they'd been shipped out of the Sierra Leone rain forest before she was born. With Acacia dead I put two and two together," Cole told them.

"And decided to keep this all to yourself?" Ezra asked.

Eli frowned. He'd been hoping that Ezra would keep their silence, that their past would not become a part of this conversation.

Nick, X, and Rome knew what had happened with them in the Sierra Leone rain forest, and Eli suspected their mates did as well. And because Ezra had used what happened to them to help Shya get better, the other FLs now knew as well. Nivea did not know and he did not want her hearing about the mistakes of his past. Not here and definitely not now.

"The why and how no longer matters."

Baxter spoke up from his spot in the corner. He moved slowly until he was standing near Elder Alamar. "This time would have come regardless of the events preceding it."

"What are you talking about?" Rome asked. "Do you know something you haven't been telling me? Something else, that is."

Eli stared at the Overseer as he came closer to the table. When Baxter looked up at him he knew exactly why. That conversation he'd thought he was overhearing weeks ago, the one that predicted the future of the Shadows, Eli had not overheard it at all. He'd seen Baxter and Elder Alamar having the conversation because he was a Seer, just as Baxter had told him. That's why he'd heard nothing but whispers when he'd put a glass to the wall. It was a vision that he had no idea when had actually taken place. But right at this moment, there was no doubt that he'd seen Baxter and the Elder talking, conversing about what they should do about Magdalena's vision.

"*A morte ea destruição. O fim completo da corrida ou uma mudança catastrófica em quem eo que somos virá. Vai chover sobre as cabeças daqueles que não tinham nada a ver com essa luta e um será encarregado de nos ver passar. Um deles será responsável para o futuro de todos nós.*" Elder Alamar spoke solemnly in Portuguese.

Baxter nodded and then looked to Rome. "It was predicted by Magdalena, the Seer of all tribes. She warned of death and destruction. The complete end of the race or a catastrophic change in who and what you all are would come. It will rain down upon the heads of those who had nothing to do with this fight and one will be tasked with seeing us through, she said. One will be responsible for the future of all."

"Why didn't you tell us this sooner?" Eli asked, his

chest still heaving at the revelation, the acceptance of what he was.

It was Elder Alamar who spoke to him this time. "The job of a Seer is to see what has been and what will be. It is not their job to change the course shifters will take."

Eli nodded, frowning at the Elder. "So they are privy to all this information but prevented from doing anything about it? That's a fucking waste!"

Rome lifted a hand to silence Eli. "It is their way," the Leader said. "It is what they were used to doing."

Everyone looked to Rome at that moment, the FLs on the speakerphone remaining silent. Kalina reached for her husband's hand. Rome laced his fingers with hers, his face grim, as he said without qualm or reservation, "We make our own future. From this moment on, we decide how this will end. We are the Shadow Shifters and we will prevail."

Chapter 16

She was unlike any woman Dorian had ever met. From the moment she walked up onto that porch and looked at him he'd known it for certain, just as he'd known that he would follow her anywhere.

"You're fucking fantastic!" she whispered, her face pressed against the wall as Dorian pumped deeply into her from behind.

They were in her hotel suite and she'd just come from the shower. He'd been on his phone, still trying to hook up with any of the surviving agents who had been at the cabin that day. Four weeks had already passed. The two agents who had been found were buried, their families still grieving their loss. And Dorian had yet to return to work. He had, however, left his sister's house about twenty minutes after Rayna had introduced herself to him.

"I've been bad, mister officer," she'd said, coming to stand between his legs just as he was leaving another message on an agent's phone.

He'd quickly disconnected the call, rising from his seat and looking at her lush naked body.

"Then you must be punished," he'd stated. "Turn around and assume the position."

She'd quickly obeyed, walking—no, sashaying her curving hips—across the room until she came to the wall where she spread her legs and placed her hands up over her head. Dorian grabbed her wrists, pressed her palms into the wall, and used his foot to kick her legs open wider.

He'd slipped into her easily; her pussy was always so wet and so tight. He was breaking all the rules he'd sworn to live by, he knew that without a doubt. But he couldn't stop it, wasn't even sure he wanted to.

"You're delicious," he whispered to her in return, his tongue licking along her ear. "Delicious and dangerous."

She'd chuckled then, pressing her ass back into each of his strokes until words escaped him and all Dorian could focus on was the slick in-and-out motions between them. When his legs trembled, release rushing through him like a tidal wave, his mind slowly began to clear.

He lowered them both to the floor afterward, curling his body around hers. They fit so perfectly, as if this was the female who had been made specifically for him. Only, she wasn't a female, at least not a human one.

"The time is almost near," she said in the quiet of the room. "What will you do?"

Dorian traced a finger from her shoulder, down her arm, to her thigh and down farther. She purred and he realized with a start that he loved that sound.

"What will you do?" he asked in return.

She moved then, just a little shift, before declaring, "Whatever is necessary."

Then there was a bigger shift. Dorian jolted back, still not used to seeing her in this form. The white Bengal tiger was big, mostly white with its black stripes darker over its back, basically disappearing toward its underbelly. Its head was that of a vicious killer, its eyes of a sultry female, the one he'd just released his essence inside of.

When she opened her mouth wide, her tongue jutting out to lick around her mouth, his dick grew harder. It was by far the weirdest thing he'd ever experienced. The woman and the cat aroused him, although he'd never verbally admit that to another living soul.

Cat people did exist.

The reports had been true and Dorian had one right here, living and breathing and making him doubt every bit of conventional sex he'd ever learned. Fleetingly he thought of what his superiors would say. The ones who had chastised him for neglecting his other cases and fixating on Reynolds and Delgado. The very ones whose faces he would laugh in once this story hit the streets.

Dorian finally stood up, one hand gripping his aching cock.

He sat on the side of the bed, legs spread, hand still jerking his length. "This is necessary," he told her. "Now."

The tiger took one step toward him, then in a blur once again became the female. She remained on her hands and knees, crawling toward him with a look of pure lust in her eyes. Goddamn, he loved that look. He loved those eyes, so eerie and yet so enticing. He inhaled deeply of the exotic scent she carried.

"You're right," she said when she was between his legs, her hands smoothing along his hair-coated thighs. "We can go over the plan later. Right now, first things first."

Her breath was warm as she opened her mouth and lowered her head, licking the tip of his dick with her moist tongue.

"Right," Dorian said, moving his hands from his length, burying his fingers in her hair, and guiding her mouth up and down. "This is definitely first." She went down on him all the way, until it felt like his tip was touching her tonsils. He gasped, tightened his grip on her hair, and thrust his hips forward. "We'll deal with them . . . after," he continued before words were lost in the deep guttural moan of pleasure.

"We're out of test monkeys," Crowe stated with finality, as if his word really carried any weight in this room. "Each time we send one out, it doesn't return. I don't know what they want me to do now. There's obviously a flaw and I can't fix it!"

The man, the great captain of the U.S. Armed Forces, was falling apart. Sweat dotted his brow, his hands shook as he dragged them through his hair. He was pacing back and forth, threatening to wear a path in the lovely dark gray carpet that lined the rooms of the suite. It would have been funny if this human's demise didn't directly affect Boden's ultimate plan.

With a resigned sigh, he smoothed a hand down the silk tie he wore. Dressing the part of a rich and influential human had become a ritual for him, the baser animalistic instincts he'd been born with still running close to the surface, however. Ready and waiting.

"The meeting is in three weeks," he stated.

"I know," Crowe whined. "I know. They won't let me forget it."

"Who will be there?"

Crowe spun around then, his lips drawn in a tight line. He wondered why Boden was asking, wondered how the man could be so calm in the face of this catastrophe. Boden knew all this and questioned why he had chosen this human to start things rolling in the first place.

"They're all going to be there!" he yelled.

Boden sat up, resting his elbows on his knees. He raised his brows, aware of how intimidating that could be with his bald head and bushy brows. He liked that look as it cultivated the calm before the storm in his mind, the normal that layered over the beast. The low chuffing sound that emanated from his chest was the icing on the cake and had Crowe stopping, rethinking his answer.

"Every high-level defense delegate in the world will be there," he said with a frown. "So far the Russians are making the top bid, but Pierson thinks the Chinese might have an ace up their sleeve. There's a lot of money riding on this deal."

"There's a lot riding on this meeting, period," Boden added. "Nothing can go wrong. Your hybrids have to be in place. Hundreds of them, ready to create the scene."

"All we need is maybe fifty good ones, fresh out of the lab, to put on a show for the delegates. They'll see what they can do without any interference and then the money will be on the table. We'll deliver the merchandise later and to hell with what happens after they've taken possession. Right?" Crowe was nodding. "Okay, we can do that. Then we'll all take our cut and get as far away from here as we can."

The man had begun pacing again. Boden simply shook his head.

"I want hundreds of them. Five hundred to be exact," he told him.

"No, that's not necessary," Crowe continued. "We just need a small amount. It's safer that way because they're so volatile. The more we create, the more unstable they become. Besides, I just told you I don't have any more test subjects. Where am I supposed to get enough DNA to create five hundred more? And in three weeks no less."

"Enough!" Boden finally raised his voice. "The stench of your panic is making me nauseous."

He stood then, pulling out his cell phone to make a call. His teeth clenched as it rang and rang until the voice mail picked up. Boden tried another number. No answer there either.

"Dammit," he muttered.

He'd been trying to reach Richard Cannon for over a week now and had not been successful. That bastard shifter owed Boden his life. In fact, his family owed Boden their lives considering all the heat he'd kept away from them by way of the Elders of the Gungi. One word, one note to the Elders that Cannon was taking their wayward youth and either killing them or selling them to Boden, and Cannon and his family would have been killed.

Boden had let the man live because he'd needed him. And now when that need was at its highest, the fool had the audacity to disappear. Well, that was not acceptable and Boden was about to show the shifter why it was safer for all involved to not try and swindle him. A hefty amount had been transferred into Cannon's account just two weeks ago. The man owed him two batches of shifter children or the "test monkeys" as Crowe called them.

The debt was real and so were the consequences for attempting to double-cross him.

"Stop pacing back and forth and make yourself useful," Boden yelled at Crowe. He walked over to the desk and picked up the hotel notepad and pen, scribbling on it as he continued to talk. "Get back to your lab and gather whatever hybrids you have left. Go to this address and bring me every breathing person in that house. Call me when the package is in hand for further instructions."

Ripping the paper off the pad, Boden turned again to hand it to the whining captain. When the man looked at him as if appalled that Boden would send him on an assignment, Boden bared his lethally sharp teeth while thrusting the paper into Crowe's chest.

"You got a problem taking orders, Captain Crowe?"

With shaking fingers Crowe reached up to snatch the paper away. The man's eyes stayed fixated on Boden, too well-trained and too proud to admit he was about to shit in his pants from seeing a living, breathing, adult Shadow Shifter.

"No problem," Crowe managed after clearing his throat. "No problem at all."

Somebody's in the house. They're breaking stuff and cursing and

The first text message ended.

I think they're going to take us

The second had come about a minute after the first and Nivea gasped, jumping out of Eli's bed.

"What is it?" he asked, sitting up instantly.

"My sister's texting me."

Eli instantly fell back against the pillows, his head turning slightly to peek at the clock on the nightstand table. "At three in the morning?"

"Something's wrong," Nivea said, hating the feel of the words clogging in her throat. "Something's happening."

She was already dialing Amina's number, hoping, no, praying that her sister would answer. When she didn't, Nivea cursed.

"I have to go to her," she said immediately, still clutching the phone in her hand as she moved to the chair where she'd begun stashing her clean clothes.

For the past three weeks she'd been in and out of Eli's bed. In the last four days she'd been more in than out, and hence her clothes now occupied the recliner chair in the corner beside his dresser, her boots and tennis shoes side by side inside his closet and her toothbrush and favorite chamomile body wash in his bathroom. He hadn't said a word about the things she'd brought into his room, no bitching and more disconcertingly—no acknowledgment. Yet, each time she'd attempted to go back to her own room, he touched her, kissed her, convinced her that this was where she belonged. Again.

Well, tonight, she knew where she had to go, despite the words she anticipated were about to come from Eli's lips.

"Are you crazy? You can't drive to New York at three a.m.," he told her, sitting up again, the sheet bunching up at his waist.

Of course he was naked beneath. Eli always slept naked and Nivea always enjoyed it. This morning, however, she was ignoring it.

"No, I'm not crazy. And yes, I can go to New York at whatever time I want if my family is in danger." She was pulling on a shirt, foregoing the bra and afterward reaching for a pair of sweatpants.

"Nivea, stop," he said, touching a hand to her shoulder as she bent over to put her legs in the pants.

"No, Eli! I will not stop!" she snapped at him with a glance over her shoulder. "Something's wrong. I can feel it. That's why I heard the vibration of my phone. A part of me knew something was going on."

He didn't argue that. She knew he was thinking about Ezra and how he had sensed something was going on with him even when his brother was all the way across the country.

"Let me see the texts," he said when she was about to push past him to get to her shoes.

"What?"

He held out a hand in front of her. "The text messages, Nivea. Let me see them."

She frowned and thought about arguing but figured what the hell, he wasn't going to stop her anyway. Thrusting the phone into his hand, she moved around him and finally grabbed her tennis shoes while he read.

"Who would want to take them?" he asked. "Your father is still locked up tight here."

Nivea looked up from tying her shoes quickly. "He wouldn't hurt them," she said. "He promised me he wouldn't touch them as long as I kept quiet and I didn't tell. I didn't tell anybody anything about what he's doing."

She knew she'd said too much the moment Eli's gaze went from confused to concerned.

"Maybe now's the time you do tell me everything," he replied.

Nivea stood. "Eli, I don't have time for this. I have to go save them. I have to stop them from being taken. I have to!"

He grabbed her by the shoulders, giving her a little shake until her lips snapped shut. "They're more than four hours away from us, Nivea. Even if we leave right this second, odds are they've already been taken."

She shook her head, not wanting to hear what he was saying.

"But I will do everything in my power to get them back for you," he continued, lifting his hands up to cup her face. "I just need you to be completely honest with me about what's going on. I can't help if I don't know who to fight for you."

Her heart was pounding, her mind whirling with possibilities. She'd made a promise never to tell. Rome had found out about part of what Richard was doing on his own, not with any help from Nivea. And Richard had gotten himself caught by daring to come visit her at Havenway. She'd kept up her end of the bargain when really, she should never have had to bargain with her father for her sisters' lives in the first place.

"I know he hurt you," Eli continued. "I want to rip his balls off for all the pain he's caused you, but I can see that you're stronger than that type of revenge. You've beaten him on all levels that he could never measure up to and for that I am most proud of you." He leaned forward then, kissing her forehead before pulling back and resting his against hers, looking straight into her eyes.

"Tell me what he's doing so I can stop him. I'll get your sisters back, I promise. I just need you to trust me with the truth."

Nivea swallowed to keep her lips from shaking and her eyes from tearing. She hated crying and hated feeling helpless. But she had to admit that being in Eli's grasp, having him say he was proud of her and that he would do anything to help her, kind of kicked helpless in the ass.

She inhaled deeply and said, "His foundation is bogus. He gets kids from the Gungi and he either sells them on the black market or kills them straight out. He hates being a shifter and would do anything to wipe us all off the face of the earth. His investors have no idea he's a murderer and neither do the Elders."

"What about Comastaz? How did he become hooked up with them?" Eli asked, a muscle ticking in his jaw.

Nivea shook her head. "I don't know. When you sent me the text with that letter from Richard to Slakeman, I had no idea what it meant. Until I saw the foundation's logo at the top of the page. One of the dead men at the cabin had a tattoo on his wrist. The tattoo is of a snake, winding its way around anything it gets close to. It's the logo for Richard's foundation. It was applied to all the children they were so-called helping, all of the ones they would threaten for the rest of their lives if they ever revealed they were Shadow Shifters."

A sharp pain coursed through her chest as she remembered seeing that same tattoo wrapping around her father's bared back, the night everything in Nivea's life had changed.

"When I was seventeen I found the pictures and a list of all the kids' names in his office. He branded all of them when they were brought over with that logo. I guess this guy was one of the few that managed to grow up."

"Yeah, he grew up and decided to get even," Eli said. "Maybe he was the one to call the meeting at the cabin in an attempt to expose the shifters to the Feds."

"That would have really pissed Richard off. He never wanted anyone to know about the shifters, never even accepted being one himself," she said.

Eli nodded, feeling like pieces to this puzzle were really starting to fall into place.

"Text your sister that we're on our way. I'll call for some backup to go with us. Try to keep her talking if you can, but tell her to be careful."

Nivea did as he said, didn't hesitate and didn't argue.

Nivea hated waiting.

Eli reached for her hand and held it. The fact that Ezra and the Sanchez brothers were standing in the truck stop parking lot looking at him only made him mildly uncomfortable. The deep, steadying breath Nivea took as a result of him holding her hand was enough to dismiss the male shifters altogether.

Amina hadn't sent another text, but Brayden had been able to tap into her phone's GPS.

"It's been hours since her last text," Nivea said, looking down at her phone again, then back up toward the road. "Maybe we should just go."

Eli shook his head, rubbing his thumb along the back of her hand. "We've been over this before. It makes much more sense for us to stay where we are considering Brayden's report that the phone has crossed from New York into New Jersey. They're heading south, so it's not smart for us to get on the road now. We're liable to pass them. We're going to wait until that signal stops and then we'll go to wherever that location is."

"What if she's not alive by then?" Nivea suggested, her worried gaze resting on his.

"She will be," he told her unequivocally. "She sounds way too much like you, strong and determined. Besides, if whoever has her wanted her dead, I'm pretty sure she wouldn't have had the opportunity to send those first few texts at all. And they wouldn't have bothered to take her cell phone with them after they'd killed her. When it's a hit, that's what they do—kill. And they don't take you and your phone with them when they leave."

"How do you know? Don't let me find out you're watching those true crime stories on TV, Eli." She gave him a withering smile and he squeezed her hand, loving her attempt to evoke humor in this situation.

"They've stopped in Maryland," Brayden announced. "The signal's been stable in one spot for the last twenty minutes so I think they've finally stopped."

Nivea's eyes widened and then she nodded. "They've stopped. Okay, we're going to rescue them from . . . who? I don't even know who has taken them," she said, looking up at Eli.

"Rogues maybe?" Eli replied.

"Why would rogues take them?" Brayden asked.

"Considering all that's been going on, I think it's safe to say everybody's a player in this game," Caleb added.

Ezra nodded. "That's what I really don't like about this situation. It's one thing to fight one enemy, but to have two or three coming at you at once?" He shook his head. "Definitely stacks the odds against us."

Eli rolled his head on his shoulders. "Not if they're all connected, which I'm almost positive they are."

"How are you so positive?" Ezra asked, giving Eli a concerned look.

Eli took a deep breath, still not ready to share the epiphany Baxter had laid on him with anybody else just yet. Especially since his gut instinct in this regard had nothing to do with any vision he'd received. Although, while they'd been riding to the truck stop, he had thought that a vision showing him where Nivea's sister was and who she was with would have been pretty damned convenient. But that would mean he was accepting what he'd been told about what he truly was. Eli wasn't ready to take that leap.

"Doesn't matter," he told Ezra. "I'm ready for whatever and I'm not scared, are you?"

"Not on your life," his twin replied.

"We're ready to rock 'n' roll," Aidan announced.

"We should get on the road so they don't have a lot of time to do whatever before we get there," Nivea told them.

She was already heading toward their truck. Eli decided to simply follow her.

"Got a bossy one there, huh, little brother?" Ezra said, clapping him on the shoulder as he walked by.

Caleb and Aidan both chuckled as they moved to their designated spots, while Brayden simply shook his head.

"I know how it feels, shifter females are a handful," he said, giving Eli a look of commiseration.

"Tell me about it," Eli replied, climbing into the backseat beside Nivea.

Twenty minutes later Brayden, who had been keeping his eyes glued to the map on his iPad, shouted an address. Aidan, who was driving, punched it into the SUV's GPS. Seconds later the younger shifter made a growling sound.

"What?" Caleb asked his brother.

"That address is deeded to Robert Slakeman too," Brayden told them.

"Like I said," Eli whispered. "It's all connected."

Chapter 17

"They're both here," Brayden said the moment he stepped out of the truck. "Rogues and hybrids. The stench is mixed and it's foul as shit."

Caleb and Aidan got out and sniffed the air, both frowning their agreement. Eli heard them from inside and scowled. He did not want her to be here, did not want her to go into that house and do what he knew would need to be done. But how could he tell her to stay behind? This was her family.

"Stay close to me," he told her instead.

"I'll make sure they're safe," she told him, as if to say she was going to do whatever she had to do regardless of what he said.

"Nivea, please," Eli attempted.

She shook her head, holding up a hand to stop his words. "This is my family, Eli. My sisters and my mother. I'm going to get them with or without you."

Her words burned through him like a torch and Eli gritted his teeth. There was no "without" him as far as he was concerned. He was not only going in there with her, but he was going to be on her like a second skin making sure she was safe, whether she liked it or not.

"Let the Sanchez brothers go up to the house first. They'll scope out the grounds, see what security we're dealing with," he told her.

She looked at him impatiently. "They'd better make it fast."

"Eli, can I see you a second?" Ezra called to Eli from outside.

"I'll knock when they're back," he told Nivea.

She nodded tightly and Eli moved in closer. He wanted to kiss her, to promise her this would be better and that once it was over he would . . . they would . . . what? Live happily ever after? Walk blissfully into the light of joining and be mates forevermore? What the hell was he going to say to her when all of this bullshit was over? More importantly, how was he ever going to walk away from her?

"Go," she whispered before looking down at her phone in her hand. "Just go."

He did as she said because if Ezra was interrupting him, it was for a good reason.

"Okay," his brother began the moment he was out in the early morning air. "Slakeman makes guns. He works with the military. Crowe is a Marine."

"Nivea's father was sending money to Comastaz and probably sending them shifters as well," Eli offered.

Ezra paused, lifted a brow, and Eli continued.

"He's been getting kids from the Gungi for years, selling them or killing them himself. Crowe couldn't get Shya and he used the one shifter he had in custody to make his first hybrids. We were wondering how he's been producing others. I think Cannon's been giving him those children."

"Sonofabitch!" Ezra cursed. "She's known this all along and she never said a word?"

His brother pointed toward the truck, his eyes blazing green with fury. Eli stood right in his face. They were the same height so they were eye to eye. "The Sanchez brothers and I followed the GPS origination signal that we lifted off the hybrids at the charity event. It was to another one of Slakeman's houses. In his office there was a letter from Cannon. *That's* how Nivea found out about her father's connection to Comastaz! And it was just a couple of weeks ago." Eli was only partially lying to his brother, but he felt like he had a good reason to. He had to protect Nivea.

"Then she should have told us a couple of weeks ago! Or you should have told us, Eli!" Ezra yelled back in his face.

"Why? So you could put her in a cell like you did her father? Hell no! She's not at fault here. She had reasons for what she did and I stand by her." No matter what, Eli thought.

"You stand by her lying to us, betraying us?" Ezra inquired angrily.

"Just like Dawn lied to you back in Sedona," Eli snapped back.

Ezra clamped his lips shut, fury still vibrating through him. But Eli knew the argument had ended. Dawn knew about the existence of the Shadows long before Ezra told her and she'd kept her mouth shut. She also knew that Crowe, her ex-boyfriend, was doing some type of developing with damiana at the Comastaz Labs. So there was no way his brother was going to stand in his face and even consider going after Nivea. No. Fucking. Way. And if he did, Eli was prepared to take him down.

"This is not over," Ezra told him. "Rome and Nick are going to be livid when they find out."

Eli still did not waver. "If they don't already know." When Ezra looked at him quizzically Eli continued, "They've been down there questioning Cannon more times than I can count and they never take either of us with them. You think Cannon's keeping his mouth closed? He's a worm, a shifter that has never been trained, never wanted to be any part of our tribe. I'll bet he's told them everything and Rome and Nick are just keeping it tight until they have a game plan ready. And if he hasn't, it doesn't matter, I'll tell Rome and Nick the same thing I just told you. I stand by Nivea."

Ezra shook his head. "Yeah, and being mated to you might be the only thing that saves her ass."

Eli didn't bother to tell Ezra that they weren't mated, that he simply understood why she'd done what she felt she needed to. He'd never tell them the reason she remained quiet, would never betray her that way.

"Nobody's guarding the outside," Caleb said, coming up behind Ezra. "There's an alarm system but I think they tried to yank it right out of the wall when they went in. I can see it hanging with wires exposed through the front door."

"So we can go in hot and go in now," Aidan suggested.

"We don't know where they are, Aidan," Brayden added. "Maybe we can have Nivea send her sister another text."

"No!" Eli said emphatically. "Enough of that. They're not driving now so they might see her texting, or they've probably tied her up and that's why she stopped texting in the first place. Let's just go in like Aidan said."

"He's right." Ezra sided with Eli, which was a slight surprise considering their most recent conversation. "We go in hard, Nivea can get to her sisters, and we can take those bastards dead or alive."

"Remember, a live one would be good," Eli started. "But don't hesitate to kill every motherfucker in there to get those women out safely."

When all the men nodded, Eli knocked on the back door of the truck and Nivea immediately came out.

"Let's go!" she said, moving quickly between all of the guys and heading up the small incline to the house.

"The rogue scent is stronger here," Ezra said, looking up at the deck that covered the entire length of the back of the house.

"We'll go in the front and handle the hybrids," Aidan announced.

The brothers ran around the other side of the house while Eli, Ezra, and Nivea stayed in the back.

"They aren't expecting us, not this soon anyway. We'll get in and get out," Eli announced. "Stay close to me."

The latter was directed to Nivea who didn't spare him a glance of agreement, making Eli think she didn't plan to do what he asked. No matter, Ezra was right behind Nivea, nodding to Eli. So the shifter took that as his cue. Lifting one arm up, he let the claws that had just extended dig into the house's siding. He did the same with the other arm and was soon scaling the side of the house, heading for the windows where lights were on. When he was at the top he hurled himself through the window, landing on his feet in the middle of an empty bedroom.

"They've been in here," he said, looking around and inhaling deeply.

"This way," Nivea yelled from where she stood already at the door and disappearing down a hallway.

Ezra shook his head as he moved past Eli. "Yeah, that's all on you, bro."

Eli frowned and followed them out. As he entered the hallway, he came to a stop right behind his brother. Standing just a few feet away, blocking any further access into the house, was a white Bengal tiger, teeth bared and ready to attack.

Ezra looked back over his shoulder at Eli. "Just like old times, huh?"

Eli shrugged. "We kicked their asses back then, we'll just have to do it again."

With that, both jaguars shifted and battled the *Lormenian* just as they had been taught in the Sierra Leone rain forest.

Nivea heard the growling and knew there was a battle going on behind her. With her heart pounding, she stood, conflicted for about two seconds before deciding that she needed to find her sisters and her mother. Eli and Ezra were well-trained. They could handle themselves until she was able to get back to help them. First and foremost, she needed to get to her family because none of them had been trained to fight rogues—or any other entity, for that matter.

As she followed their familiar scent, Nivea absolutely hated her father for denying all of them their heritage. Her sisters could shift and so could her mother but none of them had been taught any of the survival skills they needed to defend themselves against rogues or those damned hybrids. They'd act on instinct, Nivea hoped, and would at least shift into their cat form, but then what?

She ran, almost hopping down the steps to get to the room where she suspected they were. Their scent was too potent for them to be locked away, they were out in the open, right down this way. Moving through the downstairs of the large house, she came to a stop in the living room where four of the biggest, ugliest beasts she'd ever seen circled around her sisters and her mother.

"Whoa." Caleb extended an arm that landed right at Nivea's neck, blocking her from going any farther. "Stand back," he told her. "We got this."

Nivea swiped his arm out of her way. "This is my family, I've got this!" she yelled at him.

"Nivea!" Amina called to her. "Thank god you came!"

She couldn't see Amina's face, only heard her voice and saw between the gaps of the hybrid bodies that she was tied together with Serene and their mother. Without hesitation Nivea charged forward only to be lifted off the ground and turned away. As she cursed Caleb for interfering again, the hybrids moved.

Each of them came forward, as if a switch had just been turned on in their heads. They moved in perfect sync toward Nivea and Caleb. Aidan and Brayden came up behind them, extending an arm and latching onto a hybrid's neck with their claws. Caleb jumped forward, doing the same with the one closest to him. There was another and it was coming right at Nivea.

She knew how to kill them, but this one was much taller and wider than the others she'd seen. She had to get up close enough, high enough to sink her claws into its neck. Too late, he picked her up by the neck, pushing her back until she slammed into the wall, all the air in her lungs expelling in a quick whoosh that left her dizzy.

With futile efforts she swatted at the hybrid's arms but it was too strong, her blows going without any real impact. She lifted a knee and groaned when it only reached its lower chest. Her eyes were watering as he continued to choke her. She wanted to shift but wasn't sure she had enough air in her lungs to do so. When she felt herself falling forward she had only seconds to realize it was because Caleb and Brayden were attacking the hybrid at the legs from behind. The big bastard tilted back, taking Nivea down to the floor with it, still holding her by the neck. She'd just managed to come up on her knees, staring down into the ugly face of the hybrid. She was preparing to propel herself forward when the splash from its mucus guts pouring out slapped her in the face. The hands let go of her neck and Nivea fell backward. Climbing down off the hybrid quickly before it turned to ash she wiped at her eyes and headed to where she could see her sisters huddled in a corner.

She ran to them, yanking quickly at the chains that were wrapped around them. When Amina and Serene were free they both hugged her so tightly she stumbled back, tears streaming down her face and emotion welling in her chest. All that she'd done, all that she'd endured to keep them safe and this is how they finally end up, captured by hybrids and rogues, and for what?

"Why did they take you?" she asked immediately. "What did they say when they came to the house?"

Serene was shaking her head, crying inconsolably. Amina kept her arm wrapped around her as she replied, "Nothing. I mean, I didn't hear anything. When I sent you that first text it was after hearing Mom yelling at them. I think she let them in."

Nivea immediately looked to Michele Cannon who was wiping down the front of her wrinkled pantsuit as if this were just a bad fall.

"Did you let them in?" she asked, but the question was never answered since there was yelling from the other side of the room.

"We got one!" Aidan yelled. "The others are down. Get them out into the first SUV and we'll be right behind you."

Nivea still had questions for her mother but wasn't about to stand in this house a moment longer trying to get the answers. "Let's go!" she told them, pushing Amina and Serene in front of her, then reaching a hand out for her mother. Michele looked at her hand, then away, and moved quickly behind her two older daughters. Nivea didn't let it bother her, at least she didn't think she had. She ran quickly in front of them, opening the back door to the SUV she and Eli had ridden in together. She was just about to slam the door closed when Michele slipped back out, extending her hand and slapping Nivea across the face.

Eli's chest was heaving as he'd just finished loading the tranquilized rogue into the middle seat of the second SUV. He'd grabbed sweatpants and shoes out of one of the many duffle bags they always kept in the trucks just in case shifting became absolutely necessary. Only he and Ezra had shifted this time and Ezra had pulled on jeans and shoes as well. They were going to ride in this truck with the rogue, along with Caleb. Brayden and Aidan were going to drive the females. He'd been all set to climb in so they could get moving when out of the corner of his eye he saw a woman hit Nivea.

He was in motion instantly, hearing bits of the conversation.

"It's all your fault! You ungrateful brat!" Michele Cannon was saying, both of her hands going around Nivea's neck. "All we did for you, all we gave you and this is how you repay us! You're nothing but a backstabbing whore!"

Nivea had grabbed her mother's wrists, not having to use much of the strength Eli knew she possessed to push the woman back against the truck. She pulled her mother's hands away from her neck easily and stared into the woman's face.

"He's an animal," she told her in what to Eli sounded like a dangerously calm voice. "You chose to protect an animal over your own daughter."

"You're the animal!" Michele spat back. "Wanting to run around with that whole tribe, changing into beasts and walking on all fours. You never wanted to stay in the place we made for you, never wanted to be what we were."

"You are what I am!" Nivea yelled back. "You are a Shadow Shifter just like me. We share the same blood!"

Michele shook her head. "I don't share anything with you, ungrateful bitch!"

Michele lunged again but this time Nivea grabbed her arms, wrapping them behind the older woman and keeping her in a choke hold.

"How is refusing to be abused by your father being ungrateful?" Nivea asked her. "How can you stand here and say these horrible things to me after all I sacrificed, all I did to keep you and them protected!"

"Don't . . . need . . . your . . . kind of protection," Michele sputtered through the little bit of wind that Nivea was allowing to get through to her lungs. "Don't . . . need . . . you."

Nivea's entire body vibrated with those words, her eyes staring ahead, past Eli. She wasn't seeing but she was definitely hearing and she was steadily choking the life out of her mother.

"Let her go now," Eli said, coming around to stand beside Nivea. He tapped her arms. "Let her go, Nivea."

"I needed protection," she was saying. "I needed protection from him. My mother should have protected me."

"You're right," Eli said, still trying to unravel Nivea's hold on Michele. "You are absolutely right, she should have protected you."

"I always had to fend for myself, always had to do whatever was necessary to make myself happy," Nivea continued, her head shaking back and forth.

"Baby, don't do this," Eli pleaded. "Let her go, Nivea. Please."

Her arms began to shake from holding so tight and Michele's fighting began to cease.

"Nivea!" Eli yelled. "Let. Her. Go!"

He knew he was loud, knew that the fierce edge to his voice was enough to scare an entire forest of shifters. As for Nivea, she simply turned her head to face him, her eyes filled with tears that seemed to refuse to fall. "She didn't protect me."

Eli nodded. "I know, baby," he said slowly and caught Michele as Nivea abruptly let her go.

She walked back to the second truck without saying another word and without turning back to see if Michele lived or died.

Eli put Michele Cannon into the truck and made sure the woman was still breathing normally. The sisters had looked shocked by what had taken place and when they tried to assist their mother, she'd pulled away from them, shrinking into the corner of the seat. With a shake of his head, Eli slammed the door and walked to the second truck, wondering how Nivea was doing. How she'd been able to keep all this bottled up inside over the years without completely breaking.

They drove for about a half hour before Eli reached out a hand to touch Nivea's leg. She pulled away so abruptly he yanked his hand back as if he may have hurt her.

With a frown he tried something else. Turning sideways in the seat he looked at her, using a hand to smooth down the back of her head. She stiffened.

"Don't," she said simply.

"Listen, I know what you were feeling, Nivea."

She shook her head vehemently, her gaze still focused on the tinted window. "No. You don't."

"I do."

"No!" she yelled. "There's no way you can know how I feel because you've never endured what I did."

"You are right about that. I've never been abused by one parent and deserted by another. But Nivea, I do know about feeling helpless to stop the rage boiling inside. I know exactly how it feels to have shit happen to you that you don't deserve," he told her.

"But you got over it, right?" she asked. "You found some cure and you were better and your life moved on."

"No," he told her quietly. "You're wrong."

Eli inhaled deeply and let the breath out slowly.

"I'm not better. I pretend and I deny reality. But you, you've done a phenomenal job overcoming your past. You're a great guard and you're trustworthy and loyal. You are so much better than they are, Nivea."

"But I'm a part of them. I'm a part of the man that kills his own kind. Or now, is selling them to the highest bidder. For the last five hours I've been worried sick that the woman who would blame me for her perverted husband was going to be killed. I've spent all these years away from my sisters in order to protect them. I didn't send his ratchet ass to a human prison because I loved my sisters and my mother too much. What does that make me, Eli? How impossibly screwed up does that make me that I could let him get away with what he did?"

Eli moved across the seat, chancing the anger he could almost see emanating from her body, and choosing instead to try and soothe the hurt that was so evident in her voice. He wrapped an arm around her, tried to pull her against him. She didn't budge, but she didn't pull away again either.

"It makes you stronger and better than any of them, Nivea. It makes you the woman I'm damned proud to have standing beside me in battle."

She'd turned to him then, staring into his face so intently Eli thought she might see right through him.

"Right," she said quietly. "Thank you for saying that, Eli. Thank you very much."

Chapter 18

For the first time since she was seventeen years old Nivea Cannon was confused. As she sat on the edge of the bed in her room she wondered why she was here at Havenway. Why, with all that had happened to her, had she come here and trained to be a guard? She could have gone anywhere and done anything.

Still, leaning forward with her head hung low, she was unable to figure out why here, why with these people, and why on earth was all of this coming down on her now?

It had been two hours since they'd returned. She hadn't been able to get out of that truck fast enough. Her throat was raw from her heavy breathing because she'd felt like she was going to suffocate on the trip back. Eli was so close to her and saying so many things, she wanted to remember them all, to believe every word, and yet she couldn't.

She wouldn't. Ever again.

Once she'd been safely behind her closed bedroom door she'd convinced herself that she needed to shake off the self-pity and go check on her sisters, but that had been thwarted by another female that she wanted to put into a headlock.

"Orders are no visitors," Rayna told her with a smirk.

Nivea really hated this chick. For one, she looked at Eli like he was a piece of steak cooked just right and she couldn't wait to sink her teeth into him. Well, to be fair, she looked at most of the shifters around Havenway in the same manner. Tramp! And two, Nivea didn't trust her. She didn't like the glint in her cool blue eyes and that wasn't because she was a *Lormenian* either. Nivea was not prejudiced by any means. There was just something about her that screamed "watch your back" each time Nivea was in her presence. The fact that she'd managed to save Shya Delgado may have bought her some get-out-of-jail-forever tickets with Rome and Nick, but Nivea was still holding strong to her instincts.

"They're my sisters," she'd retorted, really not in the mood for this female today.

"That doesn't change my orders," Rayna insisted, folding her arms over breasts that were barely contained by the tight-ass shirt she wore.

"That's not the uniform," Nivea said without her usual calm. She'd been up for hours. A hybrid had tried to choke her out. She'd seen her sisters tied in chains and oh yeah, her mother had bitch slapped her and called her a whore. Yeah, today was really not her day.

"It's my uniform," Rayna fired back.

Nivea's fists clenched at her sides and then she exhaled slowly. "Look, just give me five minutes."

"I'll give you three to get your ass back to your room."

And that was it. Nivea was in her face, hands gripping the *Lormenian*'s shoulders as she pushed her out of the way. Rayna went along with the shove but put her leg out so Nivea stumbled, almost smashing her face into the door.

"Whoa, hold on. What's the problem here?" X appeared, pulling the females apart and directing his question to Nivea.

She heaved and pushed the hair she'd left hanging loose back from her face. "I want to see my sisters."

"You know the drill, Cannon. They're being debriefed," he told her.

"Then I should be in there."

X shook his head. "You should be in your room."

Nivea's lips went into a thin line, anger boiling just at the surface. She would respect X for the position he held but he might just get cussed out if he didn't hurry up and move away from that door.

"So I shouldn't be a part of my sisters' debriefing and I shouldn't have been a part of the meeting with all of you head honchos even though I'm personally involved in what's going on. I should just close myself in my room like a good little female."

"A good little bitch you mean," Rayna said from behind X.

Nivea didn't even bother to jump at her because she knew X wasn't going to let her punch the tramp in her face.

"It's protocol," X told her.

"You're lying," she fired back.

He sighed.

"Okay, it's Eli's call. He said he was going to come talk to you about everything that went down. He's probably waiting for you in your room now."

"Bullshit!" she yelled. "I don't have to sit around and wait for him like a good obedient—"

"Bitch, like I said," Rayna added.

"You!" X shouted over his shoulder. "You're relieved. Go. Now!"

Rayna didn't look at all bothered by the Lead Enforcer's reprimand, simply slunk her trashy self away, having the audacity to look over her shoulder at Nivea and smile. Nivea simply shook her head, rubbing her temples in the process.

"Look, X, I get it. I know the protocol, but I just want to make sure they're okay."

"They're fine. Ary checked both of them out and they've been given some food. Kalina and Caprise are talking to them now and I'm sure one of them will fill you in on what's being said. But for right now, you just need to go back to your room and sit tight."

He'd rubbed her shoulder as he said that, like a big brother. She figured it was the equivalent of patting her on the head. Deciding it just wasn't worth it to stand here and keep arguing with him, she simply turned away without saying another word.

Now in her room again she couldn't do anything but think and hate her thoughts and wonder why she was even having them in the first place. She'd come so far, had healed so much and yet, these past few weeks had felt like she'd gotten on the treadmill and run backward a kazillion miles. It was heartbreaking and she wanted to cry.

But she didn't.

She raged, she thought, she made her decision and when he knocked on her door, she didn't even move to let him in.

"Hi," Eli said when he finally used his override code to enter her room. She hated that he had the authority to do that.

She did not speak to him, did not lift her head. She just couldn't at the moment.

"Listen, Rome is going down to talk to Cannon again, to see if he'll give up who the buyer is. We were thinking it was Crowe but after checking the man's financials, it doesn't jibe. No way does he have the thousands of dollars that Cannon was being paid to deliver those shifters. There has to be a middleman."

Eli continued to talk and Nivea only half listened.

"It's possible the middleman could be a rogue. When

you told Kalina that you saw the tattoo your father used on one of the dead guys at the cabin, she contacted one of her cop friends in Cecil County and learned the names of the dead men. Of course they only recovered one body, the one with the tat had been removed. But there was a wallet with an ID at the scene that the cops were still searching. The name sounded familiar to Kalina so she ran it through the shifter database. It was Kegan Charles, brother of Darel Charles who was killed about a month ago. Darel was in deep with Sabar, if you remember. So we're really working the rogue being the third man angle."

He paused, took a deep breath, and wondered why she hadn't spoken. Nivea looked up then, staring directly at him.

"Do you want my applause?" she asked him. "Or should I simply be grateful?"

He actually looked perplexed. "What?"

Nivea came to her feet, confidence surging through her bloodstream like a drug.

"Do you want me to thank you for coming to give me this information? For allowing me to sleep in your bed, to receive your sexual prowess, when you know damned well you never intended to mate me?"

The look of surprise turned to annoyance and then to muted anger, all in the span of about ten seconds. Nivea almost smiled with amusement.

"I don't understand," he said finally. "I thought we were talking about your father and how he's connected to what's going on with us."

Nivea shook her head. "No," she told him. "I know my father is a betraying asshole and that everything he's done his entire life has led him and his family to this exact point in their lives. But thank you so much for relaying the highlights from today's meeting to me. Even though none of that comes close to talking about what's going on with us."

Eli took a step back, literally and physically. She watched him brace himself, legs spread apart, muscled arms coming up to cross over that broad and well-defined chest. He had the perfect body—slim waist, washboard abs, thick bulging muscles in his chest, biceps, and thighs. She could actually visualize him naked and aroused standing there in front of her. But she didn't. Instead she saw the shifter that had taunted her with his presence, albeit not intentionally, for more years than she could count.

Fortunately, for Nivea, that time was over.

"Okay, you're right. I've been giving this some thought." He took a deep breath and released it slowly, as if whatever he was about to say was so heavy he had to prepare himself to say it. "Why don't you just pack up all your stuff and move into my room?"

For a moment Nivea didn't think she'd heard him correctly and apparently her silence—and most likely odd glare—signaled him to expand on his little statement.

"I mean, if we're sleeping together—and since everybody knows we're sleeping together—then we might as well do it officially."

She nodded slightly. "And moving all my things to your room is making our sleeping arrangement official?"

"Yes," he said with another sigh as if this was truly hard for him. "I made it very clear to Rome and everyone else that we are together. They all know where we stand now," he continued.

Nivea narrowed her eyes at Eli, resisting the urge she had to run over and swat at him with her clawed hand. The cat inside hissed because that's precisely what it wanted to do.

"They all know that you're sleeping with me."

Now he looked exasperated, which Nivea thought was good. At least he was showing some emotion where they were concerned.

"Last time I checked we were sleeping with each other, Nivea. What is your problem? I thought this was what you wanted?"

And that was it, the proverbial straw that broke, yada, yada, yada. . . . Nivea was moving before she could think better of it. Her cat was pressing forward, taking this seemingly human situation in its own hands. With a pointed finger she jabbed directly into the center of Eli's chest.

"You are an idiot!" she yelled into his face. "We were not sleeping with each other, asshole. I was making love to the shifter I thought was my mate! Now you go and tell everybody that we're sleeping together and then come in here with your chest all poked out, spoon feeding me the information you want me to have, when you want me to have it like you're doing me some big ol' favor. Well, I've got news for you, Eli Preston. I don't need any of this and I don't need you!"

Her chest heaved, her hand wanted to shake but she willed it not to. Eli hadn't moved, the bastard. He was still standing perfectly still, staring down at her through those stupid-ass shades that she wanted to reach up and grab. The moment she tried, he thwarted the effort by gripping her wrist when her fingers were a couple of inches away from his glasses.

"Don't," he said solemnly.

She yanked away from him then, taking a step back to steady her breathing. "That's right. Don't touch Eli's precious glasses. Don't ask Eli to share any piece of himself with you that's beyond the physical. Don't expect him to get past his big dark past and move into a blissful future with you of all people, Nivea, because that's never going to happen."

He opened his mouth to say something and Nivea's hand flew up into the air to stop him. "Oh no, don't you dare," she said. "Don't you dare try to say something that you think will make this better. It will probably only piss me off to the point where I'm ready to literally knock your head off!"

She was glaring at him now, knowing full well that her cat's eyes were visible, and she didn't give a damn.

"I want you and your arrogant words and thoughts to get the hell out of my room. And if you think of coming back here without offering . . ." Her words trailed off. "No, Eli. No. Don't you ever think about coming back here or to me again. Ever!"

There was nothing he could offer, Nivea realized with a start. Nothing that Eli Preston was willing to give her that would fill the void that she'd just concluded might never go away.

That night Eli lay on his cot staring up at the ceiling until his eyes closed of their own volition. In an instant he was back in the Sierra Leone rain forest, the evening air thick with humidity beneath its thick canopy. The hut he and Ezra shared was unusually quiet and when he looked over expecting to see his brother in the bed beside him, it was instead the naked body of a female that had him sitting straight up. Breathing heavily he let his feet hit the matted floor, sweat already pouring from his mostly nude body. For endless moments he sat on the side of that cot staring at her curvaceous backside, the straight spinal cord, and long legs. Hair, dark in the dimness of the room, fell like a scarf onto the pillow. Up, down, in, and out, slowly, measured, she breathed.

When staring did not seem to be getting him anywhere and fear snaked around his neck like a noose, Eli stood. Deep inside like a pulse, the need beat slowly at first, then more persistently as he continued to watch her. It burned and when he swallowed, it felt like acid pouring over an open wound. It was so painful to want this way and to not be able to possess.

Acacia was not his. She was mated and nothing, not even the intriguing *Topètenia* twins were going to change that. Fine, he'd thought with a clench of his fists. That was the way it had to be.

Leanne was sweet and soft and accommodating, until he told her there would be no commitment. No marriage and no damned house with a picket fence to hold their children—their half-breed children. There was no future there for Eli because Leanne was a human and his gut instinct told him that humans would never understand or tolerate a Shadow Shifter. He'd been as honest with her as he could about his limitations and in the end, that honesty had killed her.

Just as the brutal honesty he'd had to face with Acacia had led to the outpouring of anger that had controlled him, forcing him and Ezra to kill her.

Now there was Nivea . . . no, he thought. Just no.

Eli turned away from the female lying on the other cot. Just as he'd done years ago after Leanne's death. He was finished with females, done with all those trappings that mating and joining and loving entailed. It just wasn't for him. It couldn't be.

And yet . . .

"Eli," she called to him, her voice like a whisper on the dew-scented air.

"Come back to me, Eli."

He was shaking his head as the words were repeated. She begged, she needed. That burning inside him ceased, as if a slow, cool trickle had tempered it.

"Eli."

Each time she spoke his name something inside him shifted. His cat reared up eagerly, intrigued by the voice, the calling. That dark pain that had been as steady a part of him as breathing lessened, until he had to completely focus on it to identify its presence. And the cool, the soothing, the need swirled around like a building storm.

When she called his name again he turned, his eyes opened wide—no sunglasses—ready and waiting to see, to reach out and maybe this time, just maybe to hold onto.

But when he looked down she'd turned onto her back and was staring up at him. Her eyes a soft brown, her cheekbones high, chin stubborn. Her hair was free, unlike the ponytail she wore when in battle. She lifted her arms to him, the scar from when Rimas had stabbed her in the shoulder long gone. And she called to him again, "Eli."

"Nivea," he whispered a split second before noticing the necklace.

Its band was a circle of pure gold. At the center was a cascade of quartz pieces surrounding a clear yellow orb like a halo. No, Eli thought with a gasp, an eye—a jaguar's eye.

"Boden," he whispered, his gaze glued to the necklace. "Boden's joining necklace for Acacia."

With a start, face damp, chest heaving, Eli sat straight up in his bed in his room at Havenway. He stared over to his dresser where he'd put the box that had been mailed to him at his shop.

He picked up the necklace, felt its heat in his palms as he held it, as if it were alive. It wasn't and neither was the one it had been meant for. With a frown he realized that's what all of this had been about.

Boden was sending him a personal message. The conniving bastard had been planning this moment, this revenge for his mate's death, all along. And now Eli would have to come full circle. He would not return physically to the place and time that had changed his life forever, but everything that had happened in the Sierra Leone rain forest was about to land right at his doorstep. He was finally going to have to deal with his past head-on, and that was just fine. If Boden wanted to try and take a piece of him, Eli was more than willing to oblige the exiled shifter. But he was certain that Boden had no idea what he was in for . . . and for that matter, neither did the rest of the Shadow Shifters.

Chapter 19

"Women," Rome said as he leaned forward, placing the phone receiver into its cradle before easing back into his burgundy leather office chair. "Female shifters, I should say, are something else."

Eli, who had been standing at the window looking down onto the streets of downtown D.C., seeing the people and cars milling about, turned slowly at the sound of his Leader's voice.

"I guess it's a good thing shifter pregnancies do not last as long as human ones," Eli replied, very uneasy talking to Rome about his mate.

Rome nodded, a smile that Eli didn't see often ghosting his face. "Twelve to eighteen weeks," he said. "Well, she's already five weeks along so more like seven to thirteen weeks to go."

The usually composed and reticent Assembly Leader clasped his hands, released them, and then used one to smooth down his goatee. He rubbed both hands down his thighs, then looked up at Eli as if just remembering he wasn't in the room alone.

"It's not all that bad, you know," Rome told him.

"What isn't? Being a pregnant female or being the mate that's waiting for said pregnant female to give birth?" He chuckled and slipped his hands into his pockets.

Eli wasn't wearing his normal guard uniform. Whenever Rome went into the office or to court, Eli wore dress slacks and a button-down shirt and tie so that he appeared to be more of a colleague than a bodyguard. Today it was all gray, a color that signified his mood. Still, he had a job to do and he planned to do it no matter how he was feeling.

"Being mated," Rome said seriously.

Eli didn't reply. He didn't know what Rome expected him to say, or what he was comfortable revealing. In the past few days he'd come to the conclusion that there was just too much that wasn't a certainty in his life and he wasn't pleased by that fact.

"You know, Shadow Shifters are born to mate. And they mate for life," Rome told him as if Eli didn't already know this part of their history.

"Like Boden and Acacia," he said without really meaning to. Ever since the dream, no, the vision where Nivea was wearing Acacia's joining necklace, Eli had been thinking a lot about that particular shifter couple.

Rome nodded. "That was an unlikely pairing, I admit. But once that connection is made there's really no breaking it. Teodoro tried and it ended badly."

"It hasn't ended," Eli snapped. "That motherfucker is here now looking for some measure of revenge."

Rome held up a hand, his elbow now resting on the desk. "Whoa, let's not get offtrack here. Boden is back and it's to bring his own brand of hell and damnation to all of the Shadows. Because he believes we all betrayed him and conspired to have him murdered. Don't think for one minute that his mission is solely aimed at you or Ezra."

Eli sighed, shaking his head. "Nah, not solely, Rome.

But he's gunning for us too. How else do you explain him sending me that necklace?"

The morning after the vision, Eli had gone straight to Ezra's room with the necklace in hand. His brother had taken the news a lot better than Eli had, possibly because Dawn had been sitting right beside him, her hand on his thigh while he held the necklace in his hands. Eli had unsuccessfully tried to ignore that little show of support. An hour later the twins had stood in front of Rome, Nick, and X, giving them a rundown of how what happened in the Sierra Leone rain forest connected to the necklace and verified Boden's reappearance. He was the only one who would have had possession of the necklace he'd intended to give his mate the night of their joining—the night that Teodoro had Boden taken away.

"Yes, he wants a piece of you and Ezra because you dared to touch his mate," Rome continued slowly. "That's precisely the point I'm trying to make to you about shifters and their mating, Eli. It's not something you can make go away or attempt to ignore."

"On the mating level, this has nothing to do with me," Eli said, knowing full well how absolutely wrong that statement was.

Rome simply stared at him until Eli found himself dropping into one of the guest chairs across from Rome's desk and resting his elbows on his gaped thighs. "Look, I know what my limitations are. I know why I'm here and what my mission is. That's what's important." He didn't look up at the Assembly Leader, didn't want to see the look of disbelief he figured the shifter would have.

"Your mate is important, Eli. That's what Nivea was trying to make you see." Rome gave a little chuckle then. "I have to admit, it's been kind of entertaining watching her give you and every other male shifter at Havenway a cold shoulder the likes of which shifters living in Siberia wouldn't be able to stand. She's been one angry cat lately."

"Tell me about it," Eli said. She'd been angry and he'd been lonelier than he'd ever imagined he could be.

"But it's because she sees so clearly what you allow to be blurred. I heard her tell Kalina she'd like to take your shades and ram them down your throat since you depend on them so much to hide who you really are and what you're really feeling. Even though I thought that was a bit drastic, I trembled at the notion that she would actually do it if given the opportunity." Rome sighed. "You hurt her, man. You hurt her pretty bad."

Eli cursed, slamming his back against the chair and looking to Rome. "I didn't mean to. The one thing that's been constant and true in my mind is that I never wanted to hurt her. There's nothing I wouldn't do to keep her from ever suffering again. Only the grace of some higher deity is keeping Richard Cannon alive and breathing in that cell."

"I hear you," Rome said with a nod. "But none of those words are what Nivea wants to hear, and I can guarantee you that none of them will ease the pain she's enduring right now."

"She's reunited with her sisters. I see them going out to dinner and shopping and whatever else they do all the time now."

"You know everything they're doing, Eli. Don't try to fool me. You're watching her more closely now than you have in the last few months."

Eli didn't speak.

"Yeah, I know you assigned Prince and Naz to guard her whenever she wasn't out in the field with you, which has been less than I would like since you're still responsible for her continued training."

Eli was about to say something but Rome stood from his chair, raising a brow that silenced him.

"What I'm saying to you is coming from the man, Eli. Not your Leader or boss or any of that crap. I'm talking to you man to man, shifter to shifter, because over these past years you and Ezra have become a part of my family." Rome had circled the desk and now leaned against its edge as he stared squarely at Eli. "Accept it. Go to her on your knees begging she forgive you for being an ignorant ass and claim her. Claim your mate and make it known to the entire tribe that she belongs to you. Because if you don't . . ." Rome paused. "Just do it, man, because it's the right thing to do and because it's painfully obvious how much turmoil you're suffering by being apart from her."

"You don't understand," Eli started to say.

Rome leaned forward, clapping a hand on his shoulder. "I understand completely about thinking you're unworthy and doubting what your true destiny is. I fought my own for years. So I know firsthand just how futile it is. Embrace what was meant to be and get ready to have your mate fight this war by your side. We're all going to need every defense we can muster and love is a much stronger one than weapons."

Sure, Rome's words sounded good, they didn't call him the Lethal Litigator for nothing. The man could deliver closing arguments that changed every mind on a jury when he needed to. And when necessary he stood in front of the Assembly of Stateside Elders and representatives from the Gungi and told them how he was going to run his division of the shifters.

That's what he'd just done with Eli. He'd laid it all out so simply and so tight that Eli couldn't figure out how to swivel around anything he'd said. He'd known Rome's words were right, but that didn't make doing what the Leader said any easier.

Luckily for Eli, there was a hurried knock at Rome's office door before it flew open, a very excited Thelma, Rome's secretary, running inside.

"Mr. Reynolds, something's happened," she said, one hand still holding the doorknob, the other fluttering at her neck. "Security came up and said they want to lock down the building. They've called the police and animal control."

"Wait a minute," Rome said to her as he walked to where she stood. "What are you talking about?"

"There's something . . . I mean, a thing . . . or I don't know, sir. I just came back from lunch and this van pulled up and soldiers got out and dropped this big . . . animal. There's blood, oh my, so much blood," Thelma finished and made a sound that said she needed to be taken to the restroom quickly before she lost her lunch.

"Okay, fine. I'll handle it. You go on and get yourself together," Rome told her. "Don't leave this floor, Thelma. I want this building locked down."

Eli was already up when his cell phone vibrated on his hip. Yanking it out of the holder quickly he answered, "Yeah?"

"We've got a problem," Aidan said. "There's a dead cougar in front of the police station."

"What?" Eli yelled into the phone, catching Rome's gaze as he pulled out his own phone to call building security. "Yeah," Eli continued. "We've got something here too."

In seconds Nick was in Rome's office. "What the hell is going on?"

"Aidan says there's a cougar in front of the police station," Eli told them.

"Let's get downstairs and see what the hell's out front," Rome said, moving past both of them.

Ezra stood to the rear of the elevator, Eli directly in front, blocking anyone else from boarding, while Nick and

Rome stood side by side between them. They rode down in silence and walked out to utter pandemonium. There were people, other tenants of the building milling about, crowding the front foyer and blocking the view of the glass-fronted walls.

Nick yanked one of the security guards nearly off his feet, yelling into the man's face, "Get them the hell out of here!"

The man whistled for his coworkers, who immediately began shuttling the people to the back of the floor, away from the doors.

"We locked the doors, sir. We didn't want people rushing in from outside and we didn't want that thing in here," another guard said, looking back at the glass with disgust.

Rome barely acknowledged him but continued on to the glass doors, saying forcefully, "Unlock it."

The guard didn't move.

Then Rome yelled, "Now!"

The security guard's body literally shook as he moved to the doors, going down on one knee to insert his key into the lock and disengaging it. The door opened and screams and sirens sounded from the outside. Rome stepped out first, Nick right on his heels. Eli and Ezra came through the adjoining door, both standing with their backs to the sidewalk as Rome and Nick bent down to look at what was lying on the sidewalk in front of their building.

"Dammit!" Rome cursed.

"What the fucking hell is this?" Nick added as he pulled back the rest of the tarp that the dead cat was lying in.

Blood marred the sidewalk, its acrid stench rising up and floating on the cool day's breeze. Ezra cursed under his breath while Eli clenched his teeth. It was a shifter. Its head and claws had already changed to that of a jaguar while the rest of its human body, still garbed in the navy blue guard uniform, signified he was one of theirs.

"Who did this?" Nick was still yelling. "I want to know right now who left this here!"

Rome stood after pulling the tarp over the shifter. "Get a team in here to clean this up right away," he told Ezra. "Eli, you get the truck and meet me in the garage in ten minutes. We're going to see what other little presents have been left for us."

By the time Rome and Nick climbed into the back of the SUV, Eli had more bad news.

"A tiger was left at the hospital. Papplin had it put in a body bag and taken to the morgue. He's waiting for X to come and pick it up."

Nick slammed a fist into the seat in front of him, while Rome remained silent.

"What else?" the Assembly Leader asked.

Eli replied, "They were each one of our guards."

"This is a state-of-the-art facility," Kalina said to Priya as she sat on the caramel-colored leather couch on the other side of Priya's office.

"I know," Priya replied, sitting back in the matching chair positioned to the right of where Kalina sat. "Your husband sure knows how to design a headquarters."

They were at the brand-new Assembly Headquarters located in Prince George's County, Maryland. It was a fifteen-story building constructed out of steel and glass, rising into the sky with its innovative design and slick contemporary décor. Priya's office was a calm and soothing range of burgundy and beige, leather and marble. Everything that represented the confidence and unequivocal reign of the Stateside Assembly.

The fact that these two females were sitting with their feet up on the glass-topped coffee table having a relaxed conversation wasn't exactly the type of business that was meant for this office, but she was the First Female; she could do whatever she wanted. And what she wanted most right now was to talk about becoming a mother.

Rubbing her hand over the belly that just five weeks ago was flat as a board but now sported a nice round bump, Kalina looked down and sighed. "I cannot believe I'm doing this," she told Priya. "I never wanted to have children before."

Priya looked over at her quizzically. "Really? I would have thought you and Rome were dying to start a family, what with the way you both dote on Shya."

Kalina shook her head. "I was an orphan and I didn't see myself having a committed relationship. I always knew I didn't want to bring a child into this world without having something rock solid to offer him or her."

"And now you've got that," Priya said. "You've got it all, Mrs. Roman Reynolds. And I know plenty of women who would line up for the chance to walk in your shoes."

She shrugged. "That's because they don't really know what it's like. I'm a shape shifter about to give birth to her first child in about thirteen weeks. I have no idea how to be a mother to a little boy or girl, let alone a shifter girl or boy. And that's not saying anything about the situation we find ourselves in now." She looked over to Priya then and said honestly, "I don't know how this is going to turn out for us. So why would I pick now to become pregnant? Why would I want to bring another life into this turmoil?"

Priya stood, going to sit beside Kalina on the couch, taking the First Female's hands into hers. They hadn't known each other that long, but Kalina had taken a quick liking to Priya Drake. It was most likely because Priya was just like Kalina used to be, career-focused and tenacious. Neither of them had thought they'd find love and certainly not with a shape shifter, but here they were.

"You and Rome are doing what is natural for humans or any other species. As for the timing, well, that's never ideal and nobody could have foreseen Crowe's hybrids or Boden's plan of revenge," Priya said. "Besides, I have complete faith that the Shadows will come out on top and dispel all the evil that's currently swirling around you . . . us," she corrected. "It's all going to come to a head soon and blow over just as quickly."

Kalina was about to agree, albeit still with her own inner misgivings, and hug Priya for her kindness when the door to Priya's office was thrust open and Jax came running in.

"Rome wants you back at Havenway, now!" he told her, reaching for her to take his hand so he could help her up off the chair.

"What's going on?" Priya asked instantly. "What happened?"

On the desk her cell phone rang. Jax looked at her. "Answer it and you'll be filled in."

He took Kalina's hand as she stood up, staring at him. "Tell me, Jax."

"Let's get you to the truck and I'll tell you what I know."

She nodded, knowing better than to stand there wasting time arguing.

"Okay, let's go," she said, grabbing her purse.

Within fifteen minutes Kalina was whisked from the office on the sixth floor, down to the parking garage, and into the back of the black Suburban she always traveled in with Jax. She was snapping her seat belt when Jax climbed in from the other side, talking as he put on his seat belt. By the time he'd given her the rundown of what had been happening while she sat languishing in the gorgeous headquarters offices, she was speechless.

"He murdered shifters and left them out in the open for anyone to see," she said quietly.

"He wrapped them up, but people on the street saw the heads and the blood, and news crews are all over the place.

Traffic's going to be rough getting out of the city, but Rome wants you safe so that's what we're going to do."

"I was safe at headquarters. We could have just stayed there until things calmed down." *If* things calmed down, she thought as she looked out the tinted window.

"No. He wants you home and I think that's best too. Don't worry, we're going to get you there," Jax told her.

But Kalina wasn't so sure. She had a sour taste at the back of her throat and the baby that had been moving steadily inside of her all day had ceased. Her hand was firmly planted on her stomach, moving of its own volition in an attempt to coax and help calm her young, but it wasn't working, she knew. Her heart was beating faster with every movement of the SUV. Beside her she heard Jax taking a call and giving their coordinates. He would either be talking to Rome personally or to one of the guards at the command station at Havenway. They would be giving the best traffic options to get her home as soon as possible.

Home, she thought as they passed cars quickly. Their driver had taken the shoulder of the road and was passing the stalled traffic completely, the SUV going much faster than what she thought was the speed limit.

Sweat had begun to trickle down the back of her neck. She leaned forward to tap on the privacy divider to tell Marc, the driver, to turn up the air when out of the corner of her eye, she noticed another SUV coming up beside them. It was also black with tinted windows so she couldn't see through them, but at that very moment the baby inside of her kicked so violently that Kalina slid off the seat, the belt tightening to painful proportions around her waist. Then there was a loud crash. The SUV was turning over and over and over and Kalina was holding her stomach. She prayed and whispered Rome's name.

* * *

With confident strides Nivea walked past the two guards at the entrance to the holding cells where both of her parents were now being kept. It had been days since what she now called her "aha" moment—when she'd realized that both her parents were assholes and the man she loved was incapable of loving her in return. Each time she'd heard about that special moment on television or via online personalities, it had represented a turning point in one's life, a new beginning or some other crap. For Nivea, it had just been a wake-up call. One which she'd answered and was now ready to put behind her.

"Five minutes," Sal, the guard at the first door said to her, his bushy brows moving as he spoke.

He was a *Croesteriia* shifter—a cheetah—but nobody would have known it by the thick build of his body. When he shifted into the long, sleek cat, nothing gave him away except the speed he also maintained in his human form. That's probably why he was placed at this door, just in case Michele Cannon tried to escape as her husband had the day before.

Sal and the other guards were still pissed as hell that Richard Cannon had been able to dig his way out of that concrete room. The fact that huge blocks of the wall had been cut away, as if someone with a circular saw had gone in and given the guy a helping hand, wasn't sitting well with the guards or the Assembly Leader.

When they'd come to tell Nivea she'd been just returning from being in the field, once again searching for Agent Wilson with Caprise and her personal guard, Tobias. Nick had looked as if he wanted to accuse Nivea of helping her father escape, but Ezra—to her shock—had been the first to remind them that Nivea had been out all day. Caprise and Tobias had verified her alibi and the Lead Enforcer had no choice but to back down from accusing her. Nivea had been relieved because the last battle she felt like fighting at that moment was with the shifter leadership.

Instead, she'd quickly made her way down to the doubly secure room they were holding her mother in. She knew that should Michele try to escape, Sal and the other guards had been instructed to kill if necessary. She wasn't going to overthink the fact that it didn't evoke any emotion in her either way.

"That's all I'll need," she told Sal and waited while he turned his back to her, punching in the code to unlock the door.

Of course they wouldn't tell her the code, even though she'd sworn many times that she had never helped her parents do anything against the shifters and wasn't about to start now.

When she walked into the room, Nivea took a deep breath and let it out slowly. Her mother's scent, familiar and slightly heartbreaking, filled the small area. There was a table in the corner with a lamp, but it was not switched on. In another corner there was a tray where Michele had received her lunch, but she had not touched it.

"Bitch." The word was hissed through clenched teeth.

Flecks of spittle peppered the side of Nivea's face as Michele stood right next to her to the left. Nivea didn't even turn to face her, but walked deeper into the room, stopping just before meeting the wall on the opposite side.

"Maybe that's what you should have named me since that is what you believe I am," she said, now looking at the tall, frail woman.

She wore a white jumpsuit that was fitted with electrical fibers that would deliver instant shocks to her body should another escape be attempted. Around her neck was a solid lead necklace equipped with a GPS tracking system and steel-reinforced layers so that if Michele thought to shift into a jaguar, she would choke to death before the change was complete. Her hair was a wild halo around her mocha-brown face, hands fisting at her sides.

"You were always ungrateful no matter what we tried to do for you. I hate you!" she yelled vehemently.

"Do you hate me or yourself?" Nivea asked her. "Because of all those nights you had to lie in that big comfortable bed, in the lavish penthouse you liked to brag so often about, while your husband was down the hall doing heinous things to your youngest daughter? That ranks right up there with something to hate yourself for.

"Or maybe, it's because you helped him transport hundreds of children and then watched as he facilitated their demise. You killed shifters, some probably from the same bloodline as your own. Again, that's a heavy burden to bear and I can easily see how one would hate herself for participating in such acts.

"Or," Nivea continued, her voice growing edgier with every word. "You could be hating yourself for being so gullible and eventually expendable. Did you know he escaped and left you here to rot, or to be killed, whichever comes first?"

"You think you're so smart. Think you are so high and mighty but they don't give a damn about you here either!" Michele spat, taking a step closer to Nivea. "Nobody cares about you, they just let you stay to do their dirty work. They knew all along who and what you were. A whore and a backstabber."

Michele lunged at Nivea and she was ready. Stepping to the side, she let her mother tumble across the floor, falling into the wall. Before she could turn around she knew Michele would try again, so Nivea moved quickly, wrapping her arms around her mother's neck, pulling her body back against hers as she squeezed. The brace around her neck was thick and Nivea felt it pressing into the inside of her arm as she continued to tighten her grip on her mother's neck. In an instant the weight of a heavy realization hit her.

She could kill Michele Cannon. With all the distaste and disappointment for what she'd done and what she'd allowed over the years, Nivea could kill her and walk right out of this room as if she'd dispatched any other enemy. After all, that's what she'd been trained to do.

With a quick motion she released her and Michele stumbled around, finally standing up straight to taunt her daughter once again.

"You can't even do that right," Michele said viciously. "Nothing you do will ever amount to anything. You will always be a complete failure. No man will want to touch you either because you're disgusting to have wanted your own father in your bed."

Nivea reacted instantly, her arm extending, fist landing against Michele's jaw, the woman's head snapping back from the assault.

"You are the bitch!" Nivea told her. "You never knew how to be a mother and instead of owning up to your faults, you tried to make us feel like the failure was ours. You're no better than him, and believe me when I say both of you will rot in hell for what you've done."

Michele made a move like she wanted to charge Nivea again, her sharp jaguar's teeth and claws bared. Nivea simply shook her head at the pitiful sight.

"I didn't kill you once," Nivea said, her voice deadly calm. "But let's be perfectly clear, that is the only chance you'll ever get."

Michele growled loudly, her arms lifting, claws bared just before her entire body trembled with the bolts of electricity soaring through her. Nivea turned to look at the door that was still closed. Had someone been watching or had Michele's actions activated something? The woman fell to the floor, still convulsing, but Nivea turned away.

She didn't give a rat's ass what was happening to her mother. But more so because there was a weird feeling assailing her at the same time. She walked to the door, opened it, and walked right past Sal without a word. Inside her cat was up, its eyes trained via Nivea's human ones on something straight ahead. She was moving but she had no idea where she was going or why she needed to get there so quickly. All she knew for certain was the scent that filled her nostrils, the warmth that coated her body, and the warning that her cat was sending was loud and clear.

Something had happened to Eli.

Chapter 20

Eli had called her more than a dozen times. Since the moment he'd raced through the garage to get the SUV he'd been trying to get in contact with Nivea. She wasn't responding.

There were three dead guards, all in uniform, all dumped at locations that either a human or a shifter were sure to find them. The thought that there would be more, that Nivea could be . . . he held the phone tightly in his hand, pressing the speed dial one more time. As it rang insistently in his ear, Eli closed his eyes. He tried to concentrate on his breathing, tried to focus on the smidgen of light he could see. It was shining amidst the dark and he knew what it was now, knew who it represented in his life. Each time he dialed her number he was reaching for that light and it was slowly diminishing, until the moment his chest constricted with the possibilities.

He could not see Nivea. No vision appeared and he wanted to curse whatever was inside him, whatever he was truly supposed to be. If it was a Seer, how come he couldn't see the one thing he needed desperately to see right now?

How come he couldn't find her wherever she was in this world to ensure that she was safe?

Ezra was speeding down the highway, trying his damnedest to get them back to Havenway as soon as possible. There'd been reports of suspicious deaths interrupting the radio stations and Ezra had finally turned it off, while in the backseat Rome and Nick kept an angry silence.

Eli was just about to dial Nivea's number again when his phone rang instead. "Yeah?" he answered, instantly hoping . . .

He turned in his seat the moment the voice in his ear began talking, his gaze connecting with Rome's.

"Fuck!" Eli cursed.

Rome sat forward, his hands gripping the leather-backed seats in front of him.

"Kalina?" he asked.

Eli was moving the phone slowly from his ear as he said, "There's been an accident."

Havenway's side doors burst open and Caleb Sanchez carried Kalina's unconscious body inside. Ary and her newest assistant, Lucas, the teenager that had come from the Gungi with her almost a year ago, were waiting right there dressed in scrubs with a gurney between them.

"I keep talking to her but she's not responding," Caleb yelled.

Lucas helped him get Kalina's bloody body situated on the stretcher, while Ary looked down in concern.

Nivea rounded the corner having broken into a run, the anxiety centered in her chest so potent. The second she picked up the scent of blood she thought of Eli and ran faster, only to stop short at the sight of the First Female lying on the stark white sheets. Blood streaked her face and down the front of the yellow blouse she'd worn. But there was more on her legs, the beige tights almost completely covered with it, her brown suede skirt twisted around her waist.

"Kalina," Nivea whispered.

"Let's get her to the medical center, quickly!" Ary yelled.

"Jax and the driver are hurt too. They're coming in the other truck," Caleb told Ary who looked around.

She wasn't panicking, not just yet, but with others milling about, shocked silence registering on her face, the *curandera* needed to act fast.

"Nivea, you come with me. Caleb, you stay here and wait for the others. Lucas, you go get another stretcher, and somebody page Papplin!" Ary instructed.

Nivea came around to the opposite side of the bed and helped Ary push it through the crowd spreading out before them. They moved quickly, running alongside the bed until they were finally at the medical center.

"Get those clothes off her while I check her vitals," Ary instructed.

Nivea moved, taking off the First Female's riding boots and tights, then her skirt, all the while her hands were shaking at the blood and the possibilities. In her mind she wished for saving mercies, that this woman who had been so strong and so nice to all the female shifters at Havenway would live. And not only her, but the baby as well.

The first child of the Assembly Leader. With emotion clogging her throat, Nivea moved slowly, using the scissors to cut the blouse away from Kalina's chest. She tried like hell not to look down at her stomach, at the pouch where the baby should be growing and breathing.

"She's lost a lot of blood, I just need to figure out where it's coming from so I can stop it," Ary was saying.

Nivea inhaled deeply and let the breath out as she looked down at Kalina, studying every part of her but not thinking about the baby or the hurt that Rome would endure if she did not live.

"There's a head wound," she said. "On this side, right here." She pointed and Ary hurried around to her side of the table.

"Superficial, she probably banged it against the window or something when the truck flipped over," Ary said. "I'll need to stitch it but that's not where all this blood is coming from."

"Flipped over?" Nivea repeated.

"Yeah, five times, across the highway. That's what Aidan said when they called."

Ary was talking as she moved, pulling out instruments and doing things to Kalina that Nivea had never seen before.

"I'm going to start an IV. Get me that cart from over there and open those packages for me."

Shaking her head to clear the visual of a truck rolling over with people inside of it, Nivea hurried to do what she'd been told. With skilled hands Ary inserted a needle and soon whatever was in that IV bag was dripping into the First Female.

"Found it!" Ary yelled. "There's a gash here at her back. I can sew it up as soon as I stop this bleeding. In the meantime her pressure's dropping."

That didn't sound good and when Ary moved Kalina's body it looked even worse as blood gushed from the wound.

"Grab those towels and get over here!" was the next order that came Nivea's way.

She wasn't trained for this, wasn't really into saving lives as much as she was defending—and usually taking—them. But this was Kalina . . . this was her family. All the family she figured she would ever have, all things considered. So she moved around the medical center, doing whatever Ary asked even when she barely understood what the *curandera* wanted her to do. It didn't matter, whatever assistance she could offer, she would, to save this female shifter and her baby because there was no way in hell she was going to walk out of that door and tell Roman Reynolds that his mate was gone.

"Where is she?" Rome asked immediately, after having pushed through the double doors of the medical center.

"Sir, she's in the back with Ary. I believe she's stable but you cannot go back there right now," Lucas said, his voice as shaky as his hands, which he finally put down at his sides in an attempt to keep them still.

"I will not wait here while she's in there . . ." Rome paused, swallowed deeply. "Get the hell out of my way!"

He pushed past Lucas, who actually stood a little firmer than anyone could have expected.

"Sir, I'm just following orders. I can't let you go back there until she says so."

"Lucas, I'm not in the fucking mood for this right now. Get. Out. Of. My. Way!" Rome yelled and pushed forward again.

Lucas used both hands this time to push against Rome's chest, trying to keep him still. Finally, it was Eli and X who took Rome by the arms.

"Give him a second, Rome." X spoke, leaning directly into Rome's face. "He's gonna go tell Ary you're here and then you can go back and see her."

X's voice was serious and clear as a whistle as Lucas backed up, then turned and ran into one of the other rooms.

"She can't be . . ." Rome began.

"She's not," Eli replied confidently. "She's breathing and so is the baby."

Rome turned to him so fast, grabbing him by the front of his shirt and slamming him against the wall. Eli let out a whoosh of breath before looking his Leader directly in the eye.

"I can hear her heartbeat and the baby's," Eli told him. "I know it sounds strange and you might not believe me, but . . . I'm a Seer, Rome. Apparently my gift from the shaman's poisonous smoke is a speedy track to my true destiny as a shifter. You're the Assembly Leader, Ary's the *curandera* and I . . . am . . . the Seer," he said with a finality that rang true through every pore of his body. His limbs felt stronger, his breath came easier, and when he looked even deeper into Rome's eyes, he saw the two heartbeats there. Deep inside this strong and powerful shifter, Eli could see the extensions of him, his mate, and his child—his family.

He lifted his hands and placed them on Rome's shoulders. "They are alive," he told him sincerely.

"She's asking for you."

Rome jerked at the female voice and moved away from Eli without speaking another word. Eli, on the other hand, closed his eyes again and heard screams echoing in his head of the female's voice, blood pumping so loudly and so fiercely through his body he actually trembled.

She was covered in blood. It was on her arms, her face, her clothes. He instantly thought of her in the forest being attacked by *Lormenians,* in that bed, wearing that necklace, calling to him. Bringing his hands up, Eli clapped them to his ears and hurriedly left the room.

He collided instantly with a body, strong hands clasping his shoulders.

"You know that this is no longer the answer," the gravelly male voice whispered to him. "Fear will feed the darkness. Love will bring back the light. Take a deep breath, shifter, and let the light in."

Eli nodded then. Hearing the words, knowing their truth. He hadn't been able to see Nivea earlier when he'd wanted to, but after hearing what Rome needed to get him through and admitting to himself and to the others in that room who and what he was, he knew the running had to stop.

This vision of Nivea, the one where she died because of events he'd set in motion. It scared the hell out of him. Scared him enough to want to make this right, to make her his.

"Eli," Nivea called to him.

She'd obviously followed him out of the medical center and most likely had heard what Baxter had just said to him.

"There is strength here." Baxter began speaking once more.

Eli stood up straight, squaring his shoulders but still not turning to face either of them.

"In the Gungi, my father was also a shaman. He could create great spells and cures. I asked him one day how he came to be so talented and he shook his head, telling me simply that the success of any spell or cure rested within the individual it was used upon. A great warrior with strength and power beyond compare would own any cure a shaman offered. You own that cure, your destiny is much stronger than any poison Dagar could have ever concocted. Embrace it, embrace what is meant to be. And she," Baxter said, pausing. "She owns your heart.

"There is no more time for this discord. The danger is real and unity is the defense. The Leader will need you both to survive this. They will all need you."

Chapter 21

Nivea let her head fall back, hot water sluicing down her throat, between the valley of her breasts. Her muscles were tight, her temples throbbing mildly, persistently. But at least her hands had ceased shaking.

There'd been so much blood and Kalina's eyes had remained closed and the monitor Ary had hooked to her stomach had been silent for ten excruciatingly long seconds. Her gaze had met Ary's and Nivea saw the tears sheening her eyes, knew they matched her own. Then the sound had begun, loud and fast and Ary gasped.

"Yes! Yes! It's breathing. The baby is breathing!" she'd said, her body shaking with relief.

Nivea had let her head fall forward, her chin touching her chest as she thanked everyone and everything higher and more powerful than them. She inhaled when she heard Ary begin to move, knowing there was more that needed to be done, and the scent of the First Female's blood permeated her senses.

As she stood in the shower remembering, the scent remained fresh in her mind. And for the second time in as many months, Nivea cried.

The sound of the shower door opening made her jump and she immediately dipped her face beneath the spray of water again. Eli stepped in so that when she opened her eyes, through the blur of the water, he was standing right there. His hands immediately went to the nape of her neck, where, for endless seconds, he just held on. A muscle twitched in his jaw as he blinked, the stormy green of his eyes clear. He pulled her closer, lowering his forehead to hers but not closing his eyes.

"Look at me," he said when she blinked slowly. "I need you to look at me."

She did and bolts of heat traveled from the spot where his thumbs rubbed along her jawline, down her neck to her breasts.

"I don't know why it was you. Or why I was the one who connected to Acacia in the jungle and needed that shaman's cure. I can't explain what being a Seer will mean to me, or to my future and I won't promise you that I will not try to protect you with every breath in my body. I'm not an easy shifter to be with," he said, snapping his lips shut tightly, his eyes blinking fiercely.

"But what I do know is that I cannot continue to do any of this . . ." He paused, took a deep breath, and let it out forcefully. "Without you."

Her chest felt heavy, like a boulder had been settled there as she tried to inhale. When the effort seemed like too much work he kissed her. Soft and slow, his lips touched hers, tilted over them, and warmed every inch of her body. His tongue licked along the seam, coaxing her to open, to acquiesce and heaven help her, she did.

Together their tongues danced and dueled, dipped and dived in and out of each other's mouths, along their lips, their chins, and necks. His hands moved down her arms to her torso, then down further to cup her ass tightly. Nivea wrapped her arms around his neck, her palms flattening on the back of his head. And she held on. For the next breath and the next, she simply held on.

Eli was fast and he was determined, his hard length pressing deep inside her the moment he'd lifted her thighs and pressed her back against the cool tiles. She locked her ankles behind his back and he pounded into her with such force, such emotion she could only open her mouth to scream, but no sound escaped. She shivered, her thighs shaking so vehemently she thought her legs would simply slip from his waist and when she was ready to hold onto the blissful release, Eli pulled out of her quickly. In seconds he was turning, lowering her to the floor of the shower, kicking the door open behind him so that her legs were half in and half out. He came down onto his knees, lifting her legs onto his shoulders and fastened his mouth on her clit, sucking until Nivea's nails scraped along the shower floor. Water pelted down onto her body, stinging the turgid nipples of her breasts, running in sensual rivulets over her stomach, pattering over the back of Eli's head as he continued to suck and lick her until her eyes closed, her body tremoring with the quick shock of release.

She was limp and believing with everything left in her that she would never move again—or at least, not in the near future. But she was wrong; Eli was on a mission. He lifted her from the floor of the shower, holding her wet and limp body tightly against his, kissing her ear and her neck as he moved them over to the sink.

He turned her to face the mirror, slapped her palms on the sides of the sink, and stared at her in the mirror.

"Not without you, Nivea," he said, dipping his head to bite the edge of her left shoulder before looking up again. "Not ever again."

She didn't know what she was supposed to think or feel at this moment, or what, if anything, Eli expected her to say. All she knew for certain was that this feeling of pure pleasure coursing through her, coaxing the cat that lived within, enticing the female that ruled, was everything she'd ever hoped for. All the counseling, the persistent will to be normal, to put her past behind her, to be better than the people who had given her life, it all came down to this exact second. The moment Eli Preston stared at her with his intense green eyes and offered her everything she'd ever wanted, and more.

"Not again," she whispered, licking her lips and straightening her shoulders. "Not ever again, Eli."

His hand was between her legs then, the other one squeezing her breast. Two fingers dipped inside her, pressing deep, spreading wide. Nivea opened her legs, going up on tiptoe with the intense waves of pleasure. But she did not look away, did not break the contact she'd waited what seemed like a lifetime to achieve.

He pumped wildly, his palm smacking against the moist lips of her pussy until her legs once again began to quiver. Faster and harder he pushed her, thrusting into her while the fingers of his other hand pinched her nipple, sending spikes of pleasure/pain all the way down to her toes. When he pulled his fingers from her abruptly, Nivea wasn't totally surprised. She'd seen the dark desire in his eyes, heard it in his breathing, felt his cat reaching for hers. She knew what he wanted and she was more than eager to give it to him. Clasping her fingers tightly on the edge of the sink she leaned farther in, her legs spread, lifting her hips in offering to him. He released her breast, that hand spreading her cheeks as his fingers, now drenched with her essence, pushed slowly into her anus. She hissed, taking her lower lip between her teeth and pressing back against his hand.

He pulled out, pressed in again, and she purred.

"Yeah," he whispered, his forehead resting on her spine. "That's my little cat. Tell her I'm here," he continued, coaxing her entrance, spreading her wider, readying her for his taking.

"*O companheiro dela está aqui, para sempre,*" he whispered, pulling his fingers out and pressing the hard length of his dick in their place. "*O companheiro dela está aqui, para sempre. Para sempre.*"

Nivea accepted him deep inside her, loving the feel of him filling her completely. His words replaying over and over in her mind.

"Her mate is here, forever. Forever."

That's what he'd said, what he was still saying as he pumped into her deeply, intensely.

When he came, she came; when he roared, she roared. And when their mating was final, when their hearts were beating wildly with Eli's arms wrapped tightly around her body, his lips pressing warm kisses down her back, Nivea sighed and repeated, "*Sua companheira está aqui, para sempre. Para sempre.*"

"I never thought I'd be here, in this emotional place with anyone," Eli said, his voice soft but gruff as they lay in his dark bedroom.

Nivea lay on her stomach, one leg tossed over his waist, an arm and her head resting on his chest. She liked to sleep in this position, he'd thought absently a few seconds ago. Now, he realized how much he also enjoyed her in this position, whether she was asleep or awake.

"This is exactly where I always thought I would be with someone," she replied before sighing. "It's the thought that kept me sane through everything."

The hand he'd had resting on her shoulder moved so that his fingers toyed with her hair. She'd been through so much and yet had come out so strong. Eli deeply admired her for having accomplished that. "I wish I'd had your strength," he admitted.

"You did," she told him, her palm flattening on his bicep and clenching gently. "You used your strength to complete your training and to come here and help Rome start the Assembly. We all have strengths and weaknesses, Eli, what counts is how we use them."

"I've always thought of that drug as a curse, as poison living and breathing inside of me," he confessed.

"But don't you see how all of that had to happen for us to be where we are now? Without that shaman's smoke, without what you went through with Acacia and then Leanne, you and I would not be here together at this moment. And you would not be the Seer that Rome needs by his side at this time."

"They have Magdalena," he replied.

"She was for the Elders and the old ways of the shifters. You," Nivea said, poking a finger into his chest, then rubbing her palm over that spot. "You are here for us, during the Stateside Shifters' time of need, you are here and you have a power that I have no doubt will help us through this."

Eli shook his head. "I don't know how to control it. When I was searching for you and wanted a vision desperately, it wouldn't come. And then when I was in the medical center and Rome was ready to tear down the walls . . ." His words trailed off as Eli sighed, remembering how intense that moment with Rome had actually been, for both of them.

"The power you needed to calm Rome's worst fears appeared. You assured him and most likely saved the walls and everyone else in that room from his wrath. It was perfect timing," she told him.

Eli kissed her forehead then, hugging her even closer to him. "You are perfect timing for me, Nivea Cannon. I couldn't do this without you, couldn't embrace—"

His words were cut short once again as she moved until

she was completely straddling him, leaning down to cup his face in her hands. "You can and you will," she said seriously. "Together, we can and we will. Together, Eli, that's all that matters."

"Yes. That's all that matters," he agreed, readjusting himself so that his now awakening arousal was closer to her warmth.

"And just so you know, I won't be promising not to protect you either. You may be very important to the Assembly as our new Seer, but to me, you're much more. You're my mate and I'll be damned if anybody or anything past, present, or future, will ever come between us."

Eli smiled. He couldn't help it. She was tenacious and headstrong and beautiful with her hair a bushy halo around her face, lips swollen from his kisses. She wasn't soft and dainty or privileged and high-minded. She was simply the female that, at some point in these last few years, Eli had fallen in love with.

His hands went to her hips, his fingers kneading the soft skin there as he looked up at her. "I think you've got it twisted," he told her. "I'm your mate so I'll be protecting you."

She smiled then, a wide and gorgeous smile that lifted her already high cheekbones and brightened her eyes. Eli's chest filled with warmth at the sight, his body reacting in a similar way.

"Don't forget I've been highly trained to protect shifters and humans," she said, then lifted her hips slightly so that her wet folds rubbed seductively over the tip of his length. "My mate would be first in line to reap the rewards of my training."

"Oh, I'll reap the rewards all right," Eli told her, grabbing her hips and thrusting upward until the tip of his dick was at the entrance of her hot pussy.

She purred and Eli felt the vibration throughout his

entire body. The sound touched every nerve ending, rubbing along his cat with a tender familiarity that had it chuffing in response.

"I was hoping you'd say that," she told him before leaning over and sucking his bottom lip into her mouth.

Eli let her control the kiss while he held firmly to her hips, bringing her down hard each time he pumped upward, filling her so completely and loving the feel of her warm essence dripping onto him.

When she pulled her mouth from his, Eli whispered, "I'm never gonna get enough of you."

Nivea licked his lips again, moving out of his reach when he attempted to trap her tongue in his mouth once more. She sat up straight, an act that increased the depth of his length inside of her and solicited a deep groan from him.

"That's good to know," she told him, settling her hips over him so that their bodies conjoined. "Because I don't tire easily."

With that she began pumping him with hard, rhythmic thrusts. Up and down, up even higher, until nothing but the tip of his dick remained in touch with her, then down until his balls rubbed against her plump wet folds. Over and over until they both were struggling for breath. When Eli's hands went to her hips this time, he moved in farther, using his thumbs to part her folds so that when he looked down, the puckered hood of her clit was bared for his view. Licking his lips he touched a thumb to the nub and rubbed. Nivea arched back farther, her hands going back to grip his thighs for leverage. Eli lifted slightly off the pillows so he could see her better, see the desire on her face, the rise and fall of her breasts, the glistening bud of her clit and the in-and-out motion of his dick still driving deep inside of her thanks to her continued pumps.

His breath came in thick, heavy pants, hers in shallow

little sounds that made him harder, his balls tightening in anticipation of release. She continued to move, her hair brushing his knees as she did. Eli pumped into her, matching her already established rhythm thrust for deliciously deep thrust. He felt the moment their cats met, the pounding inside his body as it welcomed yet another entity—his mate. He felt as if he'd jumped off a cliff and landed on a cloud, a puffy thick cloud that was now carrying him to the sweetest abyss ever. Nivea jerked forward, her palms slapping into his chest, her extended claws cutting with a sting into his skin. Her body had begun to tremble, her release pouring out, covering his dick. She leaned in farther, licking the cuts she'd inflicted on his chest and that's when Eli erupted, his release shooting into her with the force of every emotion he felt for her.

Minutes later, after they'd just begun to gather their wits, Nivea rolled off of him as they were startled by the loud voice coming from the television. Apparently when they'd come out of the bathroom from their earlier shower, their hands and mouths still affixed to each other, they'd forgotten to clean off the bed. The television remote control was what Nivea had rolled over when she'd moved, turning on the TV unintentionally.

"The Advanced Technology of Defense Convention seems to come to the capital at a time when defense discussions are most needed. With the recent uptick in violence throughout the city and the continental U.S., it is apparent that we are not doing everything we should to protect our citizens from our own, not to mention not protecting us from international threats. Hopefully, this weekend's joining of top defense experts will develop some new strategy to the unknown evil that has recently plagued our streets."

They'd both paused and listened to the reporter standing outside of the Gaylord National Convention Center located at D.C.'s National Harbor. As she spoke there was a huge banner advertising the ATD National Conference—a conference to discuss defense techniques with all the world leaders.

"Oh no," she whispered, sitting up in the bed.

"Oh yes," Eli followed, rising up beside her. "That's what this has all been leading up to. It's why those hybrids are here and most likely so is Crowe."

"He's going to sell the hybrids to the highest bidder," Nivea continued, a hand raking through her hair.

Eli nodded. "And Boden will finally get his chance at revenge."

"Boden?"

"Yeah." Eli sighed. "He's the middleman. Dammit! I should have seen it sooner. Crowe doesn't have the resources to pay Cannon for the shifter specimens. Hell, he wouldn't have even had a clue as to where to get them. Only someone—only a shifter—would have known about the children being taken from the Gungi. And only a sadistic shifter with a grudge against the entire tribe would know what was going on with those children and not open his mouth or try to save them. He would hold that information until it was of use to him, until . . . the time was right."

"I don't understand," Nivea said.

"Boden had a box delivered to my shop with a necklace that was meant for his mate, Acacia. She's the *Lormenian* that Ezra and I were involved with. I told the others about the necklace, but I didn't mention the note that was also inside. He said the unveiling was coming soon."

Nivea was no longer looking at the television, but was staring directly at Eli now. "The unveiling of what? The hybrids?" she asked.

"The unveiling of the Shadow Shifters," Eli told her, the vision flashing through his mind as plainly as if it had just been on the TV screen. "He plans to tell the world about us and take out as many of the Shadows as he can so that he will become the new leader. That would be the ultimate revenge for what the Elders did to him so long ago."

"Then he would become the rogue leader," Nivea added.

Eli shook his head. "Not as long as I live," he told her with a certainty that had his cat roaring deep inside.

This time in the conference room, Eli did not stand behind Rome. He was sitting next to Nick, Nivea on his left. Ezra sat across from his brother, X on his right, Caprise next to him. Rome and Kalina were at the head of the table. Baxter and Elder Alamar both sat at the other end of the table. Priya and Bas were there in person this time. Jace and Cole were on speaker.

"How is Boden Estevez connected to Crowe and these hybrids?" Nick asked.

Eli shook his head. "I believe he's the one who connected Cannon to Comastaz."

"So Crowe could get the shifters and the money he needed to continue with the Genesis Project," Rome added, solidifying what Eli had told Ezra the night they'd rescued Nivea's sisters—that Rome and Nick had gotten some information out of Cannon, but hadn't told them.

"Right," Eli said, deciding now was definitely not the time to question the Leader about his tactics. "But Boden's no middleman. He's in charge, of this operation at least. My thought is that all of this spawns from the fact that a dominant shifter like Boden would hold a grudge against the Elders and the tribe for running him out of the jungle. He would want to get back at them, just as he'd want to get back at Ezra and me for what he feels we took from him as well."

"So whoever helped my father escape did so for a reason. I'm guessing they needed him to get more unwanteds so they would be prepared for Boden's big showdown," Nivea added when everyone in the room was looking at Eli, trying to digest all that he'd just told them.

Eli and Nivea had been up most of the night talking about how they would approach the Assembly Leader and lay out the plan they had to thwart whatever efforts Boden and Crowe planned to make at the conference. He waited a beat for any questions or comments, but they all remained silent.

"It makes perfect sense that Crowe will be at the ATD conference this weekend," Eli continued, looking at X. "Can we check with the hotel to find out who is registered to attend?"

"Maybe not the hotel since the attendees are bound to be high-level security officials, U.S. and foreign. They may not even be privy to that information. I'd have to reach out to someone at the Department of Defense maybe," X told him. "But what Crowe is doing may be totally off the grid. This isn't something he would keep to himself. A hybrid supersoldier would draw bids from all across the world."

"So the bastard has an auction planned at a national event. Clever sonofabitch," Nick added.

"Not clever enough," Nivea told them. "They have no idea that we know about this convention or their plan. We have the upper hand."

"So what do we do now? Do we try to stop Crowe before this event starts?" Jace asked.

Priya, who had been typing on her tablet while they talked, looked up then and added, "The Gaylord has two thousand rooms. Its atrium overlooks the Potomac River. Three thousand, one hundred and twenty-three people are expected to attend the ATD conference. There are also two weddings booked for this weekend, which will probably bring in another thousand guests. Collateral damage would be huge."

"It's exactly what Boden wants," Eli said. "Thousands of people, humans, to see what he wants them to see about us."

"He's a shifter too," Cole interjected.

"He is a rogue," Elder Alamar replied. "He should have died years ago."

"Like the unwanteds," Rome said slowly. "The Elders ordered him killed and he survived to come back years later and threaten all that we have built. You segregated him because he was different and instead of protecting the tribes from him, you left us all vulnerable to the monster you created. He can hurt us more than anyone else because he knows exactly what we are and what we're capable of. He also knows our weaknesses, which he plans to exploit."

"What are you saying?" Alamar asked, flattening his palms on the table.

"He's saying you fucked up!" Nick said, frowning as Rome gave him a warning glare.

"The Elders protected the tribes in the forest the best way they knew how," Baxter began quietly. "The rules are different in the forest than in the States. I admit they realized that too late."

"Good of you to admit it," Nick chimed in again.

"That's enough," Rome said this time.

"We know now that unity is key. Magdalena has already predicted that you will need to band together to get through this," Baxter insisted.

"Magdalena is also in the forest," Rome said. "If we're going to rely on any Seer's powers and predictions, it's going to be Eli's."

There was silence once again in the room. Nivea reached for Eli's hand as he watched the other faces in the room, hoping the announcement was well received. Then again, Eli didn't really give a damn how anyone accepted the announcement. It was simple, he was a Seer. He had embraced that fact as well as his mate. Anybody who didn't like that could go straight to hell, exactly where he planned to send Boden's sorry ass.

Still, when Cole replied with an enthusiastic, "Amen to that!" Eli relaxed a little.

"The conference begins tonight," he said, getting back to the business at hand.

Not that he dismissed the wrongdoings of their ancestors, or the right they probably assumed they were doing. It happened in history over and over again. Leaders made decisions based on the information they had at the time, the remedies the situation call for in that moment. Years later, the next generation had to deal with the fallout. It was what it was and now they would do what they needed to do.

"We're not going to have a chance to strike before it begins. I think we need to find out the schedule, figure out when and where Crowe is likely to appear, and meet him head-on."

"And what about Boden?" Ezra asked, his expression that of restrained rage. "When do we get a chance at his ass?"

Eli shook his head. "I know that he's planning something, I just can't pinpoint what. I can't see it, but I feel it."

All eyes were on him now as the new Seer. They probably wanted to rely on his visions now, to be guided or forewarned by them. But Eli hadn't had one of this particular incident and he'd convinced himself that it was better not to try and force it. He would wait to see what would come to him, letting his senses do what they needed to get him the information that was required to help the shifters.

"He will be there," Eli said with confidence. "What he will do I do not know. We just need to be prepared. And once we take Boden and Crowe down, the rest of the Genesis Project will crumple."

"We should go in heavy," Nivea began, squeezing Eli's hand beneath the table. "Four teams on Crowe, four ready for Boden, and additional backup for the unexpected. Everyone should be versed in how to take down the hybrids and whether or not to take Crowe dead or alive. We need to hit hard and fast to keep exposure to a minimum."

"There's a picture of the lion found at the police station on YouTube," Priya told them. "Three-million-plus views already."

Nick cursed.

"She's right. We go in hard and fast, conceal what we can but remain focused on the ultimate goal of taking Boden down once and for all. As for Crowe, we take his sorry ass alive because he's a human," Kalina stated. "There's really no other choice."

Caprise nodded. "I agree."

Rome had visibly flinched as Kalina talked about the plan and Eli knew exactly what the shifter was feeling. He'd felt it too each time he'd looked at Nivea and known without any doubt that she planned to be a part of this battle, regardless of how he felt about it.

"Baxter, send the jet for Jace and Cole. I want them here ASAP. Bas, Nick, and X will work with Eli to sort out the teams. Ezra, you and the Sanchez brothers get down to the Gaylord and familiarize yourself with the layout. Priya or X can get you blueprints I'm sure. I'll meet you down in the training center in half an hour," Rome said, standing from his seat, his hand extended to Kalina.

She looked at him with mild questioning, but stood anyway, taking his hand. When Rome was gone, Nick's heated glare went to the end of the table where Baxter and Elder Alamar still sat.

"You two are something else," he said. "All this time you've known that this day would come and you never thought to tell any of us. Aren't you supposed to be overseeing Rome's safety? How could you let this sneak up on him?" Nick asked Baxter.

The older, thinner man stood slowly, squaring his shoulders as he met Nick's tumultuous glare.

"I have done everything in my power to prepare him for this very day. That was my job all along. You, of all people, should not doubt him now," Baxter said vehemently.

Nick stood then as well, Ezra immediately standing beside him.

"I don't doubt Rome for one minute, nor do I doubt what this newly formed Assembly can and will do in the face of danger. But I would have never kept this from him. Part of the preparation should have been to tell him that this would one day become an issue."

"That is not how life works, Mr. Nick," Baxter said in his solemn yet authoritative voice. "I have watched the three of you grow and learn, make mistakes, and grow some more. That is what life is all about. This situation will take Mr. Roman to another level."

"It may get him killed," Caprise added quietly. "Did anyone ever think of that? Rome will no doubt want to fight right along with his guards. What will happen if he is killed? What if this is Boden's ultimate goal? He would not only rule the rogues, but all of the shifters worldwide."

Nivea nodded. "That should be one of our main priorities: protecting the Assembly Leader at all costs while we are on the battlefield."

"I've always guarded Rome with my life," Eli stated firmly. "Nothing will change that."

"And Nick and I have always had his back. That stays the same," X added.

"You must think and act as one," Alamar spoke loudly. "Every plan you make, every step you take, as one, united. Or you shall all founder."

The older man left, the material of his billowing black robe swishing around his legs with each step. He left the room and Baxter followed at a much slower gait. The others simply looked after them and then to each other.

"Training center in thirty," Nick said sternly. "I have to make sure Ary and Shya are safe here. I'll speak to Rome about moving the females down to the tunnels."

"I'm going with you," Caprise told X as they neared the door.

He turned on her quickly, his face a rigid frown. Then she shook her head as if to say "don't even try it" and X stormed out, his beautiful and courageous mate behind him.

Eli stood, staring at the door, the intensity of Nivea's gaze almost burning holes in his back.

"I know you plan to fight with us," he said without turning around. He inhaled deeply, letting the thought of her going into this dangerous situation cement itself in his mind. He didn't like it. His cat didn't like it. His heart thumped wildly at the memory of his dream where she was attacked and killed . . . by Boden.

"I want you to fight by my side," he told her, the words coming slowly and unsteadily.

When she touched a hand to his shoulder, Eli warmed instantly, his heart stilling a beat.

"I would be honored to fight by your side, Eli," she said. "And I will protect you with my life."

Eli turned quickly then, taking her face in his hands. "Do not leave my side and do not do anything foolish. Do you hear me, Nivea? Just don't even think about it! If something were to happen to you . . . if you didn't make it through this . . . just—"

Nivea kissed his lips to silence his words. "I'm going to make it through this, Eli, and so are you and all the other Shadows. This is what we've been trained for, what we do.

We will protect the humans and the Shadows. We will be successful. I promise."

"It's probably for the best," Ary told Kalina as they sat at the smaller conference room table in the suite she shared with Rome.

"I know it is, but I don't have to like it," she replied. "I'm as much a part of this Assembly as anyone else and I'm trained in gun battle."

"And you are the First Female of the Assembly and carrying the first heir," Ary said matter-of-factly. "Not to mention the twenty-seven stitches currently healing on your side."

Kalina sat back in the chair, still not liking the situation but knowing that Ary's words were only solidifying what her mate had already told her.

"You will not fight, Kalina. And that is all," Rome had said the moment they'd entered their suite. When she'd opened her mouth to reply he'd silenced her with an urgent kiss that relayed all the fear and trepidation he was feeling at that very moment. Even if she'd thought she had a leg to stand on, she hadn't wanted to argue with him, not at that moment.

Nick, Ary, X, and Caprise had come in minutes later and the consensus had been the same. Ary and Shya would stay with Kalina. Jax would take them to the tunnels that had been completed just a couple of weeks ago. They ran beneath Havenway and into Alexandria. There were provisions and space in the tunnels for at least a thousand shifters to live temporarily. The cabinets were stocked with food and health supplies, there were generators and sewage lines and everything they had aboveground.

The others would go to National Harbor and defend the shifters' secret. Kalina knew it was the right thing to do but hated that she would miss all the action. Still sulking, she reached into the pocket of the jacket she'd been wearing to answer the buzzing of her cell phone. Her lips spread into an instant smile when she read the words: **Eli and I are going to be joined!**

"I thought you didn't believe in mates and joining," Ezra said as he was once again in Eli's room handing him another bow tie.

It was pink this time, a color that Eli would have never picked out for himself. But after Nivea had stopped hugging him so tightly he thought he might not breathe normally again, she'd said she had a great pink dress to wear and that he should find something to match it. They were pressed for time and needed to be in the training center in half an hour, but with all they were facing, after all that they'd both been through, there was no way Eli was going to tell her she couldn't have what she wanted, no way in hell.

Eli and Nivea had been coming from the conference room holding hands, when he'd suddenly stopped moving. He could hear Nivea calling his name but it sounded like she was a distance away instead of right beside him. Then he was surrounded by trees and the call of toucans and the laughter of monkeys. There was no sunlight and the air was damp, the crisp, fresh scent of the water cascading over the rocks. He'd taken a step, a branch cracking beneath his feet.

"Eli."

He lifted his head as she called his name. She'd been standing about ten feet away with flowers entwined in her hair, Elder Alamar standing behind her, Caprise and Kalina beside her. Her dress was long and white and cupping her silhouette seductively. A few feet away were Ezra, Rome, X, and Nick and then it clicked.

"Eli?" Nivea had called to him again, this time rubbing her hand up and down his arm.

He blinked again and immediately recognized the gray walls and tiled floors of Havenway. His breath came quickly, his lungs filling with refreshed air as all the pieces to the jumble his life had been in the last years came together.

"We need to have a joining ceremony," he'd said to her immediately. "Before we head to D.C. to face . . . whatever. This, us, we need to be official, just in case." He said the last softly.

Nivea hadn't wasted a second. She hadn't said a word in argument or protest. Instead, she'd hugged him again and the next thing Eli knew he was in his room, stepping out of the shower with Ezra sitting on the edge of his bed, a garment bag lying beside him.

"I didn't believe that foul poison would have served any good in my life, and yet it did," Eli said in reply to Ezra's question.

Ezra chuckled. "Yeah, I guess you've got a point there. But you know, we're going to come out of this all right. We're not going into battle to be killed. Unless you know something I don't." His twin lifted a brow in question.

Eli shook his head. "I haven't had any visions about the battle," he told his brother before turning from the mirror to face him. "But I did see Nivea and me joining in the rain forest. She was smiling and happy and I realized that's how I always want to see her. Not fighting against our enemies or crying over her parents' betrayal. I just want her happy and I know that this will make her happy."

"And what about you? How will it make you feel?" Ezra asked him.

"Complete," Eli immediately replied. "I will finally be complete."

Not five minutes later they all stood in the living room of Rome's suite. Kalina and Caprise stood side by side while

Ary was standing near the couch behind them where Shya slept. In front of the door was Elder Alamar, his face solemn once again, a string of beads in his right hand, a black and gold scarf thrown over his left shoulder. Baxter stood a step behind the Elder, while Ezra and Eli were to his left, all of them facing the same way.

Rome held Nivea's arm, walking her slowly the short distance from the conference room through the living room. There was no music—traditional human wedding chords or the tribal drumming that would have been heard in the Gungi. She did not wear a formal white wedding gown and Eli did not wear a designer tuxedo. There were no flowers, no gauzy white netting draping every surface, no lavish spread of food waiting for an extravagant reception later on. The room was neat and seemed personal only to those who lived there. The situation was dire and cast a heavy aura over them all.

Yet, Nivea's heart beat a little faster as she walked, her gaze fixating on Eli's until she was finally standing beside him. He took her hand and together they faced Elder Alamar.

"*Os dois vieram, coração e mente como um só,*" the Elder began, his voice low, resonating in a slow melody. "*Eles encontraram um ao outro através de todo o mundo e por muito tempo para participar deste dia.*"

He took the beads and motioned for Nivea to lower her head. Slipping them onto her neck, he pressed the emblem into her skin.

"*Topètenia* to *Topètenia,*" he whispered and nodded for her to do the same.

She cleared her throat. "*Topètenia* to *Topètenia.*"

"*Assim será abençoado,*" he said in Portuguese and then again in English. "So be blessed."

He slid the scarf from his shoulder, lifting it and nodding until Eli leaned forward so that he could fit it around his broad shoulders. When he was finished he touched the center of Eli's chest.

"*Topètenia* to *Topètenia*," he said once more.

Eli repeated, "*Topètenia* to *Topètenia*."

"*Assim será abençoado,*" Alamar said, then stepped back, holding both his hands up, palms flattened above Nivea's and Eli's heads. "*O mate é o coração, eo coração é o shifter. Estados são vida, para todo o sempre.* The mate is the heart and the heart is the shifter. United they are in life, forevermore."

"Boden Estevez will kill and destroy the world as you know it," Rayna told Dorian as they sat in his car, parked in front of the Reynolds Building.

"He is one of you?" Dorian asked, not at all surprised anymore by what was being said to him.

In the weeks since this mysteriously beautiful woman had walked up onto his sister's porch, he had learned so much. They were a different species, shape shifters, she'd called them, able to turn from human to big cat and back again. They had originated in the Amazonian rain forest and once divided, migrated to forests throughout the world. They were both an anomaly and a nightmare, he'd thought to himself.

"He is a rogue shifter. They tried to kill him off but he lived. Everywhere he goes he is sent away, but he comes back, like a disease."

"And you do not like him?"

"I abhor him," was Rayna's immediate response. "He came into my family and has been tearing us apart since day one. He's vowed revenge against the Shadows and I've vowed revenge against him."

"What did he do to you and your family?"

She turned quickly in the passenger seat and stared at him fiercely, her eyes almost translucent. He now knew this happened usually when she was upset or extremely aroused. Since they were parked in downtown D.C. on a very public street, he would have to hope for her being upset.

"He corrupted my sister. She now follows him around blindly like she is under some type of spell. It's sickening and my parents want her back," Rayna said vehemently.

"But your sister is an adult, correct? I mean, I'm just saying that oftentimes adults select persons to get involved with that their families do not approve of. It's not that uncommon and the family meddling in their business doesn't normally help."

"You do not understand. Bianca was innocent before he came. She believes she loves him, that he is her mate. But Boden had a mate and he was forced to leave her, and then she was murdered. He's angry and he's evil. He does not possess the capacity to love anymore, but Bianca cannot see that."

"If she's with him then there's a chance that she may be more like him than you think."

Her teeth bared then and Dorian instinctively reached to his side for his gun. He loved having sex with her, had never experienced anything like it before in his life, but if she shifted and attacked, he would not hesitate to defend himself. That said a lot for the bond they'd forged in the past few weeks.

"Whatever she does it is because of him," Rayna stated.

"Okay, fine. I'll take your word for it since I've never met your sister. But why did you bring us here? How does all this relate to Roman Reynolds?"

"He is what Boden is after. All that he has and is in this part of the world. Boden wants it and has planned to get it, whatever the cost."

"So he's going to attack Reynolds? Is that what you're saying? There's going to be some type of shifter war going on in my city?" Dorian had known it. Deep down he'd felt something from the second he'd seen Roman Reynolds and looked at his financial records. The pull toward this man that he now knew for certain was a beast, had been strong and persistent.

His heart pounded at what that actually meant now, what Rayna had just told him would happen. "He's going to attack Reynolds, and that means he'll also attack Kalina."

Rayna nodded. "Boden will come for Reynolds, but we can stop him. We can warn Reynolds and we can help," she said adamantly. "And then I can save my sister."

"Wait a minute," Dorian said, flattening his hands on the steering wheel. "You came to me because you want me to help Roman Reynolds?"

"You are a human," she said. "He will need the help of your kind, your law enforcement."

"He's not one of us," Dorian told her flatly.

Rayna shook her head. "Believe me when I tell you that if you could choose, it would be Roman over Boden to be a part of the human race."

Dorian didn't believe her and he didn't believe she expected him to help the man he'd sworn to take down. He also didn't want Kalina hurt. He had never wanted that, and thus this crusade against Reynolds in the first damned place. He'd always feared Kalina would become a casualty to whatever was really going on with Reynolds. In addition to that reason, Dorian was still a federal agent. It was his duty to stop any type of impending war between these animals from breaking out in his city.

Chapter 22

The time had finally come and strangely enough, Boden did not feel an ounce of excitement. There was no hum of anticipation, no anxious tingles moving throughout his body. This moment had been a long time coming. Well, the time was now. And he was ready.

"They will be here by seven, just as you asked," Bianca said, coming to sit beside him on the couch.

Yesterday she'd packed their things and they'd made the drive from the Four Seasons to the suite they now occupied at the Gaylord. Both hotels had been phenomenal in their décor and service. She draped an arm over his shoulder, her chin resting there as she used a finger to run along the line of his jaw. The touch annoyed him and Boden tilted his head out of her reach.

"How many?" he asked.

"Charles confirmed two hundred," she replied. If she was ruffled by his movements he couldn't tell, nor did he care.

Years ago, Bianca Adani had come in handy. She'd been in the right place at the right time and he'd acted accordingly, taking the body she offered and the allegiance she swore after telling him who she really was. The initial shock that he'd slept with Acacia's half-sister had first angered him. Then, after sleeping with Bianca again, he thought it fitting. Teodoro had been so smug and so arrogant that day he'd used his army of *Lormenian* soldiers to chase Boden out of the Sierra Leone rain forest. They'd forbidden him to come back, promising to do the Elders' biding and behead him if they so much as smelled his scent again.

With a second death ordered and no army to back him up, Boden had no choice but to leave. But he did not go far.

He'd hidden for months in the village just west of the rain forest until one day, he'd looked up and Bianca had been standing there. Later she would tell him how Teodoro had raped her mother repeatedly, using her as his sex slave, impregnating her twice before finally tossing her out, banning her from the rain forest as well. Her mother had taken a job as a healer with one of the local missionary groups that had no idea she was a shifter. There in that small village, she'd raised her daughters as best she could, never letting them forget that their father was the *Lormenian* tribal leader and that he had turned them away, preferring his firstborn child, Acacia.

Bianca hated the fact that Acacia was treated as a princess while she was simply tossed away by Teodoro and the tribe. She'd admitted to Boden that she'd twice come to the rain forest before he'd been exiled, and watched him with Acacia. The moment she'd heard of what Teodoro had done to him, she'd set out to find him, wanting what her sister had, Boden had thought smugly. Boden hadn't loved Bianca and he knew she'd never be his mate, but he'd seen something in her eyes the day they'd met, it reached out to a very similar trait in himself—vengeance—and that had sealed their connection.

Shortly after he'd begun sleeping with Bianca, and plotting his revenge against the Elders and the tribes, news spread that Acacia would be joined with a *Lormenian,* as per her father's wishes. That night, Boden had taken Bianca in every way possible, doing things to her that he'd never imagined with any other female. And she'd taken every whip, touch, bite, slap—whatever he dished out she took willingly, looking up at him with her ice-blue eyes and pledging her eternal loyalty. She wanted what her older sister had given up, the prestige of being with an ultimate leader. Bianca had believed in him from day one, no matter what he did with Sabar—the rogue that was so much more than his protégé—she stood by his side. She'd proven herself to him time and time again. Now, they were both about to be rewarded.

"Kegan Charles has proven much more loyal than his brother," Boden remarked absently, not wanting to think about how Bianca came to be by his side any longer.

"It was a shame to learn of Darel's death," she said. "He finally messed with the wrong shifter, I suppose."

Boden nodded, wondering what exactly Bianca knew about the shifter that had shot his son Darel and left him to bleed out in a hotel room.

"We should get dressed," he told her then, tired of the feel of her warm breath against his skin.

It seemed as if every little thing had been irritating him today. Perhaps this was his form of nervousness. No, he thought with a deep inhale. He did not get nervous. He did not worry and he did not fret. He never had. That's why he was still standing. Even with all the death orders, Boden was still alive and well and more than ready to kick some Shadow Shifter ass tonight!

Cannon had resurfaced, thanks to one of the rogues he'd sent to kidnap the man's family. The kidnapping had been disrupted by the Shadows, which on the surface had angered Boden. But the rogue that the Shadows had captured that night had saved the day. Once he'd been thrown into the cells at the Shadow headquarters, he'd recognized a familiar scent. Cannon was in a cell beside him. It had been easy enough for the rogue to strike against one of the female Shadow guards, gaining entrance into Cannon's cell, where he used his powerful fists and teeth to gnaw through the cinder block walls, setting himself and Cannon free.

Now, Crowe had more than enough hybrids and Boden had tripled the amount of rogues they needed to really shake things up tonight. His heart thumped wildly with anticipation, a grin spreading slowly across his face.

The door to the suite opened with a loud click, closing the moment the female slipped inside and pushed it shut behind her. Bianca was up in an instant, standing in front of Boden, ready to defend. She still wore the white silk robe that touched the floor and was belted tightly at her slim waist. Beneath it she wore nothing, as she had been trained to always be ready and available for him. He hadn't wanted her at all today.

Now, however, there was a surge of desire spreading throughout his body as he came forward slowly to look over Bianca's shoulder at their bold intruder. She was a gorgeous cat, one that he instantly recognized as his dick grew hard against his thigh. Her hair was long and straight, draped over her right shoulder, the wide-framed sunglasses she wore doing nothing to hide her true nature from him. If he ripped them from her face he knew exactly what color eyes he would see. She'd grown up, her body curving in all the right places—breasts high and firm, hips curving to what he knew would be a delectable ass. His mouth watered, the bland feeling that had plagued him all day long abating quickly.

"What are you doing here?" Bianca asked, surprise evident in her voice.

So she had not known that her younger sister was also here in D.C. That was interesting.

"I'm doing what I've been doing all my life," Rayna replied tightly. "Trying to save you from making a bigger mistake than you already have."

Boden tossed his head back and laughed, the sound echoing throughout the room, rumbling through his body to awaken the cat that languished inside.

"Sisters," he said finally. "Together again."

"She is no longer my sister," Bianca raged, taking a step toward Rayna. "I told you that long ago when I left that forest for good."

"You told us what he wanted you to say, Bianca. Not what you really meant. Mother was never the same after you left," Rayna said, looking as if she thought that last sentence would somehow touch her long-lost sister.

Boden knew it wouldn't. He was all Bianca had and she knew it, she accepted it. He would have it no other way. There could be no other allegiance in her life, especially not one to so-called family. If she were going to take Acacia's place in his life, she needed to pledge herself wholeheartedly to him. And she had. Poor thing.

"You can come with me now," Rayna implored. "This isn't going to turn out the way he thinks, I can promise you that. Come with me now, Bianca, before it's too late."

"I am where I belong," Bianca was saying but Boden was already pushing her to the side, moving toward Rayna.

"What do you mean this will not turn out the way I think?" he asked as he closed in on her. "What do you know?"

Her scent was heavy, sexy, infiltrating his nostrils, sending pulses of lust throughout his body. She was aroused, or had been very recently. He wondered if she would still be wet, if he licked between her long legs would he taste her sweet nectar or that of another? The thought was strange and only aroused him more, so that he was reaching for her before he could think otherwise.

"What do you know, sweeting?" he asked, his hands tightening around her arms as he pulled her close to him.

Her breasts rubbed against his chest as he lifted her off her feet and his cat purred, he could not help but acknowledge the pleasure soaring through his body. Even while he became suspicious of this little vixen.

"I know that the Shadows are going to beat you," she said to him. "No," she continued, shaking her head. "They're going to kill you. Roman won't take your head off because he's got too much class for that, but Nick? He'll kill you for sure. He'll tear your throat out and watch you bleed to death, just as Darel did."

Boden roared then, slamming her back into the wall. Her head jerked violently and the sunglasses slipped from her face. Still, she didn't look away. She stared right at him, taunting him. "When you're dead and gone my sister will have her life back. We'll walk away from your sadistic and evil ways and never look back. Our lives will finally be our own."

"You," Boden told her in a slow manner, his tongue licking along his bottom lip as he spoke. "Won't be walking anywhere."

"No!" Bianca screamed from behind. "Just ignore her, Boden. Let her go and we can continue what we've planned. I'm not leaving you. I'll never leave you. Not for her. Not for anyone."

"Shut up and take that goddamned robe off!" he yelled to Bianca without turning to look at her.

Boden kept his gaze on the pretty little vixen that thought she could come in here and threaten him, then simply walk out the door with her sister. Another poor, foolish girl.

"Take it off now!" he yelled again, because he knew Bianca hadn't done what he'd said. For the first time in years, she'd hesitated and Boden knew it was because she had an idea of what was coming.

Moving a hand to Rayna's neck he held her still, his power evident in the widening of her eyes. With his free hand he ripped the front of the dress she wore until it was hanging off her shoulders. Her breasts jiggled with the movement and he lunged quickly, taking one heavy orb into his mouth and sucking until she screamed. He moved to the next one, this time running his sharp teeth over the soft skin, loving the second it broke and the tangy taste of blood on his tongue.

"Boden, please," Bianca insisted. She was pulling on his shoulder now. "Not her. You don't have to do this to her. I'm here. Look, baby, I'm right here."

She grabbed at his face, something she would have never usually done, turning him and offering her bare breast to him instead. He roared his displeasure. "Lie down and wait!" he told Bianca. "And don't make me tell you twice!"

A tear streaked down Bianca's cheek as she backed away to the couch and lay down. She draped one leg over the back of the couch, left the other hanging down on the floor, and spread herself wide so he could see and smell, so he would know that she was waiting and willing.

But he wanted something and someone else first.

Turning his attention back to Rayna, he let her down to her feet, loving the sound of her gasping for breath as she crumpled to the floor. He unzipped his pants then, releasing his engorged sex.

"Stay right there," he told Rayna. "Open your mouth and taste what your sister fell in love with long ago."

Rayna shook her head. "Never!" she said with a mouth full of disgust.

"I will never touch you in any way, you filthy bastard!"

Those were not the words Boden wanted to hear. He grabbed her by her hair, tilting her head back until her mouth opened wide with a scream. He then positioned himself over her, putting the tip of his dick in her mouth. When she bit down hard he resisted the urge to yell out and yanked her head back so hard he pulled out a handful of hair. She screamed, releasing her hold on his now throbbing cock.

"Simple bitch!" he called to her as he dragged her across the floor toward the couch.

Bianca cried silently. Boden ignored the tears and the rapid beating of her heart he could hear over every other sound in the room.

"You need to teach your little sister some manners," he told Bianca.

She shook her head. "She doesn't know any better, Boden. Just let her go. She's not worth it," Bianca pleaded.

"I am worth it!" Rayna yelled. "And so are you! We can walk out of here, Bianca. Get up and help me, we can take him!" she yelled, her cat's claws breaking free as she reached around to swipe at Boden.

He was faster and he tossed her away like a dirty rag, watching as she rolled across the floor. When her cat pressed harder for freedom and she lunged at Boden again, he caught her with one hand, gripping her neck as his own claws and teeth were bared.

"You're too much trouble," he told her. "But I would have enjoyed fucking you."

Rayna reared back slightly and spit in Boden's face, two seconds before he opened his mouth wide and bit into the side of her head.

"No!" Bianca yelled loud and long, a sickening cry that made Boden rage.

With his claws he cut into Rayna's limp body, blood

spewing in all directions before he let her fall in a heap at his feet. When he turned to Bianca, who was still yelling and screaming on the couch, all he could see was red, all he could feel was the incessant anger of once again being betrayed. Bianca was crying but she was going to shift. She was going to turn into her tiger and come at him with death in her heart because of some meddling cat. After all he'd given her, all he'd done to get them where they were today, this bitch was going to try and kill him because of what he'd done to her sister.

Boden was faster. He was stronger, smarter, and in seconds, his jaguar was in full control, the big cat jumping onto the couch where the hysterical feline lay, unable to shift in time to try and defend herself. Her death was quick and a lot less bloody because he was too angry to care anymore, too sick of the *Lormenian* females that believed they could play him for a fool.

Jumping down from the chair, his teeth covered in blood, the jaguar roared loud and long. With his flanks heaving, Boden shifted, staying on his hands and knees until he could catch his breath. When he was breathing normally again, he shook his head and came to his feet. Moving around the blood and bodies, he went to the table where his cell phone sat.

"I need a cleanup in the penthouse suite," he said simply before dropping the phone and heading to take a shower.

He had to get dressed. Tonight was a very important night. It was finally time to take his revenge.

General Oscar Pierson, Major Randall Guthrie, and Captain Lawrence Crowe were dressed in full military regalia. Medals shined, creases stiff, hats positioned perfectly, and frowns affixed appropriately.

"The four prototypes are ready to go. I'll do a short

introduction then let them close the deal. The bidding war will start and by midnight we'll all be very wealthy men," Crowe said after emptying his glass of scotch.

Pierson and Guthrie had arrived five minutes ago, worry and anxiety making them even harder than usual to get along with.

"And you've worked out all the kinks to these proto-types?" Guthrie asked. "We don't have to worry about a repeat of the previous catastrophes in Arizona or D.C.?"

Crowe resisted the urge to snap back at the pompous bastard. These two had a lot of nerve. Neither had done a damned thing but puff out their chests and talk a lot of BS throughout the entire Genesis Project. Hell, the part of this project that was supposed to be in their control had basi-cally fallen to chance since the ATD conference had been scheduled over a year ago and the same foreign attendees with their deeply lined pockets would have been here with-out their involvement. But it was too late for regrets, too late to tell both of them to go to hell, no matter how much he wanted to.

Instead, Crowe stood his ground, shoulders squared, gaze leveled on Guthrie, the ugly motherfucker, with his cratered face, leathery skin, and hideous scar that ran down the left side of his face, curving beneath his neck. "I've done my part to make this deal a success. You just make sure your people are ready to put their money on the table once I'm done."

Guthrie frowned and Pierson nodded toward him, pull-ing the cigar he sucked on from his lips. "If anything hap-pens tonight to mess up this deal, I'm gonna personally cut off your balls and feed them to you, Crowe. You arrogant piece of crap!"

Crowe managed a smirk. "Nice doing business with you too, Pierson."

They left the room together, walking as if they were on

the battlefield with slow precision, garnering stares from guests and staff as they stepped off the elevator and headed toward the ballroom where tonight's festivities would take place. Once inside the large room filled with tables topped with black linens and crystal and china dishes surrounding huge and pointless flower arrangements, the threesome separated. Each went to their own tables in the front of the room. Crowe looked down at his table and noted there were assigned seats. Names he didn't recognize, but figured were the high rollers in tonight's little auction, were seated around him. He slipped a hand into his pocket and pulled out his cell phone, turning his back to the tables where Guthrie and Pierson were sitting and spoke quietly.

"I'm in the ballroom. Bring them down whenever you're ready, but keep them disarmed until I give you the word."

"All of them?" came the reply from the other end of the phone.

Crowe clenched his teeth. He had no idea what Boden wanted with hundreds of hybrids. But he'd had his people in the new lab working around the clock to make sure they were ready. Crowe had faced a lot in his many tours of duty. He'd aimed his gun at men, women, children, armed and unarmed, he'd watched as houses, churches, and schools were burnt to the ground and destinies changed forever, but he'd never seen anything like Boden. And try as he might, the U.S. Marine Corps hadn't taught him how not to fear a beast like that one.

"Yeah," he said tightly. "All of them."

At six thirty on Friday evening the Shadow Shifters climbed out of the black SUVs they'd arrived in. Some parked in the garage, some on National Harbor Boulevard, and others on Waterfront Street. They were coming from all directions, taking up residence at the locations that had been outlined to them by their team leaders. X and a team of five guards headed into the resort, moving to the lower level where the IT department and all the control boards for the hotel were located. They were equipped with laptops and com links, focused on taking full control of the hotel's power supply if need be, and intercepting any outgoing or incoming communications about tonight's event and the sale of the hybrids.

There were teams assigned to the roof of the resort, guards monitoring every stairwell and every bank of elevators on each floor. They blended in with the guests in the lobby, the resort restaurants, lobby bar, and penthouse club. Outside they stood at each corner, near each exit of the resort, and the parking garage. Rome had ordered full coverage and they were going to provide it.

At six forty-five when all teams had verified their positions via com link, Rome, Nick, Eli, Ezra, Nivea, and Caprise made their way to the Potomac Ballroom. The official conference activities would begin tomorrow, but defense industry guests had already begun to assemble for this ticketed event.

They spread out, each taking corners of the room, walking around, looking at and scenting the guests that filled the room. Most of them were either in full military regalia or fatigues. Even the foreign dignitaries wore their dress military gear so that the room seemed to be filled with pompous, overdressed, aging men who were on the hunt for the next best killing machine. The thought alone made Nivea angry. Sure, she believed in defense. Wasn't that what she was currently doing, dressed in a business suit and heels when she'd much rather have on her guard's uniform? But these men were specifically looking for weapons of mass destruction. That wasn't about defense, it was about killing, period. And she couldn't stand it.

"I'll be right over here," Eli said, using the private station on the e-band they both wore.

She tried not to frown because she knew it was taking a lot out of him to watch her go into battle. Last night he'd shared with her the dreams he'd had recently, as well as his guilt over the females in his life dying because of him. Of course she'd told him he was being silly on all accounts, but deep inside she recognized his fear. She too had carried fear for her sisters in the last few years. No matter how many times her therapist had told her that the abuse was not her fault and whatever Richard chose to do to anyone else was not her responsibility to stop. She'd felt different and so she'd done what she considered necessary to prevent that from happening. As such, she would not disregard Eli's feelings, nor would she judge him for them.

"I'll be in this area," she replied, looking over to make sure they made eye contact.

He nodded and Nivea smiled. Eli was wearing his shades again but they didn't bother her so much now because she knew what his eyes looked like. She'd stared into them for so long last night, when he came inside of her, when he'd roared in pleasure, and when he'd simply looked at her as if this was the first time he'd ever truly seen her. She knew the changes in color and the moods that brought it on. She cherished that knowledge, loved that he'd shared so much with her, including the fact that he'd fallen in love with her.

That had been the best.

The lights grew dim and Nivea instantly registered that her best memories were over. It was showtime.

"The doors are locked," she heard through the com link.

It was Ezra speaking and since all the guests were seated she could see all the way across the room to where she and the other shifters had come in. He was standing near the doors. Rome was closer to the podium at the front of the room, but behind him was an exit door. He sighed into the com link repeating Ezra's words, "Locked."

Nivea looked to Eli. He was about to say something when the clapping began.

"Thank you. Thank you," the man stepping to the stage said, nodding his head stiffly as his way of addressing the crowd.

"That's Crowe!" Ezra all but shouted into their ears.

Chapter 23

"We're not making a scene. Wait until there's a reason to act. Otherwise we'll get him when he steps offstage," Rome directed.

Nivea nodded, rolling her shoulders back and focusing her attention on the man dressed in the U.S. Marine Corps uniform and speaking into the microphone, acknowledging that this was how a true monster looked.

"Thank you all for graciously accepting my invitation," Crowe began. "It is not every day that like-minded individuals of our training and caliber are gathered in one place."

"He really means like-minded assholes," Caprise said through the link.

Nivea didn't even try to hide her smile.

"I won't waste time with platitudes and chitchat, but will get right to the point. Tonight I have gathered you here to allow you to be the first to witness the next phase in the world's defense. I introduce to you the Genesis Project, Prototype V."

With his words Nivea's cat reared up, her back straightening, cat's eyes widening as she focused on the center of the stage where Crowe had just stepped from the podium, his arm extended to the curtains opening in the center. There was immediate mumbling throughout the room as one of those damned hybrids stepped through the curtain, dressed in battle fatigues and even wearing a fitted cap pulled down low over its brow. To hide the eerie green eyes, no doubt.

It took long, wide strides until coming to a stop at the edge of the stage. Crowe looked to be saying something, his lips moving. And then all hell broke loose.

The hybrid stepped right off the stage, lifting its beefy arms and slamming them down on the first table in its reach, its mouth opening so that a deafening roar vibrated throughout the room. The guests screamed, some of them getting up from their seats as the curtains moved and out came two more hybrids.

"Cut the lights! Cut the lights!" Rome yelled into his com link.

"We'll take the one over here," Eli said, coming up behind Nivea, touching a hand to her back.

They moved easily through the dark, whereas the humans were still scrambling around. They couldn't see, and also, they didn't know what the hell was roaring at them or breaking all the glassware around them. Nivea ran beside Eli until the hybrid was standing directly in front of them, roaring and dripping its sickly ooze.

"On three," Eli told her, but Nivea ignored him.

Instead she leapt forward, catching hold of the hybrid's arm and propelling herself up the front of its body. Her feet slammed into its chest and it began to fall backward just as her clawed hand swung out to the spot beneath its ear, knowing she would take it down. It was quick and jolting as her body almost immediately made contact with the floor. A strong arm went around her waist and pulled her upward to her relief. The angry voice in her ear was not.

"I said on three," Eli yelled.

"Yeah, I forgot," she replied, without the shrug that would have only irritated him more. "Behind you!" she yelled just in time for him to turn and strike the hybrid in the stomach area. It barely stopped moving but the second of contact gave Eli enough time to send another blow to its arm, then its lower leg and finally, to leap onto its back and dispatch the hybrid. He jumped down before the ashes could drop him to the floor as they had Nivea. They didn't speak again but turned immediately to the continued chaos in the room, fighting, side by side.

Outside the Gaylord, the night seemed as normal as any other. Cars pulled into the garage to park, while people stepped out of the vehicles and headed into the hotel's lobby. None were the wiser, not even the woman who walked directly beside him. He almost laughed at the situation. She'd looked up and smiled when he opened the door for her.

"Thank you," she said, her long lashes blinking wildly against the smooth ivory tone of her skin.

"You're so very welcome," he replied with a smile of his own, one that revealed his long, sharp teeth.

She gasped and tried to hurry away but he was quicker. Reaching out he grabbed her, pulling her to him, chuckling. "What's the matter, baby? You don't like sharp teeth?" he asked before ducking his head and licking the cleavage she so boldly displayed through the low-cut blouse she was wearing. She let out a scream that should have broken the glass doors. And he bit her right there, teeth sinking straight into the pliant human skin, pulling his mouth away as she continued to yell, then pushing her body back until she fell onto the ground.

That one action set everything in motion and only seconds later, there were rogues and those fucking hybrids coming from every direction. They'd been in cars, behind bushes, inside the hotel, inside the garage, every one on special orders from Boden. And now, with Boden's appearance, they were free to do whatever the hell they wanted.

Oh happy day, he thought, ripping through the lobby as his human body shifted into that of a cougar and he roared to make his presence known.

"Shit! They're fucking everywhere out here! Cats!" Zach yelled into the com link. "They're goddamned cats!"

Rome's standing order was that they not shift under any circumstances. The Assembly Leader had said this time and time again, but as Zach came to a stop at the corner of Waterfront Street, after having run a block from where he'd been stationed, all he could see was pandemonium. There were cats climbing up the walls of the Gaylord, jumping through the resort windows. They stood on top of cars, crashing through hoods as they ran to the nearest human that appeared. Whoever they saw they terrorized, either by picking them up or tossing them a distance that all but assured they would be dead when they hit the ground. There was screaming and yelling and the otherwise cool air stilled with the stench that they'd all recognized . . . death.

"We don't have a choice," Zach finally said into the com link, before shifting as he ran to confront a rogue that had just pounced on the hood of a moving car.

"Shit. Shit. Shit!" Priya cursed from the back of the news van she'd been sitting in with Bas and four other guards.

Their assignment had been to wait and to monitor. Rome had been banking on exposing Crowe for his illegal arms dealing with Robert Slakeman and having Priya there to get the scoop on that story to possibly take the heat off the cat people sightings. She was sure he had no idea the scoop would *be* the cat people!

"I'm getting out," Bas yelled. "You three stay with her and drive to Havenway. Now!"

He was heading to the back door when Priya grabbed him, tears already welling in her eyes as her heart pounded in her chest. She'd known who and what he was, knew what this entire situation had meant for him and his tribe, but damn if she'd let herself believe that something would happen to him, that maybe she'd never see him again. She opened her mouth but the words wouldn't come.

"I'm coming back to you," he told her seriously. "I promise you I'm coming back."

She couldn't talk, her lips trembling as his touched hers softly. "I promise," he whispered again before disappearing through that door.

"Promise." Priya heard her own whisper as the truck pulled off. She tried to keep looking at him, to keep Bas in her sights, but there were too many of them.

They were all over the place in what seemed like seconds, like they'd simply been waiting. Like they'd laid the trap for the Shadows and were now pouncing, killing. There was a time when the reporter in her would have demanded she get out of that truck, to follow the story wherever it led. But that was before she'd met Bas and the shifters. It was before she saw what they were and realized how quickly all of this could go bad and how the world as she'd known it could change with her words and observations. She'd vowed to do the opposite of what she'd been taught at the *Post* about doing whatever was necessary for the story. Instead, she committed herself to protecting her kind and those she loved. Now, all that had seemed for nothing.

Rome and the others broke through the doors of the ballroom just in time to see more people running, this time from big cats with even bigger teeth. The roaring and chuffing sounded like they were in the middle of the jungle and not a five-star resort.

He'd heard the yelling through the com link from other Shadows. Bas and Cole had just checked in with their locations in the parking garage of the building. X had abandoned his spot at the control board and was headed out to take on as many as he could. Nick was standing right beside Rome, his cat on the verge of breaking free. Rome reached out a hand to grab his best friend's arm.

"We are Shadow Shifters," he said to Nick.

Nick looked right into Rome's eyes and nodded his head. "And we will prevail," he finished Rome's statement.

They parted ways, each of them knowing what had to be done. Eli saw the moment Rome had made his decision and Eli was right on his heels, pulling Nivea along with him. He'd been at the stairs when something stopped him. It wasn't a sound or an occurrence, but a feeling deep in his gut, a shifting of something other than his cat and he turned around immediately.

"What is it?" Nivea asked as she was pushed up against him by someone screaming and trying to get out of the building. "Eli?" she called to him again, lifting a hand to his chin, attempting to turn his face to hers.

He touched the wrist of that hand, holding her still as he continued to stare back toward the ballroom they'd just come from. Through the open doors, three uniformed men came running out, guns drawn. He remembered the first two had sat at the two tables closest to the stage and they hadn't seemed at all surprised when the hybrids had appeared. The last one had been on the stage—Crowe. He had looked cocky but Eli had sensed some trepidation in him, definitely some anxiety. Now, that anxiety radiated as fear, combining with the sickening scent of terror that permeated the air. In the next moment Eli saw Ezra, and

Eli's cat roared deep inside because he knew how this confrontation was going to end.

Lawrence Crowe had emotionally and physically abused Ezra's mate, Dawn. He'd threatened Dawn's father and had him kidnapped. Crowe had escaped when Ezra had attempted to apprehend him back in Sedona. To say there was bad blood between them that went beyond Crowe's creation of the hybrids was an understatement. Ezra shouted to Crowe and he turned to see who it was calling after him. Subsequently, he lifted his arm and aimed the gun at Ezra's head and Eli knew exactly what would happen next.

His brother shifted into the huge black jaguar with glowing green eyes that Eli knew was more powerful than just about any shifter he'd ever seen. Opening his mouth wide, he roared and leapt toward Crowe, but not before Crowe fired the gun. The cat knocked Crowe to the floor and Eli was already on his way across the hallway.

He didn't know if Nivea was still behind him because he'd released his hold on her the moment his claws extended from his fingers. Mowing people down in front of him was a necessity, his brother's life was in danger. When he came to the spot where Crowe had gone down, it was just in time to see Ezra's cat bite deeply into Crowe's skull, killing the man instantly as his paws held him down by the chest.

Someone screamed so loud Eli's ears rang. The other two military men that had been moving with Crowe were long gone as Eli looked around for them. Then he saw Nivea going to her knees, her hand on the back of Ezra's cat's head.

"Let him go," she was saying as quietly as she could through all the noise. "Let him go, Ezra. It is done."

For the first time in the last five minutes it seemed, Eli

breathed, he actually sucked in air and released it, yelling into his com link, "I need a couple of guards to the ball room, now!" he yelled. "Shifter injured. Get here now!"

He moved closer to Ezra, touching the flank of the cat where he saw the darkening of blood. "Come on, bro. Back up over here so I can look at your wound."

Ezra's teeth were still locked on Crowe and Eli watched the grisly sight, feeling the same deep grief he'd felt when they were back in the Sierra Leone rain forest, staring down at what they'd both done to Acacia and her guards.

"Come on, let's go," he said again, as both he and Nivea rubbed their palms along the cat's heaving body.

There was another roar as Ezra finally released his hold Crowe's body slumping in the pool of blood beneath it With both his arms around the cat, Eli guided his brother back into the ballroom. He didn't have to push past people this time, because nobody wanted to be near a large adul male jaguar that had just killed a man in plain sight.

"You did good," Eli told Ezra when they were finally in the ballroom, the cat lying on its side against the wall.

Its flanks heaved up and down as if it was the hardes thing it ever had to do.

"You're going to be fine," Nivea told Ezra. "Just fine As soon as the team gets here they'll take you back to Hav enway and Ary will fix you right up."

There was a hitch in her last words and Eli rubbed his hand down his brother's head. "Yeah, he's strong. He'll be fine."

Five guards came running into the room, stopping when they saw Ezra's cat lying on the floor. They looked grim barely constraining their anger.

Eli stood, directing them immediately. "Get him back to Havenway, now! Radio someone there to tell them he's coming and to be ready."

There was a nod and then the shifters were moving, liftng the cat together as if it weighed no more than a child. They moved fast across the ballroom floor over the broken glass and overturned furniture, bursting through the exit door and disappearing as quickly as they'd come.

"We have to go," Nivea said, touching a hand to Eli's back.

Eli nodded.

"Rome and Nick are heading to the garage to help Bas there," she continued.

He nodded again, his body trembling with rage, his teeth clenching to keep the cat at bay.

"Pull back! Pull back!" They both heard blaring through their com links from the Assembly Leader. "Reporters are here, humans are dying. Pull back!"

Rome was calling them off, commanding them all to stand down and head back to Havenway. They'd been exposed and there was nothing any of them could do about it. Around him Eli heard the sirens of law officials and ambulances, he heard the screams of humans both afraid and wounded, and the unmistakable roaring of big cats enraged and hunting. The two worlds mixed, human and shifter, and it was nothing like the Assembly Leader had envisioned, nothing at all.

"Eli?" Nivea said more urgently. "We must go now!"

He turned to her then, staring directly into her glowing cat's eyes. "Boden is here."

Chapter 24

Eli was moving quickly and Nivea was struggling to sta[y] behind him. He reached for her and she extended her hand to grasp his. He pulled her along, while people were ev[-] erywhere, yelling and screaming and crying. The acidi[c] stench of blood permeated her senses as she looked over and upward to see a cheetah jumping from its perch on [a] counter into the crowd, biting down on whomever it lande[d] on. Her chest clenched at the sight, her ears ringing wit[h] every cry she heard.

Each way she turned it was the same thing, a big ca[t] or one of those horrid hybrids, mowing through the crow[d] with force and destruction in their eyes. They were kill[-] ing and pillaging like some prehistoric scene come horri[-] bly to life. Her chest heaved as her cat roared inside, read[y] at any moment to break free, to defend and protect.

Something or someone slammed into her back and pai[n] radiated up her left side. She yelled out, turning her hea[d] back to see what it was and completely froze as she looke[d] pure evil directly in the eye.

It happened so quickly she wouldn't have been able t[o] stop it even if she could. In the next seconds she wa[s] wrenched through the crowd, lifted above everyone, and carried over a huge shoulder. The rogue that had her moved fast, leaping over people and slamming her into an elevator. Nivea fell to the floor and pain soared up her side. Looking down, she saw that she'd been cut. The sonofabitch had sunk his claws into her side, no doubt to cut down on her fighting back. It obviously had no idea who the hell it was dealing with.

She quickly came to her feet and faced her attacker the moment the elevator doors closed and prayed for once in her life that everything she'd learned, everything she knew would see her through this moment. She could not die, that was not an option. Not only was she more than ready to live her life with her mate, but she knew unequivocally that Eli would carry her death as his third strike of guilt over females. After seeing his brother wounded this would destroy him, and Nivea was determined not to let that happen.

Fists clenching at her sides, she was more than prepared to fight when the elevator doors opened and the rogue stepped out. It shifted into a cheetah and ran immediately to her left.

"What the—" she began to say, looking down the hall to the cheetah leaving the scene.

She was just about to turn back and get onto the elevator so she could head back down to where Eli was, but a familiar scent stopped her. Standing still for a moment, Nivea cursed under her breath. She had been looking down toward the elevator buttons, but slowly lifted her head, turning in the opposite direction from where the cheetah had gone, frowning when she saw his smiling face.

"It always boils down to you and me." Richard Cannon spoke slowly, his hands clasped in front of him as he stood at the end of the hall near a bank of windows.

"There is no you and me," Nivea told him, noting the

elevator doors closing, leaving her alone with him, once again.

He walked toward her and Nivea felt no fear at all. Richard hadn't shifted into a jaguar in years, he had no training at all, in fact, he was absolutely no threat to her. Not anymore.

So she walked in his direction, determined to show him how little she thought of his presence here and all that he'd done to her and to others in his miserable lifetime.

"You didn't think I was smart enough to get away from those shifters you love so much," Richard said to her.

They stood about ten feet apart now. He was dressed in khakis and a plaid shirt, his leather tie-ups shining, gold watch on his left wrist gleaming. He looked much older to her now, his hairline receding and the mustache he'd always worn sprinkled with gray hairs.

"Actually," she told him, "I think that's just another dumb thing you've done to be added to the long list you've been working on."

"Still so fucking smart," he snapped. "You still think you're going to win. Look around you, Nivea, you and your Shadows are going down! You're never going to make it out of here alive." He laughed at that, looking toward the windows where lights from police cars and ambulances flashed against the night sky.

"That's where you are wrong again, Richard." She said his name with all the contempt she felt for him. "Boden has been using you all along. He has no use for you now, you've done everything he required. *You* are the one who's not going to leave here alive."

"You have no idea what you're talking about, little girl. No idea what's been going on right under your nose."

"I know that you've been a liar and a pretender all your life and that the moment I threatened all by simply questioning you and what you believed, you felt like you had to shut me up, to keep me down so far that I'd never look up and see who and what you truly were. Well, you were wrong!" she shouted and dodged out of his way the moment Richard lunged for her.

He fell face-first to the floor as she turned to see him cursing and turning to get back up. Nivea moved quickly, until she was standing over him, her foot at his neck. He looked up to her then, that appalling grin spreading across his face.

"What are you going to do?" he asked, no, he taunted her. "Are you really going to kill your father, Nivea? Are you that much of a savage, an animal?"

At her sides, Nivea's claws extended, her teeth lengthening sharp and lethal as a ferocious growl escaped her throat.

"That's right, Nivea, kill the bastard who raped you. Take his miserable life so that none of us will have to see him again."

Nivea heard the deep voice behind her and didn't have to turn to verify who it was. His scent was powerful, almost overwhelming with contempt, hate, and disgustingly, lust.

From the floor Richard laughed. "She won't kill me. She can't."

To prove him wrong, Nivea leaned in, her foot pressing harder against his throat until he choked at her efforts. He lifted his hands, grabbing her ankle in an attempt to push her away, but she was much stronger than him. With two quick swings of her arms, her claws swiped at his arms until he tried to yell with the pain of the deep slashes now in both his arms. The sound was a muted growl and she pushed her foot with more force, watching as his face reddened, his eyes bulging.

"Kill him!" Boden yelled from behind her. "Kill him!"

Nivea could do it. Despite what Richard said, what he

obviously thought of her, the contempt he'd had for her all her life, she knew she could kill him. She should kill him, the miserable bastard.

But what would that make her if she did? How would it help or even justify all the counseling she'd endured, all of the training as a guard, the woman that she'd fought so hard to become?

Even as her claws retracted, her foot was easing off Richard's windpipe, her cat pulling back from its prey. She'd just taken two steps away from Richard's body when from behind her a huge white lion leapt into the air, landing on top of Richard's body where it immediately bit into his head, crushing his skull.

He couldn't find her.

One second he felt her right there with him, her hand in his, her cat running alongside his own. They were headed up to where he instinctively knew Boden would be hiding.

And then she was gone.

For the second time tonight Eli felt as if his soul was being yanked from his body. This time the sensation was much more powerful, ripping the breath from his lungs so that he made some awfully painful sound the second he turned around in the stairwell and found himself alone. Almost dislocating his shoulder, he wrenched the door open to hurry back out to find Nivea. The second he was in that hallway again he knew she wasn't there.

The scent, the one that had attempted to cocoon him since the moment he'd first sank deep inside of her, was gone. He looked back and forth, inhaling deeply but could not find her. His body began to vibrate with rage, his cat roaring inside pressing persistently against the human. It wanted release so it could go and find its mate, to kill if need be to save her. But Eli stood still, he closed his eyes and ears to everything around him and waited. Shaking all over with impatience, he continued to wait for seconds that seemed like hours. On the next inhale he picked up a scent—their *companheiro calor*. When his long sharp teeth pricked his lips, his nostrils flaring, clawed fingers wiggling at his sides, Eli knew exactly where she was and who she was with.

He went back into the stairway, running up and up, his lungs filling with air, and after a few flights he found the scent he'd searched for. With renewed vigor Eli burst through doorway after doorway, hearing the chaos going on around him and not giving a damn. The shifters had been exposed; humans were at this very moment recording everything that was going on at this resort. The killing, the animalistic nature of the beasts, the fear—it was all being documented and come tomorrow morning, nobody knew what would happen. But at this moment Eli didn't give a damn. All he wanted was to find his mate.

When he opened the next door and was attempting to step into the hallway, he was knocked back by a foot to his chest. His body fell against the door, cracking the hinges, before his weight slammed to the floor. Looking up, he stared into the glowing blue eyes of a *Lormenian* shifter.

With a vicious roar Eli propelled himself upward, grabbing the *Lormenian* by the ankle and turning it until the bone cracked, the shifter roaring in pain. Eli released him, moving past quickly as it fell to the floor behind him. Another one charged him, claws and teeth bared. Eli ducked its first blow, slamming his clawed hand into its stomach. Pulling his hand away as the shifter bent over clutching his wound, Eli swung his hand backward, his claws slashing over the back of the shifter's neck without him even looking back to see the damage.

He kept moving, her scent stronger, and his heart

pounding louder. They came at him like ants, another *Lormenian* that Eli ran up to and punched in the face, and when the shifter fell back onto the floor, he stomped into its chest until it struggled for oxygen. A cheetah jumped at him from behind but Eli heard its breathing, saw its approach in his peripheral vision, and turned in just enough time to wrap his strong arms around the cheetah's neck, choking it until it crumpled to the floor. When he turned again it was to see the cat slowly approaching.

"Your turn, motherfucker!" he yelled, running in his human form straight toward the cat. When the cat opened its mouth and came up on its hind legs to attack him, Eli jumped, twisting his body in the air and coming down into a backflip that pushed him past the cat. Landing on his feet, he jumped on the tiger's back, his hands reaching around to grab its opened jaws and with all his strength, pulled until his head literally ripped apart.

Coming back to his feet, the tiger lying on the floor in front of him, Eli's breath came in quick pants. And then he heard it. Laughter. Sick and demented laughter that could only come from one person, one shifter.

"Where's your twin?" the almost seven-foot-tall man standing at the end of the hallway asked. "I know how you two like to double-team when fighting . . . and fucking."

Eli had already turned around and now stared into the cat's eyes of the most sadistic and feared Shadow Shifter ever to walk the earth. Boden looked like a god standing there dressed in a black suit, white shirt, and red tie. His body was built, strength fairly oozing from him as he stood in all his glory as a force to be reckoned with. Eli knew his story, he knew the resilience of this shifter, the tenacity that kept him alive when others condemned him to death. His head was wide, round, void of hair on top, but his eyebrows were thick and bushy, his mustache trimmed.

Beside him was Nivea, on her knees and wearing a

necklace very similar to the one Eli had back at Haven-way, the one that Boden had designed for Acacia.

"Let her go," Eli said as he approached. "This is between you and me."

Boden tossed back his head and laughed again, his entire body vibrating with the sound.

"Poor misguided Shadow," Boden told him. "You still do not have a clue."

"I know that I'm going to rip your fucking head off and I'd rather not get your tainted blood on my mate," Eli told him, continuing to draw closer, moving slowly in case more of Boden's minions came for him.

Boden reached down, petting Nivea on the head. Her cat's teeth were extended as her mouth opened wide and she roared, nipping at his hand. There was another stronger chain around her neck with enough give to also clamp around her wrists. Eli couldn't see behind her but he was sure her ankles had also been shackled, or she would have definitely stood up from that subservient position.

"Your mate," Boden taunted him. "She's a feisty little beast. Couldn't bring herself to kill the wretched man that was her father, but that's okay. I took care of that for her." He shrugged. "I like being generous sometimes."

He again ran his hand down Nivea's head, wrapping her hair around his wrist then yanking back until her throat was bared. Nivea did not scream the way Boden was probably expecting. Instead she looked directly at Eli.

That's right, baby, focus on me, Eli told her mentally. His cat reaching out to hers, the two mated animals linking in a way that only Shadow Shifters could. *Focus on me and know that I will kill this sonofabitch for both of us.*

She didn't nod her response, couldn't. But Eli heard her cat loud and clear. *Take his ass down, now!*

"You planned this from the beginning, didn't you?" Eli

asked Boden instead. "All this time you wanted revenge against the Shadows for sentencing you to death. Against me and Ezra for taking your woman." He purposely did not say "mate." His goal was to goad the lethal shifter, to enrage him so much that he came for him, thus releasing Nivea. Saying the word "mate" while Boden held his so close might go wrong, quickly, and that would not be good for anybody here.

"I am a man of many plans," was Boden's response.

"You are a Shadow Shifter betrayed by one tribe and cast out by another. You don't belong anywhere because nobody wants you."

"You are going to be a pleasure to kill!" Boden hissed.

Eli shrugged. "I am a pleasure at so many things. Isn't that correct, my love?"

Nivea sighed her answer. "Yes, my love. You certainly are."

Her voice had deepened to a sexy moan that infiltrated the hallway, oozing over Boden so that his gaze instantly fell to her. In that second Nivea shifted, the gorgeous jaguar that she was breaking the chains at her neck and lunging at the very shocked shifter.

But Boden was not to be discounted; he was a trained warrior who fought by his own rules. He grabbed the cat by its neck before it could sink its teeth into him, tossing it across the floor. Unfortunately, that motion had called for his back to be turned to Eli. Big mistake.

Eli shifted next, jumping onto Boden's back and sinking his teeth instantly into the man's skull. As he did so, all the darkness that had been heightened in him by that shaman's smoke filled Eli completely, emptying from him as he clamped down on Boden's skull. All that anger, all that darkness seeping out like poison, should have killed the shifter, should have taken him down instantly.

But it did not.

Boden was somehow able to shake Eli off, turning with blood dripping from the back of its head.

"You can't kill me, you little shit! Not one of you stupid shifters can kill me!"

With that the man shifted into his cat. Eli had never seen a larger, deadlier-looking jaguar. And one that was so right, it would take two shifters to kill him.

In seconds both he and Nivea charged the cat, jumping at it from both sides. Boden reared up on his hind legs, roaring so that the windows around them shook. Nivea's bite went into Boden's flanks while Eli swiped at its head with powerful paws. Boden roared again and this time glass shattered, sprinkling all around them.

When the bigger jaguar came back down to his feet, Eli leapt onto its back, sinking his teeth into the top portion of its head. Boden swiped at Nivea but she wasn't to be dissuaded, she latched onto the side of his neck, biting down with almost as much strength as Eli. Boden continued to roar and buck beneath them, trying to throw them off, and yet, moving closer and closer to the open window.

In a flash Eli saw Boden in his cat form, attacking Nivea's cat in the rain forest, jumping at her again through the hut where she'd lay in that bed beside Eli wearing Acacia's necklace. Boden had always been the threat to Eli's mate. With another blink he saw Boden picking up Crowe's battered body from that house in Arizona where Ezra had thought he'd killed the human. He saw Boden and Bianca in a truck with Crowe and then Boden and Bianca sitting in the corporate office of the Cannon Group. Boden had been the archenemy of the shifters from that first day he was exiled from the Gungi.

Blinking back to reality, Eli's teeth sank deeper, he tasted the jaguar's blood at the back of his cat's throat. When Boden moved again, taking steps even with Eli and Nivea, a combined total of more than four hundred pounds hanging onto him, Eli knew where the cat would go, what he would do. He hated to do this, hated the choice he'd been given, but Eli relinquished his hold on Boden, swiping his paws over Nivea's head until her grip on the jaguar broke free as well. She turned to him instantly, growling and hissing as Boden, bleeding from multiple locations, his golden fur stained with red until it almost covered him completely, stumbled a few more steps. Eli ran toward him then, roaring with every ounce of rage, shaman's poison, and Seer's power he had in his cat, bumping the wounded jaguar with his large head until it staggered the next couple of steps before toppling over the windowsill, falling into the night.

Cats normally land on their feet and for a minute Eli worried that Boden in all his sadistic rage would somehow manage to survive that fall from eighteen floors up. But the sound of rapid gunfire and the loud roaring of other cats in the area indicated that that had not happened. Boden Estevez was dead. Finally.

The two jaguars made their way down the stairs, crossing the walkway into the garage but not before looking out to see that chaos still reigned.

Lights flashed from police cars, ambulances, and news cameras. There were people everywhere, police attempting to form perimeter blocks, yellow tape going up around bodies stretched out on the ground. When gunshots sounded from somewhere higher up, Eli pushed his cat against Nivea's, keeping her shielded as they picked up the pace. There had been guard SUVs parked throughout the garage in anticipation of the shifters needing to make quick getaways. Keys were taped behind the front wheels so that it didn't matter which vehicle was taken by what shifter.

They ran until Eli stopped at one he knew to be a guard

vehicle. He came along its side and shifted back into his human form. Hurriedly going down on one knee, he snatched the key from its hiding place and opened the back door, going straight for the duffle bags the shifters kept filled with clothes. Nivea had shifted as well and was now at his side. It was as he tossed her sweatpants and a T-shirt he thought she could fit into that he noticed her hissing. Turning toward her, he scented her blood and was ready to roar again.

Instead he touched her shoulder, turning her and seeing the blood oozing from several angry gashes at her side.

"It's okay," she told him, pulling the shirt down over the scars and putting a hand to his face to divert his attention to her eyes instead. "I'm okay, Eli. Really. Once we get back to Havenway, Ary will sew that right up," she told him with confidence.

Eli gritted his teeth.

"We don't have time to stand here, babe. We have to go," she insisted.

Eli agreed but he wasn't happy about that wound. Hell, he wasn't happy about anything that had taken place here tonight.

In the next moments they were both dressed and sitting in the front seat of the truck. He pulled out of the parking spot and was attempting to get out of the garage only to find that he was one of many. When two cougars jumped out of nowhere onto the car directly in front of them, Eli quickly put the truck in reverse and maneuvered the vehicle until it was moving around several other cars, crashing into some.

He drove like a madman, but he was determined to get them out of there. Outside there were policemen in the street, attempting to barricade the resort. But more cats appeared, more hybrids stomped along the ground like Neanderthals. The cops were outnumbered and quite possibly outpowered even though they diligently pulled their weapons, aimed, and fired at the assailants. As for Eli, he knew Rome's original order had been the correct one. They had to get out and get out now; there was no other choice for the Shadows. Vastly outnumbered and now exposed to the world, they had no other option. The world now knew who and what they were. Now everything would change.

Chapter 25

Sitting in a recliner with a cup of hot tea cooling in her hands, Kalina watched the television screen as if she expected something to jump through it at any moment. She was still a bit stiff as the stitches on her side healed. Beside her in another chair Ary sat close, rubbing her hand over Kalina's back in an effort to keep her and the baby she was carrying calm.

"He's all right," Ary said slowly, her gaze also intent on the television screen. "They're all coming back to us, Kalina. You cannot think otherwise."

"They're everywhere," Kalina said softly. "Just everywhere and they're killing whatever is in their way. Humans and shifters."

In the corner, which was his favorite spot in any room that he occupied, Baxter held Shya in his arms, rubbing his chin along the little girl's soft ebony curls. She'd flourished so much in the weeks since the blood transfusion from Ezra. Her chubby cheeks were the highlight of her cherubic face. She had a smooth, heavily-creamed coffee complexion and hazel-brown eyes. She'd even grown two teeth at the bottom front of her mouth and now held tight to the spirit-filled stick that had been converted into a rattle Baxter had given her the day she was born. Magdalena had given him the stick when he'd first left the Gungi to travel to the States with the Reynolds family. It was for protection, strength, and solace, so Baxter had given it to Shya as the firstborn of the newest shifter generation. The Seer had already sent another spirited object for the first child of the Assembly Leader upon its birth.

Watching Kalina as she worked her fingers together, then released them and started the process again, Baxter wondered if that would come to fruition. The First Female looked tired after the injuries and subsequent surgery she'd endured because of the car accident. She'd lost a little weight but Ary assured them all that the baby inside her still thrived.

"There's so much death," Kalina whispered. "So much hate."

Ary sighed. "I know. I know. But Rome is a good Leader. He'll get them all out of there. I know he will."

But even to Baxter's ears she did not sound confident.

In the next few minutes the mood in the tunnels shifted quickly. The first SUVs came barreling into the parking area. Calls came in rushed screams over the intercom system that had been installed into each room and the hallways of the tunnel. "Medical assistance needed! Medical assistance ASAP!"

Ary immediately rose from where she was seated. "You stay right here," she told Kalina. "Do not move. I'll come get you if it's Rome."

Kalina had already come to the edge of her seat, about to get up.

"Baxter, make her stay," Ary called to him.

Baxter moved slowly from the corner, going to kneel in front of the First Female. "I need you to hold Shya, while I make sure all is well. Sit back and hold the baby," he told her.

She looked up at him in a way that said she knew exactly what he was doing and wasn't fooled one bit, but she did take Shya into her arms, cuddling the little girl close to her chest. Standing, Baxter nodded to Ary and watched the *curandera* rush from the room to take care of the wounded.

Within the next hour more trucks came in with more wounded Shadow Shifters, some already dead.

When Kalina thought she would go out of her mind, and Shya had fallen asleep in her lap, she stood. With a resigned sigh and no knowledge of exactly how much time had passed, she laid Shya in the cradle that had been brought down for her. As she stood, still fighting back the tears of dread, a hand touched her shoulder. Tears fell as she exhaled slowly, her entire body filling with warmth at his touch.

"*Meu companheiro,*" he said in his deep voice and Kalina's shoulders began to shake. "Don't. Please don't cry," Rome said, turning Kalina to face him.

She fell into his embrace, holding onto him so tightly she thought she might actually break him, or her arms, in the process. "I was so afraid," she whispered into his shirt. "So afraid for you and for everyone."

He rubbed his hands down the back of her head, then cupped her face and tilted her head back until she stared up at him. "I am safe and I am here. I love you," he told her, letting one hand slip down to rub over her protruding belly.

Kalina nodded. "You are safe and I love you."

"Rome's called a meeting in half an hour," Eli said after he and Nivea had walked from their truck to the room one of the guards had directed them to. It was sparsely decorated with just a bed, one table, and one chair, but the bathroom had a shower and they were told their clothes had been brought down here. "We have just enough time to grab a quick shower, stop by the infirmary to check on Ezra, and then get to the meeting on time."

He continued to talk, not sure why it was so imperative to keep moving. Especially when he knew Nivea had come in and sat on the edge of the bed, remaining very quiet.

"Jax called me on the e-band to say that Ezra's already in surgery. Ary's working on him," he said while pulling clothes from one of the bins that had been labeled with his name. "I want to get down there as soon as possible."

Nivea still didn't speak.

"He also said your sisters were doing well," Eli continued. "I asked about your mother too."

"Stop," she said softly. "Just stop."

Eli did. He turned to face her and wanted to hit something, curse, or simply collapse at how sullen and helpless she looked at that very moment. Instead, he summoned the strength to go to her, sitting on the bed beside her and wrapping one arm around her.

"It's done," he said. "We can't go back and change it. We tried to stop it, but it's done."

Tears streamed from her eyes. Eli didn't look at her but he could smell them, salty and sad, and something clenched inside his chest tightly.

"They're dying," she told him. "I saw Pete die. That white lion took him down." Her breath hitched and more tears fell. "We couldn't stop it."

"No," Eli took her. "We couldn't."

"What will happen now?" she asked.

"I don't know," he replied honestly. "I really don't know the answer to that question, Nivea."

Then Eli moved and he lifted Nivea onto his lap, wrapping one strong arm around her waist, using his other to lift her face and cup her cheek. "All I know right here and right now is that I love you more than life itself. And I don't ever want to lose you, not in battle, not because of some disagreement or lack of communication. I just want you, always."

She looked at him through eyes blurred by tears, human eyes that had seen and experienced far too much in her young life. And he wanted to give her the world. Of course he didn't know which world that would be, but Eli didn't care. All he knew was that he was looking at his future, his life, the reason why he'd survived all that he had.

"I love you," he told her again, touching his lips softly to hers. "I love you."

She sighed into his kiss, whispering over his lips in response, "I love you, too."

"We have not been able to contact Cole," Rome said solemnly as he stood in front of what was left of his leadership team. "It is too soon to send out a team to search for him, but we will as early as first thing in the morning. Ezra is in critical condition. Zach and a number of others are dead."

At the table, Eli reached for Nivea's hand. He'd seen his brother with tubes running all over him, eyes closed as he lay in the medically induced coma that Ary assured Eli would help him heal even faster than shifters normally did. It had taken a part of him to see his other half lying so still as if he were already dead, but he'd flattened his hand on his twin's chest and felt his heart still beating. Nivea had stood right by his side, as Dawn had covered Eli's hand with her own. For as much as Eli had been against his brother mating a human, he was at that moment happy that Ezra had found someone to love him the way he deserved to be loved. So he did not move when her hand rested on top of his and when Nivea leaned in, adding her hand on top of Dawn's, his heart had swelled.

"We have been exposed," Rome continued. "The humans now know without a doubt that there are Shadow Shifters living in this world with them. There will be repercussions for that revelation and there will most likely be more death."

It was a solemn declaration, but one that was true nonetheless.

Nick and Ary stood stoically just behind Rome. Kalina sat in a chair to his right. Jax was ever-present next to the First Female. X and Caprise, who had sustained a pretty violent-looking gash at her neck, stood to Rome's other side, forming what to Eli would always be an impenetrable alliance. Baxter and Elder Alamar were all the way at the back, looking as grief stricken as the others felt.

"I'll organize the recovery teams to go out at first light to search for the others that are missing," Eli volunteered, wanting to take some of the stress off the Assembly Leader's shoulders.

"I'll help with that," Bas said, speaking for the first time since returning to the tunnels and learning that Cole was missing.

"I'm going out to look for him myself," Jace told the room in a tone that dared anyone to speak against him.

Nobody argued.

They would all go out to look for the Faction Leader.

"Right now it's best if we try to get some rest," Rome told them. "Teams will be assigned and briefed at five a.m. Then we'll go out to search for survivors."

"That's not a good idea," a new voice sounded throughout the room.

All eyes went to the man now standing in the doorway, the human who was familiar to some. He was surrounded by two shifters that had what looked like a death grip on his arms.

Nivea immediately stood. "What are you doing here?"

X and Nick both moved to the doorway to confront Agent Dorian Wilson.

"That's a damned good question," Nick said, staring into the man's face.

"I was given directions," Dorian told them. "By Rayna."

"That bitch!" Nivea whispered and Caprise nodded her agreement.

"Hear what I have to say first," Dorian insisted, his gaze seeking and resting on Rome. "You'll want to hear this before you decide how to proceed."

At eleven a.m. on a Saturday morning, Eli walked behind his Assembly Leader as Roman Reynolds, Nick Delgado, Xavier Santos Markland, Sebastian Perry, Priya Drake, and Agent Dorian Wilson were escorted into the Oval Office.

They crossed the room with solemn footsteps, their feet moving softly over the United States of America's presidential seal painted on the floor. Coming to a stop, Eli made sure to count each of the Secret Service men in the room. Their job was to guard President Wilson Reed, just as Eli's was to guard Rome.

The president looked grim as he stared at Rome.

"You lied to me," was the first thing the older man said, his glasses pushed up high on his face.

"I never lied," Rome countered. "I did not tell you what you did not need to know."

President Reed slammed his palms down on his desk. "I didn't need to know that there were damned animals roaming around my country? Are you kidding me?"

"First," Rome began. "The animals you refer to are housed in a zoo. What have been walking and mingling among the humans for hundreds of years are called Shadow Shifters. And up until last night you had no idea we existed."

"That's exactly what my problem with you is, Reynolds! I allied myself with you. I supported you and your firm and the charities you reached out to."

Rome interrupted. "Because those were the right things to do. I have always been an upstanding citizen, a successful lawyer, and a contributor to this community as well as others. There was no need for you not to offer your support just because you had no knowledge of my DNA."

"Don't give me that smooth-ass lawyer crap! You should have told me!" Reed was clearly outraged and he was afraid.

Sweat pricked his forehead and his hands shook after he'd slammed them on the desk, so he pulled them down to his lap instead. He was afraid of the shifters that now had seemingly invaded his office.

When in truth, it was Priya and Dorian who had arranged for the private meeting as a form of damage control for the United States government—to whom many countries were now looking with thoughts of terrorism against their citizens, as last night's attack involved several of their highest dignitaries. And for the shifters whose true nature had finally been unveiled . . . The president's staff had jumped at this opportunity, but Rome had insisted it be a private meeting instead of a nationally televised press conference.

"Now I want you to tell me where the rest of your kind are hiding and what you all plan to do now that you're here," Reed told Rome.

The Assembly Leader shook his head. None of them had been overly optimistic about the human government being able to come to amicable terms with the shifters. That had been one of their greatest fears with exposure. But they'd agreed to the meeting, agreed with Dorian that it looked better for them, it put forth the peaceful approach the agent now believed the shifters needed to take.

Dorian's appearance had also been a huge question. But the agent had explained how he met Rayna and how the *Lormenian* shifter had wanted to help the Shadows by exposing and killing Boden. She'd wanted her sister's safety, but she'd also wanted them to be able to live cohesively with the humans in this country. She'd left him a letter with the directions to the tunnels—which she knew because she'd been there to help them work on the construction—and she'd told him that if she did not return to the hotel by a certain time that night that he should assume that she was dead and get to Rome as quickly as possible. The agent had done just that.

"We are a peaceful species," Rome told the president. "What happened last night was not our fault."

"Big-ass cats jumping over cars, biting and killing people, that's not your fault?" Reed inquired. "When I've been told that you are yourself one of the big cats."

Rome paused a moment, the room going completely silent as everyone waited for his response.

"Yes. I am one of the big cats. I am the Stateside Assembly Leader of the Shadow Shifters," Rome said with confidence and pride.

President Reed stood then, squaring his shoulders so that his stance mimicked Rome's.

"Then I command you to release the names and locations of all these species. I demand to know where every one of you is hiding so that we can deal with you appropriately," Reed said without hesitation, his angry gaze locked with Rome's.

"I will not do that," Rome told him calmly. "There's no reason for any of us not responsible for last night's fiasco to be, as you put it, 'dealt with.' And furthermore, I will not stand for the persecution and execution of my kind."

Reed nodded as if in resignation, before saying, "Then you have made the United States your enemy."

Rome's reply was immediate and came just seconds before the Assembly Leader turned and left the room, his team following dutifully behind him.

"No, Mr. President. It is my goal to work with the humans, with your government, so that there will be no need for any of us to be enemies," Rome said seriously. "You knew my parents. You know what type of man I am. You know what I stand for and what I believe. There is no reason for us to work against each other here. The Shadow Shifters simply want peace."

Wilson Reed looked from one of his advisors to the next, then back to Rome and the others who stood with him. He sighed heavily, smoothing down his tie as he lowered himself slowly into his seat.

"I only want peace for my country," the president said to Roman. "Can you promise that from your people?"

"We only want peace as well," Rome told him. "So yes, I can promise you that. And if we all work together peace and harmony shall be what we have."